THE VIGILANTES

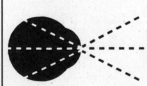

This Large Print Book carries the
Seal of Approval of N.A.V.H.

THE VIGILANTES

W.E.B. GRIFFIN
AND WILLIAM E. BUTTERWORTH IV

THORNDIKE PRESS
A part of Gale, Cengage Learning

GALE
CENGAGE Learning

Detroit • New York • San Francisco • New Haven, Conn • Waterville, Maine • London

GALE
CENGAGE Learning

Thorndike Press® Large Print Core.

The text of this Large Print edition is unabridged.

Other aspects of the book may vary from the original edition.

Set in 16 pt. Plantin.

LIBRARY OF CONGRESS CATALOGING-IN-PUBLICATION DATA

Griffin, W. E. B.
  The vigilantes / by W.E.B. Griffin and William E. Butterworth IV. — Large print ed.
    p. cm. — (Thorndike Press large print core)
  Originally published: New York : G.P. Putnam's Sons, c2008.
  "A badge of honor novel" — T.p. verso.
  ISBN-13: 978-1-4104-2775-5
  ISBN-10: 1-4104-2775-7
  1. Payne, Matt (Fictitious character) — Fiction. 2. Police — Pennsylvania — Philadelphia — Fiction. 3. Vigilantes — Fiction. 4. Philadelphia (Pa.) — Fiction. 5. Large type books. I. Butterworth, William E. (William Edmund) II. Title.
  PS3557.R489137V54 2010
  813'.54—dc22

                                              2010021361

Published in 2010 by arrangement with G. P. Putnam's Sons, a member of Penguin Group (USA) Inc.

Printed in the United States of America
1 2 3 4 5 6 7 14 13 12 11 10

★

IN FOND MEMORY OF

SERGEANT ZEBULON V. CASEY

*Internal Affairs Division
Police Department, the City of
Philadelphia, Retired*

There came a time when there were assignments that had to be done right, and they would seek Zeb out. These assignments included police shootings, civil-rights violations, and he tracked down fugitives all over the country. He was not your average cop. He was very, very professional.

— HOWARD LEBOFSKY
Deputy Solicitor of Philadelphia

I

[ONE]
1834 Callowhill Street
Philadelphia, Pennsylvania
Saturday, October 31, 7:30 P.M.

Will Curtis, a frail fifty-four-year-old, was sitting slumped against the driver's door of his rusty Chevrolet Malibu when the thoughts suddenly hit again, causing him to wince and grunt. He quickly pulled his right hand from the .45 GAP Glock Model 37 semiautomatic pistol beside him on the seat, stabbed at the dash to turn off the radio, then smacked at the brim of his grease-smeared red-and-blue FedEx cap, knocking it from his head. With the fingers of both hands, he began rubbing his sweaty temples.

Goddamn these flashbacks! he thought.

The fingertips pressed harder and deeper in a futile attempt to make the mental images vanish.

Damn them all to hell!

Only six months earlier, Curtis had been

what he'd thought of as bulky, standing at five-eleven and weighing two-ten. But now he had withered to a sickly one-sixty. His jeans, T-shirt, and denim jacket were ill-fitting, hanging on him so loosely they looked as if they belonged to someone far bigger. His close-cropped silver hair was damn near disappearing, and his formerly warm gray eyes were becoming more and more hollowed and distant in his slight if somewhat hard face.

Curtis felt he was fast becoming a miserable shell of the man he'd been. He had gone from fearing nothing and no one to being scared shitless to, now, just not giving a good goddamn anymore.

He wasn't sure what was most responsible for that — the constant stress from the mental anguish that caused the flashbacks, or the aftereffects of the intense chemotherapy treatments to slow the aggressive cancer they'd first found in his prostate.

Probably both.

Easily one or the other — especially that fucking chemo that makes me shit my shorts like some sorry bedridden invalid — but probably both.

The flashback scenes torturing Will Curtis were of the brutal sexual assault of his only child, Wendy. After leaving a pub late on the night of Saint Patrick's Day almost eighteen months ago, his beautiful, bubbly, twenty-four-year-old daughter had been attacked in her apartment.

She was just two years out of college!

Just beginning to enjoy a full life!

Triggered by the slightest of things — for example, hearing a song she liked, which had just happened as he sat listening to the radio in the Malibu, or driving past Geno's and smelling her favorite cheesesteaks — the flashbacks would suddenly hammer him. They were grotesquely lit and viciously vivid, showing the attack in her bedroom again and again from damn near every possible angle.

And they haunted him all the more because he hadn't actually witnessed the attack — rather, his imagination ran with possibilities of what had happened to her.

And what had happened to her was what the legal system termed "involuntary deviant sexual intercourse."

"Involuntary"? he thought, putting his hand back on the pistol.

Fucking-A it was involuntary!

Which of course meant rape. There'd been absolutely no question of that. The exam given by the doctors at Hahnemann University Hospital — not a dozen blocks from where he now sat parked, waiting — had determined unequivocally that that had happened. And not only vaginally, which was without doubt bad enough to have happened to his baby girl, but also what was termed in the legalese as "sexual intercourse per os and per anus."

The pervert drugged her so she passed out, then abused her body — even gave her the goddamned clap!

The revelation of all that had driven the normally levelheaded Curtis to a point of desperation he'd never believed possible.

And — *boom!* — his mind hammered with the garish image of the bastard on top of Wendy in her bed.

"Dammit!" Will Curtis said as he sat up in the dark and slammed the pistol against the dashboard.

His left hand rubbed his temples more vigorously. He shook his head.

What kind of miserable fucking animal does that?

Who takes advantage of an innocent girl like that?

He glanced out the window and looked across Callowhill Street at the office with the frosted plate-glass window. More or less centered on the window — which had a crack that ran jagged across its upper-right corner — were faded black vinyl peel-and-stick letters that spelled out LAW OFFICE OF DANIEL O. GARTNER, ESQ.

And I'll never understand why that bastard defends perverts.

Just for a lousy dollar?

But that assistant district attorney had said, "Only a matter of time before Gartner gets busted himself and goes down just like one of his clients."

So, yeah, some kind of payout, or payoff, that's for sure, because there's no shortage of scumbag lawyers like him.

He squeezed the Glock's grip.

That DA was close to right. Gartner may never have got busted, but he is about to go down. . . .

Before their world went to hell, Will Curtis and his wife, Linda, were more or less comfortably middle class. Will had driven package-delivery trucks all his career, first for the U.S. Postal Service, the last eleven years for FedEx, and Linda was a teller at First National Bank. Their idea of an exciting weekend night usually meant taking a BYOB of cheap California red wine to the $9.99 all-you-can-eat pasta and salad at Luigi's Little Italy, around the corner from their row house of twenty years on Mount Pleasant Avenue in Philly's West Mount

11

Airy section.

They had known little about what went on in the nightclubs of Philadelphia, and damn sure absolutely nothing about any illegal activities. That was, until the toxicology tests taken on Wendy Curtis at Hahnemann had come back and Will and his wife had gotten an immediate and in-depth education into what the doctors called club drugs — Rohypnol (known on the street as "roofies" or "Mind Erasers"), Ketamin ("K-Hole," "Special K"), and GHB.

Wendy's blood had tested positive for far more than a trace of GHB, which was shorthand for gamma hydroxybutyric, and called the "date-rape drug" and "easy lay," among other street names. It was a powerful pharmaceutical widely prescribed as a sleep aid and a local anesthetic. The doctors told Will and Linda that when consumed with alcohol, GHB became even more powerful. It came in the form of a quick-dissolving pill, liquid, or powder, and was odorless and colorless, sometimes with a slightly salty taste. Commonly it was slipped into the drink of a young woman at some bar — though the illicit drug was no stranger among males in the homosexual community — or even at her apartment if she made the mistake of letting a date "come up for a drink, just one only."

And just one was all it took.

Within fifteen minutes of entering the bloodstream, GHB could leave the victim completely powerless for up to four hours, during which time they had no conscious knowledge of what was happening to them. In most cases, for better or worse, it also left them afterward with no memory of what had been done to them.

Almost, the doctors explained, as if they'd had a very vague, very tragic dream.

Which, Will had tried to console himself and his wife, explained why Wendy would not talk about the attack.

She couldn't remember.

Or maybe — probably? — didn't want to. . . .

But that doctor's exam sure as hell found the physical damage.

And that's what really put her momma over the edge, screaming hysterically at the news of her baby girl hurt so badly.

Not even the damned priest could talk to her, calm her down. . . .

And then this scumbag lawyer turned it all the worse. Getting the case tossed on a technicality with the rape-kit evidence — a goddamn broken "chain of custody" in the property room.

The pervert was guilty as hell . . . then he

just walked.

Sonofabitch!

Tonight made the third time in a week that Will Curtis had been parked in the 1800 block of Callowhill Street. Each time he'd been in a different car and in a different spot, but all with a clear view of LAW OF-FICE OF DANIEL O. GARTNER, ESQ.

Callowhill was two blocks north of the Vine Street Expressway. To the south of Vine spread the great wealth of modern skyscrapers and well-preserved historic buildings that was the bustling Center City. Here, however, on this block of Callowhill, the majority of addresses were deserted. Signs in the dirty vacant windows of the decaying strips of storefronts — mostly three-story offices shar-ing a common brick façade — announced to the occasional passersby that they were for sale or lease.

Of the few that were occupied, not one was particularly noteworthy. Five addresses to the right of Gartner's law office, almost up to North Nineteenth Street, stood a soul food restaurant and bar — Curtis thought of it as "that soulless restaurant," complete with vagrants loitering nearby — and a couple addresses to his left were two other low-rent law offices, one of which had let-tering on its window stating that the firm

14

offered immigration-law services. And finally, across the street, next to a large grassy lot surrounded by chain-link fencing, was a struggling establishment named Tattoo U.

That, Curtis had thought with a morbid chuckle, was probably where Gartner's clients went to acquire "I'm a Loser Gangbanger" body art after Gartner, their loser of a lawyer, had told them their turn-in date to report to jail.

Other than that, there was damn near nothing here.

And that served his purpose tonight just fine.

It had been a little more than three hours since Will Curtis had pulled the Chevy sedan into the parallel parking space across the street from Gartner's office. In that time, he'd come to feel comfortable that the patterns he had noted on his previous two nights of surveillance were similar to what was playing out tonight.

First, most workers in the nearby offices had headed for home — *or probably a corner bar,* he'd thought — the great rush of them at the stroke of five o'clock. There were even a few who'd worn Halloween outfits. *If black tights and cat whiskers and a headband with pointy furry ears counted as a costume.*

15

Then, for the next hour, out came the stragglers. They disappeared one by one down the cracked sidewalk until, easily by six, Callowhill Street — not counting an occasional patron for the restaurant or the tattoo parlor — was more or less deserted.

Right about seven-thirty, a woman left Gartner's office, returning fifteen or so minutes later with some sort of fast food. Each night it was the same chunky woman, about age thirty and black and overweight but with a pleasant face. The first time she had carried two flat cardboard boxes with pies from the pizza joint on the corner of Callowhill and North Twenty-first Street. Tonight she'd gone a block up to Hamilton Street and come back with a couple of greasy white sacks that had Asian-looking lettering: TAKIE OUTIE TASTY CHINESE.

The thought of smelling, let alone tasting, greasy egg rolls made Will's stomach grumble. Not because he was hungry — he had almost no appetite these days — but because the chemotherapy treatments had made his gut easily upset.

Even before they found the cancer, his prostate had caused him to have to take leaks far more often than he liked. Particularly because finding a pisser was not always easy, especially while driving a FedEx truck

16

on its delivery route schedule. He couldn't keep stopping continuously — his boss would wonder why he was constantly late — so in Center City he'd swung by Goldberg's Army-Navy on Chestnut Street and bought a couple of surplus gallon canteens. The plastic containers weren't the most sanitary solution, but they worked. He could do his business while seated, then later simply crack open the door and dump out the canteen onto the street.

And that had damn sure come in handy the nights he watched the law office.

Now, for the third time tonight, Will Curtis picked up the canteen, unscrewed its top, unzipped the fly of his blue jeans, and relieved himself into the half-full container. Then he screwed the top back on tightly and dropped the canteen to the floorboard.

And heaved a huge sigh of relief.

Ten minutes later, Curtis saw the battered heavy metal door of Gartner's office swing open. The doorway opening filled with a harsh white glow of fluorescent light.

He checked his well-worn gold-toned Seiko wristwatch.

Eight o'clock on the nose.

Then, as he'd seen happen the other times here, out walked the overweight black woman. Tonight she wore a gray knee-length woolen overcoat, which only made her obesity more pronounced, and slung a black patent-leather purse over her shoulder.

Right on time.

He guessed that she was Gartner's part-time help, one who came in maybe after attending college classes or another job and worked for him till eight. Gartner's full-time assistant, a bony white woman of maybe forty, was one of the ones who left the office at five o'clock on the dot.

That meant, to the best of Curtis's knowledge, that Gartner was now alone. Which was how Curtis wanted it. He held no animosity whatever toward any of the office help. Everyone had to work for a living, he reasoned, and no one should be held accountable for what their bosses did.

Which was why he did not mind waiting so long in the car and pissing in canteens. While he knew that the spreading cancer wasn't going to give him all the time in the world — *Sure as hell not much more time left on the top side of the turf* — he felt that he did have enough time to settle some scores with the ones who deserved it.

Curtis glanced down at the Glock. The matte-black gun reminded him of the semi-automatic Colt Model 1911 .45 ACP with which he'd first learned to shoot. That had been during his short stint — two years, ten months, and twenty-two days during the 1970s, discharged honorably during a post-war Reduction in Force — in the Pennsylvania National Guard.

And that caused him to shake his head in disgust.

I joined up to fight for freedom — but damn sure not so our legal system would allow these worthless shits to do what they want to innocent girls.

No one is going to miss him.

And there's not a damn thing that's going to happen to me for taking him out — that is, if I get caught.

Then he chuckled.

Like that saying goes, "You can't kill a man born to hang."

Or, in my case, hang dead at the end of a chemo IV drip. . . .

He slipped the Glock into the right pocket of his denim jacket and opened the driver's door. As he shuffled his feet to get out, he accidentally kicked the full canteen across the floorboard. He looked down at it and made a face.

Oh, what the hell. May as well dump it out now.

Then he smirked.

And I know exactly how.

He looked over at the cracked frosted plate-glass window with LAW OFFICE OF DANIEL O. GARTNER, ESQ. He saw a couple of overhead white lights go off behind it, then there began a pulsing of different-colored lights. He'd seen that happen on the other nights he'd sat watching the office, and decided that Gartner liked to watch a little television, maybe a movie, after the help had left.

He picked up the canteen and swung open the door.

[TWO]

Will Curtis, staying in the shadows, walked up the sidewalk on the far side of the street. As he approached a parallel-parked filthy old Ford panel van — one that apparently hadn't been moved in a month of Sundays, judging by the parking tickets and fast-food restaurant flyers stacked thick under its windshield wipers — he stepped off the curb to cross the street. He turned his head left and checked for any traffic, and just as he saw that there wasn't anything coming, there came from the opposite direction the

20

sound of a roaring motorcycle engine.

He stopped in his tracks, keeping behind the filthy Ford van, and carefully peered out to look to the right.

And there he saw it: one of those high-end racing-style motorcycles designed to look at once sleek and aggressive.

He saw plenty of them while driving his truck routes — and he hated them.

The idiots on those crotch rockets are always street racing or running in packs like marauding dogs, reckless as hell, causing wrecks in their wake.

Even worse, every now and then splattering themselves on the bumper of some car, making that innocent driver carry that damn memory the rest of his life.

The motorcycle had just turned the corner at Nineteenth, but then suddenly made a fast U-turn, which explained the roaring sound he'd heard.

And then Curtis saw why the rider — *Jesus, he's small for that big bike* — had changed direction: Near the end of the block, a group of four girls wearing their parochial-school outfits of dark woolen skirts and white cotton blouses were approaching the corner of Nineteenth and Callowhill. They looked to be about age fifteen or sixteen.

As the motorcycle closed on the group, the

girls were lit by the bike's bright headlight — and they froze there in the beam, staring at the fast-approaching machine.

Scared like damned deer.

One of the girls wore a zippered hoodie athletic jacket, in blue and white, and when she turned away from the beam it lit her back. There Curtis saw the representation of Mickey Mouse stitched on the jacket, the cartoon character's head partially obscured by the hood.

Curtis had figured — and the jacket confirmed — that the group was from John W. Hallahan Catholic Girls' High School. A private institution run by the Archdiocese of Philadelphia, Hallahan was just around the corner, between Callowhill and Vine. Blue and white were its school colors, the Disney icon its school mascot.

The motorcyclist slowed, then passed the girls and did another quick U-turn.

He may be small, but the prick can ride.

That's the "little man syndrome" — insecure guys getting a hot bike or car to help them look tougher.

Or maybe it's "little dick syndrome."

As the headlight swept around, it again washed the girls in its beam. Then the motorcycle engine roared loudly and the beam moved upward as the bike popped a wheelie, the front tire rising about three feet off the asphalt. The rider, half standing on the foot pegs, drove the bike on its back tire as he roared past the group of girls.

Fucking showing off, Curtis thought.

Like he owns the street.

And wants to own one of them. . . .

As the motorcycle came closer to where Will Curtis peered out from behind the filthy Ford van, the rider backed off the gas and the front tire returned to the pavement. The headlight beam flashed Curtis in the eyes, momentarily blinding him.

He instinctively dropped back behind the van and went into a crouch. He heard the motorcycle approaching quickly, followed by the sound of skidding tires. The motorcycle's engine revved twice, then went silent.

The only sound Will Curtis now heard was in the distance, up the street. The school girls were giggling and talking — both nervously and excitedly — as they slowly walked on up Nineteenth.

And — *boom!* — the sights and sounds of the high schoolers triggered a memory.

This time, though, the flashback wasn't an unpleasant one.

Wendy had attended Hallahan. And Will remembered the last day of her senior year. She had come home with her blue-and-white athletic jacket dripping wet because, as was traditional at the girls' school, she and the rest of the senior class had jumped into the Logan Circle fountain, which was just blocks south of the school in front of the Four Seasons Hotel.

And then the Catholic school memory — *boom!* — filled his mind with scenes of attending Saint Vincent's Catholic Church with Wendy and Linda.

In addition to worshipping there, near their West Mount Airy home, Will had volunteered his time. Mostly it had been in the capacity of scoutmaster with a Boy Scout troop that the church sponsored. Never mind that he'd had no sons in the program. He liked what the Scouts did — he'd been one as a kid, working his way up to just two merit badges shy of the top rank of Eagle Scout — and, bending rules a bit, he liked taking his daughter on camping trips and other outings with the boys. He'd treated her like the others. He taught them how to handle knives and how to shoot pistols and .22-caliber rifles (though, to his disappointment, she never kept any interest in guns).

In Scouts he'd also, of course, taught Wendy how to tie her knots.

And that — *boom!* — did cause an unpleasant flashback.

Damn it!

An ugly one, a vivid one, because he knew that the morning after Saint Paddy's, after that evil date-rape drug had worn off, Wendy had awakened to find herself naked and spread-eagled — bound with nylon stockings knotted around all four of the bed-posts.

As Will Curtis's eyes readjusted to the darkness and he could make out his surroundings again, the flashback faded.

He looked across the street and saw that the motorcycle rider had nosed the machine to a stop in front of the cracked frosted plate-glass window with LAW OFFICE OF DANIEL O. GARTNER, ESQ.

The window still pulsed with colored lights from the television.

The bike was indeed an aggressive-looking racing machine. It had bright neon green plastic body panels and a neon green fuel tank, a sleek, swept-back windscreen, and bold decalcomania that damn near screamed in black lettering: KAWASAKI NINJA.

The rider dramatically swung his right leg over the seat as he dismounted. He then began loosening the chin strap of his matching neon green helmet, a full-face model with its silver-mirrored visor pushed up.

Then, suddenly, the battered metal door of the office opened.

The motorcyclist turned to look toward it.

Will Curtis thought, *All that engine roaring and rubber burning got someone's attention.*

And then he saw a familiar face in the doorway.

Curtis had amused himself the first time he'd seen the criminal defense lawyer's name listed on court papers as: COUNSELOR, DEFENSE — GARTNER, DANIEL O. He'd begun by calling him "Danny O." Then he'd switched that around.

Well, hello, O Danny Boy.

You sleazy sonofabitch. . . .

Curtis thought of Gartner, with a beak of a nose and squinty dark eyes, as a pale-faced prick. He was medium-size and in his early to mid fifties. He tried to appear much younger by dying the gray of his thinning hair, though the dye job, full of blotches, was badly done. He wore tight faded black jeans, a gray T-shirt stenciled with black arty lettering that read PEACE LOVE JUSTICE, and tan suede shoes that were open at the heel.

As his squinty eyes darted back and forth, Curtis recalled his first impression of Gartner: that he not only looked like a weasel, but projected a greasy sleaziness.

26

Gartner then said something to the motorcyclist as he was rocking his helmet side to side to slide it from his head. When he'd finally gotten it off and turned to lock it to the rear of the bike, Curtis saw yet another familiar face, a smug one.

Well, I will be goddamned! All the waiting really has paid off.

I'm going to get a twofer!

Jay-Cee, you miserable shit. You won't be smug long, not for what you did to Wendy. . . .

John "JC" Nguyen was a cocky twenty-five-year-old — half Caucasian, half Asian, small-boned, five-two, and maybe one-ten soaking wet — who didn't walk but strutted. His thick black hair was combed straight back and hung to his collar. He wore baggy blue jeans that barely clung to his hips, a long-sleeved white T-shirt, and, over the T-shirt, a Philadelphia Eagles football jersey.

The green jersey had a big white number 7 on the back and, in white block lettering across the shoulder blades, the name VICK.

Small surprise that the punk worships an overpaid jock who likes making dogs fight to the death.

But what the hell kind of justice is it that Michael Vick sat almost two years in the slam for that crime while this miserable shit abused my baby and never spent a single fucking night behind bars?

By the time he reentered the court system for the assault on Wendy Curtis, JC had had a long list of priors — more than a dozen arrests over as many years, mostly for either possession of, or possession with intent to distribute, pot and speed and other controlled substances. His first bust had been when he'd just turned fourteen, and it earned him the street name "JC," for John Cannabis, a nod to the homegrown marijuana he first sold to his South Philly High schoolmates.

Curtis had learned, primarily from the prosecutors in the Repeat Offenders Unit of the district attorney's office, that in all but Nguyen's very first cases, he had been represented by Gartner.

Curtis also had been told that that did not necessarily mean Gartner was a good lawyer. In fact, one assistant district attorney assigned to prosecute Nguyen's case said that the opposite was true.

"The one thing commonly said of Daniel O. Gartner, Esquire," the prosecutor told Curtis, quietly but bitterly, "is that he's the worst fucking lawyer in all the Commonwealth of Pennsylvania."

He'd then added, "If there existed a book titled *The Dictionary of Dirtbags,* and in it was a definition of a lawyer who not only graduated at the bottom of his class but was as dirty as his clients, Gartner's ugly mug would be beside it." He'd exhaled audibly and added, "He's always working the system."

He explained that Gartner almost never really won a case for a client. Practically all them were negotiated with some sort of plea bargain to get the charges reduced, working the system so that the sentence left the scum with a very short term in the slam. Thus, it wasn't unusual for Gartner to watch a less-than-ecstatic client in handcuffs and a faded orange jumpsuit being hauled out of court to go back behind bars.

Sometimes — thanks to the already overloaded justice system, its dockets packed, its prisons full — he managed to get only a slap-on-the-wrist sentence of probation.

And, on very rare occasions, Gartner got a case tossed out on a technicality.

Curtis had learned that the hard way in Wendy's case, with Nguyen. Gartner got the guilty bastard off scot-free. All it had taken was for him to find a breach in how the evidence had been handled.

The animal didn't even get probation. Nothing.

In the DA's office, after giving the bad news to Will and Linda Curtis, then deeply apologizing for the administrative mistake, the prosecutor sighed and said, "It's the reality of what we deal with every day. The system is broken. But like a broken watch that gets the time right twice a day, we eventually do get 'em. Meanwhile, guys like Gartner take advantage of the weaknesses to get their clients to walk."

Will Curtis saw Gartner motion for JC to come inside. JC nodded in reply, then pulled a small nylon bag from under the weblike netting on the rear end of the motorcycle's black seat.

Strutting like a rooster, he carried the bag to the open metal door, went through it, and closed the door behind him.

Will Curtis checked for traffic again and started across the street.

[THREE]
Loft Number 2180
Hops Haus Tower
1100 N. Lee Street, Philadelphia
Saturday, October 31, 11:05 P.M.

"Maybe I'm wrong about you being a cop," Dr. Amanda Law playfully whispered to Homicide Sergeant Matthew M. Payne, Philadelphia Police Department Badge Number 471, "because I'm beginning to think that you do your best work undercover."

He saw that her face was flushed and glowing as she smiled and pulled her shoulder-length blond hair into a ponytail, then threw back the soft cotton cover in question.

She leaned over and kissed him wetly and loudly on his heaving chest. Then she stepped out of bed and, after taking a moment to catch her breath, said, "Be right back, Romeo."

Twenty-seven-year-old Matt Payne — who was six feet tall, one-seventy-five with a chiseled face, dark intelligent eyes, and thick dark hair he kept trimmed short — marveled at the magnificent milk-white orbs that formed the toned derriere of Amanda Law as she padded stark naked across the hardwood flooring, then disappeared into the bathroom.

There then came from behind the door a soft thumping and whine, followed by the sound of two clicks, one of a light switch and another of the door latch softly shutting.

The whine had been from Luna, the two-year-old pup Amanda had rescued from the animal shelter five months earlier. And the thumping had been the dog's wagging tail hitting the plastic floor liner of the wire kennel crate that served as the dog's den in the massive tiled bathroom.

Luna — Matt joked that it was short for "Lunatic" due to the dog's occasional hyperness and regular talkativeness — was either a labradoodle or a genuine purebred Portuguese water dog. The two breeds could be spitting images, and had similar traits: a friendly disposition and a serious protective loud bark. It was Amanda's opinion that Luna, at forty pounds, with a dense, tightly curled, nonshedding black coat, was more poodle than lab.

Payne smiled as he thought, *What the hell? Is it possible to lose count?*

He glanced at the bedside table. There,

beside two beer bottles and a glass of white wine, was his cell phone. He looked at the clock on its screen.

It's only eleven? And we got back here at maybe nine.

Payne, his heart pounding, put his head back on the pillow.

So, that means she . . . that is, we . . .

Damn! Three times in two hours. . . .

As his chest continued to rise and fall with heavy breaths, he decided that if he was about to go into full cardiac arrest right damn here and right damn now, the luxury apartment of a medical doctor wasn't necessarily a bad place for that to happen. Particularly considering that over the course of the last two hours, said medical doctor had been party to the cause of his current condition.

I'm not about to die, but when I do, I damn sure want to go wrapped in the arms of that wonderful blond goddess.

Thank God she's gotten back so much of her old self.

And, thank God again, she seems only to have suffered a little of the anxiety that her shrink predicted — and none of the post-trauma stress he'd said would come.

He certainly underestimated her strong character and her ability to move forward and keep working.

And she loves her work.

Amanda Law, MD, FACS, FCCM, was chief physician at Temple University Hospital's Burn Center.

Matt was then jarred by the painful memory of Amanda's abduction from in front of the hospital a month before — and how close she'd come to being killed by a psychopath. And that made him think about what she'd just said about him being a cop, and that in turn made him think about her condominium and why he was really glad she had a place that he knew was safer than any place in the screwed-up city.

After what she went through, having The Fortress doesn't hurt.

If only for her peace of mind.

Hell, mine, too.

Nearly nine months earlier, Amanda Law had bought Loft Number 2180, a luxury one-bedroom, one-and-a-half-bath condominium on the top floor of the year-old Hops Haus Tower in the Northern Liberties section of Philly. The penthouse property had met her long list of requirements, starting with a good price.

"A really reasonable one, considering all the amenities," she'd said.

But, she confided in Matt, what had really sold her on the place were the incredible panoramic views.

Even from his pillow, Payne could stare out at the lights twinkling on nearby Interstate 95 and the Delaware River and, past the far riverbank, the lights of Camden, New Jersey, and, spreading out even farther east, of the Garden State itself.

She'd said she also liked the retro industrial design of the high-rise, which reflected the feel of the Hops Haus Brewery, the renovated four-story, hundred-year-old building adjacent to the foot of the tower. The wall surfaces were alternately exposed red brick and stained concrete, and the flooring was a rustic dark hardwood planking. The high ceilings had exposed fire sprinkler pipes, and the metal ductwork for the air-conditioning hung from straps out in the open. The floor-to-ceiling windows were of the same design as those of the original Bavarian brewhouse downstairs.

But what Payne liked best about the residential tower — and why he privately called it The Fortress — was that, while it was meant to appear old, the place had the absolute latest in state-of-the-art security. That included, of course, being wired with high-end closed-circuit TV cameras with overlapping fields of view so that no corner went unrecorded, as well as a multifactor authentication system for anyone who wished to access the property.

And all of it was monitored by round-the-clock private security personnel. The security chief was Andy Hardwick, a mid-forties, bald, and barrel-chested sergeant from Central Detectives who'd conveniently retired from the Philadelphia Police Department right before the development was completed. He'd known Payne's biological father and uncle, had known Matt since he'd been in diapers, and was more than happy to show him all the building's bells and whistles and bad-guy booby traps.

Hardwick had promised Payne there'd be a close but discreet protective eye kept on the primary resident of Loft Number 2180, as well as heightened surveillance, mostly via CCTV cameras, but also by occasional security personnel "performing routine safety-device inspections," of the twenty-first floor.

This place is probably tighter than a Graterford RHU, Payne thought, and then he had a mental image of the hellish super-secure Restricted Housing Units — effectively individual prisons for the worst offenders serving time in solitary confinement — at the Pennsylvania State Correctional Institution thirty miles west of Philly.

■■■■

All of the Hops Haus Tower's common-area and exterior doors were on computer-controlled locks. Every resident was issued an electronic fob, smaller than a cough drop and designed to fit conveniently on a key ring, each of which had a unique electronic signature that could be turned on — and, perhaps more important, turned off — at one of the security computers. Most residents also had electronic scans of their thumbprints saved to the security computers.

For entry, residents could unlock the common-area and exterior doors — including those on each floor of the parking garage that led to the elevators — only through a two-step authentication process: First, they used the electronic fob, and second, they submitted to a biometric thumbprint reader or manually entered a unique code on a keypad. The doors guarding each elevator bank within the building were fitted with the same certification devices.

Finally, as a last electronic barrier, there was a fob receiver panel inside each elevator, on the wall of buttons. You had to swipe the fob in order for any of the buttons to become live and light up when pushed.

Each fob was coded to be floor-specific,

which meant two things. It was noted if the resident associated with the thumbprint or keypad code at the elevator bank door got off at a floor other than the one linked to the fob, and the anomaly was flagged and archived and available in the event anything unfortunate happened.

And only residents of the penthouse floor had fobs that allowed access to that level. The fobs of every other resident could go only as high as the twentieth floor. Which was another reason Payne thought that Amanda's top-floor unit was highly secure.

Then he had an unkind thought.

Of course, no matter how high the professional standards, including Andy Hardwick's, the weak link in the most secure of facilities, whether it's a luxury residence or a super-max prison, is the human factor — the gatekeepers, whoever the hell is manning the desks and machinery.

One crooked guard on the take and the whole fucking system may as well be a bucket of rusty bolts and blown locks.

Especially with security — and certain concierge — personnel having access to that master key to every unit, the one that that effeminate manager had said "was necessary, you know, just in case of emergency, like your washing machine's water line ruptures while you're gone or your bathtub overflows and starts flooding your neighbors."

Yeah, right. And for what he didn't say: "Or there's the stench of rotted flesh coming from behind your locked door."

Still, for what it is, and where it is, this place is as good as it gets.

His pulse starting to calm, Payne sat up and heaved one last deep breath. He reached back over to the bedside table and picked up one of the beers, a half-empty bottle of Hops Haus India Pale Ale. After he and Amanda had eaten dinner in the pub on the first floor of the building, he'd bought a case of the IPA — the pub had its own microbrewery — and that case of twenty-four bottles was now down to twenty.

He looked out the tall windows again as he took a swig of beer. While he could appreciate the view, being a cop he couldn't help but look past the twinkling lights and think of all the criminals hiding out there in the shadows, masked by darkness.

His eyes followed the Delaware River up to the Betsy Ross Bridge, then beyond that. Though too far to see clearly, he knew that a few miles beyond the bridge, on State Road in the Holmesburg section of Northeast Philadelphia, some of those lights were from the Philadelphia Prison System. Its Curran-

Fromhold Correctional Facility, the largest in the system, alone processed some thirty thousand inmates, all adult males, each year, every year. The intake center operated around the clock.

But not damn near enough.

What was that figure on fugitives from the courts? Almost fifty thousand who've jumped bail and run?

Now they're in the wind . . . out there, somewhere.

They're damn sure not in church confessing their sins and praying for absolution.

Hell no. They're roaming the streets, committing more robberies, rapes, murders, whatever, at will.

They know the court system is so clogged that they can just ignore it, thumb their nose at it.

Jesus, what a mess. . . .

[FOUR]

It was no secret to the one and a half million residents of the sixth-most-populated city in America that the City of Brotherly Love was among the deadliest in America.

Philadelphia — *"Killadelphia,"* Payne heard

it called at least once every damn day — averaged a murder daily — *down from, incredibly, a two-a-day average only a decade ago* — which of course kept the police department's Homicide Unit plenty busy.

What politicians wished was more of a secret, if only because of bureaucratic bungling and intergovernmental finger-pointing, was the fact that there were tens of thousands of fugitives loose on the streets. Nearly fifty thousand miscreants — from pimps to pedophiles to robbers to rapists to junkies to every other lawless sonofabitch — who had skipped out on their bail and were on the run from facing their day in court.

As a general rule of thumb, the main purpose of a court's bail system was more or less a noble one: to let certain of those charged with crimes to remain productive family members and citizens in their community until their court date, which could be months away. This "pretrial release" reinforced the presumption that those charged with crimes were "innocent until proven guilty."

It also, conveniently, helped ease the burden on the overcrowded jails. And that, in turn, eased the financial burden on a cash-strapped city to provide three square meals a day, armed guards for supervision, and sundry other services.

The vast majority of America's biggest cities used the bail bond system, a private-sector enterprise administered by for-profit companies. In contrast, the City of Philadelphia (and the City of Chicago, Illinois, which had a similar number of fugitives from justice) used a system of deposit bail, which was government-funded and government-run.

In Philly, it was overseen by judges from the Municipal Court and from the Court of Common Pleas.

Using a worksheet titled "Pretrial Release Guidelines," an arraignment magistrate determined the severity of the crime and the risk factor of the person charged with the crime to set the bail. The guidelines would, in theory, set a bail high enough to ensure that the person charged with the crime would appear in court so as not to lose the security fee.

Once the bail fee had been set, both the bail bond and the deposit bond worked essentially the same way. Generally, depending on various factors, the person charged with the crime had to pay only ten percent of the whole security fee to get out of jail.

The main differences between the two models arose if the offender missed or skipped out on his court date. Under the bail bond model, the court went after the bail bondsman for the deadbeat's forfeited fee — the company then had a financial incentive to find the deadbeat and deliver him to the court. There was no similar financial incentive, however, with a deposit bond. The government already owned the deadbeat's IOU. It was funny money, more or less worthless unless they hunted down the deadbeat and collected the remaining fee — *if* they could find him, and *if* he had the funds to pay.

And so, not surprisingly, those who'd blown their deposit bail numbered around fifty thousand — no one knew the exact number because, due to more bureaucratic blundering, a master listing was never kept.

These fugitives collectively owed hundreds of millions of dollars for their unpaid IOUs.

Worse, in the meantime they remained at large on the streets, acting with impunity — effectively telling the City of Philadelphia and its judicial system to go fuck itself.

All kinds of craziness going on down there, Payne thought, *while I'm up here enjoying the company of this incredible goddess.*

And God knows I do love her.

But do I love being out there chasing some murderer more?

He sighed.

The answer — right here, right now — is not

no, but hell no!

And Amanda's not complaining that they pulled me back off the street and stuck me at a desk in Homicide. There's absolutely no question that deep down, all things being equal, she'd rather I do something other than be a cop, anything that didn't risk me getting shot in the line of duty, like her father, or killed, like my father and uncle.

And that obit damn sure spelled it out.

[FIVE]

While Amanda Law had been in her first week of recovery, under the shrink's orders simply to rest at home and to reconsider taking the antianxiety meds that he'd prescribed and that she'd steadfastly refused — "I don't need to be popping Prozacs and I damn sure don't need them turning my mind to putty so I just sit there and drool all over myself" — her type A personality had her brain working overtime.

Dealing mentally with the abduction and the attempt at extortion had been bad enough. But then came the knowledge that the bastards who'd kidnapped her had made a regular habit of committing sexual assaults

44

and, worse, their leader had just killed one teenage Honduran girl — an illegal immigrant whom he'd forced into prostitution.

Naturally, logically, all that had caused her to consider her own mortality — *How close had he been to killing again? He certainly threatened me* — and then that of Matt.

And in the process of working through what-if scenarios — *What happens if we continue seeing each other? What happens if we get married and move into that vine-covered cottage with the white picket fence that Matt loves to mention? And then what happens if he stays on with the department?* — she'd come up with, as her father the cop had taught her to do, a worst-case scenario.

Amanda explained all this — and more — to Matt in great detail. And then handed him the absolute worst case as it had manifested itself to her: as an obituary.

Amanda had written the obit as if she were Mickey O'Hara, the Pulitzer Prize–winning reporter who was well respected by both police rank and file and brass. Over the years, Matt and the wiry Irishman ten years his senior had even become fairly close friends.

Amanda had gotten a great deal of the details for the obit from searches on the Internet, mostly from the *Bulletin*'s online archive of articles, many of which had been articles written by O'Hara. The rest of the details had been provided by Matt's sister. Amy Payne had never liked that her brother was a cop, and had been more than happy to fill in any gaps for her old college dorm suitemate.

Payne thought that Amanda had done a helluva job putting together the obit. He hadn't been able to shake it from his mind, which was no surprise, considering the subject:

The Wyatt Earp of the Main Line:

KILLED IN THE LINE OF DUTY

Homicide Sergeant Matthew M. Payne, 31, Faithfully Served Family and Philly — and Paid the Ultimate Price

By Michael J. O'Hara

Staff Writer, *The Philadelphia Bulletin*

Photographs Courtesy of the Family and Michael J. O'Hara

PHILADELPHIA — The City of Brotherly Love grieves today at the loss of

---

one of its finest citizens and police officers. Sergeant Matthew Mark Payne, a nine-year veteran of the Philadelphia Police Department and well known as the Wyatt Earp of the Main Line, was gunned down last week in a Kensington alleyway as he dragged out a fellow officer who'd been wounded in an ambush.

Payne's heroic act amid a barrage of bullets sealed, right up until his last breath, his long-held reputation as a brave, loyal, and honorable officer and gentleman.

Friends and family say that part of what made Payne such an outstanding civil servant, one that personified the department's motto of Honor, Integrity, Sacrifice, was that he didn't have to do it.

He chose to do so.

A Family That Served — and Sacrificed

When, almost a decade ago, Payne graduated summa cum laude from the University of Pennsylvania, he could have followed practically any professional path other than law enforcement.

He'd enjoyed a privileged background,

brought up in upscale Wallingford, in all the comfort that a Main Line life afforded. After attending prep school at Episcopal Academy, then completing his studies at U of P, he was expected to pursue a law degree and, perhaps, join his adoptive father's law practice, the prestigious firm of Mawson, Payne, Stockton, McAdoo & Lester.

Instead, Matt Payne chose something else: He decided that he should defend his country.

He signed recruitment papers with the United States Marine Corps, only to discover that a minor condition with his vision barred him from joining the Corps.

Determined to serve in some other capacity, Payne joined the Philadelphia Police Department.

Again, he didn't have to. If anything, Matt Payne had a pass. But, again, he chose to.

A pass, because his biological father, Sergeant John F. X. Moffitt, known as Jack, was killed in the line of duty, too — shot dead while responding to a silent burglar alarm at a gasoline station. And Jack Moffitt's brother, Captain Richard C. "Dutch" Moffitt, commanding officer of the department's elite Highway Patrol, had been killed as well while trying to stop a robbery at the Waikiki Diner on Roosevelt Avenue.

Payne's decision to join the police department came only months after his Uncle Dutch was killed. Many believed he joined in order to avenge the deaths of his father and uncle, and to prove that the condition that kept him out of the Corps would not keep him from being a good cop.

"Frankly, all that scared the hell out of us," said Dennis V. "Denny" Coughlin, who recently retired as first deputy commissioner of police, but who was a chief inspector at the time Payne joined the department.

Coughlin had been best friends with Jack Moffitt at his death, and took upon himself the sad duty of delivering the tragic news to Matt's mother — then pregnant with Matt — that she'd been widowed.

"I can confess now that when Matty came to the department," a visibly upset Coughlin added, "I tried to protect him. I sure as hell didn't want to have to knock on his mother's door with the news that now Jack's son had been killed on the job, too. Unfortunately, that duty fell last week to First Deputy Commissioner of Police Peter Wohl."

New Cop, Hero Cop
After graduating from the Police Academy, there was no question that Matt Payne was becoming both a good cop and a respected one.

"But no matter how hard we tried throughout his career," said Peter Wohl, to whom Payne was first assigned as an administrative assistant when Wohl ran Special Operations, "Matt wound up in the thick of things, bullets flying. That said, all his shootings were found to be righteous ones."

Before Payne had even put in six months on the job, he had already drawn his pistol. It had happened when he was off duty and had come across a van that fit the description of the one used by the criminal the newspapers had labeled the Northwest Serial Rapist. When the driver tried to run him down, Payne shot him in the head. A young woman, trussed up and naked in the back of the vehicle, was saved from becoming the rapist's next victim. And headlines hailed Matt Payne as a hero.

The next incident happened during an operation that this writer covered.

Matt Payne had been assigned to provide protection for me in an alleyway that was supposed to be a safe distance from where tactical teams were staging to arrest a gang who had committed murder while robbing Goldblatt's Department Store.

"We thought that in having Matt sit on Mick," Wohl explained, "we could keep Mick out of our way and at the same time keep Matt far from any gunplay."

They were wrong.

As this writer reported then, one of the men the cops were trying to arrest came into the alleyway and began shooting. Matt Payne, his forehead grazed by a bullet, returned fire and killed the shooter.

The following day, on the front page of the *Bulletin,* the photograph I took of a bloodied Matt Payne holding his pistol and standing over the dead shooter appeared with this writer's firsthand account of Payne's heroic actions.

The photograph's headline read: "Officer M. M. Payne, 23, The Wyatt Earp of the Main Line."

A Shining — but Brief — Career
Promotion followed, but so, too, did more gunfire.

Payne became romantically involved with a young woman named Susan Reynolds and then discovered that a sorority sister of hers had become caught up with a terrorist named Bryan Chenowith, who was the target of a nationwide manhunt by the Federal Bureau of Investigation.

In an attempt to trap Chenowith, Payne asked Reynolds to lure her friend to a diner in hopes that the fugitive would follow and the FBI's special agent in charge in Philadelphia could nab him. However, the fugitive brought with him a .30-caliber carbine rifle and shot up the parking lot.

Susan Reynolds took a bullet to the head and died in Payne's arms.

Later, Matt Payne quietly admitted to a very few that the experience haunted him beyond anything he'd ever known.

Payne dealt with it as best he could, mostly by losing himself in his work. And that he did well.

When he was promoted to sergeant and transferred to the Homicide Unit, Matt Payne was given Badge Number 471, which previously had been worn by Sergeant John "Jack" F. X. Moffitt, his father.

Other dramatic incidents occurred — too many to be included here — but one of the most recent was among the most memorable, when the Wyatt Earp of the Main Line again found himself involved in a foot chase — and a shoot-out — with a murderer.

Payne happened to be at Temple University Hospital when Jesús Jiménez, a nineteen-year-old gang member, snuck into the hospital's third-floor Burn Unit and executed a patient.

When Jiménez fled the floor, Payne pursued him out onto the streets, ultimately wounding Jiménez in the thigh before he got away.

Jiménez, it turned out, belonged to a group led by Juan Paulo Delgado, a Texican, age twenty-one. And the assassination in the hospital was only a part of Delgado's reign of terror — one that stretched from the streets of Philadelphia to the dirt trails of the Texas–Mexico border.

When Delgado abducted Dr. Amanda Law for ransom, Payne, Detective Anthony Harris, and Sergeant Jim Byrth of the legendary Texas Rangers law-enforcement agency were already hunting him. Thery were accompanied by a confidential informant.

Acting on a tip from the informant, the group tracked Delgado to a dilapidated row house on Hancock Street in Kensington. The policemen confronted the occupants — Jiménez, Delgado, and their associate Omar Quintanilla — in an exchange that eventually left Delgado and Quintanilla dead. Payne and his associates rescued Dr. Law, who was found in the kitchen, her head covered by a pillowcase, her ankles and wrists bound by duct tape to a chair, and the arrests of the members of Delgado's gang quickly followed.

And so now we come to today: One final time we declare Matt Payne a hero.

This courageous, dedicated son of Philadelphia gave the city his all in last week's gun battle and selfless act in which he put down a pair of vicious criminals and saved a fellow officer.

May he rest in peace.

"We know that Matt will always be a hero to the decent and law-abiding citizens of Philadelphia," said his deeply grieving wife, Dr. Amanda Law Payne, as she held their toddler daughter on her hip and as their twin sons clung to her legs following a memorial service that overflowed with attendees. "But first and foremost, he was our family's hero. While we must move forward, our children and I shall never ever forget that."

Matthew Mark Payne is survived by his loving wife of five years, Mrs. Amanda Law Payne; his sons, Brewster Cortland Payne III and John Francis Xavier Moffitt Payne, age four; his daughter, Mandy Law Payne, age two; his sister, Dr. Amelia Payne; his parents, Mr. and Mrs. B. C. Payne II; and numerous other relatives and friends.

The family requests that, in lieu of flowers, memorials be made in Matthew Mark Payne's name to the Widow & Orphan Fund at the Fraternal Order of Police, Lodge #5, 1336 Spring Garden Street, Philadelphia, PA 19123.

Matt remembered slowly folding the sheets of paper, then handing it back to her.

She smiled weakly as tears welled, then trickled down her rosy cheeks.

Softly, she said, "Life is short, baby. Maybe too short."

II

[ONE]
1834 Callowhill Street,
Philadelphia
Saturday, October 31, 8:27 P.M.

Will Curtis, almost across the street, chuckled at the tune that suddenly played in his head. Then he heard himself start singing it softly: "O Danny Boy, the pipes, the pipes are calling, from glen to glen, and down the mountain side, the summer's gone, and all the *losers* falling . . ."

As he came closer to the law office, he realized that he hadn't given a hell of a lot of thought as to how he was going to get inside. He figured if he knocked on the door long enough and loud enough he would get a response.

Hell, then again, all I really have to do is make a lot of noise kicking over the motorcycle.

I'll bet that bastard Jay-Cee comes flying outside.

When he reached the door and had put the canteen on the sidewalk beside it, he decided, just for the hell of it, to try the doorknob.

With his right hand holding his Glock, he carefully grabbed the knob with his left hand and slowly started to turn it.

It was unlocked.

Why am I not surprised? Jay-Cee's a dumbass.

The heavy metal door swung outward with a squeak of its hinges.

And then Curtis realized why it had been unlocked: It was a common door for the multiple individual offices within the building.

He now stood in an empty corridor, a short and very narrow one, with the inner door to Gartner's office immediately to his left, a flight of well-worn wooden stairs leading to the offices on the upper floors a little farther down on the right, and, at the end of the corridor, an exit door to the alleyway.

Curtis decided to press his luck and turn the dirty tin knob on Gartner's interior door to see if just maybe JC might have left it unlocked, too. As he reached for the knob, he heard someone directly on the other side of the door, then saw the knob turn. He barely had time to flatten himself against the wall by the door hinges before the door flew open toward him, blocking his view.

Then came the sound of feet moving quickly, then the exterior door squeaking open and closed.

Curtis didn't see who had gone outside. But now he leaned over to peer through the gap between the door edge and the frame into Gartner's office.

It was mostly dark except for the glow of the television — out of Curtis's field of view, but he could hear its sound, which seemed to be a lot of heavy breathing with rock music blaring in the background — and a single short lamp on what he guessed to be Gartner's desk.

There were two other desks, smaller ones, their tops not nearly as messy, though one had the crumpled greasy Chinese takeout bags on it. Against a far wall stood a pair of old six-foot-long folding tables. They sagged at the center under the weight of loose fat file folders and white cardboard storage boxes. Under the tables, and all along the walls, were books and more stacks of file folders and piles of legal-size papers. And there was trash, or what could have been more legal papers, littering the worn, dirty industrial carpeting.

Curtis could see Gartner behind the desk — a big wooden one piled ridiculously high with papers — standing bent over at the waist with his face close to the desktop. He held something to his face and slowly pivoted his head from left to right while inhaling deeply.

Then he suddenly stood erect and, rubbing his nose, looked wide-eyed at the open office door, then spun on his heels and looked at the cracked plate-glass window.

After a second, apparently satisfied, Gartner then bent back over the desk again.

Will Curtis carefully stepped to the left so he could peer around the far edge of the open door. He saw that the heavy metal door to the street was closed. He started to move toward it to lock its deadbolts. But then he thought that might reveal him to Gartner, if only for a second or two, which would ruin the element of surprise.

Fuck it. Get it over with. . . .

Will Curtis quickly moved around the open door and, gun up and ready, entered Danny Gartner's office. As he scanned the interior — Gartner was alone — he pulled the door closed behind him. This time, he did throw the lock on the door.

Before Curtis could say anything, Gartner, his face still close to the desk, casually said, "You find it?"

When Gartner looked up for a response, his eyes became huge again. He dropped what he had in his hand and staggered two steps backward, almost tripping over his own feet.

"What the hell?" Danny Gartner asked, his voice almost a squeak. "Who —"

"Shut the fuck up," Will Curtis said calmly but forcefully, aiming at him with the Glock.

"Who —" Gartner repeated.

"I said shut the fuck up!"

Curtis glanced at the desktop. He saw the black nylon bag JC had brought. It was open, and held a plastic sandwich bag, not quite a quarter full, of what looked like ground-up chalk. Beside that on the desktop were two lines — actually, a line and a half left — of the powder, and a stub of a thin plastic straw.

Coke? Maybe meth?

Goddamn drugs.

He glanced around the room. He now had a clear view of the TV, and the pulsing lights were of a very raw pornographic scene. It was hard-core — nothing but writhing naked women and close-up shots of the sex toys probing their genitalia filled the flat screen.

Sick sonsofbitches! he thought as he walked over to the TV.

There's no end to their depravity!

He hit the ON-OFF switch and the room got darker.

Curtis looked back at Gartner, then motioned quickly with the pistol. "Step out here in front of the desk."

Gartner didn't move. Curtis saw his eyes glance out the plate-glass window.

"Where'd JC go?" Curtis asked.

It was clear by Gartner's expression that he was surprised the intruder knew JC's name. Then that expression changed to one of found opportunity.

Gartner, his tone more controlled, said, "You're after JC? I can —"

"Damn it! Just answer the question." He motioned more aggressively with the pistol. "And get your ass over here, slowly."

Staring at the Glock, Gartner began moving as told. When he was in the middle of the floor, Curtis motioned again with the gun and said, "Now, on your knees."

As Gartner complied, Curtis looked around the room quickly. Over on one of the sagging folding tables was a roll of three-inch-wide clear packing tape. He walked over and picked it up, then went back to Gartner.

"Hands behind your back," Curtis said, and when Gartner had complied, Curtis wrapped his wrists tightly together with the tape. He pulled a folding knife from his pocket and cut the tape roll free. Then he pushed Gartner hard between the shoulder blades so that he fell forward and smacked his face on the dirty carpeting.

"Shit!" Gartner said. "What'd you do that for?"

Curtis didn't reply. He put his right knee in the small of Gartner's back — and on top of the taped wrists — then quickly wrapped Gartner's ankles with the tape.

The locked doorknob rattled, followed by a knock.

"Dan!" JC's muffled voice called. "What's up?"

Will Curtis put the muzzle of the pistol against Gartner's left temple. "Don't say a word."

He looked at Gartner's eyes, then decided he didn't trust him to do as ordered. He ran the tape through Gartner's open mouth and wrapped it twice around his head.

As Curtis stood and went to the door, JC began banging on it.

"Dan! You okay in there?" JC called.

At the door, Curtis held his pistol at the point where he expected to find JC's head.

Then he reached for the knob and unlocked it.

At the sound of the click, the knob spun and the door was yanked open.

JC stood there, an envelope in his right hand and — surprising Curtis — the green plastic canteen in his left. He froze as he saw he was looking at the muzzle of a big-bore pistol.

And, judging how his facial expression changed, he recognized the angry man who was aiming the weapon between his eyes.

"Ahhh," JC said, dropping the envelope and canteen, and holding up his hands, palms out.

Curtis then noticed some kind of movement in JC's midsection. When he glanced down, he saw that the crotch of JC's blue jeans was darkening and the stain was quickly spreading, moving mostly down the inside of the right leg of his pants.

Curtis snorted.

Not so smug now, huh?

Not so tough and cocky, either.

You chickenshit. You just pissed yourself.

"C'mon," Curtis said, motioning with the pistol for JC to come in. "Strut in over there. Beside your lawyer buddy. And get on your knees."

After JC reluctantly moved inside the office, Curtis quickly stepped out and grabbed the envelope and the canteen, then pulled the door shut and relocked it.

The envelope was hefty, and packed with a thick wad of paper. Will Curtis put one end of the envelope in his teeth and tore it open. He blew into the hole, then looked inside — then whistled.

He walked over to the desk and started shaking the envelope to dump out its contents.

A stack of well-worn bills — twenties, fifties, and hundreds, easily totaling at least a couple grand — landed by the zip-top bag of white powder. He shook the envelope once more and out fell a cellophane packet of pills.

He looked at JC, who had gotten on his knees.

Curtis then went to him and said, "Hands behind your back."

As Curtis wrapped JC's wrists, he asked, "What's that bag of powder? Meth?"

JC shook his head. "Uh-uh," he said nervously. "Coke. Take all you want."

Curtis ignored that. "And those pills in the packet?"

He saw JC and Gartner exchange nervous glances. He pushed JC to the floor and put a knee in his back.

"What the fuck are they?" Curtis said.

"Tell me, or I'll just shoot you now."

"Roofies," JC said quietly, closing his eyes.

Curtis said nothing as he considered that while taping together JC's ankles.

Then, with an amused tone to his voice, he said: "*Roofies?* Really!"

Curtis then leaned over Gartner and, using the pocketknife, cut the tape that was wrapped around his head and pulled the gag from his mouth.

"I think we all need a drink," Curtis said. "I know you've got to have something here, Danny Boy."

Gartner made a forced smile. "Sure. Bourbon. Vodka. Gin. What do you want?"

"Where is it?"

Gartner nodded toward a bookshelf across the room.

Will Curtis grabbed the first bottle he saw on the bookself. It was vodka, Stolichnaya, specifically Stoli Razberi. Beside it was a bottle of Jack Black and one of Bombay Sapphire. And next to those were six somewhat clean highball glasses.

As he walked back to the desk, Curtis didn't know what pissed him off more about the vodka.

That it's goddamned Russian, or that it's candy-ass flavored.

Well, maybe the raspberry will make the pills easier to swallow.

Gartner and JC watched Curtis's every move as he splashed about an inch of Stoli into each of two glasses. Then he took from the cellophane packet four of the Rohypnol pills and dropped two in each of the glasses of vodka. There was a little fizz as the pills began to dissolve in the alcohol.

He took the bottle of Stoli Razberi back to the bookshelf, picked up another glass, then the bottle of Jack Daniel's. As he poured, he turned to glance at Gartner and JC.

"If you're getting the clear stuff," Curtis said, "then I'm getting the dark stuff. Wouldn't want to get them confused, no?"

He carried the glass of Jack Black to the desk and set it down. Then he picked up one of the glasses of vodka. He took it over to where Gartner lay on the carpet. Grabbing Gartner by the arm, Curtis got him back up on his knees. Then he held the glass to his lips. Gartner shook his head. Curtis grabbed him by his thinning gray-black hair and yanked back. Gartner's jaw dropped open and Curtis poured in the vodka, then moved his hand under the jaw and closed Gartner's mouth. It took a moment, but Gartner finally swallowed most of it.

He repeated the process with JC, though

he had to hit JC on the head with his pistol after he spit out the first glass of vodka. Curtis had then mixed two more roofies with another three inches of Stoli Razberi, then grabbed a stunned JC by his blood-soaked thick black hair and poured the drink down his throat.

Then Will Curtis went back to the desk, sat in the chair, and began sipping from the Jack Daniel's while watching the alcohol-fueled roofies take effect.

And for reasons he did not understand, particularly considering the circumstances, he suffered not one single flashback.

Maybe this is what they mean by finding peace through justice.

"Okay, let's go, you assholes."

Curtis didn't expect a reply. Under the influence of the Stoli-Rohypnol mixture, Gartner and JC were more or less out cold. Even when he kicked them in the ass with his boot toe, they barely responded.

For the first ten minutes after he'd forced them to swallow the powerful sedative, he'd watched them slowly get sleepier and sleepier. Gartner faded faster, and Curtis thought that might be because of the cocaine he'd also consumed.

By the time fifteen minutes had passed,

they'd basically become incoherent, slurring their words.

After the twenty-minute mark, with them curled up babylike on the carpet, Curtis had felt confident that they posed no problem whatsoever and had gone out to move the car behind the building.

Now, a half hour later, he struggled to get them — very groggy but agreeable, despite their wrists still being bound — one at a time down the corridor and out the back door of the office building.

He'd parked the Malibu in the dark alley and left its truck open.

He dumped JC and Gartner inside the trunk, then took the clear adhesive tape and wrapped their heads so that the tape sealed the nose and mouth of both men.

As he watched their bodies begin to convulse at the blockage of their airways, Curtis wondered, *Why don't I feel bad about this?*

Then — *boom!* — a vision came of Wendy.

It was the one of her, spread-eagled, bound to the bed with her nylon stockings.

Shit! That's the hell why!

He looked at JC.

Because of what you did to my baby and to whoever else, you miserable bastard.

Then his eyes went to the other bucking body.

And you, Danny Boy, kept him out of jail so that he could.

Kept him and who the hell knows how many other miserable shits on the streets.

Curtis, suddenly furious, shook his head angrily as he took one last look at the pair.

Then he quickly pulled from his pocket two plastic garbage bags he'd grabbed in Gartner's office and covered their heads with them. He took the Glock from his jacket and put its muzzle at the base of JC's skull, angled toward the top of his head, and squeezed the trigger.

The .45-caliber round fired with a loud *bang*, JC made a primal groan, his legs kicked out straight, and the garbage bag on his head billowed briefly, the top of it moving violently as bullet fragments flew out, accompanied by bits of brain and blood, and lodged in the trunk floorboard.

The pistol automatically ejected the empty brass casing, which flew up, hitting the trunk lid, then landed beside JC's body, near where a dark stream of blood flowed from the bag, staining the white shirt and pooling on the football jersey.

Now you won't be going after those high school girls — or any others.

Then he moved the pistol muzzle to the same place at the base of Gartner's skull and squeezed off another round.

This time the ejected spent casing landed on the concrete of the alleyway. The brass made a tinkling sound in the darkness as it tumbled to a stop against a curb.

Rot in hell, you scum! Will Curtis thought, then slammed down the lid.

[TWO]
Loft Number 2180
Hops Haus Tower
1100 N. Lee Street, Philadelphia
Saturday, October 31, 11:10 P.M.

As Matt Payne looked out of Amanda Law's penthouse window, thinking about how much damn truth Amanda had written in his would-be obituary, he took a sip from the beer bottle and swallowed hard.

So then why do I feel the pull to be out there running down those animals?

Because of what else Amanda said, long before writing the obit? That it takes cops like me and her dad to keep the city as safe as possible from the bad guys loose on the streets.

Which she'd told me, more than a little ironically, right before those shits snatched her off the street.

At the memory of finding her bound in the gutted kitchen of that abandoned row house, Payne suddenly felt his throat constrict.

That place wasn't a house. It was a slum, and a fucking prison slum at that.

But there it is: I'll take the door of any place like that a hundred times over. That may or may not make me a good cop, but bagging bad guys is the right thing to do.

Proof of that being that Amanda is alive.

And further proof being that bastard Jiménez is on the fast track to serving a life sentence in Graterford.

Following his arrest at the row house, Jesús Jiménez had confessed to killing twenty-seven-year-old J. Warren "Skipper" Olde over what Juan Paulo Delgado claimed was a bad drug debt. In exchange for avoiding the death penalty, Jiménez also ratted out everyone in their small band of thugs in a signed confession.

Payne drained the beer bottle, which helped ease the constriction. Then he grinned as he thought:

Too bad the bastard's about to become somebody's bitch.

Jiménez will hope he gets thrown alone in an RHU.

The door to the bathroom swung open and Amanda Law, still starkers, stood momentarily backlit in the doorway.

My God, she's stunning! Matt thought.

"You take my breath away," he said. "In more ways than one, it would appear."

She flashed a sly smile. "That, Romeo, is my evil plan."

She clicked off the bathroom light and said sweetly to the dog, "Good girl, Luna. Lie down."

Then she smoothly and swiftly moved across the dimly lit bedroom, completely comfortable in her birthday suit. It reminded Matt of the second time he'd met her, just last month in Liberties Bar, when she seemed to float effortlessly across the well-worn wooden floor. Clothed, of course, but even then he'd been mentally undressing her.

As she crawled back into bed, Matt smelled the delicate floral scent of her perfume. It became stronger as she moved in closer to put a hand on his chest and kiss him on the forehead. He smoothly turned his head so that his lips were on hers. She moaned softy and appreciatively, and then — hearing a brief familiar vibrating sound — made an unhappy groan.

Payne's eyes turned in the direction of the sound, to the bedside table where he'd left his cell phone. It was set to SILENT/VIBRATE. Its color screen was now casting a pulsing bluish-green glow.

Amanda playfully bit his lower lip and held it as she mumbled, "Don't you dare get . . ."

Matt, still in her grips, carefully reached for the phone, then held it more or less behind Amanda's head so he could clearly see its screen.

She bit harder.

Payne grunted as he read the text message on-screen:

```
— BLOCKED NUMBER -

YO, MATTY. HOPE I'M INTERRUPT-
ING SOMETHING REALLY GOOD AT
THIS HOUR!

GOT ANOTHER POP-N-DROP AN HOUR
AGO. TWO ACTUALLY.

COULDN'T HAVE HAPPENED TO NICER
GUYS. YOU KNOW ONE. THE BLACK
BUDDHA SAID TO GIVE YOU A
HEADS-UP.

CLICK ON FOX29 NEWS. -TH
```

Matt sighed, then turned his eyes to meet Amanda's and raised his hands up, palms out.

"I surrender," he muttered as best he could.

She let loose his lip and slipped back between the sheets.

Her tone sounding disappointed, Amanda said, "I sure hope that's not what I'm afraid it is. Especially at this hour. Please tell me it's not work."

He held the phone out for her to read its screen.

As she did, Matt thought, *Someone I know?*

What the hell does that mean?

"TH" was Tony Harris — age thirty-eight, slight of build and starting to bald — who was widely regarded as a really good guy and a really good Homicide detective. He had worked closely with Matt and Sergeant Jim Byrth of the Texas Rangers last month when they'd tracked down Juan Paulo Delgado.

And the Black Buddha was their boss, Lieutenant Jason Washington, head of the Homicide Unit. He was a great big bear of a man — six-foot-three and two hundred twenty-five pounds, with very dark skin. Washington, well-spoken, superbly tailored, and highly respected, did not consider the nickname unflattering. "I'm damn sure black, Matthew," he said in his deep, sonorous voice. "And Buddha, the 'enlightened one,' surely is a wise man. I have no problem wearing that badge with pride."

"So," Amanda said softly, "I guess since you've been working the pop-and-drops, we're done for the evening?"

Someone in the city was shooting fugitives. These particular ones were wanted on outstanding arrest warrants for crimes against women and children. He had not told Amanda that their crimes were sexual in nature.

After "popping" a sex offender at point-blank range, the shooter then transported the body to the nearest police district headquarters, "dropping" it off in the parking lot with a copy of the perp's Wanted information — a computer printout downloaded from one of various Internet websites listing fugitives — stapled to some part of his clothing.

Thus, "pop-and-drop."

Not that anyone's complaining that the scum of society is being swept from the streets for good, Payne had thought.

But as Jason Washington said, "Murder's murder, Matthew. And who knows what the

75

shooter might escalate to next?"

Matt Payne hadn't figured out how in hell the shooter had been able to get so close to any of the district HQ buildings without being caught in the act of dumping a body. So far it had happened five times in about as many weeks, and the department had been able to keep the incidents quiet — which meant away from the news media — while the brass finally found someone who was available to take the cases and try to piece together who the hell the doer or doers might be. A lucky Sergeant Payne, stuck at his desk assignment, had been chosen.

Matt turned, kissed Amanda on the forehead, and said, "Hold on, baby."

Matt reached back over to the side table and fished around in its drawer until he came up with a remote control. He thumbed the ON button and the sixty-inch flat-screen television mounted on the wall made a humming sound and its screen began to glow.

He punched in from memory the channel of the local Fox station, and it was clear a live news report was being broadcast. In the bottom left-hand corner was confirmation: A small box alternately blinked the FOX29 logotype and the phrase "News Now, News You Can Use." A white bar also ran diagonally over the left top corner of the image, and it flashed red text: "REPORTING LIVE at 11:21 P.M. from Old City."

As the red and blue emergency lights from the police vehicles flashed, the news camera panned down the narrow tree-lined street. On the red brick sidewalk were curious bystanders — Payne noticed more than a few in Halloween costumes — held back by a length of yellow crime-scene tape.

Payne's eyes went to the ticker of text scrolling across the bottom of the TV screen: *BREAKING NEWS . . . TWO MEN FOUND BOUND AND SHOT DEAD . . . ONE IS A 25-YEAR-OLD WANTED ON AN OUTSTANDING BENCH WARRANT . . . ARREST WARRANT WAS FOR FAILURE TO APPEAR IN MUNICIPAL COURT ON TWO COUNTS OF INTENT TO DELIVER A CONTROLLED SUBSTANCE . . . THE OTHER DEAD MAN IS A CRIMINAL DEFENSE LAWYER, ABOUT AGE 50 . . . BOTH BODIES DUMPED AT LEX TALIONIS OFFICES . . . POLICE WITHHOLDING NAMES PENDING NOTIFICATION OF FAMILIES OF THE DECEASED . . . BREAKING NEWS . . .*

Then the camera cut away from the shot of the sidewalk and the TV screen suddenly filled with an awkwardly tight shot. It showed the jowly face of an almost bald man wearing a dark rumpled suit coat and a wrinkled white shirt with no necktie. The emergency lights bathed him in pulses of red and blue.

"Oh, hell!" Matt said. "That's a bit more of good ole Five-Eff than I'd care to see."

Then, in a jerky motion, the camera lens pulled back.

Amanda looked at the TV screen. She recognized the man, who now was shown head-to-toe in front of a nice but old brick building. He was in his mid-forties, short and stout with a small defined gut. He had a round face and wore, perched at the end of his bulbous nose, tiny round reading eyeglasses.

He stood addressing a small crowd of news media types. Reporters held microphones to the portly man's face, almost touching his big nose, as well as camera lenses, both still and video.

"'Five-Eff'?" she repeated. "I thought Frank Fuller was 'Four-Eff.'"

Payne turned to her and smiled. He said, "*Fucking* Frances Franklin Fuller the Fifth. That makes five."

[THREE]

Matt Payne's family had known Francis Fuller's as long as Matt could remember. They had many connections, both social and professional, and while Payne did not actively dislike the man, he had on more than one occasion called him Five-Eff to his face — and that almost always had happened when Fuller was being a pompous ass.

Payne otherwise addressed Fuller as "Francis," knowing full well (and purposely ignoring) that Fuller preferred the more masculine "Frank."

Fuller boldly and shamelessly touted the fact that he traced his family lineage — and what he called its puritanical ways — back to Benjamin Franklin. Fuller fancied himself a devout Franklinite, mimicking his ancestor from his looks to his philosophical beliefs. Fuller regularly sprinkled his conversations with quotes from *Poor Richard's Almanac* and other Ben Franklin sources. And like the multitalented Franklin, Francis Fuller was involved in all kinds of enterprises, private and public.

Payne somewhat begrudgingly admired Fuller for having built on the wealth he'd been born into, because he himself had enjoyed being raised, as he called it, "comfortably" — *though certainly not nearly on the level of the super-wealthy Fullers* — and he'd seen many others piss away vast sums of money that they had done nothing to earn and, he believed, thus did not deserve.

Fuller's primary company — Richard Saunders Holdings, which he'd taken from the name Franklin had used to write *Poor Richard's Almanac* — had many entities. There was KeyCom, the Fortune 500 nationwide telecommunications corporation that he'd built city by city by buying up local community cable television providers. And KeyCargo Import-Exports, which was one of the largest leasers of warehouse space at the Port of Philadelphia, which was easily visible from another of Fuller's holdings — the Hops Haus Tower — which fell under his KeyProperties.

With so much financial wealth came a great deal of influence, and Francis Fuller had political connections from Washington, D.C., to Harrisburg to Philly's City Hall and police department. He was more or less happy to share with all both his wealth and his opinions, though sometimes far more of the latter than the former. And in terms of the latter, Fuller was a devout believer in the Bible's an eye for an eye and a tooth for a tooth.

And so Francis Fuller funded and personally promoted a nonprofit organization he called Lex Talionis, from the Latin phrase for the "law of talion," which more or less translated as "an eye for an eye" — which, of course, was the meting out of punishments that matched the crimes. The logotype of Lex Talionis had the "o" as a stylized eyeball.

The offices for Lex Talionis took up half of the first floor of a five-story brick building on the tree-lined corner of North Third and Arch Streets. Fuller said he felt the location on Arch, in the historic section of Old City, with the Delaware River just blocks to the east and the Liberty Bell on display just blocks to the west, was more appropriate than any shiny marble-and-glass high-rise office building.

Francis Franklin Fuller V's belief in the fundamental philosophy of *Lex Talionis* was strong and unwavering, and there was a good reason for it: Tragedy had struck him personally.

Five years earlier, his wife and their eight-year-old daughter had been driving home in the early evening of a rainy Saturday, when she had accidentally exited just shy of the Vine Street Expressway she'd been aiming for.

My dearest could get lost in a closet, Fuller later lamented, *and that GPS street map in the dash of her Benz may as well have been a video game for all she knew how to operate it.*

After getting off the expressway at Spring Garden Street, then driving east and crossing over the Schuylkill Expressway, she'd somehow, maybe because the rain was disorienting, made a wrong turn onto Pennsylvania Avenue. Shortly thereafter she'd found herself in the North Philadelphia West area, driving down the darkened streets of struggling and failing neighborhoods.

What had happened next was a matter of great speculation. It could have been because of the luxury convertible automobile she was driving. Or it could simply have been an unfortunate case of being in the wrong place at the wrong time.

According to two eyewitness statements, as the Mercedes waited for a traffic light to turn green, two vehicles flew up to the intersection and squealed to a stop alongside. The second car actually went up over the curb, striking a garbage can and newspaper dispenser box, knocking them over.

Angry words were exchanged between the occupants of the two cars — and suddenly a torrent of gunfire filled the air.

Then the first vehicle ran the red light, followed by the second, both racing off into the night.

The Fullers' Mercedes-Benz did not move for a couple of minutes, even as the traffic light cycled to green and back to red. Then the car began to roll into the intersection, running the red traffic light and getting struck by an old pickup truck.

The truck did not kill them, although it struck the Mercedes-Benz hard enough to trigger its air bags. The Medical Examiner's Office determined that both mother and daughter had died when struck by multiple hits of single-aught buckshot from a shotgun — or shotguns. The windows of the Mercedes, and certainly the soft fabric of the convertible top, were no match for the fusillade of lead balls.

The shooters were never caught, despite the extreme pressure Francis Franklin Fuller V placed on everyone from the police department to the offices of the mayor and the governor.

Frustrated, Fuller shortly thereafter announced his new nonprofit organization:

"That night, I lost my wife, my child — my family. Sadly, it was a tragedy that could happen to anyone. And those responsible for such harm must be brought to justice and held accountable. To help the police and the justice system do exactly that, today I have established Lex Talionis in honor of my wife and daughter and all other victims in the City of Philadelphia."

He explained that he had funded the organization with an initial endowment of five million dollars. From that, he said, "Lex Talionis will reward ten thousand dollars cash to any individual who provides information that leads to the arrest, conviction, and/or removal from free society of a criminal guilty of murder or attempted murder, rape or other sexually deviant crime, or illicit drug distribution in the City of Philadelphia. Lex Talionis will work with the Philadelphia Police Department and our courts to protect the identities of those providing the information, keeping them anonymous."

Every week, usually on Fridays, he ran an announcement restating that message in Philadelphia's newspapers and on its television stations.

"You don't like Fuller?" Amanda Law asked Matt Payne.

"Sometimes I do. And sometimes, not so much," Matt said, turning up the volume. "Here. Let's see what he's saying."

Fuller's voice filled the bedroom: "As my ancestor Benjamin Franklin wrote in the Year of our Lord 1734, 'Where carcasses are, eagles will gather. And where good laws are, much people flock thither.' And so to-night I am personally signing the paperwork for my organization" — he gestured grandly toward the cast-bronze signage listing all his companies that was embedded in the wall behind him, to the line that read LEX TALIONIS, LLC — "to transfer two ten-thousand-dollar rewards into two separate escrow accounts at PNC Bank. These will be payable immediately upon the determi-nation of who is properly responsible for the apprehension of these evildoers."

There was a smattering of loud applause in the background, and the cameras panned to show the people who were clapping outside of the police crime-scene tape.

Matt said, "Looks like Francis has the support of Batman and — what's that other character there that's the supervillain? — the Joker?"

Amanda looked at the screen and made a *hmm* sound.

"I think that particular Joker costume is

supposed to be one of our distinguished city councilmen. You can tell by his trademark black bow tie that looks like a tiny cheap clip-on. And by all those exaggerated dollar-bill bribes — they're stuffing his pockets to the point of overflowing. The handcuffs on his left wrist are a nice touch. Oh, and there's a dollar symbol on his coat, kind of like the Riddler had those question marks."

Payne recalled that the loud cries of corruption in City Hall were back in the news — if they'd ever really left.

Either way, to bow-tied City Councilman H. Rapp Badde, Jr., a thirty-two-year-old native Philadelphian who was alternately charismatic and arrogant, it was simply politics as usual. Which also meant shenanigans as usual, including the hiring of a twenty-five-year-old "highly regarded colleague" as his executive assistant and the use of funds from his election campaign for them to attend a conference on urban renewal in, of all places, Bermuda.

As luck would have it, someone happened to recognize the publicity-happy councilman during the trip. And when a photograph appeared in the news media of the councilman and his tremendously attractive assistant on the beach — wearing, as one TV news wag said, "nothing that could be considered business attire, unless they were employed in a strip club at SeaWorld" — citizens of Philadelphia were furious, perhaps the least happy being Badde's wife of seven years.

Of course, the councilman, drawing on both his charisma and arrogance, repeatedly stated that it was all being misinterpreted, that the trip had cost the city not one red cent — his excess campaign contributions covered it. Then he spun the subject to what he and his able assistant had learned on advancing urban renewal and how H. Rapp Badde, Jr., was going to change Philly's fortunes.

The behavior stemmed from the same sort of above-reproach attitude — from the hanky-panky to the deny-and-spin — that he'd learned from his father, Horatio R. Badde, Sr., who'd once held the office Junior now so desperately desired, that of mayor.

To Matt and countless others in Philadelphia, the good news in all this was that there was a genuine first-class person serving as Hizzonor. The Honorable Jerome H. "Jerry" Carlucci was no-nonsense to the point that his detractors — and quite a few admirers — claimed he governed with an iron fist. Unapologetic, Carlucci fought the culture of corruption in City Hall just as he had fought crime in the city before being elected to public office.

Carlucci had risen through the ranks of the Philadelphia Police Department, and he bragged that he'd held every rank but that of policewoman.

Payne said: "Or maybe, more appropriately, that dollar sign is also supposed to represent a scarlet letter for Badde?"

These days it's easier finding a virgin in a whorehouse than an honest politician. He grunted to himself. *An honest pol in or out of a whorehouse. With or without a scarlet letter.*

Fuller could be heard speaking again, and the camera cut back to him:

"So, to all you out there who commit crimes, or you who are considering doing so, I share with you further wisdom of Benjamin Franklin: 'Fear to do ill, and you need fear nought else.'"

There was more applause. Fuller paused, waved briefly to acknowledge it, then looked back into the camera.

His face turned stern, and he wagged the stubby fat index finger of his right hand as he went on dramatically: "Evildoers, know that you are being watched. Know that eventually you will be caught" — with all his right hand's stubby fat fingers, he gestured behind himself, where the bodies had been dumped, never taking his eyes off the camera — "and know that you will be brought to justice. By God's grace and by God's words: As it says in Exodus 23:24, 'Then you shall give life for life, eye for eye, tooth for tooth, foot for foot.' *Lex Talionis.* Thank you."

There was more applause, this time accompanied by whistles and cheers.

Matt sighed.

"'Evildoers.' Jesus! I've heard enough of that," he said, thumbing the MUTE button on the remote.

After a moment, Amanda said, "Well, I can't say I am opposed to what he's trying to accomplish."

Matt looked at her with an eyebrow raised. "But, baby, people just can't take the law into their own hands. And that's what he's basically encouraging."

She shrugged. "Sorry. I can't. . . ."

Of course she can't.

Damn sure not after what she's gone through. . . .

He nodded thoughtfully and kissed her on the forehead.

The news camera now followed Francis Fuller as he walked inside the office building. Then it panned the cheering crowd, and in the process captured some of the news media.

Payne said: "Hey, there's Mickey O'Hara.

He's working the story?"

A young-looking Philadelphia Police Department patrolman was going back under the yellow police tape next to O'Hara, who Matt noted was standing apart from the pack of reporters quickly scribbling on their pads. O'Hara had a camera of some type hanging from his right shoulder by a thin black strap. He held in both hands what looked like a cell phone, and he was tapping it with both of his thumbs.

Then Payne felt his phone vibrate again, and a new text message appeared in a box on its screen:

MICKEY O'HARA

AN OLD SOURCE JUST MENTIONED "POP-N-DROPS"

TELL ME WHAT YOU KNOW, DAMN IT, AND I'LL TELL YOU WHAT I DO . . .

MEET ME AT LIBERTIES?

"Old source" my ass — it was that wet-behind-the-ears uniform.

The kid's probably starstruck with Mickey and thought he'd show off how important he already is by sharing what's supposed to be kept quiet.

Hell, Mickey will keep his mouth shut if I ask, and if he's on the scene he probably has something good that I can use.

But Amanda is going to be pissed if I leave now to go work.

He heard her sigh, and when Matt looked to her, he saw that she'd read the screen.

He began to apologize: "I'm —"

"No," she interrupted. "It's okay. Really, it is. I can't agree that bad guys should be off the streets and then expect you not to do your job."

He kissed her forehead again.

"I'm sorry," he said, finishing the apology.

Then Payne texted "Liberties in 20" back to O'Hara.

Payne's phone vibrated once, then again. The first message was from O'Hara, who'd simply texted "OK." The second was from Tony Harris:

— BLOCKED NUMBER-

YOU JUST SEE 5-F?

I BET JASON IS FIT TO BE TIED.

GOT TIME FOR A BEER? -TH

"My," Amanda said, "aren't you the popular one at this hour. Should I be jealous?"

Payne thought, *What the hell, may as well kill two birds with one stone*, and texted back: "Liberties in 20."

She rolled over and began to slowly rub his belly.

Matt looked at her and began, "Speaking of killings —"

"You should go?" Amanda finished his sentence.

"No. What I was going to say is: I don't see the rush."

As she made another slow circle with her palm, she asked, "What do you mean?"

"Well, as far as I can tell, there's no reason to jump up and race anywhere. Mick can cool his heels with Tony at Liberties for ten minutes. And even if I do get a call about those pop-and-drops" — he reached for his cell phone and pressed a button to turn it off — "which will now go directly into voice mail, it's my professional opinion that those guys who got popped will probably still be dead ten minutes from now."

Amanda's hand stopped. Matt looked deeply in her eyes.

"'Just ten minutes'?" she said, her tone suggestive.

As he smiled and nodded, she pursed her lips.

After a moment, he felt her warm hand slide down his belly.

"I know a Ben Franklin saying, too," she said.

"Yeah? I'm afraid to ask. Something to do with moderation or saving for a rainy day, or — worse — abstinence?"

Her warm palm moved smoothly and excitingly slowly until it was just below his belly button, then a bit farther down. He grunted appreciatively in anticipation — until her fingers suddenly gripped him by the short hairs.

"Ouch!" he cried out a bit dramatically when she pulled them. "What was *that* for?"

"Ben said, 'Love, and be lov'd.'"

[FOUR]
5550 Ridgewood Street, Philadelphia
Saturday, October 31, 11:45 P.M.

Mrs. Joelle Bazelon long had lived with the dark fear, deep in her big bones, that such a terrible day would come. The dark-skinned, sixty-two-year-old widow — she was of Jamaican descent, five-foot-eight tall, and after a decade of battling diabetes, clinically obese — had prayed literally every night, down on arthritic knees, her Bible before her on the bedspread, that somehow she could figure out a way to run from it. Some way to pack up everything in time and move to a better place for her and Sasha, her just-turned-eighteen-year-old granddaughter.

But that hadn't happened.

And now, standing at the kitchen sink on what so far had been a fairly pleasant Halloween, looking out the window as she finished drying and putting up the dinner dishes, Joelle Bazelon suddenly realized that time had run out.

Earlier in the evening, she'd heard the doorbell ring again and again, the excited choruses of young children shouting, "Trick or treat!" and seen Sasha, her beautiful, slender, five-foot-seven teen, rushing enthusiastically to the door with the large plastic bowl of candies, then bending at the waist and complimenting each child on his or her costume as she put treats in their bags.

The sequence of sounds had repeated until about nine o'clock, when the kids — even the older ones, a few in their middle teens who knew they really were too old to be trick-or-treating — had stopped ringing the doorbell.

Sasha had then told her grandmother that she was going down the street to hang out with Keesha Jones, her friend since they were ten. Joelle was never completely comfortable with Sasha being out at night, especially late, but she reminded herself that the child was now eighteen, too old to be kept home, and Keesha lived just at the end of the block.

About the only thing that Joelle could do was tell her to be safe. And, as an added precaution — so that when Sasha came home it would be easier, and quicker, to come inside the house — leave the heavy wrought-iron outer door unlocked.

And now, from the sound of it, Sasha was coming home very quickly.

Too quickly.

Joelle heard the wooden front door fling open, making a stunning thud as its heavy brass doorknob smacked an interior wall.

Then she heard a clearly terrified Sasha cry out, *"Grammy!"*

Joelle got the chills. And when she heard a familiar male voice call out, "Trick or treat!" — the tone deeply threatening — her knees buckled.

Xavier Smith! she thought, clinging to the lip of the sink to keep from falling to the linoleum floor.

Ridgewood Street was in the Kingsessing area of southwest Philadelphia. Joelle Bazelon had lived there going on forty years, graduating from South Philly High, then LaSalle University with her teacher's certificate, and ultimately being assigned to Anna H. Shaw Middle School, from which she'd now retired as principal.

The school, at 5400 Warrington Avenue, was only a three-block walk from her row house on Ridgewood. She'd moved to the row house with her husband, Ray, whom she'd met at LaSalle, and later they'd reared their only daughter, Rachel, there.

About the same time that Joelle retired from teaching, Rachel, then age eighteen, had become pregnant with Sasha. The father, a year older, had stuck around for about half the length of time it had taken him to cause the actual moment of conception.

The Bazelon house — a modest thirteen hundred square feet total — became quite full.

That had lasted for only just shy of a year, however.

Ray and Rachel had been driving up from Delaware on Interstate 95 when their car's front left tire blew out, causing the vehicle to roll over and strike a bridge support. They were killed on impact.

Among many things, Joelle was tough. She had to be. And, as she had already reared one daughter and over the years taught countless other children, she had no problem with the idea of bringing up Sasha on her own.

Yet over the years, despite Sasha proving to be both as sweet and as smart as her mother had been, rearing a granddaughter hadn't been easy. As any single parent knew, the constant one-on-one time with a child exhausted energy and emotion. There had also been a money problem — Ray's income went away shortly after his burial, and Joelle's pension did not go as far as she'd have liked. Then came her health issues, including the diabetes and, because of her excessive weight, a heart condition, which not only further sapped her strength but also drained the savings account to pay for doctor's bills and medications.

And what put a painfully fine point on their problems was that southwest Philadelphia simply was no longer the same place that Joelle and Ray had first moved to twenty years before to raise a family.

At first glance, Kingsessing appeared to be the same somewhat comfortable middle-class neighborhood. Most of the residents tried to keep the row homes tidy, the small yards trimmed and free of trash.

But if one looked closely, the signs of quiet despair were present.

Practically all the residences had something not one of them had been built with: burglar bars. The heavy racks of black wrought iron had been added house by house over the last ten or twelve years.

Some of the chain-link fences were even topped with razor wire.

There was a creeping blight on almost every block: When houses burned down — not always by accident — the owners took whatever money the insurance company paid out and got the hell out of town. The city was stuck with the task of finishing off the destruction of the property, which more times than not left a dirt lot littered with rubble. A lot that oddly still had the five-tier set of concrete steps coming up from the sidewalk but leading to nowhere.

When that happened to the house next door to Joelle Bazelon's, she saw the writing on the wall. She planted a FOR SALE sign in the small ten-foot-square patch of grass that was her front yard.

Joelle Bazelon found that she was not the only one who saw that the neighborhood was going to hell in a handbasket. Three other row houses were on the market within just two blocks of her address. They all offered essentially the same property, give or take a bath or bedroom.

She'd listed the property through a Realtor, setting the asking price at ninety-nine thousand dollars. And she never got a single offer. When she asked the Realtor why not, Joelle was told that the price on one of the other row houses for sale nearby was being reduced by five thousand dollars every two weeks. Worse, it still wasn't getting any reasonable offers.

Joelle Bazelon had suddenly felt terribly trapped.

She now knew that she'd seen the start of all this decline years before, back when she'd been principal of the middle school. She'd seen kids who were on the path to no good — and parents who didn't care. And in the time since then, she'd seen plenty of punks from Shaw, from the neighborhood, who had gone on to cause trouble in high school or, worse, in one of the disciplinary schools that served as their last stop in the School District of Philadelphia.

The worst of the worst had gone straight to the temptations of the street, and there drawn the real-world version of a Monopoly game card: GO STRAIGHT TO JAIL, DO NOT PASS GO.

Punks such as Xavier "Xpress" Smith, who got his nickname selling crystal methamphetamine, and delivering it fast.

Except they didn't always stay in jail.

III

[ONE]
Loft Number 2180
Hops Haus Tower
1100 N. Lee Street, Philadelphia
Saturday, October 31, 11:48 P.M.

The irony was not lost on Matt Payne. Here, at almost the stroke of midnight on All Hallows' Eve, he was headed for Liberties Bar to spend time talking about some goddamn bad guys who were stupid enough to get themselves murdered.

What a shitty way to spend a holiday.

Even more to the point: especially when my other option was staying in that wonderful bed with the goddess.

Who, all things considered, would really rather have me there than here.

He felt his phone vibrate twice, and when he looked at the screen, there were two text messages, the first from Amanda — "Be safe out there, baby" — and the second from Mickey O'Hara — "Where the hell are you?"

He had a mental image of Amanda walking Luna on the leash out to the grassy area that the Hops Haus Tower called "the Pet Run." Matt had started calling it "Piss Park," which was the nicer of the two nicknames that had come to mind. He was convinced that the tower's four-legged residents outnumbered the two-legged ones — the vast majority of the latter, it appeared, by both sight and smell, choosing to ignore the Pet Run's garbage can, roll of disposable plastic bags, and sign reading PLEASE PICK UP AFTER YOUR PET.

As he texted "See you soon, sweetie" back to Amanda, he was reminded again of the "obituary."

She's always going to be concerned.

It's sweet. And it's somewhat worrisome — because what happens if she doesn't get over that?

Then again, what the hell happens if she's right?

He texted a reply to O'Hara: "5 mins out . . . order me a Macallan 18."

If nothing else right now, Payne did find himself enjoying the energy of those celebrating Halloween. The infectious laughter and vibrant music coming out of the bars along Second Street could be heard damn near all the way back to Amanda's place.

Most everyone he'd seen up and down the sidewalks, pub crawling, was having one helluva Halloween. In the elevator and the lobby of the Hops Haus Tower, Payne had come across quite a few twenty- and thirty-somethings in Halloween costumes, some of which were quite interesting — if not totally wild. Such as the one worn by the cute, well-built blonde in her early thirties who was having difficulty opening one of the big glass doors at the lobby's main entrance. She was dressed as Little Bo Peep. But her scant, frilly, white-and-baby-blue outfit, the ruffled skirt cut high and the push-up top cut low, was anything but G-rated. The costume gave the character a whole new meaning, especially when she kept bending over to pick up her sheepherder's staff and the outfit revealed far more than an eyeful of lovely flesh.

Bo Peep, indeed, Payne thought with a grin.

Then, as he walked down Second Street toward Liberties, Payne had also gotten a chuckle when he saw two guys more or less staggering out of a bar wearing T-shirts that, while not technically Halloween costumes, were appropriately dark-humored.

One T-shirt had a representation of the Liberty Bell with the words COME TO PHILADELPHIA FOR THE CRACK.

The other showed a white chalk outline of a human and the words:

> **A FRIEND WILL HELP YOU MOVE**
>
> **BUT A GOOD FRIEND WILL HELP YOU MOVE THE BODY.**

Either of which, Payne thought, would be appropriate to wear into Liberties for to-night's discussion on pop-and-drops with Tony Harris and Mickey O'Hara.

It certainly would not be the first time such topics had been broached in Liberties. The bar was the unofficial preferred watering hole of the Homicide Division, as well as cops from other divisions who'd discovered the comfortable old neighborhood bar that served stiff drinks and great food and — some would argue — occasionally more than a little gruff attitude.

The place has real character.

Payne then idly wondered how much longer such older establishments would survive. Because there was no doubt that this section of the city, thanks to the new Hops Haus complex and its fancy new neighbor, the Schmidt's Brewery development, was seeing its real estate prices pushed up. And that, in turn, was forcing out the longtime residents who couldn't afford to live there anymore, everybody from older retirees to young bohemian artists.

The more expensive properties that attracted young professionals were replacing the low-rent row houses and abandoned industrial areas, and the newcomers generated new jobs for others. And money spent meant money taxed, which translated to more revenue to fill the city's coffers.

Such is the rejuvenation of Philadelphia.

And Lord knows so much of it needs renovation.

Too many parts are a living hell.

That gave some hope to a lot of people — including Matt — who feared that Philly, with all its crime, corruption, and broken infrastructure, was circling the goddamned drain.

Payne knew that supporting the gentrification was one of the reasons Amanda Law bought a place in Hops Haus Tower rather than one in Center City, where Payne had his small apartment. She liked the idea of renewal and rebuilding. The location wasn't any closer to her work — the difference would have been only minutes — but she believed that it was a vibrant place where for too long there had been little more than misery.

And the fact that Philadelphia — the city Matt loved but knew so many others loved to hate — had been allowed to reach such depressing depths was something that frustrated him.

How in hell does the city that's the birthplace of the most important law of our land — the United States Constitution — become one of our nation's most lawless?

And one of our nation's most fucked up?

How does that get fixed?

How do we get back that honor and pride?

He shook his head.

Could the answer be found here?

Two major speculators, one who built Hops, the other who developed Schmidt's, had both denied for nearly a decade that they were at all interested in a lost cause like Northern Liberties.

But once one of the speculators had quietly pieced together enough property to begin a development, the renovation had begun on the Schmidt's Brewery building. Then, like a Phoenix rising above the ashes of Philly's Northern Liberties, additional two-story buildings went up, filled with expensive apartments, stores, restaurants, and, of course, office space.

Then, when that development had proved a success, the owner of the Hops Brewery site began his renovation project. And soon the twenty-one-floor Hops Haus Tower also had risen, well above Schmidt's.

People want to save this city, want to preserve its history.

And there's damn sure plenty of it. All over Philly.

But throwing all kinds of money at a problem is no guarantee of success — just look at Center City, Philly's shining star, of all places. It has parts that still look like ghetto.

Maybe this place is past the point of saving?

[TWO]
5550 Ridgewood Street, Philadelphia
Saturday, October 31, 11:50 P.M.

At the kitchen sink, Joelle Bazelon struggled to regain the strength in her knees, then moved as quickly as her legs and weight allowed. She came out of the kitchen and headed toward the sounds of scuffling at the front of the house. When she entered the living room, she came almost face-to-face with Xavier "Xpress" Smith. His left hand gripped Sasha's right arm. He had a snub-nosed chrome-plated .32-caliber revolver in his right hand.

This was not Joelle's first encounter with Smith. He'd grown up one block over, on Pentridge Street. A twenty-four-year-old black male with a short temper, he had a hard, mean face and wore baggy denim pants that hung so low that half of his brown boxer shorts were visible, a T-shirt, a zipper-front hoodie, and a New York Mets ballcap, the brim worn sideways over his right ear, in which a diamond stud twinkled.

Sasha cried, "I didn't see him hiding in the dark by the porch, Grammy!"

"Shut up, bitch!" Smith shouted at her.

As she'd done with so many students over so many years, Joelle carefully studied the punk. Though he had a pistol and was waving it, he wasn't directly aiming it at anyone.

She saw that his eyes were bloodshot, his movements jerky and hyperactive.

He's on something, she thought.

"You will not speak to my granddaughter in that manner," Joelle said in her crisp English accent, as calmly and authoritatively as she could. She felt as if her rapidly beating heart was about to burst through her chest.

Smith tried to stare her down.

"I told you this would happen!" he then shouted. "I warned you, don't talk with nobody! You old bitch, you been fucking with me all my life!"

What Joelle Bazelon had done the previous week was more or less the same thing she'd done ten years earlier, when she'd seen Xavier Smith, then fourteen years old, beating up younger boys as they walked to Shaw Middle School. After the first shakedown, she'd telephoned his house to speak with his parents. But Xavier's mother — also, Joelle then learned, a single parent — had told her that she should mind her own business, that she could take care of her own boy. Then, when Joelle had seen Xavier shake down another boy the very next week, taking his money and wristwatch, she'd called the cops.

She'd told the cops that she was saddened to see such bad behavior, but it could not be tolerated.

And she'd still felt the same way four days ago when she'd again called the cops.

The City of Philadelphia was divided into twenty-six patrol districts — twenty-five numbered ones, plus Center City. The corporal who answered the phone at the police department's Twelfth District, down on Woodland Avenue at Sixty-fifth, dispatched a pair of patrol officers to respond to the house of the complainant, one Mrs. Joelle Bazelon at 5550 Ridgewood Street.

Joelle had been waiting in the wooden rocking chair on the front porch when the Chevrolet Impala squad car pulled up to her curb. She repeated to the uniformed patrol officers what she'd witnessed: that when she'd been in the alleyway putting out trash that afternoon, she'd seen Xavier sneaking out the back of the neighbor's house two doors down. He'd been carrying the new flat-screen television that she knew the neighbor had just bought.

When Xavier had realized she'd seen him, he'd shouted at her: "Mind your own business, bitch! Or there be trouble!"

The cops asked a few questions, wrote down her statement, had her read and sign it, and then told her that they'd be in touch if they needed anything else.

And that was the last she'd heard about the episode.

That was, until tonight, when Xavier Smith, angry and hopped up on some drug, burst into her house.

"I seen that police car here!" he said. "Next I knowed, I was picked up!" Then he made an odd smile, showing his bad teeth. "But I got me a good lawyer."

He looked at Sasha and leered at her backside. "Your girl got herself one fine booty."

Sasha glared at him.

He noticed the bulge in the back pocket of her tight jeans.

"Give me that cell phone," he said, and when she didn't move, he worked it out of her pocket and put it in his front pocket.

"Xavier, please let go of my granddaughter," Joelle said as evenly and sternly as she could. "Then please leave. If you don't —"

He suddenly laughed out loud, interrupting her.

"Leave, old woman? *You* telling *me* to leave? You crazy! I ain't leaving till I show you what happens when you call the police on me! That cost me money, had to pay my lawyer and bail. I don't like losing money."

Joelle started to move toward the couch, and to the white telephone with the long cord there. "I'm going to call —"

"You not calling nobody!" he said. He waved with the pistol in the direction of the couch. "Sit there, you old bitch!"

"Xavier . . ."

He suddenly shook his head violently, as if trying to clear it, then shouted: "Don't you be trying to talk me down!"

He let go of Sasha's arm, then waved the pistol muzzle at the elderly woman as he walked over to her. He then pushed her so hard that she fell onto the couch.

As she lay there, struggling to sit up, he grabbed the telephone from the side table. He took up the slack in its cord and yanked hard, snapping it free of the wall plug.

He then went back to Joelle and pushed her back down on the cushions. After tucking the snub-nosed revolver in the hoodie's belly pocket, he grabbed Joelle's wrists and started wrapping them with the cord. She resisted, pulling apart her wrists after a moment and undoing his work.

He grabbed the pistol from the pocket and raised it above his head as if he was about to hit her.

"Don't make me do it," he said, almost in a growl, then put the pistol back in his pocket and rewrapped her wrists, then tied her ankles.

The white vinyl-coated cord pressed deeply into her loose black flesh.

He looked down at her and said, "Now I'm gonna show you what it's like when you got something to lose, too!"

He walked back over to Sasha, who was visibly shaking.

He aimed the pistol at her chest.

"Get to your knees, whore!"

Joelle, who suddenly started to hyperventilate, cried out: "Xavier, please! Don't hurt her! She's all I have left!"

Sasha started sobbing.

"Do it!" Smith said, pointing to the ground.

Sasha suddenly shook her head in defiance.

Smith hauled back his left hand, then swung forward, slapping her with an open palm with such force that it knocked her off her feet.

As she started to get up, trembling, he grabbed her by the hair, yanking her around till she was on her knees, facing his crotch.

"Go on, whore. You know what to do with it."

"No, please," she said, starting to sob deeply. "No . . ."

Joelle could be heard taking faster breaths, shorter ones.

Smith looked down at Sasha.

"Do it!"

She shook her head again, closing her eyes at the anticipation of being slapped again.

He didn't hit her but, instead, touched the muzzle of the revolver to her head and slowly thumbed back the hammer. As he did so, the cylinder rotated. The metallic *click-click* sounds made her open her eyes wide.

When he'd finished, Sasha began to sob softly.

Xavier "Xpress" Smith, still with his left fist gripping her hair and his right hand holding the pistol to her head, then terrified the beautiful teenager one last time.

"Bang-bang, bitch," he said as he smiled and squeezed the trigger.

Sasha screamed at the sound of the hammer falling forward.

But there was no bang.

There was just silence — and a great gasping from the couch. Then nothing.

Smith laughed as he and Sasha looked over to the couch.

The old woman had either fainted or was pretending to sleep.

"Next time, old woman, there be a bullet in there," he called to her.

His left hand let loose of Sasha's hair. He patted her head.

"That was good, girl. Real good. I just might make you my steady bitch."

Sasha got to her feet and bolted over to the couch.

"Grammy!" she cried as she reached her.

There was no response. Sasha shook her, but still nothing. She put her cheek to her grandmother's nose and mouth, looking for an exhaled breath, then desperately touched the inside of her wrists and all along her neck at the jawbone, hoping to find a pulse, however weak.

"She's dead!" Sasha wailed. "Oh, Grammy!"

Xavier "Xpress" Smith ran over to the couch and felt the wrist and neck of the old woman.

Sasha balled her fists and started hitting Xavier Smith on the back and arms. "Don't touch Grammy, you bastard!"

He stood up and nervously aimed the pistol at Sasha.

"Listen, bitch. Don't you say a word I was here. You hear me?"

She stared at him, a mixture of deep sadness and hatred in her eyes.

He moved quickly toward the front door and said, "Don't you forget. I can come here anytime I want. Or find you anywhere. Anytime."

Then Xavier "Xpress" Smith lived up to his nickname and fled into the dark of night.

[THREE]
705 N. Second Street, Philadelphia
Saturday, October 31, 11:59 P.M.

Tony's and Mickey's cars, Harris's city-issued battered unmarked gray Ford Crown Victoria Police Interceptor and O'Hara's new black BMW M5 sedan, were parked in front of Liberties Bar.

Inside, Matt Payne saw that the place was not as packed as he'd expected. Along the left wall were wooden tables with booths. A couple were filled, but most looked like they'd recently been vacated. They were still covered with empty and unfinished drinking glasses. Same was true in the middle of the room, where there were more wooden tables and chairs. The busboy was working busily, and would be for some time.

Matt noticed some motion across the room and looked to the century-old, ornately carved oak bar. It ran from the front window almost back to the wooden stairway leading to second-floor seating. The bar was three-quarters full, and at its right end, nearest the front window that looked out onto the street, stood Michael J. "Mickey" O'Hara.

The Irishman exuded an infectious energy, and now used that to enthusiastically wave his right hand high above his very curly red hair.

Standing next to him, wearing his usual well-worn blue blazer and gray slacks, was Tony Harris. He'd noticed Mickey's manic wave and looked over his shoulder. When Tony saw Matt, he shuffled to the left, making a place for him at the bar. His move gave Matt a clear view of Mickey — more specifically, of what he wore under his tweed jacket: a green T-shirt that had a four-leaf clover and read KISS ME, I'M IRISH.

As Payne approached, O'Hara said, "What the hell took you so long?"

Discretion being the better part of valor, I

116

believe I'll dodge that one.

"I had to walk her dog," Matt said.

"Oh?" O'Hara smiled. As he motioned suggestively with his right hand, the middle finger rubbing the top of the index finger, he said, "Is that what they're calling it these days?"

Harris chuckled.

"Screw you, Mickey," Payne said, but he smiled. He changed the subject. "Nice shirt. But wrong holiday."

"It's the closest to a costume I've got," Mickey said. "But don't be so damned sure of yourself, Matty."

"What do you mean?" Payne asked.

Tony Harris had a bottle of Hops Haus lager beer to his lips, about to sip, when he nodded and said, "He's already gotten six kisses, including two long ones from an incredibly cute, quote, angel, unquote, in all white. She rubbed Mickey's head and said he was her lucky charm."

Matt laughed, and the bartender walked up and slid two glasses on the bar before him, one with ice cubes in a clear liquid and one with just a dark liquid, both half-filled.

"First round tonight's on me," said the bartender, John Sullivan — a hefty forty-year-old, second-generation Irish-American with an ample belly, friendly bright eyes, and a full white beard. "Happy Halloween, Matt."

"I guess I should've said 'Trick or treat' to earn my single-malt, huh?" Payne replied, reaching for the glass that he knew held the ice water. He poured it into the glass that contained the dark brown liquor, mixing it fifty-fifty. "Thanks, John."

The bartender grinned as Payne held up his drink and said, "Cheers, gents," clinked the glasses and bottle of John the bartender, Tony, and Mickey, then took a healthy sip.

He turned to looked at Harris. "So tell me what the hell that was all about tonight in Old City."

Harris glanced at Mickey O'Hara. "You want to start?"

O'Hara gestured grandly, *After you.*

Harris shrugged, then nodded and said, "All off the record, right?"

O'Hara sighed. "You know you'll see what I put together before I post it online."

From the look on Tony Harris's face, it was evident that he was genuinely embarrassed for the slip of tongue. "Sorry, Mickey. Old habits and all."

[FOUR]

As a rule, cops didn't much like reporters, and, accordingly, didn't share with them more than they absolutely had to — and a good deal of the time not even that.

Those who made up the Thin Blue Line were a guarded group. Outsiders simply didn't understand what it was that they did, what their brotherhood meant, and apparently no amount of education changed that.

You either were a cop — and understood — or you weren't.

Mickey O'Hara wasn't a cop. "I couldn't get on with the police department," he joked with his cop friends, "because I knew both of my parents and knew that they were married."

But — as, invariably, rules had exceptions — O'Hara did indeed understand.

He had long ago earned the respect — and in cases like Matt Payne, the friendship — of many on the police department, including more than a few of the white shirts, some of whom even wore stars on their uniforms.

It was said of Mickey O'Hara that he knew

more people on the police force than most of the cops did themselves, and certainly more cops recognized him than could identify in a crowd the top cop himself, Police Commissioner Ralph J. Mariana.

O'Hara's history with the police was almost, but not quite, as long as his history with the *Bulletin*. He'd begun with a paper route at age twelve, throwing the afternoon edition from his bike at the stoops of West Philadelphia row houses every day after school for four years.

By the time he turned sixteen, a series of events had served to dramatically change his career in newspapers.

The series was triggered by his being expelled from West Catholic High School.

Monsignor Dooley had made it clear that gambling would not be tolerated. When he found out that the O'Hara boy had illegal numbers slips that could be traced back to Francesco "Frankie the Gut" Guttermo, and that Mickey would not rat out his coconspirator — no matter how immoral the Monsignor declared it all to be — the Monsignor said that left him with no choice but to throw Mickey out of school.

Before being caught by the Monsignor and being shown the door, Mickey had heard that the *Bulletin* had a copyboy position open.

He'd never had the time to pursue it — until now. And now he really wanted it, because it offered far more money than throwing papers from a bike, and it was indoor work, so no more riding in the rain or racing away from the snapping maws of those goddamn rabid street dogs.

Mickey actually got the position, but with a ninety-day probation period.

He took his new job seriously, probation or not. And that did not go unnoticed.

After his probation period expired, he came to be mentored by the ink-stained assistant city desk editor, who dumped on Mickey more and more of the research assignments — drudge work that no one else wanted to do. Before Mickey knew it, the research he was turning in was becoming actual articles, albeit short ones, printed under the credit "Staff Roundup."

Then, late one Friday afternoon — he clearly remembered it as if it had happened yesterday, not nearly two decades earlier — he'd been summoned to the managing editor's office. The office had a huge glass window overlooking the entire newsroom, and as Mickey approached he saw that the managing editor was looking at a copy of that afternoon's front page. The assistant city desk editor was in there, too, looking his usual deeply introspective self.

Mickey O'Hara, days shy of turning eighteen, was convinced that this was the end of his newspaper days. Clearly, his mentor had been caught abusing his official duties by helping develop the questionable skills of a lowly copyboy.

And now said copyboy was about to lose his job and be sent back to the streets.

O'Hara figured that if he was lucky they might let him pedal around town slinging papers at stoops again.

But, of course, that had not happened.

After an initial awkward exchange of pleasantries, the managing editor had tossed the afternoon paper that he was holding to Mickey. Mickey had glanced at it, recognized the headline he'd written, then under that seen his name — his *byline* there on the front page.

As Mickey O'Hara, speechless, looked between the two men, the managing editor said, "Congratulations, Mickey. Nice work. This is usually the part of the interview process when I ask, 'When can you start?' but it would appear that you already have."

O'Hara rose rapidly in the hierarchy of the *Bulletin* city room, eventually writing "Follow the Money," the hard-hitting series of articles on graft and gross incompetence in the city's Child Protective Services. It was the series that won him a Pulitzer Prize for public service.

O'Hara had thought that he was on top of the world, particularly considering how far he'd come from the day Monsignor Dooley had shown him the door. He was being paid, he'd thought, damned decently for something he enjoyed doing. And, he believed, the stories that helped better the lot of kids trapped in the hell that was CPS was alone worth it all.

But then his childhood buddy, Casimir Bolinski, showed up in town and told him he was a fool. His exact words: "Face it, Mickey, those bastards are screwing you."

"Those bastards" being the *Bulletin*'s management.

O'Hara was told that they were not paying him his due. Mickey listened to his buddy, especially when Bolinski offered to represent him as a small token of appreciation — "I can never adequately repay you" — for taking the fall at West Catholic High.

"If you'd ratted me out to Dooley the Drooler as your fellow numbers runner," Casimir said, "I'd have been out on my ass, too. There'd have been no 'The Bull' Bolinski, no all-American trophy, no scholarship to Notre Dame, no career with the Green

123

Bay Packers. And without the cushion from the Packers, both the pay and off-season time, I'd probably never have considered law school, and certainly not become a sports agent after retirement."

And as an agent, The Bull proved every bit as effective off the field as he'd been on it.

Players liked The Bull personally, but the athletes really liked what he could do for them financially. And The Bull wound up making more money by repping the sports world's top players — football, basketball, golf, et cetera — than he had earned actually playing the game.

Negotiating Mickey O'Hara's new contract with the *Bulletin* had been no challenge compared to the high-pressure worlds of sports and product endorsements.

And as happy as O'Hara had been with his new benefits — from more pay and holiday time to a new lease car every year — The Bull showed his brilliance by including an exit clause in the contract. It was brilliant because the *Bulletin* signed off on it, and because everyone believed Mickey, happy with the contract terms, would write for the paper forever.

Everyone including Mickey.

But then came the newsroom brawl, in which Mickey punched the city editor. Ros-

coe G. Kennedy was no great fan of O'Hara
— though he did grudgingly admit that
Mickey could be a helluva writer despite not
having attended the glorified University of
Missouri School of Journalism, as Kennedy
had. And there was no question that Kennedy resented the money and perks that the
unschooled O'Hara enjoyed thanks to his
buddy, The Bull, squeezing the newspaper
management.

Kennedy thought that Mickey O'Hara had
become a prima donna in his expensively
furnished office, someone who had the au-
dacity to demand more space in the newspaper for his articles and photographs than
the boss — J-school grad Kennedy — felt he
deserved.

O'Hara, who'd been at the Italian restaurant La Famiglia the night that Matt Payne
put down the two robbers who'd beaten up a
couple in the parking lot, had written a long
article for Page 1A. He'd also delivered the
photograph he'd taken of Payne in his tux-
edo standing over one robber lying on the
ground. Payne had his cell phone in his left
hand and his Colt .45 Officer's Model in his
right.

What had set Mickey O'Hara off — and it
happened in the presence of The Bull and
his wife, Antoinette Bolinski — was Ken-

nedy wanting to put a smart-ass headline on the photograph: MAIN LINE WYATT EARP 2, BAD GUYS 0 IN SHOOT-OUT AT THE LA FAMIGLIA CORRAL. Kennedy justified it by saying that Payne looked like a god-damn gunslinger who obviously liked shooting people.

O'Hara put up his dukes, then dodged Kennedy's swinging fists, putting him down with a left punch to the nose followed by a right jab to the abdomen. Casimir J. Bolinski, Esq., then grabbed his client and — with Kennedy disparaging O'Hara before the entire newsroom staff, then declaring him fired — dragged him out of the city room, never to return.

The Bull that day pulled out O'Hara's contract — the signatures barely dry — and easily negotiated with the *Bulletin* management a thirty-day cooling-off period with pay for Mickey, plus public apologies from Kennedy for the city editor's treatment of a Pulitzer Prize winner before newsroom colleagues.

O'Hara decided to use his downtime to research a book on Fort Festung — a despicable shit from Philly who had been found guilty of murdering his girlfriend and stuffing her body in a steamer trunk, where she'd been found mummified.

Mickey convinced Matt to accompany him to France in hopes of finding the fugitive — if only for a current photograph for the book.

And, toward the end of their time in France, they finally tracked down the arrogant Festung, long-haired and goateed, living comfortably on wine and cheese with a new girlfriend in a French village.

Mickey got his photograph — and it was of Philadelphia Police Department Sergeant Matthew M. Payne collaring the fugitive.

And only weeks after their return to Philadelphia, Casimir J. Bolinski, Esq., ever diligent in delivering for his clients, presented Michael J. O'Hara with the contract for his new position as chief executive officer and publisher of CrimeFreePhilly.com.

Mickey, after signing the contract in mid-September, called Matt's cell and told Matt to meet him at Liberties Bar for some good news.

As O'Hara slid in the booth across the table from Payne, he said, "You may kiss my ring, Matty, as I'm now a triple-dipper. Say, 'Congrats, Mick.'"

Matt looked at the blue T-shirt Mickey wore. In white, it bore a representation of a pair of dangling handcuffs and lettering that read MAKE HIS DAY: KISS A COP AT

"Okay, congrats. But what the hell is a triple-dipper? And what the hell's up with that shirt?"

Mickey's animated face lit up and he said: "Two weeks ago, The Bull told the *Bulletin*'s management that his client — me — was unhappy with the tepid apology, et cetera, of their city editor, and that at the expiration of the thirty-day cooling-off period, I planned immediately to execute the exit clause of my employment contract. That happened the following day, and triggered a lump payment equal to a month's pay for every year that I'd been employed by the newspaper, dating back to when I threw the rag from my bike in West Philly. So that's one deep dip into the moneymaking machine. And I just got the check, less The Bull's five percent commission, for the publisher's acceptance of my book on Fort Festung. That check makes for a double-dip."

"And the third?"

He pointed to his shirt and said, "I'm now running CrimeFreePhilly! I have a five-year contract, renewable annually, which means every year I know if I have another five to go. If I ever get canned, I walk with the equivalent of four years' pay. And I have stock options that vest if certain goals are accomplished, which gives me both incentive and a nice nest egg on top of what I walked away with from the *Bulletin*. Thus making me a triple-dipper."

"Impressive. But aren't you going to miss newspapers?"

Mickey shook his head. "Hell no, Matty. Forget that. Haven't you been paying attention? Newspapers are deader than a double-crossing gangbanger in South Philly. Just like the TV nightly news killed afternoon papers, there's this thing now called the World Wide Web that's killing all newspapers. You really should try to keep up."

Payne flashed him the middle finger of his right hand, then changed to his index finger and pointed at the T-shirt.

"I've heard about that but never looked it up."

"You should. Here's the deal. It's basically brand new. It was originally quietly funded by a philanthropist, a good citizen who's simply fed up with Philly sinking in a cesspool of crime. The idea is pretty damned simple: support the good guys and get rid of the bad guys."

"Maybe too simple, Mick. There's already a lot of money being thrown at crime. And speaking of a lot of money, I didn't think newsy websites made money."

"Most don't. Most are losing money. But profit isn't the point. Cleaning up the city is. People are fucking fed up —"

"Amen to that," Payne interrupted. "Count me among the disenchanted."

Mick went on: "— and when The Bull heard about it, he put money in. A number of his clients did, too, some of them guys who broke out of the ghetto and want to help those still stuck there. Even though CrimeFreePhilly-dot-com doesn't have to make money, I think it will. There's also the sweetheart deal it has with KeyCom."

"The cable-TV-slash-Internet-slash-phone conglomerate based here? That's Five-Eff's! Which means Francis Fulton is your secret moneyman?"

O'Hara shrugged. "Some questions don't need to be asked. All I know is I have both the funding and the moral backing of some heavy hitters to help this city. No pun intended concerning The Bull's clients."

He paused, then his infectious energy kicked in: "Get this, Matty, I can run live, breaking news on CrimeFreePhilly, and then KeyCom's massive computer servers send it — for free — out to any TV, computer, and even better, to any cell phone. Worldwide! I could never do anything like that at the *Bulletin,* where I fought for inches of copy.

Anyway, with criminals infesting every city, we plan eventually to roll out a CrimeFree-dot-com everywhere — CrimeFreeNYC, CrimeFreeLA, et cetera, et cetera. All over-seen by yours truly. Why would I ever work at a newspaper again?"

Payne nodded, then said, "You think it'll make a difference? I'm beginning to think it might be time to get off this sinking ship of a city."

O'Hara grinned widely. "Oh, yeah, Matty. It's already working. People love those cops-and-robbers TV shows. You know, like *Most Wanted in America, Homicide 9-1-1.* We're taking that a step — *steps* — further. We're a one-stop shop for fans of those kinds of shows, plus have news articles on crime and crime prevention and profiles of the bad guys. We list who's offering rewards for which criminals and for how much, and show how to search databases for criminals and submit tips on where they might be — new ones, old ones, fugitives like violators of Megan's Law — and on and on."

Megan's Law was the catchall name for any number of federal and state statutes concerning sexual predators. It was named after a seven-year-old New Jersey girl who had been abducted by a neighbor right after the pervert had gotten out of the slam where he'd been serving time for sex crimes. He raped and killed the little girl.

Outraged citizens demanded that they had the right to know when dangerous people moved into their neighborhoods, leading to the passage of sex offender registry laws, first in Jersey, then across the nation.

Payne said, "Aren't you worried that that's essentially encouraging people to take the law into their own hands, like Fuller's Lex Talionis is doing? Not that I'm surprised, considering your secret benefactor."

"Uh-uh," Mickey quickly said, shaking his head vigorously, making the red curls bounce like tiny coiled springs. "In that area, we're simply a clearinghouse of sorts for a lot of things that are already available all over on the Internet. The key to any good source of information, Matt, is making it easy on the person looking for that information, whether it's where to get the cheapest ground sirloin or how to finger a bad guy. You ever hear of a company called Google?"

"Yeah, the eight-hundred-pound gorilla of Internet search engines," Payne said. "I take your point. I'm just not convinced."

"Hell, Matt, the FBI has a page devoted to a Wanted poster for that raghead, Whatshisname the Terrorist, with a twenty-five-million-dollar price tag for his head. And all sorts of bounties for lesser criminal shits. How the hell is that any different if we add it to our website?"

After a moment, Matt nodded. "Okay, you're convincing me."

Mickey went on: "And we're also a place to give 'attaboy' accolades to cops who otherwise don't get noticed, like a patrolman walking the beat in your neighborhood who unlocks your car after you've left your keys in it." He pointed to his shirt. "Kiss a Cop."

"Now, that sounds like a stretch."

"Aw, c'mon, Matty. You ever read a positive piece on a cop? Everyone likes a pat on the back now and then."

"Well, you're absolutely right about that. Rare is the day you ever hear anything good about cops doing their job. Just mention the name Wyatt Earp of the Main Line." He smiled. "Sounds like we're on the same side of this fight, Mick, just different teams."

"Exactly."

IV

[ONE]

Standing at the bar at Liberties, Harris looked from Mickey to Matt, took a sip of beer, then said, "You remember Danny Gartner, Matt?"

Payne, his glass to his lips, raised his eyebrows in surprise.

"Really? 'The shittiest lawyer in all the Commonwealth of Pennsylvania,' as they call him in the DA's office? Never could forget a prick like that. Can't count the times in court during questioning that he tried to make me look stupid or crooked. So he's the one who got dumped at Francis Fuller's door?"

Harris nodded and said, "Gartner and one of his loser clients, a cocky little shit by the name of John Nguyen, aka 'Jay-Cee,' 'Johnny Cannabis,' age twenty-five. And mean as hell."

Then he mimed that his right hand was a pistol. He put the tip of the index finger in the base of his skull and, moving his thumb forward, dropped the "hammer" and mouthed *Bang!*

He said: "Apparently, a fairly big-bore weapon. Really made a mess of their skulls."

"I think I'm about to cry," Payne said, more than a little sarcastically, then sipped at his single-malt. He feigned wiping at a tear under his eye and went on: "Nope, guess I was wrong."

O'Hara chuckled.

Payne smiled. He said to Harris, "Should I know the punk client, too?"

"Only if you were in on any of his dozen drug busts for possession with intent to distribute. Just two of which ever went to trial — both for running roofies and other date-rape drugs — because Gartner kept playing the three-strikes game. There was also a sexual assault charge that got tossed because of a broken chain of evidence."

"Three strikes, eh?" O'Hara said. "That has to be one of the worst rules ever. Whatever happened to the notion of a speedy trial, as opposed to a speedy dismissal?"

Clearing out cases so there could be speedy trials was precisely why, at least in theory, the Municipal Court had invoked Rule 555 in the criminal court procedures.

Despite the shared name, Philly's three-strikes law had nothing to do with laws across the land which declared that if someone racked up three felony convictions, he or she was clearly a habitual criminal who hadn't learned a damn thing the first two times in the court system — and, accordingly, deserved a long sentence that essentially locked them up and threw away the key.

Philly's three strikes, in fact, could be argued to have the polar opposite effect of those laws: Rule 555 actually put criminals back on the streets.

When someone was arrested, they came before the court for a preliminary hearing. But, due to any number of reasons — busy work or school schedules, miscommunications, even having second thoughts about testifying against a known thug — not all the victims or witnesses would show up for a hearing. And if they were not there in court at the scheduled time, then the prosecutors had to inform the judge that they were not prepared and that they had to request a rescheduling of the preliminary hearing.

An occasional request for rescheduling might be manageable for the court system. But with the understaffed DA's office overwhelmed with cases, the constant juggling of hearing dates made court scheduling chaotic, if not impossible.

In response, the judges came up with Rule 555. It allowed prosecutors only three attempts at a preliminary hearing. If on the third hearing date the victims or witnesses still had not made it before the court, the judge slammed his gavel and announced, "On grounds of no evidence, case dismissed!"

And the accused walked.

Criminal defense lawyers were not held to such a standard. And the manner in which Danny Gartner and others of his ilk abused the system was equal parts clever and slimy.

One type of abuse was for the defense attorney to ask his client on the day of a hearing if he or she saw anyone waiting in the courtroom who could be called as a witness against them. If they did, the defense attorney told the accused to scram. When the judge called the case, the defense attorney came up with an excuse — "Your Honor, my client could not get free from his job" and "didn't have bus fare" were popular — and promised the court that the client would absolutely make a later court appearance — "even if I have to fry those McBurgers myself, Your Honor, then chauffeur him here." The lawyer would request a delay.

That wasn't strike one, two, or three for the prosecutor.

But it damn sure was an inconvenience for the prosecution. And especially for the victims and witnesses, who, unlike the judges and lawyers and cops, were not paid for their time in the judicial system. Accordingly, they genuinely might not be able to get another day free from their job or school duties, and would end up a no-show. And then their absence *did* trigger a strike against the prosecution.

Another type of abuse was for the accused, or an associate of the accused, to intimidate the victims or witnesses back in the 'hood so that they simply gave up on pressing the case altogether. The message — *Snitches are not tolerated* — was not lost on anyone in the ghetto. It didn't matter that such an act was illegal. It still effectively caused a case to go nowhere — and the accused to go free.

And thus Rule 555 made the DA's job of bringing cases to trial more difficult — if not damn near impossible.

"Now," Mickey said, "where were we on the pop-and-drops?"

"Tony was describing how they found Gartner and his punk pal."

Harris nodded, then said, "Well, both of the victims were bound. They had their wrists and ankles taped with packing tape. You know, it's clear and maybe three inches wide, designed for those handheld dispensers?"

"Yeah," O'Hara said, "I've got one. I just use the rolls by themselves, because every time I tried with the dispenser, that jagged row of teeth always wound up slicing my hand or arm."

Payne snorted. "I've had that happen."

"Anyway," Harris went on, "it appears that the doer also used the tape without the dispenser. Through the clear tape you actually could see dirty fingerprints that were picked up on the adhesive side."

"The doer didn't wear gloves?" Payne said.

Harris shrugged. "Unless the doer made either Gartner and Jay-Cee bind the other, or made someone else. Whatever the sequence, whoever did it left prints. We will just have to see if they match those of the deceased, or whatever prints they can lift at Gartner's office." He stopped and gestured upward with his left index finger. "Speaking of which . . ."

He paused and finished off his Hops Haus lager, then signaled the bartender for another round of drinks for all three of them.

"Speaking of which," Harris went on, "when we ID'd Gartner at the scene — his wallet, including driver's license and sixty-four bucks cash, was still in his hip pocket — we sent Crime Scene Units over to Gartner's apartment and to his office. The apartment manager didn't seem particularly upset with his demise, except for the fact he owed three months' back rent. Anyway, the manager let us in. There was no apparent sign of anything having happened in the apartment."

"And the office?" Payne asked. "Where is it?"

"Over on Callowhill, not far from the ICE office."

"Really?" Payne said, mentally picturing the building that housed the local office of Immigration and Customs Enforcement, the federal agency that was under the U.S. Department of Homeland Security. "Was Gartner into immigration law, too?"

"I doubt it. I don't think he was that smart."

"You know, those guys can be real low-lifes," O'Hara put in. "Some poor immigrant, wanting to do the right thing and become a legal citizen of the United States, willingly goes through all the hoops, including hiring an immigration attorney to help him understand all the legalese. The immigrant gives the lawyer his five-grand cash retainer, then the lawyer doesn't do shit and the poor immigrant, who probably drove a cab to hell and back to earn that five large, and now is even poorer, winds up deported. And the lawyer keeps the retainer, never again to see the client for whom he's done nothing."

Payne shook his head. "Nice."

Mickey looked furious. "If I ever find a way to put stuff like that on CrimeFree-Philly, those guys are toast, too."

John Sullivan delivered their drinks, and after they'd all had a sip, Harris continued.

"Gartner's office was a mess. But it appeared to be just a normal office mess. There was no sign of a struggle there. And no forced entry. Curiously, both the front and back main exterior doors of the building had been left unlocked, as had the interior door to Gartner's office. We found drugs on one of the desks, what looked like coke or crank in one zip-top bag, and another bag with roofies. There was even a line of powder on the desktop that hadn't been snorted."

"That's strange," Payne said. "Like someone had to leave fast. But no signs that either he or his punk client was popped there?"

Harris shrugged. "The CSU boys were

141

still working it when I stopped by on the way here. But, for now, it appears the answer is no. And Jay-Cee's motorcycle was parked on the sidewalk." He paused, sipped his beer, then said, "Something did happen there, though — something really weird."

He looked between Matt and Mickey, whose curiosity clearly was piqued.

After a moment, they said in unison: "What?"

"Piss."

"Piss?" they repeated in unison.

Harris nodded.

"There was piss everywhere," he said. "And I mean everywhere. You'd think gallons."

"Animal urine? Like some dog got loose in there?" Payne asked. "You said the doors were unlocked. Maybe they'd been open, too."

"I don't know. Maybe. Judging by the amount, though, something bigger. I mean, who has that large of a bladder?"

Mickey glanced over at a couple at the bar in a two-part cow costume.

"Cows?" he offered. Then he looked back at Harris and said, "Or maybe the doer is a deer hunter. Once, when I was up in Bucks County, I found a place where they were selling bottles of animal piss — I think it was doe urine — that hunters poured on themselves to mask their human scent in the woods. Or maybe it was meant as an attractant to draw out horny males. Or something."

Payne looked at O'Hara, raised his eyebrows, and said, "So you're thinking that fucking Bambi is the doer?"

O'Hara and Harris laughed.

Payne then looked at Harris and said, "I'm assuming there's enough piss to run a DNA analysis?"

Harris snorted.

"Enough to float a boat. There was a pool of piss in the plastic bag alone. The dope that hadn't dissolved just floated in it!"

"Was there piss at the scene at Francis Fuller's office in Old City?"

Harris nodded. "Yeah. On Jay-Cee's pants crotch. But that was more like he'd just pissed himself. Nothing like the pools of it in the office."

"Anything else out of the ordinary?"

"Define 'out of the ordinary,' Sergeant Payne."

They all chuckled.

Harris, looking deep in thought, then said, "Not really. Gartner was wearing a T-shirt that read PEACE LOVE JUSTICE."

Payne snorted. "File that under 'Irony,' Detective, not 'Extraordinary.'"

Harris shrugged. After a minute, he added, "Well, the only other thing that comes to mind is that there wasn't any paperwork attached."

"Really?" Payne said, visibly surprised. "Now, that's out of the ordinary — outside the MO of the other pop-and-drops, that is."

"Paperwork?" O'Hara asked, looking from Matt to Tony. "Like police forms?"

Then he looked at Payne.

"Wait," O'Hara said. "Back up. Explain that 'outside the others' *modus operandi* oddity thing. What method of operation?"

Payne took a sip of his single-malt, then said: "The MO in the other cases is that someone's shooting fugitives in the head or chest and dumping their bodies. Further, the dead guys — and they're only guys, so far — are wanted on outstanding warrants. A couple of them jumped bail, the others violated parole, for sex crimes against women and children. Involuntary deviant sexual intercourse, rape, aggravated indecent assault. These shits get popped point-blank, then dumped at a district station, one we assume is closest to where they got nabbed."

"None dumped at the Roundhouse?"

"None. At least not yet. That'd be an interesting situation."

O'Hara nodded as he took all that in.

"Now, the difference between those dumped at the districts and these two tonight is that tonight there was no 'paperwork' — printouts of the bad guys' Wanted info downloaded from the Internet. All the others had their paperwork stapled to them."

"*Stapled?* Like to their clothes?"

Payne nodded. "Usually. But one bastard who'd raped a ten-year-old girl had his sheet stapled clean through his prick. Multiple times."

"Ouch!" O'Hara said, instinctively crossing his legs.

Payne then said, "You know, it's funny, because your website is one place from where more than one of the Wanted posters has been downloaded. You can tell because the line at the foot of the page shows the date the page was printed and its source URL."

"That's great to know," O'Hara said. "That means that CrimeFreePhilly is working!"

"Only," Payne said dryly, "to create more crime, it would appear. As far as I know, as much as a miserable dirty rotten shit Danny Gartner was, he had no criminal record."

O'Hara shrugged. "Chalk it up to collateral damage. You associate with swine, you're going to get muddy, too."

"Jay-Cee," Harris put in, "had charges against him of involuntary deviant sexual intercourse and rape of an unconscious or unaware person in one case that Gartner got tossed."

Payne nodded, then took a swallow of his single-malt and glanced at his watch.

"I need to get the hell out of here. I'm trying to have a life outside of work," he said, then looked at O'Hara. "Okay, Mick. That's all we know at this point. Now tell me what you know."

O'Hara raised his glass. "Not a goddamn thing, Matty. That's why you're called the confidential source close to the Roundhouse, and I'm called the reporter."

O'Hara took a sip of his drink as Payne gave him the finger.

"Sorry, pal. I really wish I had something for you. You know that eventually I will. And when I do, it's yours."

They all then stared into their glasses, quietly thinking.

After some time, O'Hara suddenly said, "So, Matty, what do you think are the chances of solving this?"

"Seriously?"

O'Hara nodded. "Seriously."

"Hell, I don't know. Right now, I'd say that the odds are about as high as the number of 'r's in 'fat fucking chance.' Zilch. Which is maybe slightly better than, say, finding all those fifty thousand fugitives."

Harris said, "Hey, you got Fort Festung. He was in the wind."

"Whoopie! One down, another forty-nine thousand nine-ninety-nine, give or take, to go. And don't forget that he took almost twenty years."

Tony Harris's cell phone then chimed once and vibrated. He pulled it from the plastic cradle on his belt and glanced at the LCD screen.

"It's Jenkins," he said as his thumb worked the BB-size polymer ball to navigate the phone's screen. He rolled and clicked to where the text messages were stored. "He's working the Wheel."

The Homicide Unit had a system called "the Wheel," basically a roster that listed the detectives on the shift. At the top of the roster was the detective currently assigned to "man the desk." When a call came in with a new murder, the "desk man" got assigned to the case. The detective listed below him on the roster — who was said to be "next up on the wheel" — then became the next "desk man."

Harris pushed again, then saw the message and exclaimed, "Holy shit!"

O'Hara looked at Payne and casually inquired, "How come you don't get 'holy shit!' texts from the Wheel guy? You're a sergeant. That outranks a lowly detective like Harris."

Tony handed Matt the phone for him to read the text message.

"Correction," Payne said. "I'm a sergeant assigned to a desk. Tony gets the fun job of working the streets."

He looked at the screen.

"Holy shit!" Payne repeated, rereading the message as he said, "Well, Mickey, do you want an exclusive for CrimeFreePhilly?"

"Sure. What?"

Matt handed the phone back to Tony, then his eyes met Mickey's.

"Minutes after the last Crime Scene Unit drove off from Lex Talionis," Matt said, "another body got dumped there. Someone walking by thought it was a vagrant passed out on the sidewalk. Then they noticed all the blood."

"Holy shit!" O'Hara joined in, then downed his drink.

"You can't run with this just yet, Mickey, but there's something different with this pop-and-drop."

"What?"

"He was strangled and beaten. But no bul-

148

let wounds."

O'Hara banged the glass on the wooden bar and, making a circular gesture with his hand over their drinks, barked to the bartender: "Johnny, all this on my tab. We've got to go!"

[TWO]
Loft Number 2055
Hops Haus Tower
1100 N. Lee Street, Philadelphia
Sunday, November 1, 1:14 A.M.

Tossing his suit coat and kicking off his loafers, H. Rapp Badde, Jr., chased the beautiful and giggling Cleopatra past the floor-to-ceiling windows of the living room. His intent: to make the beast with two backs after ripping off the Halloween outfit as fast as humanly possible.

I love that there're no other high-rises near here so no one can see us through those big windows.

I can do whatever the hell I want. . . .

It wasn't the first time that the idea of doing whatever the hell he wanted — damn the consequences — had entered the mind of H. Rapp Badde, Jr.

For almost all of his thirty-two years, Badde — a fairly fit, five-foot-eleven two-hundred-pounder with a thin face, close-cropped hair, and medium-dark skin — had learned that what he could not get with his charisma or his arrogant badgering, he could always get by subtly, or sometimes not so subtly, playing his favorite card, that of being a disadvantaged minority.

It was a tactic — a remarkably effective one considering that Philly as a whole was half black, some sections up to three-quarters — that he had learned from his father. Horatio R. Badde, Sr., had used it successfully to work himself up from being a small-business owner — first a barber in South Philadelphia, then the owner of a string of barbershops throughout the city — to being elected to the Philadelphia City Council, and then, almost ten years later, to the office of mayor.

Which was exactly Rapp's planned next step: to become mayor. He was banking both on the name recognition — "Mayor Badde" still was familiar to voters despite the eight years since his father held the office — and what he considered to be his own accomplishments as a city councilman. And he was going to let nothing get in his way. There'd already been rumors trying to tie him to voter fraud, but he publicly dismissed them as exactly that — rumors that were simply a part of petty politics.

Rapp Badde did as he pleased — damn the consequences — and the Hop Haus Tower condominium was no exception.

The tax rolls of the Philadelphia County Recorder of Deeds, in Room 156 at City Hall, showed Loft Number 2055 — a year-old 2,010-square-foot, two-bedroom, two-bath condominium on the twentieth floor — as being owned by the Urban Venture Fund, in care of Mr. James R. Johnson, JRJ Certified Public Accountants, 1611 Walnut Street, Suite 1011, Philadelphia, Pennsylvania 19103.

There was similar information on the books at the complex.

The building management kept a regularly updated computer file known as PROPERTY OWNERS: PERMANENT RESIDENTS & REGISTERED GUESTS. It listed everyone who was officially on file and showed that 2055's permanent resident was named Johnson, James R., and its listed registered guest was a Harper, Janelle.

While it wasn't unusual for the names of owners and guests to be different — there were, for example, many unmarried couples who cohabited, as well as many lawfully married couples whose surnames were not the same — neither James Johnson nor Janelle Harper had a genuine financial investment in Loft Number 2055.

In fact, the apartment's official owner, the Urban Venture Fund, was a corporate entity solely owned by one H. R. Badde, Jr., 1611 Walnut Street, Suite 1011, Philadelphia, Pennsylvania 19103.

That was in technical terms.

Practically speaking, Unit 2055's permanent resident and its (very) regular guest were actually Jan Harper and Rapp Badde.

Never mind that Mr. James R. Johnson, CPA, had never set foot in the place.

And never mind that Badde had purchased, with cash, the *pied-à-terre* love nest.

And certainly never mind that the funds for the purchase were a small part of those provided to his mayoral election campaign chest by a generous businessman who believed in the politician, in his future at City Hall, and his influence therein for old friends.

Twenty-five-year-old Jan Harper — who had a full and curvy five-six, one-forty body and a silky light-brown skin tone — was down to barely more than Cleopatra's golden-colored sheer panties and plastic-jeweled collar and crown as she ran into the bedroom. Rapp was hot on her heels.

And just as she jumped on the king-size bed's thick goose-down comforter, her legs flying up and ample breasts bouncing, Rapp heard his Go To Hell cell phone start ringing in his pants pocket.

Damn! he thought.

Badde shared the number of his Go To Hell phone, one of two he carried, with next to no one — only his accountant, his three lawyers, and a select few others who were friends or business associates, or both, had the number. Even Jan didn't know it; being his executive assistant, she could call him on his main cell phone.

He'd given it that name because, when somebody who did have the number called, chances were damn good that something had just gone to hell. Or was about to.

Jan was now busily unbuttoning Rapp's white dress shirt as he quickly dug into his pants pocket.

Retrieving the phone, he looked at the screen, hissed the word "Shit," then pulled away from Jan's hands. He walked toward the windows.

"What?" she said, surprised. Then, a little

indignantly, she added, "Who the hell is that at this hour?"

He held up his left index finger to gesture *Give me a minute,* then flipped open the phone, put it to his head, and said, "Everything okay, man?"

He listened for a moment.

"Wait," he suddenly said. "Who the hell is this, and how'd you get this number?"

After a moment, he said, "Goddamn it!"

His eye caught Jan, now sitting up on the comforter with her arms crossed over her naked breasts, her head cocked, looking at him curiously.

"Hold on a minute, brother," he said into the phone.

Then to Jan he said, "I'm sorry, honey. I'll be right back."

Badde slid open the glass door in the wall of the floor-to-ceiling windows and stepped out onto the small concrete balcony.

The view from the twentieth floor was extraordinary. And for more than just the beauty of the lights twinkling in the night.

H. Rapp Badde, Jr., enjoyed the feeling he got from being up so high and seeing so many parts of the city that made up his life. It made him feel literally on top of the world, or at least on top of what he thought of as *his* world — Philadelphia.

"Okay, Kenny — I mean, *Kareem,*" Badde said when he'd closed the sliding glass door, "calm down and start from the beginning."

For his first twenty-two years, Kareem Abdul-Qaadir answered to the name Kenny Jones. That had changed two years ago when Kenny Jones, not the brightest bulb on the marquee, had gotten arrested for selling crack cocaine to undercover Philly cops in Germantown, then fled the justice system by jumping his two-thousand-dollar bond.

The Jones family, who'd lived in a brick-faced row house across Daly Street from the Baddes in South Philly, had four brothers. Kenny was second oldest, after Jack, who'd been a classmate and friend of Badde's seemingly forever.

When Kenny went on the lam, he called his big brother for help and advice. Jack then turned to his old buddy, Rapp Badde. The city councilman had connections with the authorities — "Maybe he can get the whole case thrown out or something," Jack told Kenny. And if for some reason Badde was not able to use those connections, he had other resources well beyond the Joneses'.

Badde hadn't hesitated. Beyond being old neighbors, the Jones family had campaigned hard for his election to office. He couldn't do anything with Kenny's case; that, he told Jack, was a matter involving the court system and the district attorney's office, over which a city councilman such as himself had absolutely no sway, even in a place like Philadelphia.

So he called the manager of his campaign office in West Philly, which was run from a rented row house, and told him to let Kareem live there in the basement bedroom, which had its own door to the street, and to pay him, in cash, to work as one of Badde's "community voter canvassers."

Badde even helped Kenny pick out the cover name "Abdul-Qaadir," which was Arabic for Servant of the Capable. Badde quietly enjoyed the implication of that.

At first, Kareem Abdul-Qaadir's job had been to go door to door pretending to be a volunteer with the City of Philadelphia working for the Forgotten Voters Initiative — a program that, had anyone actually bothered to investigate, would've been found not to exist. He asked the residents if they were registered voters. If they said no, he helped get them registered.

But then came his real job: the compilation of the names and addresses of all these voters, especially noting the elderly, immigrants, and others who could easily be convinced that they needed to request absentee-voter ballot forms. More important, once those ballots arrived in the mail, Kenny would help those voters with filling out the forms — specifically, under "city councilman," marking the box next to "H. Rapp Badde, Jr."

Kenny had then stumbled across an idea that had turned out to be borderline brilliant.

As he was canvassing a far section of West Philly, knocking on door after door, he walked up to a retirement community, Fernwood Manor at Cobbs Creek. The ten-story-high building overlooked the greenbelt of the small tree-lined stream — and, curiously, on the opposite side of the creek, Fernwood Cemetery.

Kenny, whose experience with retirement communities could be equated to his knowledge of quantum physics, had been excited to find the place was packed with really old people. In no time he had talked his way into its Community Activity Center, a large building that reminded him of a high school auditorium. There he found that the residents watched TV, played card games and bingo, and otherwise pleasantly passed time in their retirement before, ultimately, winding up across the creek.

At Fernwood Manor's Community Activity Center, he didn't have to go door to door. The retirees came to him. They were happy to see a nice, clean-cut young man such as Kareem. Especially the old-timers who had failing memories, Alzheimer's disease in particular, and never remembered previously meeting him — or filling out forms.

And when Kareem had explained the purpose of his volunteer work, everyone thought that the nice young man was extremely considerate to think of forgotten old folks. That, and to understand how difficult it was for them on voting day. They said visiting polling stations that invariably had long lines was very painful for their aged bodies. At the community activity center, though, they could at their leisure fill out the requests for absentee-voter forms, then later, when the forms arrived, fill those out also at their leisure.

Especially with the kind help of a nice young man like Kareem.

Kenny started visiting as many retirement homes as would let him in the door.

And then he went to nursing homes, where he found the residents were more or less unconscious — almost every one on medication that kept them in a mental fog, or worse —

so all he had to do was forge their signatures on the forms. Even easier to sign up were those who in the last year or two had fallen into their own category: deceased.

Slipping the kid or old man in the mailroom a little stash of cocaine or cash, with the promise of more, guaranteed that there'd be a telephone call alerting him when the absentee-voter ballots arrived in the mail.

Over time, Kenny Jones did one hell of a job collecting names and helping the forgotten voters of Philadelphia support Badde for city councilman — and soon, for the office of mayor.

And Rapp Badde had been impressed. Ignoring the unfortunate fact that Kenny was a fugitive charged with a felony, he'd thought that Kenny was still pretty much the good, if dim, kid he'd been when they were growing up. And in two years since his arrest — *What the hell's wrong with a little coke now and then? That probably was a bullshit bust, anyway* — he'd never gotten into any other trouble.

Until now.

"What the hell do you mean something's gone bad with you and Reggie?" he said into his Go To Hell cell as he looked out over the

159

city to the right, toward West Philly and the rented campaign-office row house.

Reggie was the baby Jones brother, but at age twenty and two hundred thirty pounds, not much of a baby anymore.

Rapp knew that Reggie had never been really normal — his mother had had him late in life, in her forties, and there'd been complications at birth — and when Reggie got mixed up with drugs, he really went off the deep end.

Worse, while Kenny had just sold dope, Reggie both sold and used the stuff. Unfortunately, a lot more of the latter than the former, and he was forever trying to pay off his dealer.

Kenny said, "I got a call from Reggie. He was crazy. Crazy scared. Crying, man. Said, 'If I don't come up with thirty large to pay the man, I'm dead.' He didn't, and next day they grabbed him."

Thirty thousand dollars! Badde thought. *Jesus!*

"How'd he get that deep in debt?" Badde asked.

"Hell if I know. Snorting more than selling? A lot of IOUs over time? And some crazy interest on top of what he owed? Adds up fast."

"Who grabbed Reggie?" Badde asked.

"The dude he bought his coke from. The man. His dealer."

Badde sighed audibly.

"So, what would you have me do about it?"

Kenny was quiet a moment, then with a tone that was incredulous said, "What else, man? You know."

"What?"

"The money. I need the money bad to get him back."

Can I quickly put my hands on that much even if I wanted? Badde thought as he looked out at the city and mentally went over his cash reserves.

There's only ten, eleven grand in my office safe.

He was silent for at least a minute.

"You still there?" asked Kenny.

Badde didn't reply.

Kenny said, "We go way back. My family's done a lot for you, man."

And I've not helped you?

And what the hell have you done that's worth thirty grand?

Kenny added, "It'd just be a loan. You name the interest, whatever."

Right. Where the hell will you get that to repay me?

"Rapp? You there?"

"Yeah, Kenny. I'm here. Isn't there any way you can work out an arrangement with this dealer, just —"

Kenny Jones interrupted him: "Are you listening, man? We passed that point. These people kill for less!"

Rapp stared off into the night, silent.

Kenny went on: "Listen, man, it, uh, it wouldn't be good for folks to find out about those ballots, you know what I'm saying?"

What? "Those ballots"?

He's threatening me!

Sonofabitch! He thinks he can finger me for the voter fraud!

He blurted: "Are you fucking threatening me? You fucking ingrate!"

"I'm just saying . . ."

Jesus! Him getting diarrhea of the mouth would start the whole house of cards crumbling, starting with the campaign for mayor. And I can kiss the housing project good-bye.

Well, that is fucking worth thirty grand.

But if I cough up the money, I can forget getting paid back, with or without interest.

And what's going to stop him from squeezing me for more?

Shit!

"Kenny, where am I going to put my hands on thirty grand?"

"Important folks like you, you got connections."

Badde kicked the concrete four-foot-tall wall that served as the balcony's railing.

Goddamn it!

"Where are you now?" he asked.

"At the house in West Philly."

"How soon do you need the money?"

"Like yesterday?"

Shit.

"Kenny, I hate to ask this, but do you know if he's still alive? Have you talked to Reggie?"

"Yeah, this morning. But he won't be if I don't do something."

Bullshit. Then they really wouldn't get their money.

Kenny, as if reading Badde's mind, added, his voice cracking: "And if they kill him, they're coming after me for it."

Well, then not paying would remove one problem immediately.

But Kenny would still be mine, especially if he went into hiding and started blowing the damn whistle on the absentee ballots.

The goddamn media would love that story. It'd become a bigger circus than the Bermuda photographs.

And even if I gave him the money, I can't keep having to wonder when dimwit Kenny or

Reggie will fuck up again, or if Kenny will open his mouth about the ballots.

"Okay, look, Kenny, it's going to take a little time. Especially at this hour. But I'll send someone first thing —"

Kenny interrupted, "No, man. You need to bring it."

He waited a moment, then replied, "Why me? Personally?"

"It'd be better. That's all."

Badde lost his temper: "Well, you can fucking forget it, Kenny! Goddamn you! You want the money or not?"

There was a long pause while Kenny thought about that.

"Fine, then. I'll be here waiting."

As Badde broke the connection, looking out at West Philly and shaking his head, he heard the glass door slide open, then Jan's voice: "Everything okay, honey? I saw you kick the wall."

When he turned and looked at her, he saw that she glistened from having just taken a shower. Now she wore a tan silk robe. It hung open, and he could see that she was completely naked beneath it.

Badde took a deep breath and composed himself.

"Yeah, just give me one more second. I've got to make a quick call. You do look incredible, honey."

"I'll be waiting," she said softly, and slid the glass door shut.

H. Rapp Badde, Jr., felt a stirring in his groin.

Is that from seeing her gorgeous naked body — or because I'm about to have someone whacked?

[THREE]
The Roundhouse
Eighth and Race Streets,
Philadelphia
Sunday, November 1, 7:30 A.M.

Lieutenant Jason Washington looked up from reading the front page of the morning's *Philadelphia Bulletin* in time to see his boss walking purposefully around a corner, making a beeline for Washington's glass-walled office. Captain Henry C. Quaire, commanding officer of the Homicide Unit, was a stocky balding man in his late forties. Like Washington he wore khaki slacks, but instead of the white button-down-collar shirt Washington had on, Henry wore a red knit polo under a navy blazer.

Jason glanced at the wall clock and saw that Quaire was fifteen minutes earlier than he had said he would arrive. They'd spoken on the telephone an hour earlier. Quaire had called Washington at home and announced that Frank Hollaran had just called him at home, asking if they could be at the Roundhouse as soon as possible.

Quaire said that Captain Francis Xavier Hollaran, the forty-nine-year-old assistant to First Deputy Police Commissioner Dennis V. "Denny" Coughlin, had told him: "Denny wants us to be prepared before we meet with Mariana and before Mariana's meeting with Carlucci. Mariana said Carlucci wants damage control, and he needs to know what we know about the pop-and-drops."

Police Commissioner Ralph J. Mariana, a natty Italian, was the top cop with four stars on his uniform. And the Honorable Jerome H. "Jerry" Carlucci, who had once been the top cop, was Mariana's boss, the mayor of Philadelphia.

Coughlin, whose three stars made him the number-two cop in the department, reported to Mariana. They were both appointed to their jobs by the managing director of the city, but served at the mayor's pleasure. Every policeman below them in

166

rank on the force — which, with some seven thousand in uniform, was the fourth largest in the country — was a civil servant.

Washington saw that Quaire was sipping from a heavy china coffee mug that bore the logotype of the Emerald Society, the fraternal organization of police officers of Irish heritage. Washington wasn't a member, but he knew Hollaran and Coughlin had belonged to "The Emerald" all their long careers.

"Well, Jason, I see you've seen the good news," Quaire said by way of greeting. He motioned at the desk and repeated the quote over the TV: "If it bleeds, it leads."

The newspaper's front-page headline at the top of the fold screamed:

THE HALLOWEEN HOMICIDES

TRIPLE MURDERS TERRORIZE OLD CITY

"Quite the colorful headline, if a bit sensational," Washington replied. "I have put the arm out for Harris and Payne, Henry. They said they should be here any minute."

Quaire nodded as he sipped. "Good. We're going to need everything Tony and Matt have to put out this fire. And no doubt more.

They're good, but this makes — what? — seven or eight unsolved pop-and-drops?"

While Tony Harris had a years-long history in Homicide, Matt Payne's tenure could be measured only in months. And if Quaire had had any say in it, Payne never would have gotten the job, certainly not ahead of three other sergeants who also wanted in and who Quaire felt were far more qualified.

It was customary for the Homicide chief to pick, or at the very least have veto power over, who got assigned to the unit. But Commissioner Mariana, looking for ways to encourage the best and brightest, had announced that the five officers with the highest scores on the promotion exams got the assignment of their choice in the department. And Matt Payne grabbed the brass ring by being not only in the top five scores, but number one on the list of those who'd earned promotion to sergeant. And Payne picked Homicide.

A less-than-excited Quaire had no say.

One thing Quaire worried about was how Payne would be received. He was only a five-year veteran and newly minted sergeant, and he was getting a supervisor position over guys who had served longer than five years in Homicide alone.

But when he brought that up to Lieutenant Jason Washington and Detective Tony Harris — among Homicide's most respected — they'd said that their experience with Matt Payne had been without problem. Both liked him and thought he was smart — "Smart enough to keep his eyes and ears open and learn how Homicide works," Washington said. And he had.

It didn't hurt, either, that he was well connected, starting with being the godson of Denny Coughlin, whom he was known to call "Uncle Denny."

Quaire did have absolute authority to choose which squad in the unit to assign Payne. And because Payne's score on the sergeant exam proved he was, as the commissioner would have put it, among the best and brightest, and because Harris and Washington already had worked with Payne, and clearly liked him, Quaire naturally put Payne in the squad led by Lieutenant Jason Washington.

"Here comes Coughlin now," Washington said, looking past Quaire.

Quaire turned and raised his china mug to acknowledge the first deputy police commissioner. Denny Coughlin, a ruddy-faced fifty-nine-year-old, had graduated from the Police Academy nearly forty years earlier. He was tall and heavyset, with a full mouth of teeth and full head of curly silver hair.

He wore his usual well-tailored gray plaid double-breasted suit, but no tie.

Washington made the educated guess that Coughlin kept at least two extra neckties — and probably another suit — as backups in his big office on the third floor.

"Good morning, gentlemen," Coughlin said once he was in Washington's doorway. "Thank you for coming in."

"Good morning, sir," Washington and Quaire now said in unison.

"And good timing, Commissioner," Washington added as he nodded toward the far side of the office. "Here come Sergeant Payne and Detective Harris."

Both Matt and Tony wore the same clothing that they'd had on when they'd left Liberties Bar with Mickey O'Hara some six hours earlier. And with baggy eyes and five-o'clock beard shadows, both looked as if they'd just awakened from a very short sleep.

"Jesus, you two look like the walking dead," Coughlin said by way of greeting. "You especially look like hell, Matty."

"Just call me an overachiever, Uncle Denny," Payne replied dryly. "I was catching a nap in the car when the long arm of Lieutenant Washington reached out for us. After Tony and I left the scene in Old City, we went to check out a hunch. The dead guy, Reggie Jones, had a sort of to-do list in his coat pocket, and we wound up staking out his house in South Philly. Thought it was a long shot, and boy was it."

"And I thought," Coughlin said, his tone suddenly cold as his Irish temper flared, "that we all agreed you would stay the hell off the streets while all that Wyatt Earp of the Main Line business died, if you'll pardon my choice of words."

There had been a flurry of new stories — from print to TV to the Internet — after the *Bulletin* had run the photograph of the tuxedo-clad Payne holding his Colt .45 above the robber he'd shot in the parking lot of La Famiglia Ristorante. And then those were rehashed when the story broke about Payne's foot chase and shoot-out with the assassin who fled Temple University Hospital. The mayor, who wasn't displeased with Payne per se but was tired of constantly defending a good cop doing a good job, simply called Denny Coughlin and suggested Matt stay the hell out of sight — and stay out of the news.

And Coughlin had sent the order down the chain of command, after telling Matt himself.

Coughlin looked from Payne to Washington to Quaire. "Well?"

Quaire began, "I take —"

"It's my fault, sir," Detective Tony Harris interrupted. "I should have known better."

"The hell it is," Matt Payne said, looking at Tony. He turned to Coughlin and added, "I invited myself along. Me and Mickey O'Hara."

Coughlin's eyebrows went up. "What the hell was Mickey doing?"

"We were at Liberties," Payne said, "when the news came in about the third dead guy. You know you can't tell Mickey 'no.'"

"Nor, apparently, you," Coughlin said to Matt, his ruddy face turning redder by the second. "When I give an order, I damn well expect it to be kept."

"Yes, sir," Matt said, his voice tired, its resigned tone sounding like that of a school-boy who'd just been dressed down by the headmaster. Which, a dozen years ago, he had been on more than one occasion.

"And you, Detective Harris," Coughlin said.

"Yes, sir?"

"Same applies."

"Yes, sir. Of course, sir."

Coughlin nodded and, with a more gentle voice, added, "I do commend you, Tony, being the low man on the totem pole here, for trying to take the bullet for everyone else,

172

guilty or not."

Harris shrugged, making his rumpled navy blazer look even worse.

"I do feel responsible, sir. I've seen Matt day in and day out at his desk up to his eyeballs with mostly paperwork from the other pop-and-drops. I wanted him to see a fresh crime scene. That thought had occurred to me earlier last night, when the scene for the first two guys who were pop-and-dropped was being worked. But for whatever reason I didn't call him. Then, when the news came about the third one, and we were having drinks at Liberties, it just made sense for him to come along and see the scene. It's a helluva lot better than reading statements, sir."

Coughlin considered that a long moment. He looked between them, then back to Harris, and nodded. "From a homicide investigation standpoint, I do see your point."

Everyone in the room knew well that, among the many other assignments he'd held, then-Captain Coughlin had been the chief of the Homicide Unit, and Detective F. X. Hollaran had been his right-hand man even back then.

He looked at his wristwatch.

"Okay, Matty, you have ten minutes. Tell me what I need to know before going upstairs to face the wrath of the bosses."

Payne nodded.

"All of the dead," he began, looking at Coughlin, then the others, "have been adult males, both the earlier pop-and-drops and the three found last night. That's where that thread ends.

"Of the first five, all were shot at point-blank range in the head. The ballistics tests on the only two bullets recovered — every other round passed through their bodies — showed them to be 9 millimeter and .45 caliber. Three were black males, one a white male, and one a Hispanic male. And all were wanted on outstanding warrants, either for parole violation or for jumping bail, for sex crimes committed on kids or women. They got popped somewhere other than where they were dropped."

"How do you know that for sure?" Frank Hollaran asked. "Is that an assumption due to lack of evidence?"

Payne shook his head and said, "Because they were all dropped, one per week beginning back on September sixteenth, at the nearest police district HQ. Correction. At *a* police district HQ. 'Nearest' is speculative on my part. Reason being: Why would you drive around with a dead body farther than necessary?"

There were chuckles.

"Stranger things have occurred, Matthew," Jason Washington offered.

Payne nodded. "I know. Anyway, the other consistency among these first five pop-and-drops is that they each had their Wanted poster attached to them."

"Their Wanted poster?" Coughlin repeated.

"Yes, sir. Like the ones we post on the police department website? Nice color mug shot with their full name and aliases, last known address, crimes committed, et cetera."

Coughlin nodded, motioning with his hand for Matt to go on.

Payne said: "Two of the five — both rapists — were printed from our Special Victims Unit page on the Internet. The rest were from the listing of Megan's Law fugitives on O'Hara's CrimeFreePhilly-dot-com."

"That's Mickey's?" Coughlin asked, his face brightening.

"That's where he went after he quit the *Bulletin*," Payne said.

"It's had some growing pains," Coughlin said, "but what I've seen I've mostly liked. Anyway, continue."

For a moment, Payne was impressed that Coughlin paid attention to the Internet. But then he realized it shouldn't have come as such a surprise. Coughlin was smart as hell, and while he could be old school, he was also always embracing whatever might aid him in his duties.

With maybe one exception: Denny Coughlin had told Matt he wasn't crazy about carrying the new department-issued Glock 17 semiautomatic 9-millimeter pistol. Mariana had successfully lobbied the city for the cops to have more firepower than the .38-caliber revolvers they'd carried almost since the Ice Age — Philly's first foot patrol began in the late 1600s.

And he said Coughlin needed to carry the Glock "to set an example."

Denny, who had never drawn his service weapon his entire career, didn't think he needed on his hip what he called "a small cannon" — and especially not one of the Alternative Service Weapons, Glock models chambered for .40-caliber and .45-caliber rounds that were more powerful than the 9 millimeter. But he followed the order nonetheless.

Payne went on: "Each dead guy had his rap sheet stapled to him. Usually to the clothing. But on one bad guy — a really despicable bastard, on the run from a charge of raping a ten-year-old girl — the doer stapled the Wanted poster multiple times to the guy's wang."

There were groans.

"Jesus!" Hollaran exclaimed.

Coughlin, now somber-faced, shook his head. "Could've been worse. I worked a case maybe two decades ago where a guy who thought that he quietly — and successfully — had ratted out a mobster was found dead on his front porch for all the world to see."

"That's worse?" Payne said.

"In his mouth, looking like a droopy third eye, was his severed penis."

There was a mix of grunts and chuckles from the group.

"So," Payne then said, "those are the ones I've been trying to connect the dots on. I have more details on each one."

"Not for now, thanks," Coughlin said.

Payne looked at Harris and said, "Tony knows about last night's batch."

Coughlin said, "Detective, it appears you have the floor." He looked at his watch. "And a little less than ten minutes."

"Yes, sir. As Matt said, all the dead are male adults. We got the call on the first two — Danny Gartner and his longtime client?"

Coughlin grunted derisively. "I know who Gartner was. No great loss to mankind there."

Harris went on: "That call came in at

177

precisely ten-oh-two last night, and the call on the third guy at twelve-twelve this morning.

"Both Gartner — white male, age fifty-five — and John 'Jay-Cee' Nguyen — Asian male, age twenty-five — were shot point-blank at the base of the skull" — Tony mimed the shooting with his hand again, as he'd done at Liberties Bar — "with a large-bore round. We believe it was a Glock .45 caliber, as a shiny spent casing — with '.45 GAP' for Glock Automatic Pistol stamped on the base — was found behind Gartner's office. Cause of death, though, may not be by gunshot. Both men had their mouth and nose wrapped with clear plastic packing tape, and both also had a plastic garbage bag covering the head and taped tightly at the neck. The same tape was used to bind both men at their ankles and wrists."

"No Wanted posters like the others?" Coughlin asked.

Tony thought, *How did he know that?*

Simple answer: Because he didn't become the second most important white shirt in the building by being a lazy cop.

The uniform shirt for all ranks sergeant and above was white, thus the expression "white shirt"; those in ranks of corporal down to police recruit wore blue shirts, and were referred to accordingly.

Now, his well-honed investigative mind has been putting together the pieces, and one piece is that Gartner wasn't wanted for any crime.

"No, sir," Tony Harris said after a moment. "None of the three last night."

"Tell them about the piss," Payne said.

"What?" Hollaran blurted.

Everyone looked at Matt, then at Tony.

"When we got the search warrant for Gartner's office — outside of which was parked Nguyen's motorcycle — we found no obvious signs anybody'd been whacked inside. But we did find piss poured all over the place."

"Tony said it had to be gallons," Payne added lightly. "We're guessing some animal's. I mean, four-legged animal."

Coughlin shook his head in wonder.

"Doesn't matter if it turns out to be from a human," Quaire said. "Urine is mostly worthless for our purposes."

"Really?" Payne said.

"Uh-huh," Quaire said. "I thought you knew it doesn't have enough traceable DNA to make it useful. It's just . . . well, piss."

There were chuckles.

"At the risk of repeating myself, Matthew," Jason Washington offered, "we do come across strange things in our business."

179

Coughlin then said, "Okay, and what about the third guy?"

"One Reginald 'Reggie' Jones. Black male, age twenty. A great big boy, maybe goes two-forty, two-fifty. And with one of those round baby faces. Well, before he got beaten up. Someone kicked the living shit out of him. Brutal beating. He could have died from that, or from strangulation. Two of those plastic zip ties — two short ones put end to end to make one long one — were cinched tight around his throat."

He paused as they considered that.

Then Harris said, "Jones was a small-time dealer. What he had was more of a consumption habit. But he did have a couple busts for selling coke. He was on probation for possession. Word is that . . . this is not exactly PC —"

"Oh, no," Payne gasped dramatically, "we've never heard something that was politically incorrect uttered in the Roundhouse!"

There were grins, including Tony's.

"Say it, Tony," Coughlin said, his face serious. "We need to know everything."

"Reggie Jones was backward."

"Backward?"

"More or less retarded," Tony said.

"And now he's deceased," Payne said,

"making him number eight."

"No warrants?" Coughlin went on.

His investigator's mind is still on high speed.

"No, sir. Not on the deceased. His brother, however, is in the wind."

"How's that?"

"Kenneth J. 'Kenny' Jones, black male, age twenty-two, skipped out on a charge of possession with intent to distribute. Jumped his two-thousand-dollar bail after getting picked up in Germantown. Like his brother Reggie, Kenny's not the sharpest knife in the drawer. Tried to sell crack cocaine to a couple of our guys working an undercover task force."

Coughlin snorted, thought a moment, then said, "Maybe the doer popped the wrong brother by mistake?"

"Possible."

"And the others who'd been pop-and-dropped all had some sexual crime component?"

"Yes, sir. All but the lawyer. And all the others had been shot."

"But not the Jones boy? He was strangled."

Harris nodded. "Correct."

Coughlin looked at Hollaran. "You're thinking what I'm thinking?"

Frank Hollaran had worked with Denny

Coughlin so many years he could finish his sentences.

"That it's possible?" Hollaran asked. "Sure, boss. If somehow they'd heard about the pop-and-drops. But I doubt it's happened in this case. Not enough time has elapsed. It can happen, probably will happen, especially with the cash rewards being offered."

"What're we talking about?" Payne asked.

"Copycats. Folks who mimic crimes they see in the news. That fifteen minutes of fame Andy Warhol talked about."

Quaire, gesturing again at the newspaper on Washington's desk, put in: "And now we have — cue the dramatic music — the Halloween Homicides."

Payne offered: "Playing devil's advocate, maybe it's not so much a copycat as it is someone taking up Frank Fuller on the hefty bounty he offers for — what's his phrase? — the *evildoers*."

"Think that through, Matthew," Washington said. "Who is going to claim those rewards? At least for the dead critters? They'd be admitting to murder."

Payne shrugged.

"Regardless," Coughlin said, "Jerry Carlucci is going to want to know what we're doing about the problem. He's planning on having a press conference at noon in the Executive Command Center. What he talks about depends on what he hears from us. And I'm sure he will denounce Fuller's bounty."

"Isn't denouncing the bounty a bit hypocritical?" Payne asked.

"In what way?" Coughlin said.

"The Philadelphia Police Department is in bed with, for example, the FBI and the DEA, which do offer big rewards for fingering bad guys. And that nationwide Crimestoppers program pays five or ten grand for information leading to a conviction — just call their toll-free number. It pays up even if you remain anonymous. It'd make my job a helluva lot easier if someone called with something on these pop-and-drops."

"We do ask for tips on catching criminals, Matty," Coughlin said reasonably, "but we don't encourage killing. There's a difference, one somebody needs to point out to Frank Fuller." He sighed deeply. "But good point. Carlucci will have to spin it in a positive way."

He glanced at his watch. "Okay, everyone follow me upstairs. This was just the dress rehearsal."

Payne didn't move, causing Coughlin to raise an eyebrow in question.

" 'Everyone' as in everyone?" Matt asked.

"Am I allowed to leave the office?"

Coughlin, his voice taking an official tone, then said, "As of this moment, Sergeant Payne, assuming you can at some point soon get a decent shower and shave, I hereby order your release from desk duty."

Coughlin looked around the office.

"Everyone think they can follow that order?"

There was a chorus of "Yes, sir."

[FOUR]
5550 Ridgewood Street, Philadelphia
Sunday, November 1, 9:35 A.M.

There were three official emergency vehicles parked at the curb in front of the Bazelon's row house, all with various doors open and the red-and-blue light bars on their roofs flashing. Two were white Chevy Impala squad cars assigned to the Twelfth District, and the third was a somewhat battered white Ford panel van that had a blue-and-gold stripe running the length of the vehicle and blue block lettering that spelled out MEDI-CAL EXAMINER.

On the wooden front porch of the row house, two Philadelphia Police Department blue shirts were on either side of a rocking chair, one a male standing and writing notes and the other a female down on one knee. The young woman cop was speaking softly to eighteen-year-old Sasha Bazelon, who sat in the rocker, her face in her hands, her body visibly shaking as she sobbed.

Standing nearby on the sidewalk was a small crowd of fifteen people, mostly adult men and women holding Bibles, all watching with looks of deep sadness or abject helplessness. A couple of the women were dabbing at their cheeks with white cotton handkerchiefs. They wore what Mrs. Joelle Bazelon would have said was their Sunday Go-to-Meeting Clothing.

Any other week, Joelle Bazelon also would have been in her church clothes, usually a dark-colored billowing cotton dress, joining the group as it made the regular walk to worship at the Church of Christ three blocks over, at Warrington and South Fifty-sixth Street.

This morning, however, the sixty-two-year-old widow's cold dead body, clad in a rumpled housecoat, was about to be removed from her living room couch and placed inside a heavy-duty vinyl bag by two technicians from the Medical Examiner's Office.

The techs were dressed alike in black jeans, white knit polos, and stained, well-worn white lab coats that were thigh-length with two big patch pockets on the front. They had transparent blue plastic booties covering their black athletic shoes. Their hands wore tan-colored synthetic polymer gloves.

The body bag was on a heavy-duty, metal-framed gurney that had been positioned alongside the couch, its oversize rubber wheels locked to prevent it from rolling.

The tech who was lifting the body by holding the lower legs — just above the swollen and bruised ankles — was Kim Soo. A small-bodied man with short spiked black hair and puffy round facial features, he'd been born in Philly twenty-eight years earlier to parents from South Korea who became naturalized Americans.

Soo had spent the last two hours carefully photographing the row house with a big, bulky, professional-level Nikon digital camera, its body badly scratched and dinged. He'd moved through the residence fluidly with the camera, documenting the scene. The strobe had been so intense that its pulsing flashes were easily seen by the small crowd on the sidewalk.

Soo's face was stonelike as he looked at

the lead technician, Javier Iglesia. Soo had known Iglesia going back to South Philly High, where Kim had been two grades behind him.

Iglesia, a beefy but fit thirty-year-old of Puerto Rican ancestry, was normally a very talkative sort, always ready with an opinion on anything. Now, however, holding the body at the shoulders, Iglesia was being unusually quiet.

Finally, Iglesia said, "I knew being a tech for the ME wasn't going to be all glory, Kim. But days like this, when it gets personal, I honest to God genuinely hate this damned job."

Iglesia looked at Soo, who said, "I know."

After getting a stronger grip on the housecoat, Iglesia said, "Ready? On three. One, two, *three* . . ."

The lifting took considerable exertion, and they both grunted with effort as the body began to budge. The "lift" was actually more of a slide off the couch, then a slight drop to the black vinyl body bag that was positioned on the gurney.

The big-boned, obese body made for a fairly tight fit in the body bag. It also made the bag more or less droop over the gurney's tubular frame.

"Principal Bazelon was a good and decent

woman," Javier said then. "I remember the year before she retired — it was my first year at Shaw Middle School. This woman was so strict, but also so kind."

Soo nodded, his face looking sympathetic.

"I'll tell you," he went on, "she was a major influence on me back then. And so many others. She taught me a lot. 'A fool thinks himself to be wise, but a wise man knows himself to be a fool.' That's Shakespeare. She got me reading him."

He looked down at the body in the bag. "And now this?"

"I'll tell you something," Iglesia said, then glanced around to see if anyone could be listening. He went on in a softer voice: "What I think is, she didn't just die in her sleep, is what I think." He paused. "No, I know she didn't. Just look at her wrists and ankles. Bruised and swollen from something. Tied with something, some rope, something that's been taken off. And that's called tampering with evidence." He paused again, then nodded as he added, "Mitchell will make it. He misses nothing."

The medical examiner, their boss, was Dr. Howard H. Mitchell, a very busy bald man with a dark sense of humor. He was usually found in a well-worn rumpled suit and tie, either performing an autopsy or dealing with

188

the paperwork of a place that had to deal with an average of a murder a day, plus the questionable deaths, such as that of Mrs. Joelle Bazelon.

Iglesia shook his head, then closed the top flap and began working the web straps over the bag that would secure the load to the gurney.

That done, he and Soo grabbed the tubular handles at each end of the height-adjustable gurney and lifted, once again grunting under the weight. They raised the top of the gurney to about the level of their waists. They wanted it high enough to have better control while wheeling it, but not so high that the center of gravity could cause the gurney to become ungainly and top-heavy and dump onto its side.

Kim Soo unlocked the rubber wheels, and he pushed as Javier Iglesia began pulling the gurney toward the open front door.

As they went, Javier shook his head and quietly said, "I was there when they threw Principal Bazelon's big retirement go-away thing. It was a big deal, it was. She was a big deal. And whatever happened to her, this just isn't right. What I think is that girl of hers isn't saying what really happened."

After Iglesia and Soo had first arrived at the

house and were processing the scene before preparing to remove the deceased, Javier had overheard a good bit of what Sasha Bazelon had been telling the two blue shirts.

Iglesia had been impressed with her — at eighteen, she was a year younger than his baby sister — and while she was just shy of hysterical, it was clear that on any other day, the slender, light-brown-skinned young woman would be absolutely beautiful.

The five of them had all been in the living room, the two cops interviewing the girl while the techs did their work.

Officer Geoffrey Pope, nineteen years old, was a rail-thin five-nine with closely cropped blond hair and a youthful face. Javier knew he had exactly one year on the Philadelphia Police Department.

Corporal Charlene Crowe was a black, stout thirty-year-old with a friendly face and warm smile. She stood a head shorter than Sasha, and she had to look up at the girl while asking questions. The shoulder patches of Crowe's blue uniform shirt had two blue chevrons outlined in silver.

In fits and starts, interspersed with crying jags, Sasha had told Corporal Crowe, "I came home late last night from my friend's house down the street. Grammy was sound asleep on the couch, snoring. So I quietly went to my room. When I came downstairs this morning, she was still there. But no longer breathing. When I checked for a pulse, her body felt cold and hard."

And then came the waterworks.

And then she'd basically repeated what she'd said.

And then came the waterworks again.

Javier found it curious that Sasha almost never looked Corporal Crowe in the eyes, and when she did it was for only a split second — then she'd bury her face in her hands and sob.

It wasn't that he felt the tears were not authentic.

The girl was clearly in deep emotional distress, and damn near inconsolable.

She's shaking to her core, she's crying so much.

But . . . there's something that's just not right, something that's missing, not being said.

Yet when asked if anything at all suspicious had happened in the last days, weeks, even months, she'd said there'd been nothing.

She said, "Grammy got sick a lot, mostly from her diabetes. And her weight. I guess . . . I guess her heart just couldn't take it anymore."

Kim Soo and Javier Iglesia rolled the gurney

out the front door and the wooden boards of the porch creaked under all the weight. The two uniforms talking with Sasha Bazelon looked over their shoulders and made eye contact with the medical examiner techs.

Sasha looked up from her hands, saw the packed body bag strapped to the gurney, and let out a wail.

"Officer Pope," Javier Iglesia said, "when you get a moment?"

Javier dipped his head once sideways, in the direction of the white Ford panel van.

Pope nodded.

Soo and Iglesia wheeled the gurney past the small crowd, trying to remain professional and not make eye contact. But then a tiny, ancient-looking black lady — Javier thought she easily could be in her nineties — held her Bible up to her forehead and cried, "Go with God, sweet Joelle. Rest in peace. Praise be the Lord!"

Javier saw that she was clearly upset, but unlike the other younger women had her crying under control.

A strong and brave lady, Iglesia thought as they made eye contact, and with sad eyes and thin pensive lips, he nodded. *Far braver than I.*

"Amen," he said softly to her.

■ ■ ■ ■

As Kim swung open the two rear doors of the white Ford panel van, Javier said, "You know, this and South Philly have been my home all my life. And it's all changing. It's all slowly going to shit."

"Mine, too. The whole city is," Kim replied. "So, what's your point?"

"My point is, good people are getting hurt. And someone needs to step up, is my point. I mean, I know we did pot and stuff at South Philly High. But now dealers are selling to middle schoolers, and not just pot, but bad stuff like candy smack."

"Candy smack?"

"Yeah. I mean black tar heroin, is what I mean. Cheap deadly shit from Mexico, mixed with sugar. And other junk. And then the kids get hooked, then need money to go score more, so then they go rob some old lady, maybe tie her up and kill her. That's what I mean, man!"

Kim Soo looked wide-eyed at Javier Iglesia.

"You don't know that's what happened to her," Soo said, glancing at the body bag.

Iglesia glanced up at the row house porch, then turned and stared Soo in the eyes and said, "I know two things. One, that girl knows something that she isn't telling about Principal Bazelon. And two, I'm not going to sit around while my neighborhood goes to hell."

He gazed down the block. Across the street, three houses down, he noticed that another group had gathered. Five boys. They were sitting on a short brick wall and watching the activity at the Bazelon house. They looked to be teenagers, a couple maybe a little older, and in their baggy jeans, oversize gangster jackets, and hoodie sweatshirts, they did not appear to be on their way to church.

The only thing they worship is trouble.

"See these punks?" Iglesia said as he nodded at the group. "I guarantee you they're up to no good. Ten bucks says they're using, five says selling. And who knows whatever the hell else."

Kim Soo turned to look, then faced Iglesia and said, "Aw, hell, Javier. You don't know that. A lot of kids do that gangsta-from-the-'hood look. We used to hang out in high school wearing tough looks, too."

"Uh-uh," Iglesia said, shaking his head. "It's different now, is what it is."

Soo shrugged his shoulders.

After a moment, Iglesia added, "You see any of the speech that Ben Franklin rich guy gave last night on the news? While Jimmy's team was at the Old City scene of the first two pop-and-drops?"

"Pop-and-drops?"

"Yeah, that's what a sergeant I know in Homicide says they're calling them. There was five to start. Now there's eight. And they're all stacked up in the meat locker, waiting for Mitchell and his buzz saw. The Homicide sergeant came by the office one day and took a look at them."

"Yeah, I saw that eye-for-an-eye guy's speech right before I hit the sack. He's paying ten grand for anyone bagging a bad guy — 'evildoers,' he called them!"

"Yeah!" Javier Iglesia said, his face lighting up.

Soo realized that Javier was quickly getting his talkativeness back.

Javier went on: "Now, *that's* what I'm talking about! I mean, someone has finally had enough of the city going to hell and they're stepping up to help fix it, is what I mean. Ten large per 'evildoer' is some seriously high stepping up."

He paused and looked down at the body bag.

"Too damn bad it's too late for Principal Bazelon."

Javier then softly repeated, "Rest in peace.

Praise be the Lord."

He shoved the gurney, causing its framework to collapse as it rolled up and inside the rear of the van. Then he gently, respectfully, closed the left door, then the right one.

Police Officer Geoffrey Pope was standing on the curb, behind where the right door had been open, making Javier wonder how long he'd been there and how much he'd heard.

"Hey, Geoff," Javier said to him. "You standing there long?"

"Long enough to hear the news flash that the city's going to hell. And your short prayer for the deceased." He paused, then added, "You don't look too good, Javier."

"I'm —"

He stopped as he glanced at the small crowd on the sidewalk. A few were watching the conversation between the cop and the tech with rapt interest.

"Step around here," Javier said, walking around to the far side of the van to block the view of the curious.

Javier pulled out his wallet and from it extracted a business card. He held it out to Officer Pope.

"Here's my card, Geoff. It's got my cell phone number on it. I live eight blocks away, the other side of Warrington, over where the middle school is."

"Yeah, and?"

"And if there is anything I can do to help get this girl to talk, as a citizen, as a concerned neighbor, whatever, you let me know."

"I'm not sure I should share anything —"

"Who the hell am I going to tell anything?"

Pope held up his hands chest high, palms out. "Hold up, Javier. I'm just —"

"Look, Geoff. My baby sister is her age, and I know when she's holding something back. And I'm telling you, that poor girl is holding something back."

"You don't think she did it, do you? What'd be her motive?"

"Maybe she gets the house?"

"That banshee cry of hers is deep. It's not contrived."

"Whatever it is, she's lying."

Pope shrugged.

Javier said, "I mean, I don't think it's a malicious lie, I don't. But there's something not being said."

"There always is, Javier. Welcome to police work."

V

[ONE]
2620 Wilder Street, Philadelphia
Sunday, November 1, 9:02 A.M.

Will Curtis drove the rented white Ford Freestar minivan up onto the cracked South Philly sidewalk, braking to a stop in front of the tiny, run-down, two-story row house.

He studied it and thought, *Hope this sonofabitch is in there.*

I can't believe that last sonofabitch's address was so old the house was completely gone, burned to the damn ground.

Don't want two dead ends to start my day.

Curtis wore his Federal Express uniform, complete with the grease-smeared FedEx cap. The driver and front passenger doors of the minivan each had a three-foot-square polymer sign displaying the red-and-blue FedEx logotype and the words HOME DELIVERY. He knew his makeshift package delivery van wouldn't pass muster with anyone back at the distribution warehouse, but so

198

far it had looked like the real deal to everyone else.

Curtis got out from behind the steering wheel and glanced around the neighborhood.

It wasn't that early in the morning, but the street was quiet. There were only the sounds of dogs yapping down the block and, not too far off in the distance, the horn blare from a SEPTA light-rail train.

He saw a skinny, mangy gray cat across the street. It was eating Halloween candies that had been dropped and squashed on the sidewalk.

Probably stolen from some poor kid.

But who'd go door to door for candy in this dump of a place?

For drugs, sure. Which is why it's quiet now.

Damn lowlifes up all night chasing ass and doing dope.

But catching them now all good and sleepy will be some sort of justice.

He reached back inside the door of the minivan. There was a stack of six thin white paperboard envelopes on the dashboard, and he pulled the top one off the stack. Each of the envelopes bore the distinctive FedEx logotype, as well as a clear plastic pouch holding a bill of lading.

Stepping carefully, Curtis carried the envelope toward the front door of the row house.

Parts of the crumbling sidewalk were broken down to bare dirt, and there were knee-high dead weeds in the cracks.

The house itself, built of masonry blocks with a front façade of red brick, was also in really bad shape. There were several holes in the wall where bricks were completely missing. The house hadn't been painted in far too many years, leaving bare wood that had rotted in places. Racks of rusty burglar bars covered the solid metal front door and the four double-windows — two upstairs and two at street level — and the first-floor windows were fitted with poorly cut pieces of weather-warped plywood.

To the right of the concrete steps, on the sidewalk and up against the foot of the house, Curtis saw five or six black trash bags. They were packed full, piled high, one on the bottom with a big torn hole. They looked to have been there for some time, easily days if not weeks.

Curtis went up the flight of four concrete steps leading to the battered front door. He saw out of the corner of his eye what at first he thought were two black cats. They'd been along the wall behind the trash bags. Then they'd bolted away, running behind some weeds in front of the small wood-framed window of the basement.

Those aren't cats. They're goddamn rats!

He now noticed that the basement window was open, pulled inward from the top. The rats had disappeared into it.

Curtis shook his head in disgust.

As he reached the bar-covered metal door, a breeze blew past, bringing with it a vile stench. He gagged.

He looked at the garbage bags.

Jesus! Whatever it is has to be in there.

It's worse than raw chicken — or maybe dead rats — that's gone bad.

He looked to the window where the rodents had run inside.

Or . . . could it be coming from the basement?

What a shithole!

He pulled back his sleeve, testing the air. The breeze had stopped and the stench had subsided.

For now.

I need to see who's home, then get the hell out of here. . . .

There was no doorbell — just a crude little hole where it had once been mounted — so he balled his fist, reached between the bars, and pounded on the metal door.

As he waited for some kind of life to wake up inside — other than the vile vermin — he glanced at the FedEx envelope in his hand.

Its bill of lading had a return field that read:

```
United States Department of the Treasury
1600 Pennsylvania Avenue, N.W.
Washington, D.C. 20500
```

Will grinned. He knew that was the address of the White House, and had listed it as an inside joke. He had no idea where the hell the U.S. Treasury had its main office — and didn't give a damn, because he knew the "recipient" wouldn't know, either.

The field for "Recipient" read:

```
Kendrik Mays
2620 Wilder Street
Philadelphia, PA 19147
```

Also on the bill of lading was a bold black X in the box beside the line that stated: GOVERNMENT-ISSUED ID & PERSONAL SIGNATURE OF RECIPIENT REQUIRED FOR DELIVERY.

After knocking again and waiting another few minutes, he'd yet to hear anything moving inside the house.

Dammit! Not even another rat.

Another dead end.

Move this one to the bottom of the stack with the other dead end.

Maybe try again later. At least there's a house at this address.

Just as he turned to go down the steps to the minivan, he saw movement in the left downstairs window, where he noticed a knothole in the warped wood.

So you use that as a peephole, eh?

Nervously, he readjusted the .45-caliber Glock that he had stuck under the waistband of his pants, right behind the buckle of his heavy leather belt.

This morning's work wasn't wasted after all. . . .

Curtis turned back to the door.

At five o'clock that morning, Will Curtis had awakened and gone downstairs to the kitchen to make his coffee, just as he'd done every day for as long as he could remember, easily twenty years.

All the while careful not to wake up his wife.

Not even a week after Wendy had been attacked, Linda had moved into her old bedroom. It was on the back side of the row house's first floor. It had not exactly been left as a shrine after Wendy had moved out and gotten her first apartment — if only because Wendy had needed a lot of the furniture and other items to kick-start her new independence — but it still had a lot of her personal items from growing up, things like the many trophies she had won playing soccer in junior and senior high school. And the walls were practically covered solid with framed and pushpinned photographs of Wendy and her countless gal pals, from birthday parties to summer trips at the Jersey shore, all from various points of her teen years.

A lot of memories for Linda to recall as she lay there. And, ever more the recluse, she spent more and more time in Wendy's old bed. (They'd told Wendy that a new life required a new bed, and among the apartment-warming gifts they'd given her had been a queen-size bed — the one she'd been attacked on.)

I don't know who's going to take care of Linda when I'm gone, but I do know she won't want for anything.

Especially with the house being paid off and the fat payout from my life insurance policy coming.

Which is damn convenient, because she's barely holding on to her teller job.

And I'm feeling worse every day.

As the coffee brewed, Will Curtis went down into the basement.

Shortly after moving into the house, he'd begun converting the basement into a recreation room. It had a pair of soft, deep sofas that faced a monster flat-screen plasma TV. In the corner was a freestanding bar he'd built himself. And just about every nook and cranny was filled with Philadelphia Eagles memorabilia — he'd started the collection in his youth and later had help from Wendy, who'd grown into a genuine fan, too.

And, in the corner of the rec room, his desk held a desktop computer.

Every morning, by the time he'd finished checking his e-mail, the pot of coffee would have finished brewing. He'd then go up and pour a big cup to bring back down and drink while catching up on e-mails and then reading phillybulletin.com, the online edition of the *Philadelphia Bulletin*. Up until a couple years ago, he would go out to the front stoop and pick up the paper version that he'd subscribed to forever. But, as it had never arrived until at least six in the morning — and, on rainy days, arrived wet — he'd let the subscription lapse after getting in the habit of reading the news online.

And not just news.

Lately, he'd started following a new website, the name of which he really liked: CrimeFreePhilly.com. It had news articles, but also a lot of information about crime and criminals. And so, in the last month, it had become an indispensable tool for Curtis.

Now, a cup of freshly brewed coffee in his left hand, he used his right hand to click onto CrimeFreePhilly.

The morning's lead headline was:

THREE DEAD IN OLD CITY

POLICE HUNT GUNMAN IN "POP-AND-DROP" MURDERS

Three dead? had been Curtis's first thought as he sipped from his coffee cup.

Then: *Pop-and-drop? That's an interesting way to put it.*

He noticed that Michael J. O'Hara had written the news article. Curtis had seen the byline in the *Bulletin* for a long time, and he liked the articles the O'Hara guy wrote. But he hadn't seen O'Hara's name in some time, and he'd wondered if something had happened to the reporter. But now, here was his name appearing on this new website.

Curtis read O'Hara's news story. It was

short, only six brief paragraphs stating the basic information that three men had been left dead in Old City at Lex Talionis. It didn't list the victims' names or how they'd been killed.

And it mentioned absolutely nothing about the pop-and-drops at the police stations.

Curtis saw that the article referenced both the reward offered by Lex Talionis and the speech made by Francis Fuller. Both references were underlined, meaning they were links to other pages with more information. When Curtis clicked on <u>Francis Fuller</u>, the page with the pop-and-drop article was replaced with a much longer piece on Fuller's speech on the "evildoers," written by someone named Dick Collier. He skimmed it, then went back and read it in its entirety.

Then he went back and clicked on the underlined <u>Lex Talionis</u>, and the link took him to the page at LexTalionis.com announcing the ten-thousand-dollar-reward program for information leading to the arrest and conviction of an evildoer. He knew about the program, but he read the page anyway to see if there was anything new.

There wasn't, and Curtis again clicked back to O'Hara's article on "Three Dead in Old City."

Where the hell did the third body come from?

A coincidence? Oh, sure. Someone just happened to have one lying around, and dropped it off on Halloween!

Is some asshole copying me?

Except they're not dumping bad guys at the police stations. Not that I know of, anyway. There haven't been any stories about those, mine or anyone else's.

In deep thought, he drained his coffee cup. Then he slammed the cup on the desk.

Some asshole has to be copying me!

What does that mean?

Well, for starters, it means more dead perverts.

Not that I have a problem with that.

But there's gonna be cops on every corner looking for me and whoever else is dumping bodies.

And that means, if I'm going to enforce the law of talion in whatever time I have left, I'm going to need to do something different.

[TWO]

Will Curtis had his balled fist inside the iron burglar bars and was again banging on the

208

filthy metal door.

"FedEx delivery!"

Now he could hear footsteps inside. They were moving toward the door.

Then came the sound of a chain rattling against the back side of the door, then a deadbolt unlocking, then the doorknob turning.

The door cracked open, just barely.

Judging by the sliver of a gaunt face that Curtis saw through the crack, it was a woman old enough to be Kendrik Mays's mother. She stared at him with only her left eye, and she looked absolutely awful.

Well, what the hell did you expect to find here? Miss America?

Curtis held up the envelope so she could see the bill of lading.

"Got an express delivery for a Kendrik Mays."

The lone visible eyeball darted between Curtis and the envelope.

"Ain't today Sunday?" she asked.

"Look, I don't like working weekends any more than the next guy."

She nodded as she considered his answer.

After a moment, the woman said with a shaky voice, "He down at his cousin's. Don't know when he come back. You leave it with me."

She pulled the door open wider to where the chain became taut and stuck out a badly bruised hand, fingers clawing for the envelope.

Now Curtis could see more of the woman. The entire right side of her face, including all around the right eye, was deeply bruised. She stood, her feet bare, at maybe five-two. She was clearly malnourished, and couldn't weigh a hundred pounds. Torn and dirty black jeans and a ratty T-shirt hung on her.

Curtis, trying to get over his initial shock, pulled back the envelope.

"I'm sorry," he said, "but it's gotta be signed for by the person it's addressed to."

She squinted her sunken eyes and looked harder at the envelope. "Who it from?"

Will Curtis turned over the envelope, pretending to read from the bill of lading. "Says the U.S. Treasury in Washington."

"*Treasury?* You sure you got the right address?"

He read it off the envelope, then said, "Kendrik Mays, right?"

She said, "Think that may be a check?"

In a tone he hoped showed he was uninterested, he replied: "Yeah, that'd be my guess. Pension check, IRS refund, maybe some of that stimulus money the government's been giving away. That'd be a good reason they

210

want it delivered to the right person."

Will Curtis looked her in the eyes and could see she was considering her options.

She said, "I sign for it. Kendrik my boy. I see he gets it."

Curtis shook his head. "Sorry, ma'am. I'm just a delivery guy. And I got to follow rules. I guess I'll come back —"

She slammed the door shut in his face.

What the hell? he thought.

Then he could hear the chain clanking against the inside. The door swung all the way open.

"Hurry up," she said shakily. "Maybe he got money, he don't beat me no more. Maybe he move out for good."

Curtis looked around the inside of the house. It was a shambles. The only furniture was a threadbare sofa with torn cushions and two white plastic patio chairs.

"You know that's not right. No one should beat you."

She said, "I knows. I do. But he don't mean to. It's drugs. They make him mean. Different, you know?"

"No, ma'am, I don't know. I can't begin to understand it. Where is he?"

She pointed to the floor, indicating the basement, and started to cry. "He was such a sweet little boy. The street turned him

211

bad . . ."

"That, I know."

"What?"

He held up the envelope, then grabbed the tab at the top, peeling it open. He reached in and pulled out a sheet. It was a Wanted poster from the listing of Megan's Law fugitives at CrimeFreePhilly.com, one he'd downloaded and printed in his basement.

Next to a color mug shot of an angry-looking young black man with a full beard and dreadlocks was:

Name (First, Middle, LAST):	Kendrik LeShawn MAYS
Description:	Black Male, 5'9", 200 lbs.
Date of Birth:	10/19/1988
Last Known Address:	2620 Wilder Street
City, State, ZIP:	Philadelphia, PA 19147
Convicted of:	3123 Involuntary deviant sexual intercourse & rape of an unconscious or unaware person
Phila Police Dept Case No.:	2008-18-063914

Kendrik LeShawn Mays's mother raised her eyebrows. But she did not appear at all surprised. Nor at all concerned that Will Curtis had her son's Wanted sheet.

She sighed.

"Yeah," she said, "that him. Guess he lied. Said he took care of that."

She looked at Curtis. "No check, huh?"

More like a reality check, Curtis thought.

He shook his head.

"No check."

Will Curtis went down the unstable wooden steps into the basement. His left hand slid along the wooden handrail, and his right hand, holding the .45-caliber pistol, followed the wall of mostly busted Sheetrock.

There was some light from the small window at the far end of the room — the one the rats had gone through — but not enough for him to make out anything but vague shapes in the pitch dark.

There was a stench, although not like the putrid smell that had assaulted his olfactory senses at the front door. The odor here was a sickly sweet stench that became stronger the farther down the stairs he went. So far, though, it hadn't triggered his gag reflex, and he was grateful for such small favors.

At the foot of the stairs, Curtis stopped

and listened. He could hear snoring about midway in the room.

That's two people snoring!

One deep as hell.

He felt around on the wall for a light switch. As best he could tell there wasn't one, just busted-up drywall.

He took another step, reaching farther down the wall, then felt his foot catch on a rope or cord or something.

Some kind of trip wire?

He carefully reached down with his left hand till he felt it.

It was a vinyl-covered electrical extension cord that had been run from upstairs. When he tugged on it, something attached to its far end started sliding across the basement floor toward him.

He pulled and pulled, and finally found at the end what had once been the guts of a lamp. All that was left from the lamp was a threaded metal rod attached to the receptacle that held a lone bare lightbulb. His thumb found the stick push-switch on the receptacle, and after positioning himself in a crouch and aiming his pistol in the direction of the snoring, Curtis pushed the switch on.

The bare bulb burned brightly, damn near blinding him until his eyes adjusted.

The only response from the middle of the room was another loud, deep snore.

After his eyes adjusted, Will Curtis could not believe what he was seeing.

The basement was the worst thing he'd ever seen in his life. It was completely trashed. The Sheetrock walls were all busted, as if someone had taken a sledgehammer to them in search of whatever treasure might be hidden behind them. And then he saw why: The wiring had been ripped from the wall power outlets and light switches.

It probably was cheap aluminum, not copper, wiring, making the effort mostly worthless. Idiots.

Desperate idiots . . .

Trash was strewn all across the floor. There were piles upon piles of dirty clothes that hadn't been touched in years. Dust and dirt were everywhere. And, in a far corner by a plastic bucket, he saw the source of the sickly sweet stench: mounds of dried human waste.

Indescribable filth!

Animals wouldn't live in this!

Just then, a rat ran across his booted feet, away from the light and toward the darkness of a far corner, along the way scattering what looked like rolling waves of cockroaches.

Jesus H. Christ!

This place should've been condemned a decade ago!

Then he looked to the middle of the room, to the source of the snoring.

There he saw a dirty and torn mattress set up on wooden pallets — presumably to keep it safe from the sea of cockroaches below — and on the mattress were two human forms lying side by side.

One, the deep snorer, was a black male whose coarse face made him look older than his picture in the Wanted mug shot. His hair was cut short, and he had a goatee.

The other was a very young black girl.

Twelve? Thirteen?

That sonofabitch!

Both were naked, the girl curled under a dirty bath towel she used as a makeshift blanket. Kendrik had a rolled-up jacket under his head, his right hand under it and his left hand resting on the girl's exposed bony buttock. It looked as if they had been spooning but the girl had crawled forward, away from Kendrik.

They look so dirty — so foul.

Will Curtis called out: "Kendrik Mays!"

Mays didn't move. The girl's left eye opened suddenly, then closed. She pretended to still be asleep.

Curtis walked closer to Mays, then kicked

the mattress. "Kendrik!"

He saw a groggy Mays struggle to turn his head. Then he opened his right eye to look at whoever was disturbing his sleep.

From under his jacket he suddenly pulled out a small snub-nosed revolver.

Oh, shit! Curtis thought as he instinctively leveled the Glock at Mays.

Then Curtis saw that Mays's hand was shaking so severely he couldn't keep a grip on the gun.

Curtis kicked the hand, his heavy boot causing the pistol to fly across the basement. It landed in a pile of dirty clothes.

"Sit up, you sonofabitch!" Curtis barked at Mays.

It took Mays forever to comply.

When he had finally done so, the girl turned to look at Curtis.

And Will Curtis ached.

She was as badly bruised as Kendrik's mother. She wasn't as young as he'd thought — *she can't be over seventeen, eighteen* — and she was terribly skinny from the drug abuse. Her skin sagged from her small frame, and Curtis could see her bones clearly delineated under the loose flesh.

When Kendrik moved his hand to scratch his head, the girl flinched.

She's conditioned to getting hit for the slight-

est thing. . . .

"You," Curtis said to her, kicking a ratty dress toward her. "Get dressed and get the hell out of here!"

She looked back wordlessly, her sunken eyes wide.

Then she looked to Mays, seemingly for permission.

Mays, his head cocked, stared belligerently at Curtis, his look saying, *Who the fuck does this honky think he is, aiming a fucking Glock at Kendrik Fucking Mays?*

Curtis motioned with the pistol toward the female. "Go! Now!"

Kendrik said, "Go on, bitch. I deal with you later."

She slid the dress over her head, not bothering to put on any panties, and then moved to the wooden stairs. She looked back over her shoulder, then turned and went upstairs as fast as she could.

Curtis, the pistol aimed at Mays's face, handed him the Wanted poster.

"This you?" Will asked.

Mays looked at it, then at Curtis. Then he smiled.

Will Curtis thought: *Jesus! What rotted teeth!*

At least the ones he still has.

He must be living on crystal meth.

Kendrik then said: "Fuck you! What if it is, old man?"

He spat on the floor.

"You do what it says you did?"

"Fuck you!" he repeated.

He tried to stare down Curtis. But then he suddenly started to shake uncontrollably.

After a moment, he said, "Maybe. What's it to you?" He shook again, then tried to puff out his chest. "Yeah. I done it. All that and more. Two years ago. Why you here now?"

"I'd say, 'May God have pity on you,' but I think you're past that point."

Kendrik barked: "Fuck you, mother-fucker!"

Will Curtis nodded.

And he squeezed the trigger of the Glock.

The .45-caliber round entered Kendrik's right cheek, making an entrance wound just below the eye that looked like a pulpy crimson hole.

Kendrik LeShawn Mays's eyes rolled back as he suddenly slumped onto the filthy torn mattress.

When he got to the top of the stairs, Will Curtis found Kendrik's mother standing solemnly in the middle of the shabby living room. She had her head down, her face expressionless. Her arms were tightly crossed over her chest, her hands squeezing her biceps. The girl was nowhere in sight.

"I'd like to say I'm sorry for your loss," Will Curtis said evenly. "But you lost your boy a long time ago. That wasn't him down there."

She shook her head. "No, it wasn't. You right. It ain't no good. Ain't none of it no good."

She looked up and met his eyes. He saw that hers were stone cold.

"Had it coming to him," she said. "He hurt a lot of folk, good folk, not just me. That girl? He abuse her a long time. Months. Now he won't. And I won't be beat up no more for his meth and shit."

Will nodded.

He walked toward the door, then paused.

What the hell. I can't take it with me. And Linda's set for life.

He reached in his pants pocket and came up with a wad of cash folded over and held together with a rubber band. He peeled off five twenties and a one-dollar bill.

"This is for you," he said, handing her the twenty-dollar bills.

Then he pulled a FedEx ballpoint pen from his shirt pocket and on the one-dollar bill wrote, "Lex Talionis, Third & Arch, Old City."

"You find someone to help you get Kendrik down to here. There's a ten-thousand-dollar reward" — he paused to let that sink in — "for criminals like him. You won't go to jail; if I have to, I'll call and say I did it. But you make sure you get the reward money. Maybe it will help you start a new life."

Then Will Curtis turned and went through the front door.

Behind the wheel of the rented Ford mini-van, Will Curtis pulled the next envelope from the top of the stack on the dashboard. He read its bill of lading. Under "Recipient" was:

LeRoi Cheatham
2408 N. Mutter Street
Philadelphia, PA 19133

Kensington — what a lovely part of town!
As least when the damn drug dealers aren't having shoot-outs on the street corners. . . .
He put the rented Ford minivan in gear and accelerated off the busted sidewalk.

[THREE]
Executive Command Center
The Roundhouse
Eighth and Race Streets,
Philadelphia
Sunday, November 1, 12:04:01 P.M.

"You're on in fifty-nine seconds, Mr. Mayor," Kerry Rapier said.

The master technician was seated in a wheeled nylon-mesh-fabric chair behind a black four-foot-wide control bank, also on wheels, that had a series of panels with buttons and dials, its main feature a keyboard with a joystick and a color video monitor. A fat bundle of cables ran from the control bank to the wall and, ultimately, to a rack of video recording and broadcasting equipment, including the soda-can-size digital video camera that, suspended at the end of a motorized boom, seemed to float overhead.

Rapier, a police department blue shirt whose soft features and impossibly small frame made him look much younger than his twenty-five years, had shoulder patches on his uniform bearing two silver outlined blue chevrons. He manipulated the joystick and the camera overhead zoomed in to tightly frame the face of the Honorable Jerome H. "Jerry" Carlucci, who stood at a dark-stained oak lectern.

Carlucci, his brown eyes smiling, said, "Son, are you sure you're even old enough to be a policeman, let alone a corporal?"

Corporal Rapier grinned.

"With respect, Mr. Mayor, that's not the first I've heard that."

Carlucci's brown eyes, depending on his mood, could be warm and thoughtful or intense and piercing. Large-boned and heavyset, he was a massive fifty-one-year-old with dark brown hair. He wore an impeccably tailored dark gray woolen two-piece suit with a light blue, freshly pressed dress shirt and a navy blue silk necktie that matched the silk pocket square tucked into his coat.

Standing shoulder to shoulder behind Mayor Carlucci was a veritable wall of white shirts: Police Commissioner Ralph Mariana, wearing his uniform with four stars, and Denny Coughlin, with the three stars of the first deputy police commissioner, were directly behind the mayor. And standing on opposite ends of them were Homicide Commander Henry Quaire, whose uniform bore the captain's rank insignia of two gold-colored bars, and Homicide Lieutenant Jason Washington, with the insignia of one butter bar on his uniform.

Looming on the wall behind all of them was a grid of flat-screen TVs. The screens alternately displayed either an official seal of the City of Philadelphia — the newly designed one, a golden Liberty Bell ringed by CITY OF PHILADELPHIA LIFE LIBERTY AND YOU in blue lettering — or the blue Philadelphia Police Department shield, which bore the older seal of the city and HONOR INTEGRITY SERVICE in gold lettering.

(Earlier official city phrases had been "The City of Brotherly Love" and "The Place That Loves You Back," the latter falling into disfavor after some wits in the populace reworded the slogan to read "The Place That Shoots Your Back" — and worse variants thereof.)

Carlucci was about to give a prepared statement concerning the previous night's triple murders and the first five pop-and-drops. In order to lend weight to his speech, the mayor of the City of Philadelphia was borrowing from the playbook of the police commissioner by using the Executive Command Center.

Ralph Mariana held almost all of his press conferences in the ECC, a state-of-the-art facility that held an impressive display of the latest high-tech equipment. The electronics made for terrific photo opportunities — and more important, as Mariana said, helped give the public a sure sense of confidence that the police department had the best tools to safeguard its citizens.

During a crisis, the ECC's main objective was to collect, assimilate, and analyze during a crisis a mind-boggling amount of wide-ranging raw information — people and places and events and more — in a highly efficient manner.

And then to act on it — instantly, if not sooner.

"And that's exactly what the hell we're doing this morning," Carlucci had bluntly told Mariana when he'd asked for everyone to gather in the ECC. "If this goddamn situation escalates, it has the potential to turn the city into something out of the Wild West."

The bulk of the ECC was given over to a massive pair of T-shaped conference tables. Each dark gray Formica-topped table seated twenty-six. And each of these fifty-two seats had its own multiline telephone, outlets for laptop computers, and access to secure networks for on-demand communications with other law-enforcement agencies — from local to federal to the international police agency, Interpol — as necessary.

Along the back walls were more chairs to accommodate another forty staff members.

The focal point of the room, however, were three banks of sixty-inch, high-definition LCD flat-screen TVs. There were nine TVs per bank on the ten-foot-high walls. Mounted edge to edge, the frameless TVs could create a single supersize image, or could display individual pictures — each TV could even be used in split-screen mode.

Usually, when the screens were not showing live feeds from cameras mounted in emergency vehicles at the scene of an accident or crime, they showed continuously cycling images from closed-circuit TV cameras that were mounted all over the city — in subways, public buildings, and main and secondary roadways — and the broadcasts from local and cable TV news stations. Images could be pulled from almost any source, even a cell phone camera, as long as the signals were digitized.

The ECC fell under the purview of the Science & Technology arm of the Philadelphia Police Department, which included the

Forensic Sciences, Information Systems, and Communications Divisions. Its two-star commander, Deputy Police Commissioner Howard Walker, reported to Denny Coughlin.

Acting on an order issued that morning by the mayor, Walker had alerted the local news media that a live feed of Mayor Carlucci would begin at precisely 12:05 P.M. Eastern Standard Time. The timing gave the TV news programs the opportunity to start their noon newscasts with the announcement that an important statement by the mayor of Philadelphia concerning the rash of recent murders was coming up in five minutes.

"Stay tuned. We're back with that breaking news right after this commercial break."

"Thirty seconds, gentlemen . . . ," Corporal Rapier said.

Four hours earlier, when Coughlin had led his group into the Executive Command Center, he'd found the mayor and the police commissioner already seated at Conference Table One. They had heavy china mugs steaming with fresh coffee before them on the table. Mariana's mug read SCIENCE & TECHNOLOGY EXECUTIVE COMMAND CENTER. The mayor's mug read GENO'S STEAKS SOUTH PHILLY, PENNA.

Everyone in the ECC was casually dressed. Even the usually stiffly buttoned-down Carlucci wasn't wearing a necktie, and he had his shirt collar open. And Matt Payne and Tony Harris still looked rumpled and messy, the result of having been up most of the night running down leads in the death of Reggie Jones.

"Good morning, gentlemen," Carlucci said in a solemn tone suggesting he meant that it was anything but a good morning. He did not move from his chair except to grab his coffee mug handle.

There was a chorus of "good morning"s in reply.

Mariana added, "Fresh coffee in there." He waved with his mug across the room, indicating a door that led to a kitchenette.

Carlucci then said, "Sergeant Payne, no offense, but you and Detective Harris look like hell."

"Considering what we've been through, Mr. Mayor," Payne said dryly, "hell sounds like an absolute utopian paradise. I enjoy the thrill of the chase as much as the next guy, but this one's a real challenge. Right now we don't know if we're dealing with a single shooter-slash-strangler, or if there are others — that is, as someone put it earlier, Halloween Homicide Copycats."

228

Ordinarily, a lowly police sergeant speaking so bluntly to the highest elected official of a major city would be cause for disciplinary — if not more drastic — measures.

But Carlucci's relationship with Payne, and most everyone else in the group, was anything but ordinary.

Back when he'd been a cop, Carlucci had known and liked Matt's biological father. And that went way back, to when Sergeant John F. X. Moffitt had been the best friend of a young Denny Coughlin before being killed in the line of duty.

Mayor Carlucci was also well acquainted with Matt Payne's adoptive father, whom he also liked very much, and not only because Brewster Cortland Payne II was a founding partner of Philadelphia's most prestigious law firm.

And there was another connection between Matt and Hizzonor.

Carlucci had been Coughlin's "rabbi" — his mentor — and had groomed the young police officer with great potential for the larger responsibilities that would come as he rose in the ranks of the department.

Denny Coughlin had gone on to groom Peter Wohl, son of Augustus Wohl, Chief Inspector (Retired). And then Peter Wohl — indeed among the best and brightest, having at twenty graduated from Temple University, then entered the Police Academy and, later, become the youngest staff inspector on the department — had been in recent years Matt Payne's rabbi.

And, more or less completing the circle, the elder Wohl had in his time been the rabbi of an up-and-coming police officer — a young man by the name of Jerry Carlucci.

"If I didn't know better, Matt," Mayor Carlucci now said, his face and tone suggesting more than a little displeasure, surprising Payne, "I'd say you were on the street working all night." He paused to make eye contact with the white shirt he'd mentored decades earlier, then went on: "*But* I do know that must not be the case, because we'd all agreed that the Wyatt Earp of the Main Line would stay the hell out of sight for a certain cool-down period." He looked again at Denny. "Or am I mistaken?"

Mariana, Quaire, and Washington — the direct chain of command also somewhat directly responsible for seeing that Payne drove a desk so as to stay out of the news — looked a little ill at ease.

Payne saw that Howard Walker was more than a little interested to see Denny Coughlin in the mayor's crosshairs.

But Coughlin, while deeply respectful of

Carlucci, and cognizant of Carlucci's iron fist and occasional temper, was not cowed by him. Over the years he'd learned a lot from his rabbi, and one of the most important lessons was to make a decision, then come hell or high water to stand by that decision.

Time and again, Carlucci had told him: "One's inability to be decisive gets people killed. Make up your goddamn mind — based on the best available information, or your gut, or better both — and move forward."

Denny Coughlin now said evenly, almost conversationally, "Jerry, I had the same initial reaction earlier this morning. But in light of what we're dealing with, I decided to end the cool-down period as of today. Matt's been all over the paperwork on these pop-and-drops, and if we have any chance of quickly figuring out who's doing what — and we need to, or it's likely going to get ugly very fast — we need to be able to put him back on the street."

Carlucci looked thoughtfully at Coughlin a long moment, then at Payne, then back at Coughlin. He grunted and put down his china mug with a loud *thunk*.

"For the record, Denny, color me not completely convinced. Maybe it's because I recently spent so much time trying — key word 'trying' — to dissuade the media that we have a loose cannon in our police department." He exhaled audibly. "But I do know better than to micromanage the people in whom I have absolute trust."

With a deadly serious face, he looked at Payne.

"Just try not to add to the goddamn body count. Got that, *Marshal?* I don't want to have to answer any more questions from the damned press about you."

Payne nodded. "Yessir. Duly noted, sir."

Carlucci met his eyes and added, "That doesn't mean that I don't support you in what were righteous shootings. You were doing your job, and you did it well."

"Thank you, sir."

"Okay, everybody have a seat," Carlucci then said. "Let's hear what you've got on the pop-and-drops, Matt."

"Yes, sir," Payne said. "But, as you noticed, Tony and I have been up all night. I can't speak for Tony, but I could use some caffeine."

"I'll get 'em," Harris said, heading across the room as the others sat down at the conference table.

[FOUR]

Sergeant Matt Payne drained his second cup of coffee, then made a grand sweeping gesture at one of the banks of TVs.

On its screens were images of the first five dead fugitives — both their Wanted sheets and crime-scene photos from where they'd been "dropped" — as well as detailed maps and lists of data showing where the bad guys had lived, where they had committed their crimes, and, ultimately, where they had been found dead.

He looked at Mayor Jerry Carlucci and said, "And that is essentially what I put together from the files of the first five pop-and-drops. There's no question that they were targeted killings by the same doer. But the new ones from last night don't quite fit the profile."

" 'Targeted killings'?" the mayor repeated.

Payne nodded. "Today's buzzword for 'assassination.'"

Carlucci made a sour face. "Let's stick with 'targeted killings,' in the statement and elsewhere. Or even just 'murders by perps unknown.' At least for now."

He looked around the ECC conference table, and everyone nodded agreeably.

"You said," Carlucci went on, "that with the exception of one of the first five, all were dropped by the same doer at the district PD closest to the critter's Last Known Address. And all had the same MO?"

Payne pointed to one of the TVs. "Yes, sir. That's shown on Number 8. All were bound at their ankles and wrists. All shot either in the chest or head. And all with the same doer's fingerprints. Which makes us" — he glanced at Tony Harris — "believe that we will find he's also responsible for at least two of the three dropped last night. He left prints everywhere. Prints and piss."

Carlucci cocked his head. "Did you say piss?"

When Payne explained about the "gallons" of piss all over the lawyer's office, Carlucci shook his head and said, "If I'd known, I might have contributed. Never did like that Gartner."

Matt chuckled.

Carlucci went on, "So, piss and prints. Could be the doer's just careless or stupid — or worse."

"Or maybe he wants to get caught?" Harris offered.

Payne raised an eyebrow. "Maybe. He's

234

damn sure leaving ample opportunity for that to happen. Just a matter of time . . ."

"So," Carlucci said, "again, all we have for sure is one doer linked to the first five pop-and-drops —"

"That's correct," Payne said.

"— and maybe at least two of last night's three — the two who were shot — if we find that the prints on them match those prints on the first five. Same for the third, even though he wasn't shot."

"Exactly," Payne said.

"Strangled and beaten," Carlucci then wondered aloud. "What could be the significance of that?"

Payne shrugged. "Maybe the doer ran out of bullets."

Carlucci snorted.

"Let's hope so," he said. "If not, then we have two or more goddamn doers to collar. So when do you get the prints that were taken last night back from IAFIS? Before noon, in time for the statement?"

IAFIS, the FBI's Integrated Automated Fingerprint Identification System, was the largest biometric database in the world. It held the fingerprints and other information collected from local, state, and federal law-enforcement agencies on more than fifty-five million people. Law-enforcement agencies could access it at any time and run a search with the fingerprints they lifted from a crime scene. It wasn't uncommon, provided the submitted print or prints were clean, to get a response in a couple hours as to whether there was a match in the database.

Payne shook his head. "We're still waiting for Forensics to process the prints that were lifted. You know what their motto can sometimes be . . ."

"Enlighten me," Carlucci said dryly.

" 'If we wait until the last minute to do it, it'll only take a minute.' "

There suddenly was a cold silence in the room, and Payne then realized from the furious look on Walker's face that, given difference circumstances — say, the absence of Walker's three immediate bosses — he would have reamed the hotshot Homicide sergeant a new one.

Nice job, Payne ol' boy, Matt thought. *Forensic Sciences belongs to Walker.*

Screw it. Maybe this will get them moving faster.

Payne remembered one night at Liberties Bar when, more than a couple of stiff Irish whiskeys under both their belts, Coughlin had let slip that he was not a fan of Walker's. Walker, who spoke with a cleric's soft, intelligent voice, cultivated a rather pious air. Coughlin felt that Walker used all the bells and whistles of Science & Technology as smoke and mirrors to disguise his incompetence.

"But Ralph said he had his reasons for asking me to give Walker the job. And, write this down, Matty, never argue with your boss. Still, I'd love to know what angle Walker is working on Ralph."

Mayor Carlucci guffawed, breaking the tension.

"I'm going to have to remember to use that line back at City Hall. Nothing gets done there, not even in the last minute. It's always late, if at all."

There were the expected chuckles.

"Okay," Carlucci said, "then I won't ask about NCIC. If we don't have prints to run, we don't have a name to run."

The National Crime Information Center — also maintained by the FBI and available to law enforcement at any time, day or night — had a database containing the critical records of criminals. Additionally, NCIC tracked missing persons and stolen property. Its data came not only from the same law-enforcement agencies that provided IAFIS, but also from authorized courts and foreign law-enforcement agencies.

"I'll go stoke the fire under them for those

prints," Walker then offered lamely. He stood and went over to use one of the phones at the other conference table.

Bingo, Payne thought. *That'll get 'em moving faster.*

Ralph Mariana then spoke up: "Jerry, what should be done about Frank Fuller?"

Payne put in: "I've had an unmarked sitting on Fuller's Old City office."

"That's fine, Matt," Mariana said, "but I meant what should be done about his now-infamous rewards."

Carlucci, his face showing a mixture of anger and frustration, said, "I've spoken with Fuller privately about that bloodthirsty reward system of his. I've tried to dissuade him, suggesting that it's encouraging criminal activity. He said he didn't care, that he'd spend his last dime on lawyers defending that eye-for-an-eye thing —"

"The law of talion," Payne offered.

Carlucci shot Payne a look of mild annoyance for the interruption, then went on: "— especially, he said, after what happened to his wife and child."

"What happened to his family?" Mariana asked.

Quaire offered: "I had that case in Homicide. It never got solved, primarily because, we believe, the doers involved killed each other before we could get statements, let alone bring charges. Anyway, the wife and the girl, a ten-year-old, I believe, made a wrong turn at the Museum of Art and wound up a half-mile or so north in the wrong neighborhood at the wrong time. Cut down in a crossfire of single-aught buckshot."

"Jesus!" Mariana said, shaking his head. "That's tragic."

The table was silent a moment.

Carlucci then said, "But I have no choice but to denounce him, or at least what he's accomplishing with his reward."

Denny Coughlin cleared his throat.

"You have something, Denny?" Carlucci said. "Say it."

"Just a point, Jerry. Giving credit where it's due, Matt did bring up that for us to condemn the reward system would be somewhat hypocritical."

Carlucci made an unpleasant face.

"You can't be a little pregnant," Payne said.

"What the hell is that supposed to mean?" Carlucci asked, looking at Payne.

"We can't say that Five-Eff's paying out ten-grand rewards —"

" 'Five-Eff'?" Carlucci interrupted.

Payne nodded. "Francis Franklin Fuller the Fifth long ago had his name boiled down

239

to simply Four-Eff."

"You said 'Five,'" Carlucci challenged.

Payne looked around the table, and all eyes were watching him with more than a little curiosity. He thought there may have been a trace of wariness in Coughlin's.

Payne raised an eyebrow, then said, "Francis can be pompous, as you well know, and when he annoys me, I call him Five-Eff, short for Fucking Francis Franklin Fuller the Fifth."

Carlucci guffawed again. A couple others followed his lead by chuckling. Coughlin shook his head.

"All right," Carlucci said, "as he's come to annoy the hell out of me, I'll now say: How does my denouncing Five-Eff make me pregnant?"

Payne grinned. He knew Carlucci understood what he'd meant by the analogy.

"My point is, sir, that our department has partnerships with other agencies that offer rewards. The FBI Violent Crimes Task Force, for example."

He gestured with his thumb in a southerly direction. The FBI's office, at 600 Arch Street, across from the Federal Reserve Bank, was damn near outside the back door of the Roundhouse.

"And I'm sure you'll recall that we have

our own tips hotline," Payne went on, "that, through the Citizens Crime Commission, pays out rewards that go from five hundred bucks or so on up to thousands. And when a cop gets murdered, the FOP administers rewards for info that leads to catching the doers. So we already do what Five-Eff does. We just don't, as was pointed out to me" — he exchanged glances with Coughlin — "encourage the killing of the critters."

Carlucci started nodding. "All right. I take your point. We can massage that in the message, so to speak. Now, let's boil all this down to what I'm going to say."

"Thirty seconds, Mr. Mayor," Corporal Kerry Rapier said from behind the control panel.

Jerry Carlucci scrunched up his face and assumed a serious expression.

Corporal Rapier said, "In five, four, three, two . . . ," then pointed to Mayor Carlucci. On the monitor, Mayor Carlucci was perfectly framed in a tight shot of his face, with Mariana and Coughlin looking over his shoulders.

Carlucci said: "Good afternoon, citizens of the great city of Philadelphia. Thank you for letting me into your homes today. I respect your time, and will be brief.

241

"While it saddens me to have to appear here today to address a rash of murders, I must tell you that I am very proud to be speaking to you from the Roundhouse in the company of some of the finest law-enforcement officials anywhere.

"As you may be aware, in the last month, five known criminals — all fugitives guilty of sexual offenses — have been killed and brought to the door of the Philadelphia Police Department. And last night, three more murdered men were left at the door of an organization that offers rewards for the capture of criminals.

The City of Philadelphia and our police department are grateful for any help in keeping our communities safe. We encourage citizens — who can remain anonymous — to provide tips that lead to the arrest and conviction of criminals. Simply call 911, or 215-686-TIPS. Depending on the case, there are cash rewards for information that leads to a criminal's conviction.

"While we do applaud the removal of any criminal at large in our free society, we cannot condone any such act that results in death. That is murder, and those responsible will be prosecuted to the fullest."

He paused to let that point sit with the various audiences.

"Since I have served both as your police commissioner and now as your mayor, crimes have declined in our fair city. Major crimes, such as homicides, by as much as half. While we are not where we would like to be — one robbery or murder or rape is one too many — we are committed to crime prevention and criminal apprehension. It is what we are well trained to do. And I believe the statistics prove that we do it exceptionally well.

"Now, in response to last night's criminal activity, today I am pleased to announce that Police Commissioner Mariana has formed a special task force to capture the armed and dangerous perpetrator. Operation Clean Sweep will be led by Homicide Unit Sergeant M. M. Payne —"

Carlucci paused as his image was replaced for a three-second count by one of Matt Payne and Carlucci. Payne, in a crisp Brooks Brothers two-piece suit and tie, was shaking hands with Carlucci. Their left hands held up a plaque that at the top was emblazoned with the words VALOR IN THE LINE OF DUTY.

"— whose name you may recognize as one of our highly decorated officers. He could not be here in person, as he already is fully immersed in the investigation."

Carlucci now gestured to the white shirts

behind him and went on: "Sergeant Payne will be fully supported not only by the Philadelphia PD, but by any other state and federal agencies whom we partner with in such initiatives as the FBI Violent Crimes Task Force.

"And of course Operation Clean Sweep will have the full force of all departmental assets, which are legion."

He motioned to the panel of TVs.

Corporal Rapier worked the control panel, and each screen instantly was replaced with images of nearly everything in the department's arsenal. There was a pair of the Aviation Unit's Bell 206 L-4 helicopters hovering over a grassy field, their floodlight beams lighting up a suspect, his hands up, as uniforms on the ground converged. Members of the Special Weapons and Tactical (SWAT) Unit were rescuing a hostage. A Marine Unit's twenty-four-foot-long Boston Whaler, its light bar on the aluminum tower pulsing red and blue, was screaming up the Delaware River. And more dramatic imagery of the police department in action.

"You have my word that our dedicated police department will apprehend the perpetrator, and soon.

"Again, thank you for your time and for your confidence. May God bless you and keep you safe."

At least long enough for us to catch the damned murderer, Carlucci thought as he stared somber-faced at the camera as the boom swung, pulling back from him.

Payne was standing with Harris and Walker behind Corporal Rapier and the control panel.

As he heard Corporal Rapier say, "And . . . we're clear, off the air," Payne felt his telephone vibrate.

He looked at its screen and saw the call was from the uniform he'd stationed in the unmarked in Old City.

He answered it: "Payne."

Then, after a moment, he said loudly: "What? Oh, shit!"

He felt eyes on him and looked up to see that everyone was indeed looking at him. Particularly Carlucci.

Payne was shaking his head as he listened to the phone, then after another moment he said, "What's the CCTV ID number there?"

He took a ballpoint pen from his pocket and, not quickly locating any paper, awkwardly held the phone to his ear with his shoulder while he wrote the code on his left palm.

"Thanks. I'll get right back to you."

He held out his left hand in front of Corporal Rapier.

"Kerry, please punch up the feed from this CCTV on the main screen."

Payne nodded at that bank of TVs, which had a real-time feed of the front façade of City Hall.

As Corporal Rapier's fingers flew across the keyboard, the main screen went to snow-like gray pixels.

"What is it, Matt?" Carlucci asked.

"You are not going to believe this. Looks like Five-Eff has received another charitable donation at his doorstep."

"What the hell are you talking about, Matty?" Coughlin blurted.

"Not ten minutes ago, a woman arrived at the offices of Lex Talionis in a gypsy cab. It was a minivan — an older-model tan Toyota — and when the side door opened onto the curb, the woman got out. She met the driver at the rear door of the van, and together they wrestled a rolled-up carpet out of the back. They rolled it onto the sidewalk. Then the woman handed the driver his fare like it was something she did every day, and he sped away."

Gypsy cabs — their drivers unlicensed, unregistered, and usually uninsured — were illegal. But they were plentiful because they charged far less than legit cabbies. And they were everywhere, making them hard as hell to crack down on.

The TV screen came alive with the all-too-familiar view in Old City: the office building at Arch and North Third that housed Lex Talionis. Everyone looked to it.

They saw that on the sidewalk by the front door four uniforms had formed a perimeter of sorts around a blood-soaked ratty carpet. It had been unrolled — and on top of it was the motionless body of a naked black male.

Just to the left of the carpet and its perimeter of cops was a frail-looking black woman. She was gesturing wildly with a sheet of paper at the office building's front door while another uniform, both hands shoulder high with palms out, tried calming her.

Payne, to no one in particular, announced: "Well, that makes pop-and-drop number nine. Shall we assume the old lady is our doer?"

Harris said, "You can't be serious. You don't really think —"

Payne turned and looked at him.

"Hell no, Tony. Not all nine, anyway. All I know is that my uniform in the unmarked just now said that that paper she's waving is a Wanted sheet, and she's screaming at that uniform on the sidewalk, 'I want my reward!' "

"Is that Mickey?" Jason Washington suddenly asked.

Matt and Tony turned and saw the wiry Irishman with a video camera in his hands. He was holding it high above his head, clearly recording the confrontation between the uniform and the woman. He now wore the blue T-shirt with the white handcuffs and MAKE HIS DAY: KISS A COP AT CRIMEFREEPHILLY.COM.

Payne grinned.

Sonofabitch must have been staking out the place, too.

Going to take some doing to get him to sit on that video — if that's even likely.

Then he felt his cell phone vibrate, and he looked at the text message on its screen:

AMANDA LAW

"ARMED & DANGEROUS"?

WHEN WERE YOU PLANNING ON TELLING ME, MATT?

LAST I HEARD WAS THAT YOU WERE GOING TO LIBERTIES TO "TALK" ABOUT THE POP-AND-DROPS.

"Oh, shit!" Matt said again.

"I have to agree with Matt," Carlucci said.

" 'I want my reward'? Oh, shit!"

[FIVE]
Loft Number 2055
Hops Haus Tower
1100 N. Lee Street, Philadelphia
Sunday, November 1, 12:14 P.M.

H. Rapp Badde, Jr., wearing baggy blue jeans and a red sweatshirt with TEMPLE LAW across the chest in white lettering, was seated at the large, rectangular, marble-topped table in the breakfast area adjacent to the gourmet kitchen. He had the television remote control in his right hand and was aiming it at the flat-screen that was mounted to the living room wall. He stabbed at the MUTE button as he looked with some disgust at the image of a solemn-faced Mayor Jerome Carlucci.

Keep it up, Jerry, and you'll make it even easier for me to kick your Italian ass out of office.

Badde turned his attention to Janelle Harper, who stood across the table from him, skimming a mass-produced flyer titled "Pennsylvania's Property Rights Protection Act & You." She was wearing a spandex sport outfit, black with purple accents, that clung to her curvy frame like a second skin, and athletic shoes. She had her hair pulled back and wore a pair of black-framed Gucci designer eyeglasses.

"More murders," he said almost happily. "I can probably run on the crime issue alone and get elected mayor."

She looked away from the flyer and at him. "You're not really taking any joy out of those people being killed, are you?"

"Sorry, honey. But only because they're already dead. Hell, if nothing else, I've probably lost a voter."

Or not, if whoever takes over for Kenny can register their names to vote absentee.

Speaking of Kenny, I wonder what the hell happened to him.

He glanced back at the television, and there was now a live shot from Old City showing policemen stringing up yellow crime-scene tape. The text at the bottom of the screen read: *FOURTH HALLOWEEN HOMICIDE . . . MOTHER TURNS IN FUGITIVE SON'S DEAD BODY AT LEX TALIONIS OFFICES FOR $10,000 RE-WARD . . . MOTHER SAYS SON'S DEATH WAS DRUG-RELATED . . .*

"Jesus Christ!" Badde said.

Jan looked at him, then at the TV. "Oh my God! How awful!"

"They're animals out there," Badde said, then was quiet a moment. "Hell, look at the silver lining. At this rate, the outcry over all these killings might get so bad that Carlucci resigns and I get appointed to take his place."

Jan looked at him. "Don't hold your breath."

Badde gestured at the massive three-ring binder thick with loose-leaf pages at her elbow. Its cover had in black block lettering the title PHILADELPHIA ECONOMIC GENTRIFICATION INITIATIVE.

"When are we supposed to get the second wave of fed funds for PEGI?" Badde asked, pronouncing the acronym "Peggy."

PEGI was a special program devised by the Housing and Urban Development Committee, one of dozens of such committees of the Philadelphia City Council. The city council

251

had seventeen members: ten elected in their respective districts, the remainder elected at large in the interest of balanced racial representation. The seventeen chose a council president from among themselves, and the president then decided which council members would serve on which committees.

As the number of committees far exceeded the number of council members, it was common for the president to appoint each member to six or eight committees, occasionally even more.

Ask any council member, though, and they'd quietly admit that the sheer workload of serving on just one damn committee was daunting; serving on many others became a logistical impossibility. Thus, it was common for council members simply to choose a favorite committee and pay only lip service to all the others to which they'd been appointed.

Not surprisingly, any oversight by fellow council members within the committees was replaced by an unspoken agreement: *You pay attention to the business of your committee, and I'll pay attention to mine.*

In other words: *Mind your own goddamn business.*

And so the chairman of each committee more or less had free rein. He or she completely controlled the committee's dealings with commerce in and out of City Hall, the letting of contracts, the hiring of vendors, and so on. It actually proved to be an efficient model in the sense that it avoided the frustrating back-and-forth process of committee decision-making. Instead, the chairman made a decision and — *voilà!* — it was done without further debate.

To the City of Philadelphia Housing and Urban Development Committee, the president of the city council appointed City Councilman (At Large) H. Rapp Badde, Jr., as its chairman.

HUD chairman Badde, upon returning from an urban-renewal conference in Bermuda, conceived the Philadelphia Economic Gentrification Initiative. He then funded the special program with a modest fifty thousand dollars from HUD's "exploratory" budget line — all of it federal monies — and immediately entered into an open-term vendor contract (thereby avoiding a lengthy low-bidder selection process) with Commonwealth Law Center LLP of Philadelphia.

The law firm, its practice heavily vested in real estate law, would assist Chairman Badde and his committee — in effect, only Badde and his executive assistant — in the exploratory steps for two major gentrification projects: Volks Haus and Diamond Development.

The latter created what was termed "a multipurpose professional entertainment venue." It would be an indoor coliseum with a retractable roof and convertible flooring. It could house sixty thousand fans of everything from sports (football, basketball, hockey, soccer, motocross racing, et cetera) to music concerts. It was planned to be built just west of Interstate 95 in the upper end of Northern Liberties. Thus, it would displace thousands of residents in order to demolish a vast chunk of city.

The former, Volks Haus, was to serve as one solution for the relocation of those residents. The "People's House" would be low-income housing constructed on ten square blocks a few miles to the west, in the Fairmount area, reclaiming what Chairman Badde called "a damned unsightly black hole of money-losing federal government property" — otherwise known as the Eastern State Penitentiary, which happened to be a United States Natural Historic Landmark smack dab in the middle of a struggling residential neighborhood.

The exploratory process was completed within twenty-four hours — although on paper the period was listed as three months — and two minority-owned construction firms were awarded contracts conditioned on federal dollars fully funding PEGI and the completion of the eminent-domain process.

Janelle Harper looked over the upper rim of her Gucci eyeglasses at Rapp Badde.

She said, "Those additional fed monies, I was told, after I finally got my calls returned from Commonwealth —"

Badde interrupted. "Why can't you just say her name?" He paused and shrugged, and with a weak smile said, "Wanda's not that bad."

"Why? I'll tell you why: Because *your wife* treats me like your little girlfriend — actually, sometimes more like your little 'ho' — and not like your goddamned executive assistant." She pulled at the spandex at her hips, adjusting it, then added, "I'm damned tired of it. She's not the only one with a law degree from Beasley."

Temple University, and its Beasley School of Law, was a couple miles west of the condo tower, on North Broad.

Jan met Rapp's eyes and said, "She needs to be your *ex*-wife."

Badde suddenly sat up, almost spilling his coffee.

"Are you kidding?" he said, his voice almost squeaking. "Do you know what the hell that would cost me? I mean, not only in money. I'd lose political capital, too!"

"So? You don't want to do right by me? Make me an honest woman?"

"Yes! I mean, no!"

Jan put her hands on her hips and cocked her head. "Well, which is it?"

He sighed. "It's not that simple, honey."

"Don't goddamn 'honey' me, Rapp."

"It's just better this way. If I sued for divorce, a lot of things would change." He knew how much Jan liked living in the luxury high-rise, especially for free. "This condo would go away, for one."

She considered that a long moment.

"What if she sues *you* for divorce?"

"For what?"

"For infidelity. Everyone saw that photograph of us in Bermuda."

With more than a little confidence, if not arrogance, he shot back: "Pennsylvania courts don't give a shit about cheating. And my wife knows it. How do you think I got away with that photo being run?"

He saw Jan eye him more carefully.

Suspiciously.

Like that was painful proof that she ain't the first regular piece I've had on the side.

Or maybe not the last . . .

"I know because I asked," Rapp went on, more evenly. "My lawyer told me."

"Even if the photos are *in flagrante delicto?*"

"In what?"

"In the act, Rapp. *Screwing.*"

"Oh. Yeah. Even that. I asked."

Now, why the hell did she ask that?

Would she go that low — send Wanda photos of us fucking — thinking she could become Mrs. Mayor instead?

"But she could sue for other reasons. Could even say you beat her, if she got mad enough to go after you."

He didn't say anything.

Jan quoted, "'Hell hath no fury like a woman scorned.'"

Badde sighed and said, "She won't."

"How can you be so sure?"

"She's got the Badde name, got all that money, and everything that comes with it. Why change?"

"What if she blows the whistle on PEGI?"

"Oh, now, that won't happen. She likes the money too much. Once you been broke, you don't ever want to go back. If all the padded payments from PEGI go, so do all those billable hours the Commonwealth Law Center gets from handling the business that will

257

come from Volks Haus and Diamond Development. And she can kiss goodbye those big steady retainer checks Kwame Construction has paid from the start."

Jan looked at him a long moment and shook her head.

"Rapp, I'm telling you that wives get revenge for a lot of reasons. And they're not thinking about money when they do it."

"I'm telling you, she won't," he said smugly. "Look, we're kind of like the U.S. and Russia were with that Mutual Asset Deduction."

"The what?"

"You know, with missiles aimed at each other. To knock each other out. One fires, both sides are toast."

After a moment Jan figured it out, and corrected him: *"Mutually Assured Destruction."*

He looked at her and shrugged. "Same difference. If she tells on me, I tell on her, and away goes all her money and her license to practice law or anything else. It'd be suicide."

Their met eyes again.

Badde thought: *And if you haven't realized it yet, honey, you and I are now in the same boat.*

You know that kickbacks are funneled through Commonwealth, which also happens to be a nice contributor to my campaign for mayor.

And you're helping funnel them.

After a moment, she nodded.

"Okay. I guess you're right, Rapp. I sure hope so."

She pointed at a thin sheaf of papers stapled at the top left corner.

"The fed funds for PEGI, at least the low-income-housing matching dollars, were due here last week. As was the paperwork that turns over possession of the prison to PEGI and the Volks Haus Initiative. We need those funds before the next step there. We've already cut checks for the first empty properties in Northern Liberties — bulldozers began some demolition last week — and then we'll be cutting checks for those holdouts. Maybe the bulldozers will convince them it's time to take the money and move on, and we won't have to evict."

"And tell me again: What's the next step at Volks Haus?"

"Same as it was for the Diamond project." She handed him the thin sheaf of papers.

He glanced at the cover sheet. It had the expected familiar letterhead:

Commonwealth Law Center
1611 Walnut Street, Suite 840
Philadelphia, PA 19103

The law center office, he knew, was two floors below his accountant's office.

Below that was printed in large lettering:

TITLE 26 EMINENT DOMAIN

Just Compensation and
Measure of Damages

"Eminent domain has two stages," Jan said. "The first is to prove that it's legal to take property and, meeting that, the second is to determine a fair price for the property."

He nodded, then turned to page two of the document, a table of contents, and began reading:

---

26 PA.C.S.A. # 701 JUST COMPENSATION; OTHER DAMAGES

26 PA.C.S.A. # 702 MEASURE OF DAMAGES

26 PA.C.S.A. # 703 FAIR MARKET VALUE

He felt his eyes start to glaze over, then scanned the rest, stopping at the last one:

He tossed the papers back onto the table.

"Jesus, I'm glad I hired you to deal with this bullshit." He smiled at her, and when she smiled back, he added: "Hope we don't have any trouble with that last one. I mean, what's a fair price for abandoned buildings?"

"*Condemned* buildings," she corrected him. "The Supreme Court fixed that for us with the *Kelo vs. City of New London* decision. There won't be any Fifth Amendment problems with the properties."

Badde then motioned at a long cardboard tube on the table.

"Has the Russian seen the architect's drawings?"

"Yuri had his assistant personally messenger them over from the Diamond Development office in Center City."

She grinned slyly, then added, "You know, I think that messenger boy of his is really his concubine."

"His what?"

"His young lover, his concubine."

Rapp stared at her with an incredulous look. "You shitting me? What's a billionaire Russian businessman doing with something like that? I mean, I've seen him with some incredibly hot women."

She shrugged. "Female intuition."

"Maybe. Just don't say anything to him. He has a mean goddamn temper."

"Guess that's how you get to be a billionaire," Jan said as she pulled the large sheets of architectural drawings from the cardboard tube.

Badde got up from the chair and walked around the marble-topped table. As he stood behind Jan, looking over her shoulder at the architect's renderings for Volks Haus, his hands slipped down to her waist. He rested his chin on her shoulder as he squeezed her hips.

"Pay attention," she said.

"I am paying attention," he said as he buried his nose in her neck and inhaled her lightly scented perfume. "Attention to you. I'll pay even better attention with this fancy outfit of yours off. . . ."

She giggled, then let her head drop back toward his. Just as she said, "I surrender," Badde's Go To Hell cell phone started ringing.

"Dammit!" Badde said, grabbing it and quickly checking the caller ID. It read UNKNOWN CALLER. "Dammit!"

He stepped back from Jan and started walking toward the sliding glass door to the balcony. "Yes?" he said into the phone.

The caller was yelling so loudly that Badde had to hold the phone away from his ear.

Jan could almost clearly hear what the caller was telling Badde: "Reggie's dead! They're coming after me!"

VI

[ONE]
5550 Ridgewood Street, Philadelphia
Sunday, November 1, 12:45 P.M.

Javier Iglesia parked his silver Dodge Avenger across the street from the Bazelon row house.

He counted at least a dozen teenagers and slightly older thuggish types milling about on the sidewalk — a handful of whom he'd seen earlier — and almost that many teens, mostly girls, sitting on the wooden porch and steps. Sasha Bazelon sat in the same rocker she'd been in when he'd wheeled away her grandmother three hours earlier.

At first glance, he mused, someone could easily think that a crowd of troublemakers had swooped in to take advantage of a poor teenage girl right after the death of her only kin.

But Javier now knew they weren't trouble-makers, at least not all of them, because he was very well acquainted with at least one person on the porch — his baby sister, nineteen-year-old Yvette — and was familiar with a handful of the others, including Kee-sha Cook, who was sitting between Sasha and Yvette.

They're here supporting Sasha, is what they're doing.

And not trying to take advantage of her during this dreadful time.

Even these punks, who are looking at me suspiciously.

Javier got out of the car and made eye contact with Yvette. As he started walking across the street, she popped up out of her chair and went quickly down the steps toward him.

He was surprised. *What the hell is up with her?*

But knowing his baby sister as well as he did, nothing she did should ever have come as a surprise to Javier Iglesia.

What the very petite Yvette Iglesia lacked in physical height — she stood four-feet-ten — she more than made up for with a bubbly, oversize personality. She spoke almost non-stop, mostly in rapid-fire bursts, gesturing wildly with her hands to make her points. She had straight black shoulder-length hair framing a pretty face that clearly showed her Puerto Rican heritage. Her dark eyes were full of life. And her small mouth was impressive not only for its dazzling smile, but also for the raw expletives that came out of it when she was angry, ones that Javier said "would embarrass a Port of Philly longshore-man."

"Don't forget," Yvette often said with a smile, almost as a provocation, "that dynamite comes in small packages."

Three hours earlier, just as Javier had backed up the van carrying Principal Bazelon's body to the Medical Examiner's Office, his cell phone had pinged, alerting him to a new text message.

When he had looked at the phone's screen, the message surprised him:

```
YVETTE

HEY, BIG BRO . . . SO SAD
ABOUT PRINCIPAL BAZELON

MUST BE VERY UPSETTING FOR
YOU TO HAVE PICKED HER UP

YOU'RE IN MY THOUGHTS &
PRAYERS

LOVE YOU!
```

His first thought: *What a sweetheart.*

Then: *How the hell did she find out so fast?*

After processing the body of Mrs. Joelle Bazelon into the system that was the Medical Examiner's Office — putting the body bag in one of the stainless-steel refrigerator compartments, then entering the report and photographs taken at the scene into the computer filing system — Javier had called his sister.

"Hey, I got your text. Thanks."

"You're welcome," she said, her usual bubbly tone gone. "It's . . . it's all just so awful. . . ."

"Yeah. She was a terrific lady. How'd you find out so fast? And that it was me? I mean, I'd barely left the scene" — he paused and thought, *Wrong word* — "that is, Principal Bazelon's house, when you sent that."

"Some guys walking around the neighborhood saw the ME van and stopped to watch."

She knows those thugs watching from across the street?

Maybe Kim Soo was right. They were wannabe gangstas-from-the-'hood.

"You know those guys?"

"No, not really. They think they're bad news. Jorge's little brother, Paco, he hangs with them, which makes Jorge mad."

Then I was right and Soo was wrong.

I knew I had that gut feeling they were up to no good. . . .

Yvette went on: "Anyway, Paco told Jorge he saw you at the Bazelons', and Jorge texted me about the ME van and Principal Bazelon dying and all."

Javier knew only vaguely of either Ramirez brother.

"And then Keesha called crying."

"Keesha?"

"Keesha Cook."

"Oh, that Keesha. How's she connected?"

"She and Sasha live on the same street. *Longtime* neighbors and friends. And you know Keesha used to come over and hang out."

"Yeah, I remember that. Okay, it all makes sense now."

"Word's gotten out *fast,* Javier. I mean there's already a *big* memorial at the middle school by the back door. People coming by and leaving flowers and stuffed animals. There's these big white bedsheets that they're drawing on and writing poems and memories and stuff about her. And there's already a memorial page dedicated to her on the Internet. People from around the world — and I mean *around the world,* Javier, like *China* and shit — are writing about what an influence she was to them. Someone's even made a page with a map of the world, and every time someone writes one of those notes or posts a photo of them, one of these red pushpins pops up on the map showing where these people are in the world — Africa, Europe, all over. Most of them are in Philly, though, real thick red here, then it gets thinner going out."

"That's amazing. All in — what? — just two hours? Amazing, is what that is."

"I just texted Keesha, and she's headed over to Sasha's. I'm going to go over, too. Talk her up, you know? I remember how terrible I felt when we lost our *abuela,* and even then we had each other to lean on. Sasha's so very alone now."

"Yvette, you know Sasha real good?"

"Sort of. Sure. Why?"

"Is she in any kind of trouble that you know of?"

"Sasha? No! Never. Why?"

"While I was there, I heard her answering questions from the police. What she told them wasn't much. Just that she came home late last night, saw her grandmother was asleep on the couch, then went to bed. When she came down next morning, her grandmother was dead."

"Yeah? And?"

"Look, I think there's more. I *know* there's more."

"Like what, Javier?"

"Somebody had tied Principal Bazelon's hands and wrists —"

He heard Yvette gasp.

He went on: "But when we got there, whatever they'd been tied with was gone. Just bruises left."

"You think Sasha did something to her? I can't imagine —"

"No. But I do think something happened that she won't tell anyone, especially the cops."

"Nobody talks to the man, Javier. Not if they're smart and don't want no trouble. No offense, big bro."

"I know that. Look, I'm not saying Sasha did anything wrong. But something is not right about those bruises on her grand- mother, ones Dr. Mitchell is going to see and question. If he thinks the death wasn't as simple as just an old lady going to sleep and never waking up, he'll have to tell the police. And then Sasha might get in real trouble."

"Oh my God, Javier. That's terrible!"

"I'm not saying she did anything to hurt her. Just that she's not telling everything that happened to her grandmother. Sasha *is* deeply hurt. No question she's hurt. But there's more than just sadness in her eyes. There's . . . *fear,* is what there is."

"Fear of what?"

Javier sighed loudly, then said, "I don't know."

"What do you want me to do?"

"Maybe just keep your eyes and ears open when you go over?"

There was a long silence. Then she said: "Okay. Sure. Anything."

"I'd like to stop by, too. I didn't get a chance to tell her how sorry I was."

"Okay. I'm walking over now."

"See you shortly."

Yvette Iglesia ran to intercept her brother

in front of the Bazelon row house. Javier glanced at the crowd of tough guys on the sidewalk and saw that they were following his every step. He recognized Paco Ramirez and thought he'd look like the nice kid next door if not for the wannabe gangsta clothing. Javier nodded at him, and Paco nodded back.

As Javier reached the sidewalk, Yvette met him. He saw that her eyes were tearing. As she hugged him, she softly said, "You were right, big bro."

"About what?"

She took a step back, crossed her arms over her chest, and looked up at Javier.

"She's only told Keesha," she said, "and Keesha's only told me."

"*What?*" he asked quietly.

She turned her back to the boys on the sidewalk, then, keeping her voice low, practically spat out: "That fucking shit Xpress — Xavier Smith?" She paused, and after Javier nodded that he knew him, went on. "He was here last night getting revenge on Sasha's grandmother for calling the cops on him. She saw him stealing a neighbor's TV. He hid on the porch last night, and when Sasha got home from Keesha's, he forced his way inside."

She sniffled, then wiped at her nose and cheek.

Javier said, "What happened then?"

"You were right about Principal Bazelon being tied up. He used the phone cord. Then he . . . then he put a gun to Sasha's head and made her —"

Javier saw the tears flowing faster.

She angrily wiped them away and finished: "That fucking shit make her blow him and made her *abuela* watch! *That's* what killed her!"

"Jesus Christ!" Javier said softly.

He looked over his baby sister's head to the porch. Keesha was stroking Sasha's hair.

Her abuela *died of a real broken heart.*

Dr. Mitchell told me about those, where stress damages the heart muscle, especially an old, weak one, to the point of triggering a deadly cardiac arrest.

Jesus!

Yvette added: "And he threatened Sasha, said not to tell nobody, that he could come back anytime, and that he could get her anywhere."

Javier shook his head and said, "No wonder she's terrified. Now she has no family and is constantly worried that Xpress will come back."

She nodded. "We're going to get her away from this. Walk over and see the memorial at the school, you know? Maybe that'll make her feel a little better."

They both glanced back at the porch. Sasha was moving down the steps with Keesha Cook at her side. Everyone along the way stepped back, making a path for her.

When Sasha and Keesha reached Yvette and Javier, Javier said, "I didn't get a chance to say earlier how much your grandmother meant to me, Sasha. I am terribly sorry for your loss, I really am."

Sasha looked him in the eyes and simply said, "Thanks."

Javier looked at Keesha and said, "Good to see you. Glad you can be here for Sasha."

Keesha nodded. Then she said, "You going over to the memorial at the school?"

"I wouldn't miss it for anything."

He gestured for them to lead the way. But when they turned to walk to Fifty-fifth Street, Sasha looked toward the intersection and froze, her wide eyes terrified.

And from deep inside her came a gut-wrenching moan that turned into a wail.

Coming toward them, having just turned the corner, was a medium-size black male in baggy jeans, his head covered by the hood of his black sweatshirt. When he looked up at the sound of the scream, the hard face of Xavier "Xpress" Smith was clearly visible — and, judging by its shocked expression,

clearly caught off guard by the crowd at
Sasha Bazelon's house.

Javier thought Smith's eyes — now huge —
looked particularly bloodshot.

He's hopped up on something. . . .

"He's come back!" Sasha then cried out,
and she started bawling uncontrollably.

Keesha, holding her arm, struggled to keep
her from collapsing to the ground.

Yvette, gesturing wildly at Xavier Smith,
exploded: "That bastard stuck a fucking
gun to Sasha's head last night! Made her go
down on him in front of her grandmother!"

The eyes of the crowd were all on Yvette.
Everyone was either not sure they'd heard
what they thought they'd heard, or was processing the incredibly awful news.

"What?" Paco Ramirez asked.

"It's true!" Yvette said. "Almost killed
Sasha, too!"

Then the eyes turned to Xavier Smith.
He'd already started walking away from the
group. Now, glancing over his shoulder —
and looking guilty as hell — Xavier Smith
bolted across Ridgewood.

"And that no-good nigger just tried to get
Sasha again!" Keesha screamed.

Yvette started running. "Don't let him get
way! C'mon!"

Oh, shit, Javier thought. "Yvette, wait!"

When she didn't, Javier took off after her.

Two male teenagers ran to a small red Ford pickup truck. They got in and, tires squealing, roared up the street.

Almost everyone else took off to follow Yvette, who was furiously sprinting.

Everyone but Keesha, who now sat on the sidewalk consoling a sobbing Sasha.

"See?" Sasha said. "He said he would. Anytime . . ."

A crowd at least twenty strong closed in on Smith, who now ran down the middle of Fifty-fifth Street. Barely dodging a Chevy sedan, its horn blaring and tires squealing, he then bolted across Beaumont Avenue, looking as if he were going to take a shortcut through the asphalt parking lot of Shaw Middle School.

There was a small group by the door to the school, looking at and adding to the makeshift memorial for Principal Joelle Bazelon. They turned and watched Smith approaching, then saw the angry mob that was chasing him — and fled the school grounds.

Xavier Smith turned to look over his shoulder, and as he glanced back he tripped on the uneven surface of the parking lot. He went down fast and hard, hitting the asphalt face-first. It dazed him.

The crowd, still led by Yvette Iglesia, caught up in no time.

They circled Xavier Smith. He remained motionless.

"Not much of a bad ass now, are you?" Yvette yelled between gasps for breath.

"We're sick of your shit, *pendejo!*" Paco Ramirez said — and suddenly, angrily, began kicking him.

Others immediately joined in, shoes and boots striking him on his back and legs. Some of the girls were throwing their weight into their kicks, their arms swinging with the exertion.

Smith recoiled. He pulled into the fetal position, protecting his face with his arms.

Oh, shit! Street justice! Javier thought.

The punk's getting what he deserves. But . . .

The rest of the crowd joined in, and Javier could see that the frenzy was building on itself.

They're going to kill him!

And then their lives are really ruined. . . .

Smith managed to roll over and reach underneath his sweatshirt. He pulled out a chrome-plated, snub-nosed .32-caliber revolver.

He waved it up at the crowd. "Back off! Now!"

The circle of angry teens instinctively took a couple steps backward.

Two of the older males pulled out knives. And another — Javier recognized him as the driver of the pickup, which he now saw was parked close by — came up to the circle carrying a baseball bat.

Xavier Smith jumped to his feet, but stayed in a crouch as he cradled his torso with his left hand.

They must have fractured or broke some ribs, Javier thought.

Smith waved the pistol at the crowd.

Then one teenage boy in the crowd laughed. He taunted him: *"Woohoo!* You crazy, Xpress!"

Smith aimed the pistol at him as the boy went on: "You got only five, maybe six bullets in that gun. There's a whole lot more of us than that!"

"And you ain't getting no chance to reload," said another teenage boy.

Smith jerked the pistol to aim it at him.

Then a teenage girl added, "Yeah, you can't shoot us all!"

He aimed the gun at her.

Then another laughed and said: "You must be snorting too much of your own shit!"

Suddenly, someone in the crowd behind Xavier Smith threw a broken red clay brick, one that had once been part of the old school building's wall. It struck Smith square in the back of the skull, causing him to crumble to the cracked black asphalt. He dropped the pistol as he went down. The gun bounced twice but did not go off.

As the circle again closed in on Smith, a lone hand reached down and grabbed the gun. The pistol disappeared into the mass of teenagers.

Now they are going in for the kill! Javier Iglesia thought.

"That's enough!" Javier shouted. "Stop, or you'll kill him!"

"So?" one teenage male in the crowd shouted in reply.

"Yeah, after all the things this shit has done to people?" another voice added.

The beefy Javier started muscling his way into the circle, grabbing elbows and pulling shoulders. He forced open a path to the center. Just as he reached the limp and bloodied body, Javier saw an elbow swinging toward him. He failed to duck in time, and the elbow caught him in the corner of his right eye.

"Shit!" Javier screamed out in pain, instantly covering his injured eye with his right hand. He swung his left hand over his head. "Goddamn it, everybody just fucking stop! Yvette, get them to stop!"

Paco Ramirez stepped next to Yvette Iglesia and waved his arms at the crowd. "Hey, everybody stop! Who hit Javier?"

It took a moment for the momentum to slow — there were a couple last kicks at Xavier Smith — but finally the crowd stood still. And stared down Javier.

Javier said, "Listen to me! You kill him, you're going to run from that the rest of your lives —"

"It'd be worth it!" a male teen in the crowd shouted.

Javier went on: "It's *not* worth it, is what I'm telling you. You need to let him get arrested, get charged with murdering Principal Bazelon."

"No cops," Paco said. "No way."

The reward! Javier suddenly remembered. *Let that rich guy Fuller turn him in. . . .*

He said: "Take Xpress in and get that ten-thousand-dollar reward!"

Yvette looked at her brother, and her face lit up as she said, "That's right!"

Then she looked at the crowd and said, "Javier's right! This piece of shit actually *is* worth something. And we can share the reward with Sasha."

She looked again at Javier. "Where's the place?"

He thought back to the Medical Examiner's Office unit that had picked up the three bodies the previous night. "In Old City, Arch and Third. Place is called . . . what the hell was it? . . . *Lex Talionis*."

Yvette nodded.

She then turned to the male with the baseball bat and said, "Go get your truck!"

He ran to the red Ford pickup, got in, and sped back.

Two teenage males were already waiting with the unconscious Xavier Smith in their hands. Everyone watched as the pair threw his limp body into the back of the truck like some sack of trash, then climbed in after him. Five others followed, filling the small truck until its rear seat sat low with their weight.

Then the truck roared away.

Yvette turned to Javier. She reached up and gingerly pulled back his right hand, inspecting the injury.

"Oh, wow," she said, wincing. "That's going to be a nice shiner." Then she smiled and added, "Big bruise for big bro."

"Great. Just what I need," he said. He pulled out his cell phone, scrolled the list of stored numbers, and called the one he'd entered as SGT PAYNE.

Wonder what the odds are of Xpress being alive when they get there?

[TWO]
Homicide Unit
Interview Room II
The Roundhouse
Eighth and Race Streets, Philadelphia
Sunday, November 1, 1:11 P.M.

"I want my reward," Shauna Mays repeated to Sergeant M. M. Payne.

"Yes, you've said that. And I've told you we need some questions answered about Kendrik's death."

Payne felt his cell phone vibrating. He carefully pulled it from his pants pocket. He glanced at its screen but did not recognize the caller ID number, so he let the caller get routed into voice mail.

"And I want these damn handcuffs off," she said. "I ain't done nothing wrong."

Interview Room II was small, ten by twelve feet, and held only a single bare metal table and two metal chairs, all pushed up against one wall. The chair that Shauna Mays sat in was bolted to the floor. One end of a pair of handcuffs was clipped around a bar on the seatback, the other cuff around her left wrist. On the opposite wall was a four-foot-square one-way mirror.

The room was harshly lit, and it was cold. Shauna Mays, her arms and legs crossed, shivered in her dirty, loose-hanging T-shirt and torn black jeans. Payne was not sure if the cause was the clothing or her obvious lack of a recent bath, but she gave off a musty odor that reeked of filth. He tried not to come too close to her.

There was a handheld digital audio recorder on the table between them. But the real recording equipment, audio and video, was behind the one-way mirror, in the small viewing room. Tony Harris, watching the interview with Jason Washington, was running the camera.

It had taken no time at all to bring in Shauna Mays — Third and Arch was only four blocks from the Roundhouse — particularly after Mayor Jerry Carlucci let loose with his famous temper when he saw her and her dead son on the bank of TV monitors in the Executive Command Center.

After saying "Oh, shit!" his very next breath had been: "Get that damn uniform to arrest her right damn now on suspicion

282

of murder and bring her here for questioning! I damn well just said that those responsible for any death will be prosecuted to the fullest — and goddamn it, that's what's going to happen!"

Matt Payne now looked down at the gaunt and badly bruised woman, and took pity.

Someone's really slapped her around, especially in the face. And her hand, which she must have tried to use for protection.

She could barely stand on her own two feet while they were rolling her fingers for prints and checking her hands for gunpowder residue.

The only person she's a danger to is herself. . . .

He said, "I'll remove the cuff, but one thing goes wrong and it goes back on."

She nodded.

Taking out his handcuff key, Payne asked, "Who hit you?"

"Who you think? Kendrik."

He nodded.

"Can I get you something to eat or drink?" he asked as he removed the cuff.

"Maybe a soda?"

Payne looked to the one-way mirror. He couldn't see anyone — except, of course, the reflections of himself and Shauna Mays — but he knew that on the other side of the glass they'd see him looking, and that they'd

283

bring the drink from the small refrigerator that was kept stocked in the unit.

A moment later there was a knock on the door, and when Payne unlocked and opened it a crack, a massive black paw of a hand reached in with a screw-top plastic bottle of grape-flavored soda and a snack-size bag of Tastykake.

"Thanks, Jason," he said, taking them, and then closing and locking the door.

Payne placed both on the table before Shauna Mays. As she reached for them, her bruised hand trembled.

He said, "Would you like me to open them?"

She nodded.

She ate the whole bag of Tastykake in about three mouthfuls, washing it down with half the soda in two swallows. Then she loudly belched.

She looked at Payne but said nothing.

Payne pulled from his pocket a small notepad and pen, then reached over to the recorder and pushed its red button to begin recording.

He glanced at his wristwatch and said, "Today is Sunday, November first. Time is one-twenty P.M. This interview is being held in the Philadelphia Police Department Homicide Unit, and conducted by me, Sergeant

M. M. Payne, badge number 471."

He looked at Shauna Mays, who seemed to be mesmerized by what Payne had just said.

Either that, or all of a sudden the sugar and salt in her system is throwing off her blood sugar balance.

He said, "Would you please state your name?"

"Shauna. Shauna Mays."

"And where do you live, Ms. Mays?"

"In Philadelphia."

"Okay. And your address is?"

"Uh, over on Wilder."

"That would be 2620 Wilder Street, Philadelphia 19147."

She nodded. "Uh-huh. That right."

"Have you been read your Miranda rights, Ms. Mays?"

"My what?"

"You have the right to remain silent, the right to have an attorney —"

"Oh, yeah," she interrupted. "That first cop did that."

"And you're freely willing to now answer any questions?"

"Yeah. Sure. Just so I gets my reward."

"Right. We'll get to that, Ms. Mays. First, Kendrik Mays is your son, correct?"

"Yeah. He my boy."

"Can you tell me what happened to Kendrik?"

"He got hisself killed."

"Yes, ma'am. I'm aware of that. How did it happen?"

"He was doing bad. Long time. He had it coming."

"Because he beat you? You did say he's responsible for the bruises on your body."

She looked at him oddly. "I don't understand."

"Did you kill him?"

"No! I told that first cop that!"

"Okay, then how did it happen, Ms. Mays?"

"I guess that bullet killed him."

Payne exhaled audibly. "Okay, let's start from the beginning. Who had the gun?"

"A delivery guy. He come in with Kendrik's paper. That paper I had that the cop took?"

"The Wanted sheet?"

"Yeah, that's it. He come in and — No, wait. First he say he got a check for Kendrik. And when I let him in, he give me the paper. The sheet. Said there was no check."

"This began at what time?"

She cocked her head. "Time? This morning, all I know. Ain't no clocks in a crack house!"

Payne nodded as he wrote that on his note-pad and thought, *Right.*

If something's not nailed down, it's sold for drugs.

My God, what a way to live.

"What did this guy look like? And was he alone, anyone else in the house?"

"Just him. Old white guy, maybe my age. Tall. Kinda skinny."

Payne wrote that down and asked, "He give you a name? You ever see him before?"

"Nope," she said, shaking her head. "I think Kendrik did something bad to this guy. Or maybe to his family. Robbery, rape, something. Once my boy got in the drugs, he was no good."

Payne noted that on his pad, then said, "This old white guy your age — anything unusual about him? Anything at all special or different you remember about him?"

She thought about that for a moment. Then she grinned.

"He give me money. A hundred dollars, he did! How many times *that* going to happen? Some white guy come in your house and give you a hundred dollars, then tell you how to get *ten thousand* more!"

She's almost giddy.

The sugar must really be kicking in.

She squinted her eyes at Payne and wagged

her right index finger at him. "And I want my reward!"

"This man had a gun?"

She looked at Payne with an expression that suggested he was nuts. "How else Kendrik get shot? Had to! I never saw it. But it made a loud noise. Sounded like a cannon boom in the basement."

"That's where Kendrik was shot, in the basement? Do we have your permission to go through it and search your whole house?"

She nodded, then snickered. "If you want. Sure. Just try not to make a mess." She looked at Payne and said, her tone flat, "That was a joke."

Now she's feeling so good she's a damn comedienne.

Payne nodded, then said, "You do know it's against the law to tamper with the scene of a crime, remove or otherwise alter evidence?"

She shrugged.

Payne raised an eyebrow, then went on: "Okay, do you know the cabbie who helped you?"

She shook her head. "No. He just the first one who'd help me. Had to walk four blocks till I found him on Reed Street. Only charged me twenty bucks. Said he was sorry for me but glad to see Kendrik got what he deserved. Nobody liked that boy."

Payne wrote that as he asked, "And this cabbie helped you do what?"

"He's a really big guy. He took that rug and rolled Kendrik up in it, then carried him to the car."

"Ms. Mays, that's the tampering with evidence I'm referring to. You should've called 911 and —"

She laughed. "Call 911? What? I ain't got no phone. And I sure as hell wouldn't call no police if I did."

Payne stared at her.

Amazing. You get beat to hell and back, someone blows away your son in your basement, but whatever you do, don't call the good guys. . . .

He went on: "Are you also aware it's against the law to harbor a fugitive?"

"Harbor?"

"Let him live with you."

She sat up in the chair, puffed up her chest, and in as loud and angry a voice as she could muster said, "I didn't *let* him live with me! I throwed him out over and over. But he come back. And when I try throwing him out again, after he been in jail, that's when he beat me really bad. What can I do? I got no money to move out, so I just deal with it all . . ." Her voice trailed off. She reached for the soda bottle and drained it.

Then she crossed her arms and glared at Payne. "I want my reward!"

Payne looked back at her, then glanced at his watch and said to the recorder, "Interview paused at one-forty P.M."

He stood, stuck his notepad in his pocket, and said, "I'll be right back."

He left the handcuff off her but, using the sliding bolt, locked the interview room door from the outside.

Only Jason Washington was in the small observation room when Payne entered.

"The minute you got her permission," Washington said, his deep, sonorous voice answering the unasked question, "Tony went to get a Search and Seizure warrant signed by the judge and sent the Crime Lab to her house."

"If that house is anything like its resident, I doubt we're going to get anything of real use. Other than maybe a bullet fragment. The shooter probably collected his shell casings."

Washington nodded and said, "You're probably correct, Matthew. But you know to 'never say never.'"

"And 'always check the rock under the rock,'" Payne said with a smile, citing Washington's well-known rule of thumb for conducting thorough investigations.

"I learned you well, Young Matthew," Washington said mock-seriously.

Payne looked at Shauna Mays through the window and parroted her: " 'I want my reward.' "

Washington chuckled, but then in a serious tone said, "And she should get it, considering the hell she went through."

Payne looked at him, then back at her.

After a long moment he said, "Jason, are you thinking what I'm thinking?"

"She didn't do it," Washington immediately answered. "She's arguably guilty of a whole host of other mistakes in life. But murder isn't one of them. And after one look at her physical condition, the DA isn't going to go after her for harboring a fugitive."

Payne nodded. "We could throw tampering with evidence charges at her, or even accessory to murder. But why?"

"I doubt the DA would press charges if they caught her jaywalking," Washington said. "We'll hold her till we see what, if anything, they find at the scene. Then let her loose to collect her reward."

They looked at her again.

After a moment Payne said coldly, "I'm betting this won't be the last we hear of Shauna Mays. And not alive."

"Great minds follow similar paths, Matthew. I agree. There're ten thousand reasons why."

"The whole 'hood will be after her money."

Matt Payne then felt his phone vibrating again. When he pulled it out, he saw the call was from the same number as the call he'd ignored earlier.

He looked at Washington, shrugged, and said, "Excuse me." He answered it: "Payne."

After a moment he said, "Hold on," then hit the SPEAKERPHONE key.

"You still there, Sergeant Payne?" Javier Iglesia's voice came over the speaker.

"Yeah, Javier," Payne said. "I'm here with Lieutenant Jason Washington —"

"Hey, Lieutenant," Javier interrupted. "Haven't seen you in quite a while."

"How are you, Javier?" Washington asked.

"Not real good. I was just telling Sergeant Payne that I'm near my home in Kingsessing — southwest Philadelphia?"

"We know it," Payne said. "What's this you just said about a Principal Bazelon being murdered?"

"We got the call from Twelfth District this morning that she'd died in her sleep," Iglesia began. "But I just found out she really died during a home invasion by a really bad dude named Xpress Jones . . ."

". . . and now part of that crowd is taking Xpress down to collect that ten-grand reward," Iglesia finished some five minutes later. "It being a homicide and all, I thought you'd want to be the ones who grabbed him."

"Give me this animal's name again, Javier," Payne said, pulling out his notepad and flipping to a clean page.

"Xpress Smith. *Xavier* Smith, aka Xpress. Black male, twenty-four."

Payne wrote it down. "Okay. Got it. Any unusual features to look for to ID him?"

Javier snorted. "Other than being attached to an angry mob of wannabe gangbangers? And the ten-g price tag on his head? Don't worry, Sergeant. You can't miss him. Xpress is pretty messed up."

"Thanks, Javier. We've already got someone down there. I'll give him a heads-up."

"Later," Javier said.

Payne broke the connection, then slipped the cell phone back in the left front pocket of his pants.

Matt Payne looked at Jason Washington and said, "So we have a mother bringing in her dead son, and now we have street-justice punks cashing in a really bad guy? And those first eight pop-and-drops. *Killadelphia,* indeed. The vigilantes — and now we know there's at least one — are everywhere. Worse, I'm beginning to think Operation Clean Sweep has been commandeered by Five-Eff."

"Well, Francis Fuller's reward system is certainly superior to ours in attracting attention," Washington said. "To start with, he's not a cop. And, as we well know, nobody on the street wants to talk to cops."

Payne grunted.

He said, "Carlucci is really going to blow his cork when he hears about the street vigilantes turning in this thug and that Kendrik's doer is still loose and, we can presume, still active. Next time you see my head, it'll probably be on a platter."

Payne looked at Washington a long moment, then sighed. He said, "You're smarter than I am, Jason. What the hell do I do next?"

"Applying for the monastery ever cross your mind?"

[THREE]
Jefferson and Mascher Streets, Philadelphia
Sunday, November 1, 1:55 P.M.

"Bobby, what the hell does five fucking minutes matter?" Thomas "Little Tommie" Turco glanced at his wristwatch and anxiously tapped his steel-toed work boot. "The permit says two o'clock start time. We're wasting daylight, not to mention burning rental money. Go on and swing it."

Puffing on a stub of a cigar stuck in the corner of his mouth, the bulky, thirty-eight-year-old Turco — who was anything but little — stood on the step outside the cab of a red-and-white Link-Belt crane he'd rented two hours earlier. A weathered cardboard sign, cut somewhat square, was taped to the door of the cab. It was poorly hand-lettered with a black permanent-ink marker: TURCO DEMOLITION & EXCAVATION. NOT FOR HIRE. UNDER CONTRACT WITH CITY OF PHILA HUD.

"You got it, boss," said Bobby "the Ball-

295

buster" Bucco, who was sitting at the controls. He fired up the Link-Belt's diesel engine.

Little Tommie then gave a thumbs-up to Jimmy "Dirtball" Turco. His cousin was at the controls of a massive Caterpillar D3K bulldozer that sat next to a pair of Bobcats with front-end loading buckets and a line of five heavy-duty dump trucks waiting to haul away debris. The bright yellow, nine-ton dozer roared to life. Then its twin tracks and giant front blade began kicking up clouds of dust as the dozer started pushing into piles the scattered, busted debris of the onetime residential neighborhood.

This was the second time in the last ten days that Turco's beefy crew — not one of the men weighed an ounce under two-fifty — had worked this Northern Liberties job site.

The first time, during a solid week of working dawn to dusk every day but Sunday, they had taken almost the entire block down to bare earth. Little Tommie himself would have admitted that it wasn't really all that impressive an accomplishment, if only because over the years almost half of the row houses had burned and their shells had been removed by crews from the City of Philadelphia. Turco's equipment only had to scrape up and truck off the concrete footings, and sometimes not even those were left, just weed-choked dirt.

The reason Turco's crew had not been able to finish the job all at once — and had to return today — could be explained in part by the signs recently posted on the property.

There were four shiny new large ones, four-by-eight-foot sheets of plywood painted bright white and nailed to four-by-four-inch posts, each erected on a corner of the block. Lettered in black was:

MOVING PHILLY FORWARD!
COMING SOON TO NORTHERN LIBERTIES:

3,000 NEW JOBS!

PROJECT COST TO TAXPAYERS:

ZERO!

ANOTHER FINE DEVELOPMENT FOR YOUR FUTURE FROM THE PHILADELPHIA ECONOMIC GENTRIFICATION INITIATIVE

A PROJECT OF THE CITY OF PHILADELPHIA HOUSING & URBAN DEVELOPMENT
COUNCILMAN H. RAPP BADDE, JR., CHAIRMAN

And there were a score or more smaller signs that had been made with a stencil. They had been spray-painted on the exterior doors and walls of the last five standing row houses on the block, all of which were in a group at the southwest corner of the job site.

The stencils read:

```
OFFICIAL NOTICE!
CONDEMNED PROPERTY!
CERTIFIED UNFIT FOR HUMAN
HABITATION UNDER
STATE OF PENNSYLVANIA URBAN
REDEVELOPMENT LAW
NO TRESPASSING!
```

Forty-five days earlier, the entire block had officially been declared a blight and then condemned.

Every owner of the individual properties had been served a notice of condemnation that week, and all — except for the five holdouts — had let expire the thirty-day period for challenging the condemnation.

They had taken their checks — most of the owners grumbling that PEGI paid them only pennies on the dollar for their properties, never mind that many of the houses had been genuine hazards and public nuisances, or damn close to it — and moved on.

They understood that they were powerless to fight the inevitable. And change was inevitable. They'd spent at least the last year looking at the looming twenty-one-story Hops Haus complex just three blocks to the south and right next to the fancy new Schmidt's Brewery development.

The five holdouts, however, were not easily persuaded. They had protested every day, marching with signs and chanting, even as Turco's crews and their heavy equipment created an intimidating environment while tearing down the rest of the block right up to their doorsteps.

The holdouts had even plastered home-printed handbills all over the neighborhood, including on the brand-new bright white signs at the four corners of the block. The handbills displayed a crude image of a black politician wearing a tiny black bow tie above the words:

COUNCILMAN RAPP BADDE
WANTED!
FOR CRIMES AGAINST THE
POOR & DISADVANTAGED OF PHILLY!

> LAST SEEN STEALING HOMES &
> TEARING DOWN NEIGHBORHOODS!
> HELP STOP HIM, OR YOURS IS NEXT!

But then Little Tommie had gotten the call that the holdouts had finally been dealt with, and that Turco Demolition and Excavation had the green light to reduce the remaining properties to rubble.

That call had come in two days earlier, after office hours on Friday afternoon, and it had been from some fellow who announced to Little Tommie that he'd been "tasked at HUD as the new expediter for PEGI projects."

"He said we're all good to go," Little Tommie had told Bobby the Ballbuster after he'd hung up the phone. They were sitting in Turco's office cutting the dust of the day with a couple glasses of Scotch whisky. "But I just turned that damn crane back in to the rental shop!"

Turco had then had to call and reserve another crane, a slightly smaller one that at least was cheaper than the one he'd just turned in. But he wasn't overjoyed with the news that the earliest it could be available was Sunday noon.

"I hate working Sundays," he'd said when he'd slammed down the receiver.

Now, from his seat in the cab of the rental crane, Bobby the Ballbuster could see a few of the protest signs the holdouts had carried. One that he could clearly see read: "Eminent Domain = Theft by Gov't!" Another said "5th Amendment Yes!" and had the international symbol for "no" — a red circle with a red backslash — across the words "Philly HUD" and "PEGI."

The signs were in the dirt beside the first two-story row house he was about to tear down using a four-thousand-pound forged-steel wrecking ball.

The pear-shaped ball was on a rusty hook at the end of the thick, heavy steel cable that hung from the tip of the crane's sixty-foot-high boom. A secondary steel line attached to the top of the wrecking ball ran laterally to a drum right beneath the cab. The drum had a clutch that, when released, would allow the drum to turn freely — and the two-ton ball to swing like a pendulum. After the ball struck the building, the drum would reel it back so it could be released again to knock another hole in the structure.

And so on, until nothing remained but rubble.

Now aimed at the brick siding of the faded-red row house, the ball was positioned ten feet above the ground and directly in front of the cab's windshield. Bucco could almost reach out and touch it.

Instead, he put his hand on the lever that worked the clutch on the lateral drum.

"What're you waiting for?" Little Tommie said as he removed the cigar from his mouth and spat out a piece of tobacco leaf.

Bobby the Ballbuster threw the lever, and there came an ear-piercing metallic screech as the drum spun and the wire cable unspooled. The two tons of forged-steel wrecking ball swung toward the row house. The ball struck more or less on target — and sailed right on through the brick siding. The impact caused the ground to shake.

Bucco then threw the lever to engage the lateral line drum's clutch. The crane's huge diesel engine roared. There came another screech as the wire cable wound back on the drum. The pear-shaped ball appeared in the pear-shaped hole it had made, then slowly returned to its position in front of Bucco.

"Go again!" Turco said impatiently.

Bucco threw the lever. The drum screeched and the ball swung, and the row house shook on impact.

This time, though, the kinetic energy

punched a hole in the wall that was three times the size of the ball itself. Wood splinters flew. Turco dodged one of the small pieces that managed to fly all the way to the crane.

The crane's diesel engine roared again as Bucco retracted the ball.

As it came out, they suddenly saw a small tan mongrel dog peering out of the big hole on the second floor. It had no collar. It looked around nervously, then jumped down to the ground, tumbling when it hit. The dog got to its feet, shook its head, and ran off as if it were on fire.

"Oh, for Pete's sake!" Bucco said. "I thought these houses were finally cleared!"

"Looked like a damn stray," Turco said reasonably. "And now the mutt's gone."

Bucco looked at him and said, "I don't know, Tommie. I'm getting a bad vibe. Maybe I'd better go and double-check."

Turco looked at his watch, then said, "It was just a fucking mutt. Just swing it again. We can knock these shit-for-houses down in a couple hours, and I can return this crane by five and only pay for a half-day rental. Then we can get the hell off this job and on to the next one."

Bucco looked at him a long moment, then at the big hole in the wall, then back at Turco.

He shrugged and said, "Awww, all right, you're the boss."

The next swing of the two-ton ball took out almost all the rest of the upstairs exterior wall, which caused the roof to partially collapse.

And again Bobby the Ballbuster threw the lever that caused the drum to begin reeling in the lateral line.

This time, though, there was something stuck on the ball. Bucco and Turco knew it wasn't unusual for either the ball or the cable to snag something — anything from electrical wiring to abandoned furniture — and carry it outside.

But as the ball exited the massive hole in the second-floor wall, it was clear that this wasn't any building material.

As the ball was reeled closer to the cab, they had a stomach-turning view of what had gotten snagged.

"Shit, shit, *shit!*" Bucco said as he stared through the cab windshield at the wrecking ball — and at the limp body of one of the male holdouts, his jacket caught on the rusty hook that held the ball.

His lifeless eyes stared back at Bucco.

Bobby the Ballbuster struck Little Tommie with the cab door as he flung it open. Bucco's vomit splashed all over Turco's steel-toed work boots.

[FOUR]
Executive Command Center
The Roundhouse
Eighth and Race Streets,
Philadelphia
Sunday, November 1, 1:54 P.M.

"Thank you, Commissioner Walker," Sergeant Matt Payne said into the receiver of one of three multiline telephones on the conference table in front of him. He looked at Detective Tony Harris, seated next to him, and rolled his eyes as he added, "I'm really grateful for your having pushed the processing of those prints."

He looked past Harris and saw that not only had Corporal Kerry Rapier caught the unflattering gesture, he was grinning at it.

He's not one of his starchy boss's biggest fans either.

Payne looked at the "desk sign" on the conference table between him and Harris. As sort of an inside joke, Payne had fashioned it out of a sheet of legal-pad paper he'd folded lengthwise twice to make an inverted V. Handprinted on it was TASK FORCE OPERATION CLEAN SWEEP.

The sign reminded Payne that Deputy Police Commissioner Howard Walker had been among the first to flee the ECC after Mayor Carlucci had stormed out, still fuming over Kendrik Mays's mother bringing in his bloody body for a ten-thousand-dollar reward.

Police Commissioner Ralph Mariana had then told Payne: "What Jerry announced about you having the full support of the department wasn't just thrown out there for the benefit of appeasing the public." He'd paused and smiled. "I think, though, that the part about calling in the FBI and others for help *was*. Jerry's never been a fan of the feds coming in and telling us how it's supposed to be done. I know I'm not."

Mariana had looked from First Deputy Police Commissioner Denny Coughlin to Deputy Police Commissioner Howard Walker to Captain Henry Quaire to Lieutenant Jason Washington. All were standing in a loose group near the doorway, and all nodded their agreement.

"Whatever you want, Matt, you've got. Just say."

"I appreciate it," Payne had said. "But I

believe that right now what I have" — he motioned to Harris and to Corporal Kerry Rapier seated at his control panel — "is all Operation Clean Sweep needs. Running lean and mean to start will help keep us focused, and the confusion to a minimum. I can always add people as I go. But if I get too many people in here too fast, we'll spend more time and effort keeping the navel-gazers busy than actually hunting the doer."

"Understood. Your call. All I ask is for someone to keep me posted so I can keep Jerry in the loop." Mariana nodded once and went out the door.

Walker had then said, "Kerry, you heard him. Anything Sergeant Payne needs."

And he'd looked at Quaire and Washington and added, "If there's anything I can do, let me know." Then Walker had bolted.

Payne had seen the exchange of looks between Coughlin, Quaire, and Washington. While not one of them would have said it aloud, Payne knew what they were thinking: that Walker was headed to Forensics to chew out in his snooty manner whomever he deemed responsible for the delay in processing the Halloween Homicides fingerprints — and the resulting egg on his face before the mayor of Philadelphia.

Coughlin had simply said, "Let us know,

Matty," and they were all gone.

Payne had walked to the door and swung it almost completely closed. Then he'd turned and looked between Tony Harris and Kerry Rapier and said, "Either of you buy that lean-and-mean bullshit?"

They had grinned.

"Me neither. I haven't a fucking idea of what to do first." He gestured at the banks of TV monitors that showed all the images of the pop-and-drop victims, the volumes of evidence, and live feeds that included a video of Shauna Mays being handcuffed. "Except, after interviewing this woman Hizzonor wants to make an example of, to run a fine-toothed comb back through everything."

Payne took a sip from his china mug of black coffee, then said: "Kerry, would you please punch up" — he glanced at the second bank of nine sixty-inch, flat-screen TV monitors — "number seventeen, Reggie Jones's file, on the main bank?"

The monitor still displayed various images and data from the first eight pop-and-drops — the five from the previous month and the three from last night — now all collected on the monitors numbered ten to eighteen. And, within the last hour, Rapier had added that of Kendrik Mays, including the video of

Payne's interview of Shauna Mays.

The third bank of nine monitors, numbers nineteen through twenty-seven, now showed the rotating feeds of video from the department's various cameras around the city, as well as feeds from two local TV news broadcasts.

"Yes, sir," Rapier said, and his fingers flew across the keyboard.

The image from TV monitor number seventeen was then duplicated — nine times larger — on the main bank of monitors. The image was from a digital video recording that had been shot at the crime scene the previous night, and showed the Old City sidewalk with the battered body of Reggie Jones lying inside the yellow police-line tape. The scene was brightly lit by a pair halogen floodbeams that were mounted high on the side of the Medical Examiner's Office panel van, which also held the video camera.

In the bottom right-hand corner of the image was an ID stamp:

Richard Saunders Holdings/Lex Talionis
Third & Arch
0105 hours, 01 Nov

Corporal Rapier then typed a few more keystrokes, and up popped another text box. It contained:

Name: Reginald "Reggie" JONES

Description: Black male, age 20, 5 ft. 11 in., 260 lbs.

L.K.A.: 725 Daly St, Phila.

Call Received: 01 Nov, 0012 hours

Prior arrests: 4 total: Possession of cocaine (3) and distribution of cocaine (1). On probation for possession of crack cocaine.

Cause of Death: BLUNT FORCE TRAUMA and/or STRANGULATION.

Case No.: 2010-81-039613-POP-N-DROP

Notes: Badly beaten by Suspect(s) Name Unknown. SNU 2010-56-9326 SNU 2010-56-9327. Ligature strangulation caused by plastic zip ties (two (2) 24-inch-long zip ties put together to make a single 48-inch-long tie). Mildly mentally retarded. Body transported to Lex Talionis, Old City. Brother is Kenneth J. JONES, black male, age 22, a fugitive wanted on warrants for crack cocaine possession with intent to distribute.

Payne and Harris were looking at the image and reading the text.

"Still using 'Pop-n-Drop' as the code for the master files, Kerry?" Payne asked.

The youthful corporal grinned, then said, "Yes, sir. It just made sense to stick with the obvious."

"What about the fact that Jones wasn't shot?"

"Hey, getting beat up can be called getting 'popped,'" Rapier said reasonably. "Besides, I didn't want to have to recode all the others to fit. This way, it's consistent from the start." He looked at Payne, who was still studying the main screen, then felt he needed to explain better: "With the master files all linked by 'pop-n-drop,' the system can build on any of the previous composite reports, tables, graphs, maps, et cetera, that you created with the information from the earlier case files."

Payne turned to him and nodded. He said, "Okay, Kerry. I really have no problem with that. It was just an idle question."

"Yes, sir," Rapier said.

Rapier knew that Payne was well versed in how the system worked. That it went into the digital files and took key words — names, locations, weaponry, et cetera — and attempted to cross-match them first to the files coded "pop-n-drop," and then to all the other master case files in the system. If the system found a possible connection, it would generate a digital report citing those cases and the connections.

And, of course, it was able to then feed all that information to the FBI's National Crime Information Center and attempt to cross-match with NCIC's vast criminal database that was constantly updated by law enforcement across the country.

"So there's Commissioner Walker's handiwork in the Notes section," Tony Harris said casually, pointing with his ink pen in the direction of the text box on Reggie Jones's image.

"And it's not good news," Payne said, looking at it. "Forensics, it appears, has found more than one doer's prints on Jones."

"Well, then," Harris said with a smile, "on the positive side, that means we have twice the chance of getting lucky with IAFIS putting a name to those SNUs."

IAFIS was the FBI's Integrated Automated Fingerprint Identification System. SNU was the abbreviation for Suspect Name Unknown.

"Kerry," Payne said, "would you click on Reggie's SNUs?"

"Thought you'd never ask, Marshal," Rapier said.

Payne ignored the curious sudden reference to his nickname, Wyatt Earp of the Main Line, but saw out of the corner of his eye that Rapier was grinning.

Then, on the monitor, over the text box, a cursor appeared — and he immediately understood.

"It is different, Kerry," Payne said.

Harris snorted.

The digital pointer on-screen was not the usual black arrow. It was an actual image of a Colt .45 ACP Officer's Model pistol. Rapier knew it was Payne's favorite sidearm.

"I thought you'd like it, Marshal. Changing the cursor image was easy enough. This next part took a little work."

All the underlined words in the case file were hyperlinks that allowed a system user to access additional information on the case.

Corporal Rapier moved the Colt pistol over the underlined SNU 2010-56-9326. When he clicked on it, three things happened in rapid succession. First, the sound of a pistol firing emanated from the speakers. Second, a puff of smoke appeared and disappeared from the muzzle of the pistol cursor. And, third, a box popped up that was headlined "Suspect Name Unknown #2010-56-9326."

It held digitized images of fingerprints that had been lifted from Reggie Jones.

Now Harris laughed out loud. "That's great!"

Payne looked at Rapier and said, "Have a little extra time on your hands lately, Corporal?"

Rapier looked back, appearing a little embarrassed, and shrugged. "Didn't take that long. You don't like it?"

"No, I think it's great, too, Kerry."

Payne returned his attention to the big monitor, and Rapier moved the cursor to the underlined SNU 2010-56-9327. After another click of the cursor, complete with "firing pistol" effects, a second box popped up with digitized images of fingerprints, this one headlined "Suspect Name Unknown #2010-56-9327." As in the previous box, there was a hyperlink — REGINALD "REGGIE" JONES CASE NO.: 2010-81-039613-POP-N-DROP — referencing back to Reggie Jones's master case file. That meant, at least for the moment, that the two sets of fingerprints were associated with only a single crime — his murder.

"Well, the good news is that both doers left really clear prints, even if they're far from a full set," Payne said. "IAFIS should have no trouble with them."

"Assuming there's a match on file," Harris said.

Payne grunted. He knew that had been the problem with the first five pop-and-drops. When they ran the prints though IAFIS, nothing came back. It was possible — though hard to fathom, Payne thought, considering the shooter had killed five people — that the doer had never been fingerprinted.

"Well, we should know in a couple hours," Payne said.

He turned to Rapier and said, "Let's see what we've got on Gartner." He looked at the second bank of monitors. "Looks like lucky number thirteen."

Kerry Rapier worked his control panel, and the image from TV monitor number thirteen replaced the main screen's image of Reggie Jones. It was somewhat similar to Jones's — a brightly lit shot of the sidewalk outside Francis Fuller's office building in Old City.

But this image from the medical examiner's video recording showed two bloodied bodies, with the smaller of the two slightly grayed-out and blurred so it was instantly clear which of the dead was Gartner.

The bottom right-hand corner ID stamp was also slightly different:

Payne, Harris, and Rapier read the text box that next appeared:

Name: Daniel O. "Danny" GARTNER

Description: White male, age 55, 5'9", 160 lbs.

L.K.A.: 1834 Callowhill St, Phila. and 1014 Hall St, Phila.

Prior Arrests: None.

Call Received: 31 Oct, 2202 hours.

Cause of Death: GUNSHOT and/or SUF-FOCATION.

Case No.: 2010-81-039612-POP-N-DROP

Notes: SNU 2010-56-9280 Gartner was a criminal defense lawyer. Found dead with a client, one John "JC" NGUYEN Case No.: 2010-81-039611-Pop-n-Drop. Large-bore gunshot to head. Clear packing tape wrapped around head, covering mouth and nose. Garbage bag over head sealed with packing tape. Packing tape also bound wrists and ankles. One

(1) spent shell casing Glock .45 caliber found in alleyway behind Gartner's law office. Also recovered from inside law office were zipper-top bags, one containing cocaine and one with 53 tablets of Rohypnol. And a large volume (possibly in excess of a gallon) of urine, source unknown, poured around office. Body transported to Lex Talionis, Old City.

"Well, no surprise there," Matt Payne said.

"Why's that, Matt?" Harris asked.

"Kerry, go ahead and click on his SNU. I think I know where this is going."

The Colt pistol pointer fired and smoked over the hyperlink. A box headlined "Suspect Name Unknown #2010-56-9280" popped up. It had seven different sets of fingerprints, some with two or three fingers, one with only a finger and thumb. And it had seven case file hyperlinks:

Daniel O. "Danny" GARTNER Case No.:
 2010-81-039612-Pop-n-Drop
John "JC" NGUYEN Case No.:
 2010-81-039611-Pop-n-Drop

"Holy shit!" Tony Harris said. "The prints are from the same doer."

"Yeah," Payne said, his tone frustrated. "I thought I recognized that SNU number when I saw it."

"And not a single hit with IAFIS?"

"Nope, not one," Payne said. "The problem is all we get with this guy's fingerprints is more of his fingerprints. He makes no effort to cover his tracks. It's incredible."

"And piss," Corporal Kerry Rapier said. "Don't forget the piss."

"Right," Payne said. "And the useless piss."

Payne looked at the list.

"I can damn near recite from memory everything about those first five, mostly because what little we have on them is pretty much the same. Starting with, of course, whoever the hell shot them. All male fugitives — three black, one white, and one Hispanic, an illegal alien — with a history of sex crimes against women or children. All shot either in the head or chest at point-blank range. The only autopsy results we have so far are from them. Rivera" — he gestured at the second bank of monitors — "there on number sixteen, had two full-metal-jacket 9-millimeter rounds in his chest. Whitey Walsh, on number fifteen, the lone white guy, must have had one helluva hard head, because somehow a jacketed hollow-point .45-caliber round went in at the base of his skull and stayed there after scrambling his brains."

"Jesus!" Harris said. "That's the kind of thing that generally happens only with a .22-caliber round."

"Yeah," Payne said. "Which suggests that maybe — just maybe — our doer is loading his own ammo and making light loads for his targeted killings. Or just a bad round. Either way, shot from a Glock. Ballistics, of course, caught the unique scoring made by the rifling in Glock barrels."

Harris nodded. "There was that Glock .45-cal shell casing behind Gartner's office.

It'd be a long shot, but wouldn't surprise me to hear the doer's prints also came off that brass."

"Yeah," Payne said, nodding thoughtfully. Then he went on: "And get this: The autopsies also found that all five had STDs."

"How nice," Harris said dryly. "The gift that keeps on giving. Especially when you rape someone. Damned animals."

Payne said: "Which I've come to learn is not that unusual, particularly in certain circles."

Rapier offered, "The stats are that one out of five people over age twelve in America has herpes."

Harris shook his head. "Unbelievable."

"One in five over twelve?" Payne repeated. "That'll put the fear of God in you. How'd you become such an expert on the subject, Kerry?"

"You know what they say: 'Forewarned is forearmed,'" Rapier replied mock-formally. Then he smiled and lightly added: "If I were you, Marshal, I wouldn't worry much about those odds."

Payne and Harris exchanged glances, then Payne looked at Rapier. He raised an eyebrow and said, "Okay, I'll bite. Why shouldn't I worry?"

"Well, normally I would counsel caution,

faithful use of condoms and all." He paused. "But I'm almost certain you can't get STDs from your palm."

Harris burst out laughing.

"This one?" Sergeant Matt Payne asked innocently, showing Corporal Kerry Rapier his right palm. Then Payne immediately turned it and folded all but the middle finger.

"That's what I think of your counsel, Corporal."

Both exchanged grins.

"And the other thing they all had in common," Payne continued, "is the Wanted sheet. They were all printed on the same paper stock. Same bond. Same whiteness factor — or lack thereof. Really cheap paper, almost gray. Wanted sheets for everyone but Gartner and Nguyen." He motioned at the main bank of monitors. "Kerry, can you punch up Nguyen's?"

The Colt pistol pointer floated over John "JC" NGUYEN Case No.: 2010-81-039611-Pop-n-Drop. The pistol fired and smoked, and the image from monitor number fourteen appeared in place of Gartner's. The time-stamp ID was identical, and the paused image was almost so, the only difference being that in this image it was Gartner's body that was grayed out.

They read the text:

Name: John "JC" NGUYEN

Description: Asian male, age 25, 5'2", 110 lbs.

L.K.A.: 1405 S. Colorado Street, South Philly.

Prior Arrests: 14 total: possession of marijuana (10); possession with intent to distribute Methamphetamine (2); possession with intent to distribute gamma hydroxybutyric (GHB) (1); Involuntary deviant sexual intercourse & rape of an unconscious or unaware person (1). On Probation for GHB distribution. Sex crime charges dismissed due to technicality: broken evidence chain of custody. Outstanding bench warrant for failure to appear in Municipal Court on two counts of intent to deliver a controlled substance.

Call Received: 31 Oct, 2202 hours.

Cause of Death: GUNSHOT and/or SUFFOCATION.

Case No.: 2010-81-039611-POP-N-DROP

Notes: SNU 2010-56-9280 Found dead with his criminal defense lawyer, Daniel O. "Danny" GARTNER Case No.: 2010-81-039612-POP-N-DROP. Large-bore gunshot to head. Clear packing tape wrapped around head, covering mouth and nose. Garbage bag over head, sealed with packing tape. Packing tape also bound wrists and ankles. One (1) spent shell casing Glock .45 caliber found in alleyway behind law office of Gartner. Also recovered from inside law office were zipper-top bags, one containing cocaine and one with 53 tablets of Rohypnol. And a large volume (possibly in excess of a gallon) of urine, source unknown, poured around office. Body transported to Lex Talionis, Old City.

"So," Payne said after studying the information for a moment, "with the exception of Gartner, all the dead have a sex-crime component. And the exception to that being that Gartner got his client off on a technicality. Ergo, our doer" — he looked at the text box and read aloud from it — "'SNU 2010-56-9280,' whose prints are linked to seven of the eight pop-and-drops —"

"Make that nine," Kerry Rapier interrupted, pointing to the third bank of monitors. "Here comes Xpress on number twenty-six."

He manipulated the console panel, and the video feed from the department's CCTV camera at Eighth and Arch in Old City appeared on the main bank. It showed a small red pickup packed with teenagers pulling up in front of Francis Fuller's office building — and being immediately surrounded, first by plainclothed policemen, then by uniforms.

Using the control panel's joystick, Rapier first panned the scene, then zoomed in to look inside the open back of the pickup. After a couple teenagers hopped out, the camera had a clear view of a motionless, bloodied black male lying there.

"This would appear to be one Xavier 'Xpress' Smith," Rapier said. "I pulled his sheet earlier."

"Who doesn't really count in our manhunt of the pop-and-drop doer," Payne said. "Miracle of miracles, we're right now looking at the guys — these street-justice vigilantes — who popped Smith. Wish our other doer was so damn easily collared."

Rapier said, "His rap sheet shows twenty-two cases of petty robbery, possession of stolen goods, and possession of and intent to deliver crystal meth."

"To which," Payne said, "we can add a charge of murder. At least according to Javier Iglesia. Assuming, of course, Xpress himself is not dead. He's not moving at all in the back of that truck."

They watched the CCTV feed as the uniforms began handcuffing the very unhappy teenagers.

After a moment, Payne said, "Getting back to what I was saying about our SNU whose prints are linked to seven of our eight" — he exchanged glances with Rapier — "our *nine* pop-and-drops, the doer is targeting criminals with a history of sex crimes against women and children." He looked at Harris. "Ergo, Plan A, the obvious thing to do would be to list every critter fitting that profile, then have their Last Known Address immediately put under surveillance."

Kerry Rapier offered, "I can generate a report listing them."

Harris looked at him, then at Payne, and said, "Then just wait for the doer, or doers, to show up? That's not going to work. I mean, at least logistically."

Payne nodded. "I know, I know. If even one percent of the city's fifty thousand fugitives were sex offenders, that'd mean we'd need five hundred guys on the street to stand watch. And that's for just one shift. It'd take fifteen hundred to go round the clock. And then there's the Megan's Law offenders."

Harris shook his head. "No way we could

325

get that kind of manpower. We may as well put in a request for a magic wand to wave."

Payne sighed audibly. He said, "So, Plan B."

"Which is?"

"What they say to do when nothing goes right."

Harris shook his head.

"'Go left.'"

Harris looked at him a long moment, then said, "Back to square one."

Payne nodded. "And looking under the rock under the rock."

VII

[ONE]
2408 N. Mutter Street, Philadelphia
Sunday, November 1, 4:08 P.M.

Driving up North Mutter Street, a narrow one-way lane that ran through Kensington, Will Curtis thought that this godforsaken section of Philadelphia looked not only like time had forgotten it, but also like it had suffered curses worse than all the biblical plagues combined.

Lice, disease, death of firstborn, hail and fire . . . hell, it's all here and more.

Finding the row house at 2408 had been no problem whatsoever.

It's the only damn house standing in the entire 2400 block!

Curtis bumped the tires of the rented white Ford Freestar over the curb. He stopped the minivan opposite the house where a set of marble steps was all that remained of one row house, and threw the gearshift into park.

He was still sweating profusely despite having had the windows down to let the chilly November air flow inside. He dropped his head back against the top of the seat and let out a long sigh.

Never thought I'd get here.

He was only a little more than three miles from the Mays row house on Wilder Street. But after leaving the Mays house, he had barely made it six blocks down Dickinson Street before his stomach had twisted into a nasty knot.

Curtis wasn't sure if the cause of his distress was the chemotherapy treatments for his prostate cancer or his confrontation with Kendrik Mays. Or both.

While the physical exertion of tracking down the bastard in that basement had worn

327

him out, the mental aspects had taken a genuine toll on him, too. He'd been deeply disturbed by the filthy living conditions and by seeing that poor teenage girl being held captive in the basement and sexually abused.

Which of course had made him think of Wendy, and her being bound and attacked by that pervert John "JC" Nguyen.

Who now will never harm another.

He and Mays and all the others are in that corner of hell reserved for such miserable scum.

What had not bothered Will Curtis — either mentally or physically — was the actual killing of Kendrik. He'd found that shooting vile perverts troubled him less and less each time. Especially when he saw that eliminating them forever freed others — such as the young girl and Shauna Mays — from their awful abuse.

Whatever the cause of Curtis's distress, it was the effect that he was more concerned about right now.

And if he didn't do something fast, it was going to get ugly.

Speeding down Dickinson, he desperately looked for someplace that was open on a Sunday morning and would have a toilet he could use.

But in this residential stretch of Dickinson, there was no gas station, no fast-food restaurant.

Nothing!

He'd just about decided that he would have to take a chance and knock on the door of a random house when he saw something a block up on the right: a big red church.

Thank God!

Literally . . .

The church — he couldn't readily tell which denomination it was — had no parking lot, and there were no spaces along the curb available, so he nosed the minivan up on a basketball court at the rear of the building.

And then he awkwardly bolted for the church door with signage reading BAN-QUET ROOM. He passed a few parishioners, but no one appeared to give him a second thought.

He found two restrooms in the corner just inside that door.

Thank God, he thought again.

As he was leaving thirty minutes later, he saw a small crucifix and a collection jar by the door he'd come in. He reached into his pants pocket and pulled out his wad of cash, then put a twenty-dollar bill in the jar and crossed himself.

Once back in the minivan, he started to sweat heavily, then felt faint.

What the hell is going on?

He turned the van to head back up Passyunk Avenue and made it as far as the Geno's Cheesesteaks before feeling like he really was going to pass out. He found an open parking spot at the edge of a park across the street, and quickly pulled into it and shut off the engine.

He took a deep breath, inhaling the smell of cheesesteaks from Geno's. Then he exhaled slowly and decided he should close his eyes for a second.

He awoke four hours later.

Groggy and weak, it had taken him some time to get his bearings — where he was and how the hell he'd wound up parked near Geno's. But then it had all come back to him. As had, very curiously, he thought, his appetite.

Has to be the damned chemo.

They said it causes some really weird things to happen.

Shakily, he got out of the minivan and made his way across the street. At Geno's, he ordered his and Wendy's favorite — a provolone cheesesteak with extra grilled onions, a side of freedom fries, and a Coca-Cola with the crunchy pellet-size ice.

Will Curtis, having slurped the last of the

drink, now chewed on the tiny ice pellets as he looked at the run-down row house on Mutter. Clearly there once had been wall-to-wall row houses all along the block. But now only one house was still standing. Some ramshackle fencing — a mix of chain link and four-foot-high rotted wooden pickets spray-painted with gang graffiti — surrounded a few of the abandoned lots. The fenced lots held nothing more than weeds and trash, everything from piles of old car tires to a couple of discarded water heaters.

Curtis thought that the lone row house, two stories plus a basement that couldn't total fifteen hundred square feet altogether, looked like it could fall at any moment. Especially without the added support of the row houses that once had been on either side. The red brick of its front — tagged with gang graffiti — had a spiderweb of gaping cracks that ran from the sidewalk all the way up to its sagging roof.

The rusty white front door was visible through the upper half of an aluminum storm door, where the window glass was missing. The storm door was partly open and hung crookedly. To its left, the downstairs window barely held a battered air conditioner that looked as if it had been targeted for theft more than once.

Curtis thought it was odd, particularly in a neighborhood as rough as Kensington, that there were no burglar bars mounted over the windows and doors of the structure. Then he decided that the occupants likely could not afford the iron bars, and even if they could pay for them, there was probably nothing of real value inside to protect against theft.

Why bother?

There was a short flight of three marble steps from the narrow sidewalk up to the front door. The steps had been painted red long ago, and now the paint was faded and chipped. Someone had drawn on the steps with white chalk — and very recently, as there were two broken stalks of chalk lying next to the drawings.

The drawings clearly had been made by a child. They showed three stick people: a tall one, a medium-size one, and a small one that was maybe toddler size. The child had drawn the sky with a couple clouds and a disproportionately enormous sun. The sun's rays — a heavy series of chalk lines — were shining down on the three stick people.

Despite this squalor, the poor kid seems to have some sort of "sunny" optimism.

Or maybe it's a quiet despair, and the kid wishes those rays would shine on his family.

Well, if the chalk "family" is any indication, the

good news is that someone's in that house.

He took the top FedEx envelope from the stack on the dashboard and glanced at the name on its bill of lading: LEROI CHEATHAM.

Wonder if one of those larger stick figures is supposed to be LeRoi?

If it is LeRoi, the kid'll soon have one fewer stick figure to draw.

And maybe the other large stick figure can go collect a ten-grand reward.

Curtis remembered that Cheatham, a big eighteen-year-old with droopy eyes and a goatee, hadn't even completed middle school. The Wanted sheet inside the envelope stated that he was a fugitive from Megan's Law, having failed four months earlier to register as a convicted sex offender after enjoying an early release courtesy of the prison parole board. Unsurprisingly, it also stated that Cheatham had failed to maintain contact with his Pennsylvania State Parole Agent, an offense for which there was an additional warrant.

LeRoi had the habit of snorting bumps of crystal meth, then entertaining himself during the adrenaline rush that followed by raping the first female he could snatch off the street and drag into an alley or park.

He'd stupidly dragged his last known victim, the one who'd helped finally put him behind bars, back to his bedroom in the stand-alone row house on Mutter Street. The police found him there hours later, passed out and naked on the floor, after the fifteen-year-old victim had escaped and led them back to the address that was impossible to miss.

Curtis thought he detected movement in the house. He looked back, first to the artwork on the steps, then to the doors. The rusty white front door was swinging inward.

A very skinny black boy about five feet tall stepped into the opening. He looked to be ten, maybe twelve, and was drinking from a yellow plastic cup that covered most of his narrow face. He wore oversize khaki pants with the cuffs rolled up, a faded and stained navy sweatshirt, and dirty white sneakers.

His dark almond eyes darted in the direction of the white FedEx minivan parked across the street, but he didn't seem concerned about it. He then pushed on the storm door and stepped outside.

Could he be the medium-size stick person?

Which would mean there's maybe an adult and an infant inside?

The cup still to his face, the young boy

pushed the storm door shut, then sat down on the top step. Curtis saw that he'd situated himself so that his back was mostly to the FedEx minivan but he could still see it out of the corner of his eye. Then he put down the cup, picked up a piece of the broken chalk, and went back to working on his art project.

Curtis slipped the Glock .45-caliber pistol under his waistband behind his belt buckle, then stepped out of the minivan, carrying the envelope addressed to LeRoi Cheatham.

When he was halfway across the street, Curtis called out, "This is the Cheatham home, right, young man?"

The kid did not look up, but just shook his head. He kept drawing, his eye darting a couple times to follow the approaching deliveryman.

"That's nice art," Curtis said as he stopped at the steps. "Who are the people?"

The kid didn't reply.

Curtis pointed to the smallest figure. "Is the little one your baby brother?"

The kid shook his head as he scratched out another cloud.

"Your sister?" Curtis pursued.

He shook his head again. He tapped the stick figure with the chalk, then proudly declared, "It be me, muthafucka!"

What? Curtis thought.

He found himself somewhat shocked, first by the out-of-the-blue expletive from the young boy's mouth, and then by the disconnect between what he saw in the drawing and what the boy said it was supposed to be.

Weird. The kid has no sense of scale.

But wait . . . a twelve-year-old drawing stick figures?

He must really be backward.

Maybe some mental defect from his mother smoking crack when she was pregnant. Or from bad diet. Or just being dropped when he was a baby.

Maybe he's got that — what's it called? — Tourette's syndrome.

Then again, he probably hears people swearing all the time, and no one tells him not to do it himself.

The kid went back to drawing clouds.

"Nice clouds," Curtis said. "What's your name?"

"Michael," the boy said. Then he nodded once, as if making a point.

Michael? Well, at least something's normal around here. But I bet it's probably spelled weird, like Leroy is "LeRoi."

"Michael what?"

"Michael Floyd," he said, and again nodded once.

"Nice to meet you, Michael Floyd."

The kid suddenly pointed to the medium-size stick figure. "That be Mama," he said.

"Very nice. Who is the other one? Your father?"

The kid shook his head and said, "That my uncle."

"Does he live here?"

Michael shook his head again.

"What's your uncle's name?"

"Uncle LeRoi," he said, punctuating that with a nod.

Ding-ding! We have a winner! Will Curtis thought as he glanced at the door of the house. *And if he's in the "family" drawing . . .*

He said: "LeRoi Cheatham? Is he home?"

"Don't live here no more. Told you that, muthafucka."

"Is your mother home?"

He shook his head.

"You're home alone?"

He nodded.

"Look, Michael, I have this very important envelope for your uncle." Curtis held it out toward the boy, who turned to look at it. "See? Says right here, 'to LeRoi Cheatham.' Do you know where I can find him so he can have his mail?"

The boy nodded. "He at Demetri's."

"Can you tell me where that is" — Curtis motioned with the envelope — "so I can give him this?"

"It that way," Michael said, pointing with the chalk to the south.

"What's the address?"

He shrugged.

"Is it close? Can you show me?"

He shook his head, then said, "Don't walk there no more."

"Why not?"

"Gangstas. Muthafuckas hit me. Kick me."

He gets beat up?

"Nobody will bother you with me around, Michael."

The boy shook his head vigorously.

Well, he must've really gotten his ass kicked.

No surprise. Law of the jungle is to prey on the weak.

"Michael, listen to me. This envelope is very important. I'm sure your uncle would really want to have it."

Curtis pointed to the minivan.

"You want to ride in my new delivery vehicle? You show me where he lives, we'll give him the envelope, then I'll bring you back here."

The boy jerked his head to look across the street. His eyes grew wide. Then he turned back to Curtis and nodded enthusiastically.

"Yeah, muthafucka! I ride to LeRoi! I tired of drawing."

[TWO]
Executive Command Center
The Roundhouse
Eighth and Race Streets,
Philadelphia
Sunday, November 1, 4:29 P.M.

"Okay," Matt Payne said, rubbing his eyes, "let's bring up the last one, Kendrik Mays. Not that it's likely we'll find anything new on him yet. But in the spirit of leaving no stone under the stone unturned . . ."

Matt felt a brief vibration in his front pants pocket, and he reached in and pulled out his cell phone.

He looked at the screen. It read: "(2) TEXT MESSAGES FROM AMANDA LAW."

"Oh, shit!" he said aloud. Then he thought, *Two? I never felt the damn phone vibrate before.*

As he started thumbing the phone to read the texts, he saw the signal-strength icon.

Not even one goddamn nanobit or -byte or whatever of signal!

He looked at Kerry Rapier and said, "Is it just me, or is the cell service in here worthless?"

"Just you, Marshal," Rapier said with a straight face.

Harris snorted, then said, "My signal reception's lousy, too, Matt."

Payne eyed Rapier, who smiled back.

"Seriously," Rapier then added, "it's ironic that we have some four million bucks' worth of high-tech commo equipment in here but, except for over there by the window, we can't get decent cell service." He paused, then added: "If it's any consolation — as in, misery loves company — I heard the top guy at AT&T couldn't get a signal in his Hops Haus Tower penthouse. So he personally ordered that a cellular antenna be added on the roof of the building — and he still couldn't get a reliable connection!"

Payne shook his head.

"Gotta love technology," he said, his eyes falling to his phone's screen. The text message, which had a time stamp of 2:45 P.M., read:

```
AMANDA LAW

HEY, BABY!

SORRY FOR THE TONE OF MY LAST
MESSAGE.

I KNOW YOU HAVE A JOB TO DO.
I WAS JUST CAUGHT OFF GUARD BY
THE MAYOR'S ANNOUNCEMENT.

I HOPE YOUR SILENCE IS BECAUSE
YOU'RE BUSY — NOT BECAUSE YOU'RE
UPSET WITH ME.

XOXO -A
```

Payne felt his throat tighten.
What a wonderful woman.
All I had to do was shoot back, "Sorry, I'll make it up to you" — or something.
But, being a cad, I didn't. And still she sends this.
I damn sure don't deserve her . . .
Then he scrolled to her most recent text message:

```
AMANDA LAW

SORRY TO BOTHER YOU AGAIN,
BABY.
```

```
THINK YOU MIGHT GET A BREAK?
MAYBE DINNER?

WOULD LOVE TO SEE YOU, IF ONLY
FOR A MOMENT.

I HAVE TO RUN BY THE HOSPITAL
BUT WILL BE BACK BY 6 TO LET
OUT LUNA.

HOPE YOUR DAY IS GOING AS WELL
AS IT CAN!

XOXO -A
```

Damn, it's nice to have someone like her to look forward to after a day like this.

Hope I don't manage to fuck up this relationship.

Matt had a mental image from the previous night of Amanda walking completely naked toward the master bath, her thick ponytail of wavy blond hair bouncing as her toned, athletic body floated fluidly across the room.

What a goddess. Then he grinned at the thought of a reply: *"Love to see you too, baby — starkers!"*

He buried his face in both hands, rubbing his eyes again. As he did so, he felt the stubble on his face.

And I do need a break, if only for a shave and bath.

He thumbed the REPLY key, then typed out:

```
HEY, SWEETIE . . .

I AM REALLY SORRY. I GOT YOUR
FIRST MESSAGE RIGHT AS CARLUCCI
WAS BLOWING HIS CORK. I MEANT
TO REPLY . . . BUT FORGOT. I'M
SORRY. REALLY.

AND . . . THERE WASN'T TIME BE-
FORE CARLUCCI WENT ON THE NEWS
TO LET YOU KNOW ABOUT MY HEAD-
ING UP THE TASK FORCE — WHICH
RIGHT NOW IS JUST ME, TONY
& KERRY, THE ECC TECH. SOME
FORCE, HUH? WORSE, WE'VE MADE
NO PROGRESS. JUST KEEPING UP
WITH THE BODY COUNT HAS BEEN
CHALLENGING ENOUGH.

I'LL SEE IF I CAN MAKE A BREAK
BY 6. FIRST NEED A SHAVE &
SHOWER.

BE CAREFUL OUT THERE!
```

He reread what he'd written, hit SEND, then stuck the phone back in his pocket.

Harris, trying to stifle a yawn, was saying, "Even as much as Howard probably reamed those guys in the forensics lab, I doubt they've had time to pull anything off Kendrik Mays yet."

Payne looked at him — noticing that he, too, had a face dark with a five-o'clock shadow — and nodded.

"Number eighteen coming up," Kerry Rapier said.

The main bank of monitors then showed an image of Kendrik Mays on the blood-soaked carpet on the sidewalk at Francis Fuller's Old City office building. Then an inset image popped up. It was his Wanted sheet mug shot, which showed an angry young man with foul-looking black dreadlocks and a full black beard that was matted. It was not difficult to see his nasty stubs of teeth and bad gums, both severely eroded by the caustic chemicals used in the manufacturing of crystal meth.

The bottom right-hand corner ID stamp read:

Richard Saunders Holdings/Lex Talionis
Third & Arch
1241 hours, 01 Nov

The text box read:

Name: Kendrik LeShawn MAYS

Description: Black male, age 20, 5'9",
200 lbs.

L.K.A.: 2620 Wilder St, Phila.

Priors Arrests: 8 total: possession of
marijuana (7); possession with intent to
distribute Methamphetamine (3); Conviction of and time served for Involuntary
deviant sexual intercourse & rape of an
unconscious or unaware person (1).

Call Received: 01 Nov, 1230 hours.

Cause of Death: GUNSHOT to head (99
percent probability).

Case No.: 2010-81-039614-POP-N-DROP

Notes: Fugitive. Shauna MAYS, mother
of deceased, stated in interview that he
was killed by SNU in basement of L.K.A.
She described SNU as a skinny white
male approximately her age (40), and suggested his motive was that someone in
his family may have been robbed or raped
by Kendrik Mays. Assailant left Wanted
sheet with body. Body transported to Lex
Talionis, Old City.

"Well, no surprise. No SNU number yet," Payne said. "And even if it was our doer, all we'd know is that he's added another bad guy to his exclusive death club. We'd still be no closer to figuring out who the hell he is."

Then Payne glanced back at the image and saw that 2620 WILDER ST was blinking.

"That what I think it is, Kerry?"

Corporal Kerry Rapier said, "I'll bet dollars to doughnuts that we're now getting a live feed coming in from the Mays crime scene."

Rapier typed a couple commands on the keyboard, then clicked on the blinking address with the Colt .45 Officer's Model cursor. After the pistol fired and smoked, the big-screen image of Kendrik Mays returned to monitor eighteen. Then two new images appeared on the main bank of monitors, which Rapier had turned to split-screen mode.

The top row of three monitors had a stationary digital image of the exterior of the Mays house. In the bottom right-hand corner was a white orb that contained the image's numerical designation, "1a." Next to that, a text box read: 2620 WILDER STREET — EXTERIOR.

The middle and bottom rows of monitors — each with a black "1b" in a white orb next to the text 2620 WILDER STREET — INTE-RIOR — displayed the feed from a portable digital video camera. The shaky image was mostly black as the camera's lone beam of light pierced a circle in the darkness, light-ing up bits and pieces of the trashed house.

"My God!" Payne said. "It looks as if they're going down into some hellish black hole."

Harris said, "Yeah, like out of a horror movie."

The unseen technician who carried the camera was carefully walking down a flight of unstable wooden steps. As he went, the beam of light showed busted-up Sheetrock and exposed wooden studs on the wall. Then, when the technician was almost to the bottom of the stairs, the lens caught im-ages of roaches and a black rat scattering.

"Unbelievable," Payne said.

Then the room began to fill with more ar-tificial light, and when the tech panned the camera back to the wooden steps, another tech could be seen slowly descending. He wore blue jeans, a light blue T-shirt with a representation of the Crime Scene Unit patch — a cartoon Sherlock Holmes and basset hound sniffing the Philly skyline — on its left chest, and transparent blue plastic booties and tan-colored synthetic polymer gloves. A white surgical mask covered his nose and mouth. He carried a pair of telescopic lightpole stands — each of which had two halogen floodlamps burning brightly at the top and a power cord snaking back up the steps — and a telescopic tripod.

The tech reached the bottom of the steps. He then set up the stands at opposite ends of the basement, adjusting the brilliant floodlamps so that the entire room was more or less evenly lit. Next he set up the tripod, and the tech with the camera walked to it. The camera image shook, then became stabilized as it was mounted on the tripod. The camera's lens was adjusted so that the entire room was visible.

The brilliant halogen lights clearly showed all the incredible filth. There were clothes scattered everywhere, pile after pile of pants and shirts and more, and stacks of suitcases. The walls were mostly bare wooden studs.

And in the middle of it all: a stack of wooden pallets with a blood-soaked, torn mattress on top. On the wall behind it, the exposed brick and the wooden studs were covered in blood and brain splatter that resembled some sort of morbid Rorschach inkblot test.

"Well, there's where Kendrik Mays went off to meet his maker," Harris said.

"More like to meet Satan," Payne said, shaking his head out of disgust. "Though this place looks like hell on earth. No wonder Shauna Mays looked and smelled so damn awful."

"Someone busted all the Sheetrock off the walls," Rapier said.

"Probably to pull out the electrical wiring," Harris said. "Pretty common if it's copper wiring. And they also rip the copper from air-conditioning units to sell it as scrap."

Payne then remembered thinking, after Shauna Mays had said crack houses didn't have clocks, that everything not nailed down got sold for drug money.

And here's proof that even things that are nailed down get hocked.

Unbelievable. . . .

"And all the suitcases and clothes?" Rapier asked.

"From home invasions," Harris said. "Those wheeled suitcases make it easier to haul off all the loot. The clothes cover up whatever they stole, and they're easy to sell, too."

"They don't sell the suitcases?"

"Some are sold, some reused. Who knows about the rest. Maybe it's hard to hock them if they have someone's name written on them in Magic Marker." Harris shrugged. "Hell if

I know. Hard to say what dopeheads think — or don't think, as the case may be."

Harris then pointed to a far corner of the basement. "Is that what I think it is?"

"A shit bucket," Payne said disgustedly.

The first tech, who had carried the video camera down, came into the frame. He held a professional Nikon digital camera with a squat zoom lens and an enormous flash strobe.

They watched as he began putting out the four-inch-high inverted-V evidence markers. The first yellow plastic marker bore the black numeral "01." It was placed in the middle of the bloody mattress, next to a pair of torn women's panties. He then raised the Nikon to his eye and took a series of four photographs of the panties and marker, overlapping the angles of the shots so that later a computer could create a three-dimensional rendering of the evidence.

A couple minutes later, after repeating the process with three other markers, the tech bent over in a corner of the basement. He placed an inverted-V marker bearing the numeral "05" next to a shiny black metal object that was on a dirt-encrusted, sweat-stained T-shirt.

"It's a pistol," Kerry Rapier said.

The tech raised the camera and popped

four overlapping images of the pistol.

Then he reached down with his gloved hand and carefully picked it up.

Now they had a better view of it on the TV monitor.

"A snub-nosed revolver," Rapier added. "Looks like maybe an S&W Model 49?"

"Uh-uh," Payne said, shaking his head. "The Bodyguard has a hammer shroud. And that hammer is not only exposed, it's cocked back."

"Then it's a Chief's Special," Rapier said with more conviction. "At least both are .38 caliber."

"Yeah," Payne said absently.

They watched as the tech, with what obviously was practiced skill, put the thumb of his gloved right hand on the knurled back of the hammer and, keeping a steady pressure with the thumb, squeezed the trigger with his index finger. The released hammer rotated forward — but slowly, the pressure from the thumb preventing it from falling fast enough to fire off a possible live round.

Then he thumbed the release that allowed the cylinder to swing open and carefully removed the round that had been under the hammer. It was a live one. He shot another series of four photographs of the pistol in that position. Then he extracted all the bullets from the cylinder — three spent rounds and two live ones — and photographed them. He threaded a plastic zip tie through the barrel and clasped it in such a way that it was visually obvious that the gun could not be fired, either accidentally or on purpose. Finally, he put the fired and live rounds in a clear plastic evidence bag, put the pistol in a separate clear bag, and labeled both bags.

Payne sighed.

"Okay, I've seen enough," he said. "It will take some time for them to process all of that hellhole."

"And then even more time to begin updating these master case files with the information and images," Rapier said.

After a moment, Rapier added, "What do you think are the odds of that being the doer's weapon?"

Payne shrugged.

"Who the hell knows, Kerry. You heard Kendrik's mother say in the interview that the gunshot made a big 'boom.' Arguably, a .45 is a helluva lot more of a 'boom' than a .38 — a .38's more like a 'bang.' But what does she know? A damned cork popgun would probably sound like a boom to her." He looked at the video feed of the basement. "Maybe there's a .38 embedded in the wall there with Kendrik's blood splatter. Or maybe it's a .45-cal. round, which could bring us back to our mystery shooter" — he looked at his notes — "good ol' SNU 2010-56-9280, who now has, at last known count, seven notches on his gun. But, if there is a .38 in the wall, maybe there's another doer's fingerprints on that snub-nosed Smith and Wesson. Which means another candidate for Task Force Operation Clean Sweep. And on and on. Until we get lab results, we're basically in hurry-up-and-wait mode."

"And we're at least an hour away from getting a response from IAFIS on the two prints taken off Reggie Jones."

As Payne looked at him and nodded, he felt his cell phone vibrating. He pulled it from his pants pocket, read the caller ID on the screen, and said aloud, "Wonder what's on the Black Buddha's mind?"

He put the phone to his head and said, "Boss, I sure as hell hope you're not calling for a progress report on Task Force Operation Clean Sweep. Because we've yet to make any ground."

"Matthew," Jason Washington said, "we just got a call from the Twenty-sixth District. More bodies were found a little over an hour ago. Three dead."

"Jesus! More pop-and-drops? Wait — the

Twenty-sixth? That's north of here, not Old City."

That news caused Harris and Rapier to look at Payne curiously.

"No, they're not pop-and-drops in Old City," Washington said. "In fact, quite interestingly, there's no obvious cause of death at all with two of them. They say the third looks like he succumbed to blunt trauma. May or may not be a connection with your doer, but because Carlucci says your Op Clean Sweep gets priority, you are hereby officially in the loop."

"Where's the scene, Jason?"

Payne pulled out his notepad, flipped to a clean page, and wrote "Jefferson & Mascher" on it.

"On our way," he said. "Thanks."

[THREE]
2408 N. Mutter Street, Philadelphia
Sunday, November 1, 4:35 P.M.

Michael Floyd, sitting up in the front passenger seat of the Ford Freestar, was grinning from ear to ear under the brim of Will

Curtis's grease-smeared FedEx cap.

Curtis steered the minivan off the curb. Because Mutter was a one-way street northbound, he headed for the next street up, Cumberland.

"No! No!" Michael began shouting.

Will slammed on the brakes, forcing them both against the shoulder straps of their seat belts. The FedEx cap flew off Michael's head and landed on the dashboard.

Michael pointed over his shoulder and said, "That way."

Curtis pointed out the windshield. "This street is one-way."

Michael looked at him with an expression that suggested the statement was meaningless to him.

"He live that way!" Michael then said, pointing south again.

Well, Curtis thought, *he probably only knows how to get there by walking.*

If I drive around until I find a street that has southbound traffic, he may not have the first idea where he is.

Oh, hell. "This is a one-way street, Officer? But I was only going one way."

Will Curtis drove up on the sidewalk, checked his mirror for traffic, then cut the steering wheel hard left to make a U-turn. He had to back up once to make the turn on the narrow street.

Curtis was somewhat surprised that they'd had no trouble driving the wrong way down Mutter, then the wrong way down Colona Street. And at Mascher Street, he was relieved to find that it was a one-way going the right direction, south. But then, a block later, at Susquehanna Avenue, they reached a dead end.

They were looking at a park.

Curtis turned to his navigator, who was pointing straight.

"There," Michael said.

"Through the park?" Curtis said, incredulous. "Oh, for chrissake!"

"That way!" Michael said.

Well, hell, that's the way he walks.

Then that's the way we'll drive.

Curtis checked for traffic, then drove across Susquehanna Avenue and hopped the curb. There was a concrete walkway crisscrossing the park, and he followed it.

Michael Floyd seemed to be thoroughly enjoying the drive. He scanned the park as they cut across it. About three-quarters through, he suddenly pointed to a small stand of maple trees.

"Gangstas," he said.

Curtis looked. There in the maples' shadows were four or five tough-looking teenage boys, hoodlums in baggy jeans and hoodie sweatshirts and sneakers.

Those must be the ones who beat him.

He expected Michael to recoil, or at least hide, but the next thing he knew the kid was rolling down his window and throwing the bird with both fists at the punks.

Then Michael Floyd yelled at the top of his lungs, "Fuck you, gangsta muthafuckas!"

Now what the hell else is going to happen? Will Curtis thought.

That Tourette's, if that's what it is, is going to get him killed. . . .

He accelerated, not waiting to find out if there would be any gunshots from the gangsta muthafuckas.

At the far end of the park he picked up Mascher again and, following Michael's pointing, drove south another nine blocks. Crossing Oxford, Curtis noticed that the block on his left, south of Oxford, was somewhat like the 2400 block of Mutter Street — basically barren but for a clump of the last remaining row houses.

"There," Michael said, pointing to the end of the block.

Will Curtis followed the direction of Michael's finger and saw that there were five houses altogether on the southwest corner of the block.

He also saw that there were police squad cars everywhere.

"*There?*" Will Curtis repeated.

He stood on the brakes and studied the scene.

He saw other emergency vehicles, including a big van with CRIME SCENE UNIT lettered on its side, and a bunch of heavy equipment — a tall demolition crane, a big Caterpillar bulldozer, and heavy-duty dump trucks.

"Wow!" Michael said, pointing at them.

"What the hell?" Will said aloud.

Ahead at the next intersection, Jefferson Street, was a squad car, its every exterior light flashing white or red or blue. It was parked at an angle to force traffic onto Jefferson and away from the other emergency vehicles. A policeman in uniform was beside it directing traffic. He signaled for the FedEx van to keep moving down the street toward him.

"Don't like no cop," Michael said. "LeRoi say cop bad news."

Curtis looked at him.

No surprise there.

And no surprise that generation after generation in the ghetto grows up hating cops — it's all they know, all they're taught.

Then Will realized he hadn't considered

what he would do with Michael if they actually caught up with LeRoi.

I can't let him see me take LeRoi out. Michael's done nothing to deserve that.

The only lesson he needs to learn from this is: You do bad, you pay a bad price.

Shit. I'll have to figure that out.

Will Curtis reached over, grabbed the FedEx cap from the dashboard, and put it on the boy's head.

"That'll keep you hidden from the cop, Michael."

Michael considered that, then nodded once.

As they rolled up to the intersection, the traffic cop waved for the van to take the turn. Curtis did so, and avoided making any eye contact.

Michael suddenly yelled: "Don't like no cop, muthafucka!"

"Michael!" Curtis barked.

He checked his mirror and saw the cop look at the van, but only for a second before he turned back to directing traffic.

If the cop heard that, probably wasn't the first time.

At least the kid didn't throw him the bird, too.

Curtis, his heart beating fast, shook his head.

That was close. . . .

He looked over at Michael, who now was pointing down Jefferson to the next intersection, Hancock Street.

"There LeRoi house!" he said, indicating the boarded-up row house on the corner. "Got wood window."

And just beyond the house, Curtis saw someone peer out from around the corner.

He drove on, and as they came to the corner, Curtis saw that there was more than one person. Standing in an alleyway behind the boarded-up row house were three young black men, including a great big one with droopy eyes and a trimmed goatee.

"And there LeRoi!" Michael said excitedly.

Well, I'll be damned.

He's been standing and watching those cops work that scene back there. Just hiding in plain sight.

And the cops don't have any idea that there's a fugitive living just fifty yards away.

But then, how could they? So damned many punks in this city, there's no way to keep track of them all.

Michael suddenly moved quickly, rolling down his window again. He stuck out his head, the hat hitting the top of the car's frame and falling to the floorboard.

"Lookit me, LeRoi!" Michael shouted, pumping his right fist. "I be *riding,* muthafucka!"

LeRoi Cheatham was momentarily caught completely off guard. He did not immediately know how to react to the sight of his twelve-year-old nephew hanging out of a FedEx delivery vehicle and yelling his name at the top of his lungs. Especially with who the hell knew how many cops only a block or so away.

But the two other teenage punks standing with LeRoi were more quick-witted. In a flash, they hauled ass across Hancock Street and disappeared into a wall of huge, thick bushes that had grown wild on the deserted lot.

Curtis saw LeRoi watching his buddies run away. Then LeRoi looked back at the van, then back to the bushes. As LeRoi started to cross Hancock to follow his buddies, Curtis held up the big square envelope to the windshield and tried to mime that it was intended for him.

It didn't work. LeRoi kept walking.

"Michael," Curtis said as he turned the minivan onto Hancock and drove up on the cracked sidewalk, "tell your uncle he's got a package."

Michael yelled, "You gots a package, LeRoi!"

LeRoi slowed and warily looked over his shoulder.

Curtis motioned again with the envelope, stopping the minivan at the alleyway and putting it in park. He rolled down his window and with a raised voice said, "This is my last try to find you. You don't sign for it, the check gets sent back today!"

At the mention of money, the expression on LeRoi's face changed.

As LeRoi Cheatham started back toward the alley, Curtis felt for his Glock under his shirt, then opened the driver's door. He walked around to Michael's door and opened it.

"What up?" Michael said.

Curtis took a ten-dollar bill from his wad of cash and showed it to Michael as he watched LeRoi coming closer.

"You know what a lookout is?" Curtis asked.

"For cops?" Michael said. He nodded. "Yeah. LeRoi pay me to say if I see one."

"Right," Curtis said, folding the ten-spot and handing it to the kid. "Go stand around the corner and let me know if any cop comes this way. I will come tell you when we're finished here."

Michael nodded once, took the money, and ran back to Jefferson Street.

Will Curtis turned in time to see LeRoi Cheatham come around the front of the minivan.

"What this shit about a check?" LeRoi said, looking at him hard.

Those are some seriously bloodshot eyes, Curtis thought.

Wonder what he's on?

"You're LeRoi Cheatham, right?"

"Damn right." He nodded his head once.

So that's where Michael got that nod from.

"Need to see some government ID. . . ."

"*Shit,* man," he said, staring at Curtis with a look of disgust. Then he turned and spat behind him into the alley. He turned back and, as he began digging in the front pocket of his pants, said, "Just gimme my damn check."

Curtis remembered what he had thought when Shauna Mays realized there was no money in the envelope. This time, as Curtis pulled the Glock from his waistband and aimed it at LeRoi's chest, he said it.

"Sure. Here's your reality check."

Then he squeezed the trigger. Twice.

LeRoi fell backward into the alleyway.

Not thirty seconds after that, Michael Floyd came running back and called out, "Cop!"

After putting the warm pistol back under his shirt, Curtis walked to intercept him. He tore open the envelope and pulled out LeRoi's Wanted sheet.

Michael looked around.

"Who got shot?" he asked. "Where LeRoi?"

"In the alley," Curtis said. "But don't go in there."

Curtis put the Wanted sheet on the van window, then took his FedEx ballpoint pen and wrote "Lex Talionis, Third & Arch, Old City, $10,000 reward" on the back. He handed the sheet to Michael.

"Give this to your mother. And do what the cops say. Cops are good. They will get you back home. Okay?"

Michael Floyd, looking confused, took the sheet and stared at the mug shot of his Uncle LeRoi. After a moment, he pointed to the Last Known Address.

"My house," he said.

"Right, Michael. That's from when LeRoi lived there. That sheet says he did very bad things. And when you're bad, you have to be punished." Curtis paused to let that sink in.

"That what Mama said." He was still looking at the sheet. "That why LeRoi live here."

"You be good, Michael."

Michael Floyd looked up at Will Curtis, then finally shrugged and nodded once.

As Will Curtis drove two blocks north, he heard sirens coming from the vicinity of where LeRoi Cheatham lay dead.

His pulse racing, he quickly stopped the minivan and got out. He peeled off the magnet-backed FedEx signs from both front doors, then hid them under the floor mat in the rear cargo area. Back in the car, he pulled on his denim jacket to cover his FedEx uniform shirt, buttoning it up as he drove.

He turned left on Cecil Moore Avenue and, still hearing sirens, had another idea. After two blocks, he turned down Second Avenue and followed it five blocks to where Second fed into the new Schmidt's Brewery entertainment complex.

As calmly as possible, Curtis pulled the minivan into the line of other cars waiting at a red traffic light to enter a parking garage.

The traffic light turned green. But the brake lights of the vehicles in line stayed lit as their drivers waited for a police car — an unmarked gray Ford sedan with its emergency lights flashing from behind the top of the windshield — to come flying past, its horn honking a warning.

Five minutes later, Will Curtis had parked the minivan in an open slot between a pair of full-size SUVs and begun walking toward the complex's multiscreen movie theater.

[FOUR]
S. Sixtieth and Catharine Streets, Philadelphia
Sunday, November 1, 5:01 P.M.

A frustrated H. Rapp Badde, Jr., at the wheel of the black Range Rover registered to his Urban Venture Fund, squealed its tires as he pulled a fast U-turn on Sixtieth and parked at the curb in front of the rented row house that served as his West Philly campaign headquarters.

It took for damn ever to get here — and I really don't want to be here.

City Councilman Badde tried to keep at least two levels of separation from those who worked in his various campaign offices. The separation afforded him a godlike persona, so that when he finally went to the offices and met with his worker bees, he was looked upon as the all-powerful one coming down from the holy temple that was Philadelphia City Hall.

More important, though, the levels of separation gave the ass-covering politician a buffer for when something invariably went sour. Badde had plausible deniability that he had knowledge of any lower-level act, which could easily and credibly be blamed on "a well-meaning but unfortunately overzealous campaign volunteer."

Ever wary, he knew that coming to the campaign headquarters effectively removed that buffer and that he had to be careful. The last thing he wanted to do was face the media's questions of "What did you know, and when did you know it?"

Yet when Roger Wynne called — "You need to get here as soon as possible to see what's happened and deal with this Kareem situation before it blows up in our faces" — he was really left with no option.

He couldn't get across town fast enough.

But just getting out of the Hops Haus Tower had turned into one helluva challenge.

First, he'd had to try convincing Janelle Harper that she hadn't heard anyone screaming over his cell phone about somebody getting killed, and that he wasn't rushing off to see his wife or another woman.

He'd been completely unsuccessful in persuading her on either count.

Then, to reach his Range Rover, he'd had to wait an eternity for one of the three elevators to ride down to the multilevel parking garage in the belly of the building. Then he had to drive the luxury SUV around and around, circling seemingly forever to reach street level. And then he'd had to wait for the metal overhead security door to slowly *clank-clank-clank* up and out of the way.

The sign affixed to the door told drivers to wait until the door was completely raised before exiting. But Badde, after some smug self-congratulating, had used the maddeningly long wait to hit the lever that caused the air suspension to lower the vehicle's height. And as soon as the SUV barely had cleared the rubber gasket on the door's bottom lip, he floored the accelerator pedal.

Only then to have to hit the brakes for a variety of other delays.

Driving from the far eastern side of Philly — the Delaware River was only blocks from the Hops Haus complex — to far West Philly was only a matter of five or so miles. But it was a Sunday. And that meant that Sunday drivers were out — and in no particular hurry. It also meant that there were Sunday pedestrians, among them tourists to the City of Brotherly Love who apparently were unclear on the concept of using crosswalks at the appropriate times.

Badde had felt compelled to help educate them all and freely laid on the Range Rover's very loud "by appointment to Her Majesty the Queen" British horn.

The horn did not help after he picked up the Vine Street Expressway and immediately hit stop-and-go traffic due to road construction. But crawling along had given him time to think before speaking privately with Roger Wynne.

As far as Badde was concerned, the "Kareem Abdul-Qaadir/Kenny Jones situation" had kicked into damn high gear very early that morning when Kenny had called his Go To Hell phone and tried extorting him for thirty grand.

Then it became even more dire when Kenny had called just after noontime, screaming that Reggie had been killed.

After Jan Harper had heard that, Rapp had gone out on the condo's balcony with his Go To Hell phone and slid the door shut.

He'd said, "Okay, Kenny. Tell me what's going on."

"Reggie's dead!" he'd repeated.

"You made that perfectly clear the first time. How?"

"Jack called and said that the police came by the house. He had to go down to wherever they take killed people —"

"The Medical Examiner's Office," Badde had provided.

"— yeah, that was it. He had to go down, say if it was Reggie or not. It was. And Jack said he'd been beat up really bad. And choked to death."

"I'm sorry, Kenny," Badde said, trying to sound like he meant it.

"And now they gonna come after me, man!"

"Listen to me, Kenny —"

"Rapp, they gonna do the same to me!"

"Kenny —"

"I need that money bad, man! And now it's thirty-five."

Thirty-five thousand dollars? Badde had thought. *Damn!*

"I thought you said it was thirty large!"

"It was. Now they added more interest. And a penalty for having to deal with Reggie."

"Where are you now?"

"Uh, in West Philly."

"How soon do you need the money?"

"Like yesterday?"

Badde had taken a long time to consider all that, then he'd said, "Listen to me carefully, Kenny. I'll start working on the money. You stay there out of sight."

And that's when Badde had tried to call Roger Wynne. He planned to tell Wynne to make sure Kenny stayed in the row house basement. But he'd been routed to Wynne's voice mail, and instead left a terse message: "Call me immediately. Extremely important."

And then Badde had called an old acquaintance, saying he knew the whereabouts of a fugitive who could easily be grabbed and asking if maybe the acquaintance had a friend who might be interested in making ten grand for turning in the bastard.

The Vine traffic finally cleared at the Schuylkill Expressway, which Badde followed to Walnut Street. He took Walnut through the heart of the University of Pennsylvania campus — honking when delayed by strolling students — and all the way out to South Sixtieth. There he turned down Sixtieth and followed it the fourteen blocks to where it intersected with Catharine Street.

His West Philly campaign headquarters was on the northeast corner of the intersection, directly facing the funeral home across the street.

The row houses in this neighborhood were fairly large — four- and five-bedroom, with three levels totaling up to three thousand square feet. They were set far back from the wide two-way street and tree-lined sidewalk, each with a concrete walk that had two tiers of steps leading up to a wooden front porch. The homes were fairly nicely maintained, their yards mostly kept trimmed.

When Badde shut off the engine and looked to the campaign house, he saw that Roger Wynne was already coming down the first tier of steps of the long walkway. Nailed to the porch railing behind him was a campaign poster: MOVING PHILLY FORWARD — VOTE RAPP BADDE FOR CITY COUNCIL.

Wynne — a short, pudgy, mostly bald thirty-year-old who wore blue jeans, a tan cardigan sweater over a black T-shirt, and tan open-toe sandals with black socks — had a look of concern as he puffed heavily on the pipe he held in his left fist.

Badde thought that he could easily see Wynne teaching a political science course at the University of Pennsylvania — which Wynne had done until tiring of the struggle for tenure and going to work for Rapp Badde as a "political advisor" while continuing to teach part-time at U of P. Badde was not nearly as impressed with Wynne as Wynne was with himself, but felt that he served some purpose in helping Rapp get legitimate votes — and keeping any questionable ones quiet.

Wynne pulled the pipe from his teeth as he offered Badde his hand.

"Good to see you, Rapp," he said. "Sorry to make you come all the way out here."

Badde shook the hand and said, "Miserable damn day to be out driving. But you said it was important."

Wynne nodded as he took two heavy puffs of his pipe. "It'll be better if I show you."

Badde followed him down the sidewalk to the side of the house along Catharine Street. There was a weathered wooden door with another Badde campaign poster on it. Badde knew that this was the separate entrance to the basement; another was inside the house, under the stairwell that led to the upper floor.

Wynne unlocked the door, went inside, and flipped on a light switch. Badde followed — and immediately saw what Wynne wanted him to see firsthand.

The basement, which Kenny had set up as his combination bedroom and office, was completely trashed. The mattress was overturned. The old wooden desk was up on its side. And all three of the rusty and battered metal four-drawer filing cabinets had been ransacked. Some of the drawers still contained papers and folders, but most were empty.

"When the hell did this happen?" Badde asked.

Wynne puffed on his pipe once, then exhaled smoke as he said, "Sometime in the last twenty-four hours. It was okay after lunch yesterday when I was down here."

"You don't know exactly when? This had to have made one helluva racket."

"I told you on the phone that I didn't get back here until after I got your voice mail. That's why there was the delay."

He looked at Badde and saw anger.

Roger Wynne took two hard puffs on his pipe.

Then he got mad, too.

"What the hell, Rapp? Last night was Halloween, and there was a great party at U of P. I live here. I'm not a prisoner. Nor am I a goddamn warden, watching that moron Kareem. I never liked the idea of him being here when you first forced him on me. But you said it was an important political favor and that he'd be fine in the basement. And I reluctantly agreed. Which, of course, I obviously now regret."

Roger Wynne then made a sweeping gesture at the destroyed room. "How the hell was I supposed to know this was going to happen?"

Badde glanced at him, then looked back at the destruction and sighed audibly.

"Okay, Roger, besides the obvious, what's the damage?" He pointed at the filing cabinets. "What was in them?"

"Mostly Kareem's logs, the lists of all the voters he collected. And he also had many of their absentee-voter cards or forms. I was dumbfounded how he could collect so many. He wouldn't tell me. He just showed them to me and said it was because he was a hard worker and you were going to reward him for that."

Badde raised his eyebrows at the word "reward."

I do have a reward in mind for you, Kenny.
Just not the one you're probably expecting.

Wynne continued: "So, I, uh, came down here one day while he was out 'canvassing' for the so-called Forgotten Voters Initiative. I had a little look around and found all the records. In addition to going door to door, he'd gone to retirement homes and signed up voters en masse. Then he'd moved on to nursing homes."

Badde already knew this, of course, but

replied, "Really? Well, you have to give him credit for thinking outside of the box."

Badde walked over and pulled an official-looking governmental form from one of the metal file drawers. The letterhead had the familiar crest of the City of Philadelphia and:

CITY COMMISSIONERS
COUNTY BOARD OF ELECTIONS
ROOM 142, CITY HALL
PHILADELPHIA, PA 19107
215-686-3469 215-686-3943

The first line of the sheet read: "Absentee Ballot Application & Requirements."

He read farther down and saw the requirements for "Alternative Ballots": *If you are a registered voter who is disabled or age sixty-five or older AND who is assigned to an inaccessible polling place, you are qualified to vote using an Alternative Ballot.*

Badde looked up at Wynne and said, "And I do give the bastard credit. He found groups of voters who probably really had been forgotten by the system. Well . . . some, anyway."

Wynne shrugged and went on: "Then,

some weeks back, Harvey Wilson across the street —"

Badde shook his head at first, but then he recognized the name: "The mortician?"

Wynne nodded. "He came banging on the front door. Said he'd caught Kenny in his office at the funeral home."

"What the hell was he stealing? Drugs? Do they even have drugs?"

Wynne shook his head. "No drugs. And Wilson said he wasn't really stealing any-thing, per se. At least nothing of real value to Wilson, as they were just records. But Wilson didn't like the idea of Kenny just making himself at home in his office, and told me to keep him the hell away."

"So, what was Kenny doing?"

"He got caught going through their files."

"Why?"

"He was methodically copying all the names and addresses of Wilson's recent clients."

"Identity theft of the dead?"

Wynne nodded. "Not that any of them were about to complain. If he could apply for the absentee-voter cards before the city got notice that these people were dead — and you know how muddled and long that kind of bureaucratic process can be — then he'd have even more quiet voters."

Badde grinned. "Smart. Never would've expected that from the dimwit."

Wynne nodded. "Yeah. And for all his faults — and there were many — Kareem was a stickler for detail. Maybe it was because he had so much time on his hands. He logged and filed everything."

Badde nodded toward the upturned filing cabinets.

"And took it all with him," he said.

"Stating the obvious, as long as those records were in there, and you already had been elected to office —"

Badde, affecting a bit of a French accent, authoritatively said, "It would have been *faint plea,* of course."

Wynne cocked his head as he puffed his pipe.

"A what?" Wynne said.

"You know, a *faint plea* — the French saying for 'the cow is out of the barn,' or even 'you can't get the toothpaste back in the tube.' It's a done deal, and you can't go back."

"You mean *fait accompli,*" Wynne said. "An accomplished fact."

"That's it," Badde said.

Wynne noticed that Badde was wholly unembarrassed by the correction.

"Anyway," Wynne said, "if someone pulls those forms down at City Hall, or wherever the hell they're warehoused, they're going to see a lot of the same signatures at the same mailing addresses."

They exchanged a long glance.

"And then," Wynne went on, "it's not *fait accompli,* because if there's voter fraud, the courts get involved. And then . . ."

Badde nodded slowly at the implication.

He said: "And you think Kenny, Kareem, whatever the fuck you want to call him, has the forms?"

"As your political advisor, I think it's important that we proceed as if he does. Him, or someone more dangerous. . . ."

City Councilman H. Rapp Badde, Jr., inhaled deeply, then let it out slowly.

Then a cell phone rang in his pants pocket, and Badde quickly grabbed his Go To Hell phone. But when he looked at the screen, there was nothing.

And the ringing was still coming from his pants pocket.

Other damned phone.

About time it's not the Go To Hell phone.

He exchanged phones, then looked at the caller ID.

What does Jan want?

"Whut up, honey?" he said into the phone.

"Damn it, Rapp, I thought I told you not

to do things with PEGI without my knowledge," she said with absolutely no pleasantries.

Uh-oh. Bad tone.

She's way beyond pissed.

*Now all I have to do is figure out which thing
I've done without telling her.*

That list could be endless.

"I'm sorry, honey. But —"

"Don't goddamn 'honey' me, Rapp. What's
this about an expediter?"

"'An expediter'?" Rapp repeated.

"Yeah, the one who just got us in a whole
helluva lot of hot water."

"What expediter?"

"Apparently, someone's saying he's the new
expeditor at HUD and PEGI. One I didn't
hire, and I thought you put me in charge of
this."

"I did. I mean, I didn't. I didn't hire anyone, is what I mean. And I did put you in
change, honey."

"Knock off the 'honey' crap, Rapp. I know
where you are, who you're with."

"I'm out at the West Philly row house,"
Badde said somewhat piously. "Want to talk
with Wynne?"

Smiling smugly, he exchanged glances
with Roger Wynne.

Jan said: "Don't change the subject, Rapp.

We got problems here."

H. Rapp Badde, Jr., then looked at the empty filing cabinets and thought, *Honey, if you only knew . . .*

VIII

[ONE]
Jefferson and Mascher Streets, Philadelphia
Sunday, November 1, 5:12 P.M.

Speeding down Girard Avenue, just past the Schmidt's Brewery development and just before the Hops Haus complex, Sergeant Matt Payne pulled a hard left onto Howard Street, putting the unmarked gray Ford Crown Victoria Police Interceptor into a tire-squealing four-wheel drift.

Moments earlier, Jason Washington had reported that not only were there three dead at the Northern Liberties scene, but a call had come in saying that a blue shirt at the scene reported another shooting had just taken place a block away.

Matt had floored the accelerator pedal.

Out of the corner of his eye, he saw in

the rearview mirror that the maneuver had thrown Corporal Kerry Rapier against the right rear door.

"Hey, Marshal," Rapier said, his tone casual, "think you might want to take it a little easier on the car?"

Detective Tony Harris chuckled.

"This thing's a tank, Kerry," Payne replied calmly as he steered in the direction of the skid to correct it. Then, squared up, he stepped harder on the gas pedal and the engine roared. "Heavy Dee-troit metal. Big iron block V-8. And you couldn't throw a turn like that back there without the rear-wheel drive. It's not as nimble as my Porsche, but then I wouldn't attempt a PIT with my 911. These cars are built to take it."

Rapier knew that Pursuit Intervention Technique was basically tactical ramming. In a PIT, the reinforced nose of the Police Interceptor smacked the tail of the car being pursued so that its driver suddenly lost control, turning sideways or spinning out before skidding to a stop.

"Not built to take the way you handle cars," Rapier replied. "I heard you got that nice sports car all shot up."

Harris chuckled again. "He's got you, Matt. By the way, what's up with your 911? That happened months ago."

"Still mired in the purgatory known as insurance adjuster arbitration," Payne said. "I hate insurance companies. The bastards don't want to write me a check for what it's worth to replace. I don't know if I'll ever get it back. So, while I was killing time stuck at the desk going over the pop-and-drops, I found out a half-dozen unmarkeds were about to go back to the feds — they were on loan to Dignitary Protection from the Department of Homeland Security — and I managed to get this one's transfer paperwork 'misplaced' for the foreseeable future."

Harris grinned. "Smooth move. It'll take the feds forever to figure out one's missing."

"Yeah, and my conscience is clear. Thanks to budget cuts, we don't have near enough cars, and we're at least putting this one to good use. The paperwork showed the other five are just getting parked, either warehoused or 'tasked to a possible high-value target.'"

"Translation being," Harris said, "left sitting empty with the wigwags flashing outside the U.S. Mint or Fed Reserve here to give the impression that one of the alphabet agencies under DHS is on the ball."

"Exactly."

Kerry Rapier went on: "Did you guys know

these are about to become dinosaurs? Ford's not going to make the Crown Vic anymore. And no Crown Vic means no Crown Vic Police Interceptors. They're going to be replaced with a hopped-up Ford Taurus."

"What? A scrawny V-6 front-wheel-drive like our Impala squad cars!" Payne said, making a mock gasp. "Horrors! You, Corporal Rapier, have ruined my joyous thoughts of being forever able to abuse police pursuit vehicles. I may as well put in my transfer to the Bike Squad."

Payne saw in the mirror that Rapier was smiling out his window.

And then he saw that Rapier wasn't wearing his seat belt.

When they'd first gotten in the car at the Roundhouse, both Payne and Harris had climbed into the front seats. It wasn't lost on Rapier, as he automatically went to latch his seat belt, that Matt and Tony had sat on their seat belts. The belts had already been buckled across the seats.

"Hey, guys, didn't your mothers teach you to always put on your seat belts?"

Payne was putting down the unmarked squad car's two sun visors so that they would be visible at the top of the windshield from the outside. On the driver's visor was a white sticker with red block lettering that spelled POLICE. Strapped to the passenger visor was a light bar with red-and-blue strobes. The twelve-volt DC power cord for the emergency lights was snaked over the stalk that held the rearview mirror to the windshield and ran down to the cigarette lighter.

As Payne stuck the plug in the lighter receptacle, he said, "Yes, but that was before dear ol' Mummy knew that I'd be carrying a pistol on my belt."

"What's that got to do with it?"

"I was going to say, 'Didn't they teach you at the Police Academy . . . ?' then realized that if they had, it would have been on the QT."

"Why quiet?"

Payne, badly mimicking a Shakespearean actor, said: "To buckle or not to buckle, that is the question. Whether 'tis nobler in the mind to suffer either the slings or the arrows" — he went back to his normal voice — "the slings in this case being seat belts, the arrows being bullets."

Harris put in, "You really butchered that, Matt."

"You people clearly have no couth," Payne said. "Simply put, then: It's a judgment call as to which you consider the safer option: wearing a seat belt so that you're better off in case you're in an accident, or not wearing one so that you can exit the vehicle and draw your weapon faster when going after a bad guy. Having numerous times had to exit vehicles in pursuit of bad guys — some of whom thought it a good idea to shoot at us — certain of us have chosen not to buckle."

Payne, looking in the rearview mirror, had seen Rapier considering that.

And now, as they had turned onto Jefferson, he saw that Rapier was sitting on his seat belt.

Payne braked hard, bringing the Crown Vic Police Interceptor to a screeching stop not far from a Crime Scene Unit van. A Medical Examiner's Office van was parked farther down Jefferson, and a gurney holding an obviously full body bag was being rolled into its rear cargo area.

Unrestrained by seat belts, the three men were almost instantly out of the unmarked shiny gray Police Interceptor.

"That's one massive steel ball," Kerry Rapier said, looking up at the towering red-and-white Link-Belt crane that in the late-afternoon light was casting a huge shadow across the dirt. "Must weigh two, maybe three tons. Could be a contender for the largest murder weapon on record."

Harris snorted. "If in fact it was the cause

of death. Remember that the Black Buddha said the other two victims showed no known cause of death."

With Payne leading, they walked past a big, bright white sign announcing a Philadelphia Economic Gentrification Initiative project by City Councilman Rapp Badde and the coming of three thousand new jobs.

That's a lot of jobs, Matt thought. *Especially here.*

Probably another political lie.

Payne couldn't help but notice that the sign was plastered with homemade flyers that bore a crude representation of the city councilman.

"Badde wanted for crimes?" Kerry Rapier then wondered aloud.

"Everyone's got their own idea of what constitutes a crime," Payne said. "As far as I know, Badde hasn't broken any laws on the books. Arguably, he's bent the living hell out of a few, but then that's what politicians do."

Payne saw that except for a line of five row houses — *Make that four and a half, considering that hole in the one on the end* — only smelly, raw earth remained on the once-residential city block. There was some heavy equipment and the white PEGI signs in each corner of the block. And that was it.

Yellow POLICE LINE tape was strung from the half-fallen wooden back fence of the semidemolished row house to the rear of the red-and-white Link-Belt crane, then to a four-foot-high iron pole in the concrete sidewalk that once held a parking meter, then past the Medical Examiner Office's van and all the way down the sidewalk to the farthest row house at the corner of Jefferson and Mascher.

Payne looked at the small group gathered beside the crane and saw a familiar face, Detective Harry Mudd of the Crime Scene Unit.

Mudd — a muscular, five-foot-eleven thirty-five-year-old with fiercely inquisitive eyes and salt-and-pepper hair trimmed short — was a ten-year veteran of the department. Payne knew him to be a no-nonsense and damned thorough investigator.

Mudd stood with his arms crossed and head somewhat cocked as he listened to one of the three beefy men who looked like construction workers.

Or heavy-equipment operators, Payne thought when he saw the sloppily hand-lettered cardboard square sign — TURCO DEMOLITION & EXCAVATION — that was taped to the side of the crane.

Mudd's eyes darted to Payne, who was leading Harris and Rapier toward him. He held out his right index finger as a *Hold that thought a moment* gesture to the beefy guy who was doing the talking. Then Mudd turned and started moving to intercept Payne.

"Sergeant Payne, good to see you," Detective Mudd said, offering his hand.

"It's 'Matt,' Harry," he said, taking it, then he gestured to the others. "You know Tony Harris. And this is Corporal Kerry Rapier."

"Harry Mudd, Kerry," he said, shaking the corporal's hand.

Kerry Rapier nodded, more than a little impressed by Mudd's grip. He was almost afraid he was going to pull back his hand and find his fingers crushed to a bloody pulp.

"Nice to meet you, Detective," Rapier said.

Tony Harris said, "How they hanging, Harry? It's been a while."

Mudd nodded. "It has. And if you mean, how are the bad guys hanging, I wish I could say by a noose. Otherwise, the answer's the same, one lower than the other."

He and Harris exchanged grins.

Payne looked over at the three men standing beside the Link-Belt crane. The tallest one, who appeared somewhat pale and had his chin almost to his chest, had a real look of gloom. The shortest of the three, who had a cigar stuck in the corner of his mouth, glanced at his wristwatch as he anxiously kicked the raw dirt with his boot toe, then glared in Payne's direction.

"I'm assuming one of those guys is Mr. Turco?"

Mudd glanced over. "Yeah, two actually. The tall one's name is Bucco, Bobby 'The Ballbuster' Bucco. He was running the crane when the ball found the deceased. The owner of the company is the short one who's sucking on the cigar stub. Thomas 'Little Tommie' Turco. And he's ten kinds of pissed off."

"What's his problem?"

"You."

"*Me?* I just got the hell here."

Mudd nodded. "And that's why he's pissed. I told him I was under orders to wait for the head of the homicide task force to get here. You're here in that shiny undercover car — nice wheels, by the way; where'd you steal them? — and he's probably guessing that I'm talking with The Man."

Payne decided it best to ignore the hot-car question. But the fact that Mudd raised it indicated that it wouldn't be the last time someone was going to ask how he came by a nice new vehicle when almost everyone else in the department was driving battered hand-me-downs with six digits on their odometers. It damn sure wasn't the kind of vehicle that was going to hide in plain sight very well.

"So," Payne said, "I still don't get why he's pissed at me."

"He wants to return the crane to the rental place, which he says is now charging him Sunday double time. But I told him I couldn't release him or his equipment until you gave the go-ahead."

Payne raised his eyebrows.

"Like I said, Matt, I'm just doing what I was told. You know how antsy the department's chain of command gets when Mayor Carlucci holds a press conference. And that shit flows downhill so fast."

Payne nodded. "Understood, Harry. You know I have full faith in your skills, so we can skip the formalities. What the hell is going on here?"

Mudd pulled out his spiral notepad and began, "Thomas 'Little Tommie' Turco's company was hired by HUD to turn the whole block back to dirt —"

"— and he's really pissed at 'that expediter sonofabitch who's really going to pay for all this,' " Mudd finished a few minutes later.

"So, three dead?" Payne said. "But no idea

why they were in the condemned buildings and no idea what killed the other two?"

Mudd was shaking his head. "No idea. And of course, until we hear from Dr. Mitchell's autopsy, we won't know for sure if the third died of blunt trauma. The one thing that is clear, however, is that there were people living in these houses right up until sometime today."

"Really?"

"Yeah, these folks were holdouts. They didn't want to move. They refused the buyout from PEGI." He pointed down the street. "That middle house? We found one of the dead at the kitchen table, slumped over with his face in a bowl of apparently just-made tomato soup."

"Possibly putting the time of death around noon?" Payne asked.

"Possibly," Mudd said. "Who knows?"

Payne looked at Harris and Rapier.

"Any thoughts, gentlemen? You know as much about the cases as I do."

Kerry Rapier shrugged, then grinned. "Death by drowning?"

Harris and Payne groaned.

"Only the obvious fact," Tony Harris then said, "that this doesn't fit the pop-and-drop MO in any way at all. Unless we're missing something. . . ."

Mudd glanced at the line of five remaining row houses and said: "Do you want to take a look inside?"

"Not right now," Payne said. "It's going to be dark soon. Let's talk about the other dead guy."

"Even better," Mudd said, "let's go over to the scene."

Payne gestured that Mudd should lead.

As they started walking along the sidewalk in front of the half-demolished row house, they heard an Italian-accented voice bark, "Aw, what the fuck, youse guys?"

When they all turned, they saw a frustrated Little Tommie Turco standing with both arms above his head, palms up.

Detective Harry Mudd held up his right index finger again, this time in a gesture meant to signal *Back in a minute.*

They heard Turco then bark, "Oh, for fuck's sake!" and watched as he tore the cigar stub from his mouth and threw it to the dirt.

[TWO]

As they rounded the corner from Jefferson to Hancock, Matt Payne saw that there was yellow POLICE LINE tape strung between two boarded-up row houses, blocking the entrance to an alleyway.

The first thing Payne saw behind the yellow tape was the blood trail. He took another step forward, his eye following the trail up the alleyway until he saw in the shadows the body of a very big black male. On the concrete beside his head was an inverted-V plastic marker with a black numeral "01" on it.

Parked on the street, blocking off the alleyway, was a Chevy Impala squad car. The right rear door was open, and a young black boy was sitting in the rear seat, turned so his back was to the scene.

"That's the deceased's nephew," Mudd said. "He says he didn't see the the shooter, which I doubt. We're trying to find his mother."

Payne nodded.

Poor kid is probably in shock.

As he glanced around, he thought, *Three dead back there. Another dead — a possible pop-and-drop — here.*

Two crime scenes two blocks apart. Or is it just one big scene?

And all this is going on just three blocks from The Fortress.

Then he thought: *Oh, shit, Amanda!*

He tugged back his left shirtsleeve cuff and checked his wristwatch.

Almost six?

He pulled out his cell phone and pounded out a text message with his thumbs:

HI, BABY . . .

SORRY I'M JUST NOW GETTING BACK TO YOU.

GOOD NEWS & BAD NEWS.

BAD FIRST: I OBVIOUSLY CAN'T MAKE IT BY 6. JUST GOT TO A SCENE WITH MORE DEAD.

GOOD (OR MAYBE MORE BAD) NEWS: IT'S ONLY BLOCKS FROM THE CONDO.

REALLY GOOD NEWS: SO, SEE YOU SOON?

SORRY, BABY . . .

He hit SEND. As he started to put back his phone, it almost immediately vibrated with the reply:

AMANDA LAW

OK. SEE YOU WHEN I SEE YOU

XOXO -A

Uh-oh. Do I read between the lines?

That was a fast reply.

Like she was waiting.

Correction: a fast and terse reply.

Or dismissive?

On the one hand, she shouldn't be pissed. She said she understands why I have to do this.

The damned pop-and-drop body count is probably up to nine. Then there's the three dead next door. Someone's got to stop it. . . .

But on the other hand, Amanda's emotional because she's not completely over her abduction — which I can understand — and she's not happy with my job and the idea of my being in danger.

Having been shaken to her very core, she's wisely questioning where things will go for her — for us. And, ultimately, who will I owe my allegiance to in five, ten, twenty years?

To the police department of a wild city whose crime rate doesn't seem to be improving?

Or to the goddess who's the loving mother of my children?

His thumb hovered over the REPLY key while he contemplated what he should say.

I can't lose this woman.

I should say something, I just don't know what's —

"Matt, you need to see this," Harris called.

Payne looked up, then glanced at the phone — then slipped it back into his pocket.

Nice job, Matty ol' boy.

You just proved once again that you don't deserve her.

"What is it, Tony?" Matt said as he walked toward him.

Harris was pointing in the direction of another evidence marker, this one somewhat obscured by weeds and shadows. It was close to the yellow tape. Next to it was a pair of spent shell casings.

"Any chance they're .45 GAP?" Payne asked.

"They are," Mudd offered. "Just two of them. But .45-cal. Glock."

Kerry Rapier said, "Number nine? Our mystery shooter strikes again?"

Payne exhaled audibly, then looked at Mudd.

"Well, hell, Harry, let me guess," he said, gesturing toward the alleyway. "The guy's got a history of sex crimes."

Mudd stepped over to the Impala, reached in, and from the front seat picked up a plastic evidence bag. He handed it to Payne.

Payne looked through the clear plastic at the Wanted sheet and its mug shot of the huge, goateed, droopy-eyed LeRoi Cheatham.

"You got it, Matt," Mudd said. "Cheatham served time for rape and was out on early release. Then, because he thought he could make only one visit with his parole agent, he got on the Megan's Law list."

"There's just no damned end to these perps," Payne said.

He read the back of the sheet. Handwritten in blue ink was: "Lex Talionis, Third & Arch, Old City, $10,000 reward."

"Check out the back," Payne said, handing the bag to Harris. "I'd say Kerry's right: number nine for our mystery shooter. Or ten, if Reggie Jones turns out to be his handiwork, too."

Harris held up the bag, then passed it to Rapier and said: "And, as Kerry likes to say, I'll bet dollars to doughnuts that we'll find the same doer's prints on that sheet. Looks like the same cheap gray paper stock as the others."

Mudd said, "The kid said the doer told him to give that to his mother."

"Well, that's evidence, so it's not going to Mama. She'll have to figure out how to convince Five-Eff to cough up the ten large without it."

Mudd looked at him, clearly confused.

After Payne explained that Five-Eff was

Francis Fuller, Mudd made the connection to the reward.

Mudd then went on: "Cheatham had a hundred twenty-two bucks cash on him. A rusty switchblade knife that didn't really switch itself open. And two eight-balls of what we suspect is crystal meth. Which the Wanted sheet tends to confirm, as he has a history of doing meth, too."

Payne glanced at the young boy in the back of the squad car.

"And what about him, Harry?"

"The kid's name is Michael Floyd, age twelve or age four, depending on the direction the wind's blowing."

Now Payne, Harris, and Rapier looked confused.

Payne held out his right hand, palm up, and wagged his fingers in a *Let's have it* gesture.

Mudd made a sour face. "He's a simpleton. Backward, you know? May even have a bit of brain damage. He isn't saying much. But even if he did say something we might be able to run with, I'd be very skeptical of it."

Payne glanced at the kid and said, "Well, he's got to be in shock seeing his uncle dead."

Mudd shrugged. "Then again," he said,

"it could all be an act, at least the backwardness. Just playing dumb, you know? Reason I say that is, one of the blue shirts, who was directing traffic at the first scene" — he pointed eastward, toward Mascher Street — "saw a white minivan with FedEx logos roll past a minute before he heard the two gunshots. We asked the kid about that, and" — he flipped a couple pages on his notepad and read from it — "he said, quote, What be a FedEx, motherfucker? end quote."

Payne raised his eyebrows, looking at Michael for a moment before turning back to Mudd.

Rapier handed Mudd the evidence bag with the Wanted sheet.

Mudd said, "He pointed at Cheatham's Last Known Address on here and said that's where he and his mother live, not Cheatham. He said his uncle lived in this abandoned house here."

"Maybe the kid's mama got sick of her brother's bullshit," Payne said. "Must be difficult enough raising a kid with a mental disability."

Payne then bent over to look at the spent shell casings.

They're damn near still warm.

We were that close!

Harris said, "What're you thinking, Matt?

400

Payne looked up at him and said, "How close we were."

"And now," Harris said, "how close we're not again."

Payne stood erect and, clearly in thought, stared at Tony a long moment.

"Nothing personal, Detective Harris, but you look like shit. And I'm beginning to feel like it. We've been banging away at this" — he glanced as his wristwatch — "hell, I can't even do the math. I think we need to take a break. Clear our heads. As a very wise person once told me, 'These guys will still be dead in the morning. You don't need to make a mistake and join them.'"

"That was me, Matt," Harris said.

Payne smiled. "I know."

He turned to Mudd and handed him his business card. "That's got my cell number, Harry. Let me know if you find something."

"Will do."

As they walked back to the gray Crown Vic, Payne thumbed out a text message:

```
HEY, BABY . . .

ON MY WAY. BE THERE SHORTLY.
```

He hit SEND and thought, *Hope you're still there — and still talking to me. . . .*

[THREE]
Hops Haus Tower
1100 N. Lee Street, Philadelphia
Sunday, November 1, 7:01 P.M.

It was well past dusk as Matt Payne drove up the cobblestone drive to the circle entrance of the high-rise condominiums. After dropping Harris and Rapier at the Roundhouse, he'd run by his tiny apartment on Rittenhouse Square, grabbed a fast shower and shave, and changed into an old comfortable pair of clean khakis, a long-sleeve navy cotton polo shirt, and boater's deck shoes. His shirttail was out, concealing the Colt Officer's Model .45 tucked under his belt on his right hip.

Parking in a slot across from the massive water fountain on the circle drive, he looked up and marveled at the impressive main entrance. The soaring three-story, stainless-steel-framed wall of thick clear glass gave a fantastic view of the lobby, all the more striking at night with its brightly lit gleaming marble floors and walls.

Payne walked through the main entrance doors and waved to the concierge on duty behind the main marble-topped desk. David Suder was a dark-haired, dark-eyed twenty-eight-year-old with a muscular frame that looked as if it had been forged from hardened steel. He wore a nice two-piece dark woolen suit, a starched white shirt, and a dark necktie that almost looked out of place on him.

"How you doin', David?" Payne called out.

"Good," he replied, smiling. "How goes it with you, Sarge, I mean, Mr. Payne? You look like you've had a rough one."

"It's 'Matt,' David. And indeed I have. But it's getting better by the moment."

"Glad to hear it. Check six, Matt."

"You, too, David," Payne called back as he reached the heavy sliding glass door that led to the elevator bank.

He punched in the unique code for Unit 2180 on the keypad. In mid-October, Amanda had changed it to 0-9-1-0 for September 10, the day she said her life had been profoundly changed — the day when Matt had saved her from her murderous abductors.

The glass door whooshed open sideways. Inside the elevator, he entered the code again and hit the 21 button on the panel for the penthouse floor.

As he rode up, he thought about the day that he'd met David Suder, who he knew wasn't really a concierge. As a general rule of thumb, concierges didn't address guests as "sergeant" and caution them to watch their back for bad guys — "check six" being good-guy jargon that meant for them to be wary of who might be sneaking up behind them, also known as their "six o'clock."

Suder now worked for Andy Hardwick, and Hardwick had introduced them when he'd told Matt there'd be extra protective eyes watching the penthouse floor and the owner of Unit 2180. But until recently, David had been Philadelphia Police Department Officer Suder, a rising star assigned to the elite Narcotics Strike Force. Earlier in the year he had taken the corporal's exam and passed both oral and written parts with scores high enough to put him in the top ten percent, and on "The List." Only those on The List got immediate promotions; everyone else would have to wait for a slot to open, which could take weeks, months — or maybe never even happen. After The List expired in two years, those not promoted would have to retake the exam with a new group of candidates.

But there was one caveat: funding. And because of severe budgetary cutbacks this year, there were fewer corporal slots, and only the top five percent had been immediately promoted.

Officer Suder had not been happy about that, to put it mildly.

Shortly thereafter, Andy Hardwick had been buying a few rounds down the street at Liberties Bar, catching up on Roundhouse scuttlebutt with old buddies still on the force, and he'd heard all about Suder's displeasure at getting the shaft thanks to City Hall bean counters.

The next day, Hardwick had taken Suder to lunch. Before they'd even been served their desserts, Hardwick had effectively poached him from the Philadelphia Police Department with the offer of a salary that was almost twice what any corporal could ever dream of earning.

But I simply could never do residential security, Payne thought.

Fortunately, I don't need the damn money. That's moot.

But more to the point: Where the hell's the thrill in private security? The satisfaction?

What'd be the equivalent of what I'm doing now?

Heading up Task Force Operation Poolhouse Clogged Toilet?

"Ma'am, the sign clearly states that no per-

sonal sanitary items are to be flushed. I'm afraid we're going to have to write you a ticket on this one."

He snorted as the elevator made a *ding*, stopped, and the doors parted on the twenty-first floor.

Then again, Marshal Earp, no one would be shooting at you.

And you're not exactly going gangbusters with collaring the doers in Op Clean Sweep.

As he put the key in 2180's heavy brass dead-bolt lock, Matt could hear Luna softly whining on the other side of the door. Her wagging tail was thumping against the door.

Having her so happy to see me is a nice welcome after a long lousy day.

Now I only hope that I can get Amanda to wag her lovely tail, too.

When he turned the knob and pushed the door inward, Luna stuck her black nose and curly-haired muzzle around its edge. Matt reached down to scratch her head as he opened the door.

"Good girl," he said. "Now take me to your gorgeous master."

As he stepped inside the doorway, Matt heard Amanda's sultry voice: "She already has."

He looked up from Luna and saw Amanda

standing there. She was barefoot, but wearing a stunning gold sequined cocktail dress. It clung flawlessly to her well-toned body, as if it was almost a second skin. And it shimmered miraculously. The front was cut low and wide, generously enough to show a great deal of incredible suntanned cleavage while not revealing more than a sexy suggestion of her marvelous bosom. Her thick wavy blond hair, hanging free and full, was silky and luminous.

Wow! Payne thought. *The goddess glows!*

She looks so full of life, her eyes so warm and inviting.

And that dress! It radiates like a sea at sunset.

Sorry, Luna. Your greeting just got bested.

Far, far and away . . .

And he saw that Amanda — *Perhaps even better, though it'd be the absolute last damn thing I'd ever admit to* — was holding a cocktail napkin wrapped around a squat, heavy crystal glass that was dark with what had to be an intoxicant.

"Glad you could make it," she said, her tone warm, genuinely meaning it. "I was beginning to worry."

As she turned her head slightly to the right, offering her left cheek, Matt said, "Sorry, baby, crazy day," and kissed her affectionately.

She held out the glass and flashed her dazzling smile.

"Macallan Eighteen, half water, two ice cubes."

He took it and grinned. "You not only have an incredible mind, but also a very dangerous memory."

She smiled again. "I'll take that as a compliment. Thank you."

"That said, you're not only an angel but a lifesaver. I've been longing for one of these all day."

As he took a big sip, she reached for his other hand and tugged him toward the interior of the condominium.

"Come on and sit down. Relax."

With Luna leading the way, they went into the living room and sat on the big, soft, black leather couch. It faced the floor-to-ceiling windows, and the lights of the city twinkled far into the distance. From the high-fidelity digital music player that Matt had bought Amanda when she started spending so much time at home came the soft, soothing voice of Diana Krall singing "Besame Mucho."

Matt looked at Amanda, thought, *Kiss me much, indeed* — then leaned forward and kissed her on the cheek again.

She smiled almost shyly.

He sat back and suddenly said, "You're not having anything?"

"Oh, yeah," she said, brushing her hair behind her ear and glancing back toward the kitchen.

She pushed herself up off the couch and said, "I'll be right back."

"How was your day, baby?" Payne asked as she went.

Amanda called back, "Interesting. Thanks for asking. I was going to tell you about it. But first enjoy your drink."

Uh-oh.

Was that a red flag, or maybe a yellow caution one, that just went up?

Matt watched over his shoulder as she disappeared into the kitchen. As he looked back at the lights outside, he could hear the sounds of her getting something out of the refrigerator and unwrapping it.

Oh, shit. She's had food prepared.

So she was waiting for me to reply when I sent that text.

But I was up to my ass in alligators. . . .

Then that made him think: *Surreal.*

Four dead just three blocks from here.

Absolutely surreal . . .

He heard the soft padding sound of bare feet approaching.

"Here you go, sweetie," Amanda said, putting an enormous platter of antipasto on the low marble table in front of the couch. Her other hand held a crystal stem, its huge goblet full of red wine. "I thought we could do this instead of any dinner."

"It looks marvelous. I love it. Thank you."

He reached down and grabbed a giant black olive and wrapped it in a large, thin slice of salami, then shoved the whole thing in his mouth. He chewed, nodding appreciatively at her, his eyes following her as she dropped back onto the couch.

She scooted closer beside him, holding her wineglass up and then tucking her bare feet under her golden-sequined fanny.

Just beautiful, he thought. *And so damn sexy.*

He touched his glass to hers, and said, "Cheers!"

He then watched as she reached to the table and picked up a salad fork.

She attempted to delicately spear a prosciutto-wrapped rectangle of cantaloupe. Twice. On the third attempt, made very slowly, she hit her target. She chewed the morsel and followed it with a very generous gulp of her wine.

Over the top of her glass, she made eye contact with him. When she'd swallowed the wine, she smiled.

My God, she truly is a goddess.

But why do I suspect that may not be her first glass of vino?

Or her second?

And that is a huge glass. . . .

Matt drained the rest of his eighteen-year-old single-malt.

"I'll make you another, sweetie," she said, immediately kicking her feet out from under her.

He leaned over and kissed her on the forehead to keep her seated.

"You stay. You've already made all this. I can pour my drink. Think I'll move on to the cheap stuff."

He walked over to the wet bar. He filled his glass with ice cubes, then poured a hefty double of Jameson's Irish whiskey. He looked over to the couch. Luna now had her head in Amanda's lap as Amanda absently petted her and looked out the window while sipping more wine.

This is certainly getting interesting.

She's clearly in thought about something.

And damn near in her cups.

He caught himself suddenly yawning.

Oh, shit. Hope I don't fall asleep. That will really ruin the mood.

And leave it to me to really piss her off.

411

"I don't see you forever and the few minutes you're here, you fall asleep!"

As he sat back on the couch, Amanda was holding the glass by the stem and swirling the wine around the goblet.

Kind of anxiously . . . nervously.

Then he noticed her left foot moving back and forth.

If that was attached to a churn at an Amish dairy, she could be making butter for all of Lancaster County.

Amanda turned to him.

"Want to talk about your 'crazy day'?" she said. "It's horrible that more people are dead and just up the street. Do you know who did it? And are they — you, I guess I mean — close to catching them?"

Matt took a sip from his drink, then said, "The simple answer is 'no' — to all that. No, we really don't know who. And I'm really mentally racked from thinking about the whole thing. So that means I'd really rather not talk about it. I hope you don't take that the wrong way."

Amanda smiled.

"Oh, not at all," she said. "I do understand. Sometimes you have to step back."

"How about you? Anything at the hospital?"

She nodded. Then she leaned forward and

412

put her wineglass beside the antipasto platter on the marble table.

She really is in deep thought.

She turned to him, and suddenly he could
see tears starting.

*My God. What the hell has got her so
upset?*

"Matt, you saved my life. I will never forget that terrifying moment I realized who
they were and what they'd done — and knew
that was the end for me. But then . . . then
you suddenly were there. And I heard your
voice calling out to warn Tony Harris, 'It's
me, Matt Payne!' I truly thought I was hal-
lucinating."

Oh, shit. In vino veritas. . . .

Matt stared into her eyes and felt his throat
constrict.

And I remember that moment, too.

*Inside that pillowcase they'd taped over her
head, she whimpered.*

*When I cut her free, the last person in the
world I expected to find a prisoner in that hellhole was the woman I loved.*

It was an unimaginable moment.

She reached back for her glass, took a big
sip, and said, "You saved my life, Matt. Now
it's my turn."

[FOUR]

"How does survivor's guilt fit?" Matt Payne was saying, reaching for another slice of salami and wrapping it around another big black olive.

Even though the platter was now nearly three-quarters empty, all the meat and cheese and fruit he'd eaten wasn't keeping up with the alcohol he was washing it down with. He was starting to feel a bit tight.

Or maybe it's a combination of that and being exhausted.

He'd made them both fresh drinks.

Luna was asleep at their feet, snoring softly.

"Survivor's guilt," Amanda Law said, "because Skipper died and Becca didn't."

Twenty-five-year-old Becca Benjamin, just shy of two o'clock in the morning on September 9, had been sitting in her Mercedes SUV waiting for J. Warren "Skipper" Olde, her twenty-seven-year-old boyfriend, to come out of a seedy Philly Inn motel room. Which he did, right after the meth lab inside had blown up the damn place, turning it into an inferno. The blast demolished the Mercedes.

Becca suffered a head injury from the blast that had almost killed her. Skipper was critically burned.

Matt had known them while growing up, since they were all at Episcopal Academy. Both came from families of significant means. And both had a history of getting in trouble with booze and drugs.

Because of the severity of their multiple injuries, both had been taken to Temple University Hospital's advanced burn center, where the chief physician was one Amanda Law, MD, FACS, FCCM.

"Matt, I'll never tell anyone else this," Amanda said, "but it's my brutally cold assessment that Jesús Jiménez probably did Skipper a favor by killing him. Skipper was either going to die from his burns or suffer a long recovery and never be the same again."

Matt nodded.

"But Becca," she went on, "nonetheless is feeling responsible, saying they wouldn't have been there if Skipper hadn't wanted to make her happy with some of those goddamned drugs. To get past this damned survivor's guilt, I sent her to Amy."

"That's interesting," Matt said. "Amy never mentioned she was now Becca's shrink."

"She's a doctor, sweetie. Just because she's your sister doesn't mean she's going to tell you and break the physician-patient confidentiality."

He shrugged.

Amanda said, "There can be a variant of survivor's guilt among doctors. They get a guilty feeling that they didn't do enough to save a patient. Luckily, I've never had it. But that doesn't mean I don't understand it. And I know that those who *do* have it need to look at the glass as being half full, not half empty, confident in their skills that they did the right thing."

I've had a few of those myself, Matt thought.

It wasn't that long ago that I held Susan Reynolds in my arms as her very life poured out from that bullet hole in her head.

And I loved her like I love Amanda.

Right down to the roadside cottage with the picket fence.

I endlessly questioned if I could've done anything different to save her from that madman of a killer.

And, bottom line, the answer was I couldn't.

Still, finally realizing that didn't ease the pain of loss.

He took a sip of Scotch as he glanced at Amanda.

Am I about to lose Amanda . . . ?

Amanda was saying: "I also understand that sometimes things play out the way they do no matter what anyone does. In fact, in some cases we probably prolong the inevitable by taking the heroic measures. Which was why someone in a wise moment came up with DNRs."

"Do Not Resuscitate orders," Matt said.

She nodded.

He sipped his drink again and tried to understand where she was going with this.

Maybe it's her body clock ticking. The abduction was a real wake-up call for her sense of mortality.

And maybe that's some manifestation of survivor's guilt — in part because she lived while that young teen Honduran girl, after being forced into prostitution, died a brutal death.

Then she said: "Two months ago, Matt, I went to Hawaii for an M and M."

I know she can't mean candy.

"It's a conference doctors attend," she went on, as if reading his mind, "Morbidity and Mortality."

This is about mortality!

He said, "I heard those conferences are really just an excuse to write off trips to fancy

417

places, like Hawaii, so you can play and take a business deduction."

"The idea of M and Ms is peer review. We look at how others cared for patients and how it could have been done better. Particularly cases in which a mistake was made and the patient died. Being head of the burn unit, I tend to be the one doing the reviewing. It's not exactly a pleasant task. No one likes to be told they screwed up, but we do want to do right by our patients — *First do no harm* — and the peer review, while sometimes painful, does help. You learn to modify behavior. And avoid repeating mistakes."

She looked at him a long moment.

"Matt, I don't like repeating mistakes. I can't."

"Of course not. I understand. There're lives at stake."

"Yes, there are. Ours."

What?

She said: "We're at a critical time in our lives. I feel we've both been given second chances, and I want us to get this next one right."

"Oh."

"I had a long talk with my father."

Matt had met Charley Law only once, but had heard stories about him from Jason Washington, who'd known Law during his twenty years with the department in Northeast Detectives. Washington had said that her old man always had been full of commonsense gems, that he'd been a good cop because he could quickly strip away the bullshit and cut right to the chase.

Law had been off duty when he took a bullet to the hip. He'd walked in on a robbery of a gas station on Frankford Avenue. Returning fire, he'd shot the critter dead then and there — and wound up being offered disability and retirement. And he'd taken it, saying he was glad to get the hell out, if only to get past all the lame jokes about his name — "Well, well, here comes *The* Law."

When Matt had first tried dating Amanda — right before the abduction — she had made it damn perfectly clear what a toll her father's job had taken on their family. She told him about the daily pain of watching him go to work, and fearing that that would be the last time they'd see him alive.

Amanda went on: "When I turned thirteen, Dad sat me down at the kitchen table. He said, 'This is your birds-and-bees speech. Pay attention. We're on this planet basically to do two things: eat and reproduce. And we eat in order to have the energy to reproduce. Everything else — your clothes, TV, music, vacations, whatever — it's all filler for between the reproduction times. That's what we're hardwired to do. Understanding that, you will know that boys want nothing more than to get in your pants and will tell you whatever you want to hear to accomplish that. So, understand that you — and only you — can control who gets in your pants.'"

Payne avoided eye contact as he took a long, slow sip of his drink.

Then he said, "I'm afraid to ask, but am I supposed to respond to that?"

She smiled. "No, I'm just trying to paint a picture."

He chuckled nervously. "That's one helluva picture."

"The picture I'm painting is that my dad and I have a close connection. And recently, Dad and I were talking about relationships. He told me that 'nobody has the first damn answer why two people ever get together,' only that there was the hardwiring. But he could offer me the benefit of looking back, at his marriage and those of others. His experience.

"He said, 'Amanda, so many women go into a relationship thinking they're going to change the man, make him better. Civilize him. It just doesn't work.'"

Matt looked in her eyes, then said, "I need

420

civilizing?"

Amanda shook her head. "No, it's not that at all. It's more that both people in the relationship need to be in concert from the start. Not, as my dad said, have one trying to 'fix' the other along the way."

Matt took a sip of his Scotch and nodded. "I fully agree with that."

Amanda was silent a long moment.

Oh, shit! Did I just paint myself into a corner?

"Then why won't you quit playing cop, Matt? And trying to get yourself killed?"

I wonder if she's been talking about this with Amy, who's been banging that drum forever?

The smooth voice of Diana Krall was now singing "The Look of Love," and Matt thought, *She's got the player on shuffle. Has she been playing those CDs all night?*

Amanda took a sip of her wine, then said, "Okay, now the fun part."

"What?"

"Bear with me," she said. "Not too long before she died at seventy-three, looking gorgeous even at the end, Anne Bancroft —"

She paused and looked at him questioningly.

Matt said, "Sure. Wife of one of the funniest guys ever, Mel Brooks."

"Not just a wife. She was a successful actress on her own, you know."

"Really? Like what?"

"She's one of the few with a Tony, an Emmy, and an Oscar to her name. And you *still* only know her as Mel Brooks's wife?"

Payne shook his head. "Sorry."

"She was Mrs. Robinson."

"Mrs. Robinson?"

"The Graduate?"

"Never heard of it."

Frustrated, she sighed. "Matt! You can't be that dense."

He grinned. Then he started whistling the Simon & Garfunkel hit tune from the soundtrack, appropriately titled "Mrs. Robinson."

Amanda punched him in the shoulder. He thought it was somewhat playfully done, but the sad look on her face didn't seem to support that.

"Oh, you are just impossible!" she said, her tone exasperated, then upended her wine stem, emptying it.

He made an attempt at a smile, but she was having none of it. Then he leaned forward, touched her chin with the thumb and index finger of his right hand to lift her head, and kissed her on the cheek.

"Sorry. I was just playing. What were you going to say?"

"Well, Matt, I'm not playing. Goddammit, I'm serious."

She inhaled deeply, exhaled, then said: "Not too long before Anne Bancroft died — and she didn't say it because everyone knew she had cancer; she was very private, and no one knew she was dying but Mel Brooks and her doctors — she was asked in an interview what the secret was to her successful — and quite clearly loving — forty-year marriage."

Oh, shit. I think I see where this is going.

He said: "Okay . . ."

"And what do you think she said, Matt?"

Watch out, Matty, ol' boy.

This is a minefield.

Step carefully or . . . BOOM!

He thought for a long moment, then said, "I don't know. What with being married to a brilliant writer, actor, director, probably something about patience. And about re-spect. And real love, of course."

"Yes and no."

"She said 'yes and no'?"

"*No!* What she said was all that you said — and more. But she didn't list them. It was the way she phrased it."

With his right hand, somewhat anxiously, he made a gesture that said *And that was?* Then he saw her face, and immediately re-gretted it.

Amanda said, "Didn't you just in your last breath suggest that patience was a virtue to have in a good lasting relationship?"

Well, KAAA-FUCKING-BOOM, Matty!

Nice job. You may as well have just taken a running dive onto that minefield.

"I'm sorry, baby."

"Well, damn it, Matt! You should be. Because this is really important to me. Because you're important to me."

She paused, and she looked deeply, and genuinely lovingly, into his eyes.

It was powerful, and he felt his throat tighten.

She truly is a goddess.

And I truly am a complete and utter ass.

"Amanda, I'm sorry."

"What she said was this: 'When I hear the tires of his car come crunching up the stone drive of our house in Connecticut, I visualize him and think, 'Now the fun begins.'"

Amanda stared Matt in the eyes again.

"Do you see?" Amanda said softly. "There was an excitement to their relationship. They weren't together for any reason other than enjoying one another. Love, too, but enjoyment."

He looked at her and thought, *The way it is in the beginning, when just the thought of your mate makes your heart beat faster.*

She added, "Theirs was a true companion-
ship. A real relationship. Joyful."

He nodded.

"Now the fun begins," she repeated. "I want
that, Matt. I need that. Now, and especially
later, when most don't have it."

She looked down a moment, then back up
at him, and softly added: "I *felt* that when I
heard your key in the lock earlier. *Now the
fun begins. . . .*"

They looked each other in the eyes, and
after what seemed like a very long time,
Amanda said, "You don't have any response
to that?"

Matt didn't trust his voice to speak.

He raised his eyebrows, then cleared this
throat.

"Only," he said carefully, "that I really ad-
mire Mel even more now. And, yeah, I want
that, too."

They stared at each other for a moment.

"It sounds like there was a 'but' coming,"
Amanda said. "Do you think it's possible?"

He hesitated, then rolled his eyes.

"Nah," he said. "Obviously, only in the
movies."

Her eyes grew wide with shock. "What?"

Then he smiled, held her hand, and said,
"Baby, not yes, but hell yes it's possible."

He wrapped his arms around her. She

rested her head on his shoulder.

As he gently squeezed, he said, "I do want that, too. I want you, Amanda, more than anything."

Did I just prove her father's point — that I'll say anything she wants to hear? Particularly to get her naked?

But it's more than that.

I meant what I said. I do want her.

I just have no damn idea what to say if she asks about me quitting the department.

He felt her arms wrap around him, and she squeezed gently back. She buried her nose behind his ear and softly kissed his neck.

As he thought he heard her begin to sniffle, he picked her up and carried her into the bedroom.

"I've Got You Under My Skin" came softly from the speakers.

IX

[ONE]
2027 Fairmount Avenue,
Philadelphia
Sunday, November 1, 7:22 P.M.

H. Rapp Badde, Jr., sitting in his Range Rover parked at the curb near the corner of Corinthian and Fairmount Avenues, knew that his sudden dark mood had not been caused by his view of the medieval Eastern State Penitentiary. But the haunting and imposing two-hundred-year-old structure damn sure wasn't helping his attitude, despite the signage he'd days earlier ordered bolted to its massive stone walls.

The sign — one of a dozen fabricated by the same local company that did all of PEGI's projects — was a four-by-eight-foot sheet of plywood painted bright white. Its bold black lettering read:

MOVING PHILLY FORWARD!
COMING SOON TO FAIRMOUNT:
THE VOLKS HAUS
AFFORDABLE APARTMENT LIVING
FOUR 500-UNIT HIGH-RISE
TOWERS!
ANOTHER FINE DEVELOPMENT
FOR YOUR FUTURE FROM
PHILADELPHIA ECONOMIC
GENTRIFICATION INITIATIVE
*A PROJECT OF THE CITY OF
PHILADELPHIA
HOUSING & URBAN DEVELOPMENT
COUNCILMAN H. RAPP BADDE, JR.,
CHAIRMAN*

Though PEGI had not yet received the paperwork from the bureaucrats in Washington, D.C., releasing the decrepit property to them, Badde felt enough time had been wasted and had given the go-ahead for the posting of the signs.

It had taken more of his political skills than he'd expected for his Housing and Urban Development Committee to take over the property from the nonprofit historical association that oversaw it. And he'd really wanted to rub it in the faces of the people who'd tried tripping him up every step of the way.

"For chrissake, Jan," he'd said in the beginning, "even those damned do-gooders call it a 'preserved ruin.' If we have to, we can play the eminent-domain card and say it's a neighborhood hazard, a danger that needs to be condemned. Who the hell wants something that ugly in their neighborhood that's not even being maintained? Not when we can take federal funds and build housing for our voters."

To fight the battle for possession, Badde had educated himself about the property. And knew far more than he really wished he did, like that the prison's Gothic architecture was intentionally harsh. The medieval style of the dark ages was meant to intimidate those incarcerated — as well as anyone who might consider committing a crime.

Which, he thought, staring at it, *damn well may be why it's bothering me right now.*

The prison had been conceived in Ben Franklin's house in 1787 and opened in 1829. It promoted a new type of incarceration, one encouraging rehabilitation by locking up prisoners by themselves. It was believed that being alone in the cold, hard cells would force inmates to consider their crimes, and perhaps find God as they sought penance — thus the word "penitentiary." The cells each even had a small skylight, a simple glass pane — the "eye of God" — that was meant to remind the prisoners that they were always being watched.

Probably the only thing about the place that Rapp Badde really found fascinating was that at one time it had housed the infamous Al Capone. Badde appreciated that, even behind bars, the ruthless gangster broke rules. Thumbing his nose at the system, Capone had packed his cold hard cell with creature comforts from woolen rugs to fine linens, even a small library with reading lamps and a wooden secretary desk for his writing.

The prison started going downhill after being abandoned in 1971, when prisoners started getting sent to the new Graterford facility outside of Philly.

"Then some moron gets it made a national historical site?" Badde had said to Jan incredulously. "It's controlled by a nonprofit organization. What part of not-for-profit doesn't anyone understand? Rather than subsidizing a damned ancient eyesore that's taking up valuable land in the middle of the city, we can put the place to good use for our citizens. Which means for us, too."

And, against the odds and the protests, he'd flexed his considerable political muscle to make the People's House a reality.

At least this far, he thought.

Which could all fall apart if I don't make these problems go away.

Badde's office cell phone rang, and the caller ID announced JANELLE HARPER. Since leaving the basement of the West Philly row house, Badde had been using both cell phones almost constantly. At one point he'd been on both at the same time, requiring him to manipulate the Range Rover's steering wheel with his left knee.

First he'd had a long talk with Janelle Harper, then an even longer one with his personal lawyer, then another call with Jan to report the gist of what the lawyer had said, which basically had been next to nothing — he'd said he was going to have to think it all over thoroughly. Then, as Badde pulled ten grand in cash from his office safe and stuffed it into a black duffel bag, he'd set up the rendezvous here at Eastern State Penitentiary.

And now Jan was calling again.

"Yeah, honey?"

She said: "The Russian just called and said now that the Diamond property is cleared, it's time to talk. What do you think he meant by that? I mean the 'cleared' part?"

Badde said: "I don't know what he meant.

Just that he was pissed it'd taken so long with those holdouts. We'll be there. Where and when?"

"He suggested Vista Fiume at ten-thirty," Jan said. "That's the nice new five-star. Make sure you change into nice clothes."

"Ten-thirty? Damn, that's late! But okay. I'll pick you up."

Rapp then heard his Go To Hell cell phone ring. The caller ID read: JACK JONES.

About damn time.

"Honey, I've got to take this one. I'll call you back when I can. Meantime, you get ready for dinner, okay? We need our game faces on for this one. And I think the Russian really likes you."

He broke off that call, then in his smoothest politician's voice said into his Go To Hell phone, "Thanks for calling back, brother."

He wanted to add: *And thanks for taking your sweet goddamn time.*

"Whut up, Rapp," Jack Jones replied, his tone depressed. "You know all about Reggie, right?"

"Yeah, Kenny told me. I need to talk to him. That's why I called. Know where he's at?"

"Kenny?"

Yes, Kenny.

What the hell's wrong with you, Jack? You're

not making sense.

Shock, maybe?

I do the bastard a favor and this is what I get.

And what the hell is that noise in the background? Bingo games?

"Yeah, I mean Kenny. I know he's in trouble, Jack. When's the last you heard from him?"

"Why?"

"Didn't he tell you that I'm trying to reach him and arrange for the money?"

There was nothing but silence on the other end.

Badde went on: "Look, Jack, I really need to get in touch with him."

He then remembered that Kenny, when he'd called screaming that he was the next to be killed if Reggie's drug debt went unpaid, said that Jack was the one who'd gone to the Medical Examiner's Office to ID the brutally beaten body.

"You know, we can't let what happened to Reggie happen to him."

There was another long moment of silence.

"No shit, Rapp," Jack said disgustedly. "You wouldn't believe how bad they beat him, man. About the only way I could tell for sure it was him was those scars on his

433

ass from that dog that bit him when we were in middle school. There was nothing recognizable of his face. The medical guy said he thought they'd used a baseball bat, then poured some kind of acid on him. Nobody deserves that, Rapp."

Rapp heard a *tap-tap* on the window of the Range Rover's front passenger door. He looked and saw Allante Williams standing just outside the door. Williams was a nicely dressed, clean-cut black male in his late thirties. He was also Badde's second cousin. While Williams tried to project a straight-laced, professional appearance, in reality he'd just gotten paroled after serving seven years on a ten-year rap for murder. He now ran what he called a "private security business." And, throwing family a bone, Badde had had Urban Ventures put him on retainer.

Badde reached for the master door-locking button and pressed it. Williams opened the passenger door and climbed into the seat. With his right index finger, Badd made a gesture that meant *Just one more second,* then after Williams shut his door hit the master lock button again.

"Look, Jack. Make goddamn sure Kenny calls me ASAP. Got it? This is a lot of money, and I just can't wait for him. Later."

He broke the connection, then made a fist with his right hand and bumped knuckles with Williams.

"Good to see you, Rapp."

"You, too, man."

Badde then reached into the backseat, where he had his Italian black leather brief-case beside a small black duffel bag. He pulled from the briefcase two of the ten photocopies he'd made at the campaign house. They were all the same, copies of the bogus badge that Kenny Jones had laminated in clear plastic. It was strung on a black metal bead chain taken from one of the ceiling fans at the West Philly row house. The badge showed a color head-shot of him with long locks and a full beard, underneath which was:

KAREEM ABDUL-QAADIR
COMMUNITY REPRESENTATIVE
CITY OF PHILADELPHIA
FORGOTTEN VOTERS INITIATIVE

"Here's the most recent photograph we have of him. Real name is Kenny Jones" — he paused as he watched Allante pull out a small notepad and pen — "and he grew up at 726 Daly Street, where his older brother,

Jack, who I was just talking to, lives with their parents. His younger brother, Reggie, got whacked last night. Kenny's on the run. He jumped bail a couple years back after trying to sell crack to some cops."

Allante snorted. "Brilliant dude, huh?"

"Right. Anything but. Anyway, first thing you need to do, Allante, is find him. I already told you about the drug debt we're supposed to pay. I've got an idea how to play that. But first I need to get back some sensitive files, voter records, that he stole from my campaign headquarters."

"Okay."

"When he gets turned in for the reward, I can't have it come back to me. . . ."

"I understand."

"I'm just saying."

"You know I got your back, Rapp. I'll handle this one myself."

Rapp Badde nodded, then heard his Go To Hell phone ringing again. The screen read: CALLER ID BLOCKED.

"Yeah?" Badde snapped as he answered it.

"Yo, Rapp. It's Kenny," he said, his tone flat.

Badde's eyebrows went up. He pointed at the phone and mouthed to Williams, *It's him.*

Badde went back to his smooth politician's voice: "Hey, brother. Hold on a second while I get rid of this other call."

Badde, putting his left index finger to his lips, signaled to Allante for silence. Then he hit SPEAKERPHONE.

"Where are you, Kenny?" Badde said casually.

Kenny ignored the question. "You got the money?"

"I've got something even better."

There was a long pause.

In the silence, Badde could hear a familiar sound.

What the hell is that in the background? Badde thought.

That is a bingo game!

That means that bastard Jack is with him.

Badde then said: "Kenny, did you know the basement of the house got broken into?"

Kenny was quiet another moment.

"Really?" he finally said, unconvincingly.

"They took whatever was in the filing cabinets," Badde went on.

"Don't know why," Kenny said, clearly lying. "Just old voter files. Don't know why anybody'd want those." He paused, then said, "What's the something better? You got the money or not?"

"I got the cash. Wasn't easy."

437

"Good man, Rapp," Kenny said, his voice suddenly more chipper. "I knew you'd pull through."

Badde looked at Williams and rolled his eyes.

Bullshit, he thought. *You're prepared to burn me at the stake.*

"Look, Kenny. What's this guy's name we're paying off?"

"Oh, no, man. He'd pop me just for saying names."

"Kenny, I don't have time for these games. It's my money, and I want to know where it's going. You don't want to end up like Reggie, you goddamn well better tell me what I need to know."

Kenny was quiet a long time while he considered that. And Badde definitely heard someone calling "bingo!" in the background.

"Dude's name is Cicero," Kenny then said.

"Cicero?" Badde repeated. "A drug dealer named Cicero?"

"Uh-huh. I think it's Marcus Cicero. We just call him Cicero."

Badde looked at Williams, who shook his head, not recognizing the name.

"Okay, Kenny, here's the deal. I'll do even better than the thirty-five thousand."

"What's that?"

"I've got a forty-five-thousand-dollar pay-day for you."

"How much?"

"Ten Gs more than the thirty-five owed."

He was quiet another long moment.

"Okay, Rapp, you got my attention. Talk."

"You know the place where they found Reggie in Old City, Lex Talionis?"

"Uh-huh."

"You're aware that whoever took him there is eligible for a ten-thousand-dollar reward because Reggie had a long rap sheet?"

"Say what?"

Rapp Badde explained that, then said, "And it can be paid anonymously. So you could pop this Cicero guy, turn him in, and clear your debt, then get the reward."

Kenny was quiet again. "What's the catch?"

"The catch, Kenny, is grabbing Cicero and getting him signed, sealed, and delivered to Old City. But my guy is going to help you do that, too."

Stupid bastard doesn't realize the same can happen with him.

I get Allante to pop them both, and it's twenty large in his pocket.

And my problems disappear.

439

"Listen, Kenny, I'm going to give you my guy's number — he goes by Big Al. He's going to bring the money. Make sure you touch base with him right now."

"Okay."

After he'd given Kenny the number, Badde broke the connection, then reached in the back and grabbed the duffel.

"There's ten grand cash in there, enough to look like a lot of money before they try counting it. Should buy you plenty of time."

Allante Williams nodded, then took the bag. "I'll be in touch."

As he was closing the door, his cell phone rang. He answered it: "Big Al."

Badde took a long last look at the intimidating ancient prison walls and thought *I may never win another election. But I sure as hell am not going to jail.* He dumped the Range Rover in gear and sped away.

[TWO]
Hops Haus Cinema de Lux
1111 N. Front Street,
Philadelphia
Sunday, November 1, 8:01 P.M.

Will Curtis had been having a fantastic dream, one of those he called Technicolor dreams because they seemed so extraordinarily real and cinematic. In it, everything was bright and pleasant, complete with amazing sensations that made him feel warm and relaxed.

That was all abruptly interrupted by someone shaking his shoulder.

"Hey, mister, you gotta wake up," a teenage boy's voice was saying. "C'mon, wake up! You've done slept through the movie twice. Nobody likes Stan Colt flicks that much."

The movie star Stan Colt — real name: Stanley Coleman — promoted himself as being as rough and tough as his hometown of Philadelphia.

A groggy Curtis cracked open one eye.

441

He was sitting in the highest row of the movie theater's stadium seating, all the way up and back in a corner. He saw that the theater lights were all up and below him all the seats were empty. There was a large soft drink cup in the cupholder of his seat's armrest.

Oh, yeah . . . still in NoLibs.

He remembered that he'd come into the Northern Liberties cinema after the shooting, both to hide and to await the safety that the dark of night offered.

He stared back at the pimpled face of a lanky kid who looked to be Asian and was maybe thirteen. The kid wore black slacks and a white shirt, and he held a trash bag and a four-foot-long trash-collecting device that he spun on his arm like some kind of nunchuck.

"Manager finds out," the kid said, "you're gonna have to pay twice."

Will Curtis nodded. He put his hands on the armrests and, when he leaned forward to push himself up to stand, suddenly felt a stickiness in the seat of his pants.

What?

Did I spill my drink when I fell asleep?

No, it's in the cupholder.

He stood. And then he smelled it.

Dammit!

442

That dream's warm fuzzy feeling was me shitting myself!

Goddamn greasy cheesesteak . . .

The kid now looked at him with a wrinkled, soured expression.

He went to the far side of the theater and, occasionally looking over his shoulder, began sticking the pole between the theater seats and pulling out discarded candy wrappers and paper cups.

As carefully as he could, Will Curtis made his way down the carpeted steps of the theater, then out into the corridor. He stopped, looked to the right, then to the left, and saw a pair of restrooms two screening rooms away.

He found the men's room empty. After grabbing some paper towels, he entered a stall, closing and locking the door.

He unbuttoned his denim jacket, then reached under his shirttail to pull out the Glock. He looked around the stall but could not find a flat surface to put it on. And he could not simply set it on the floor as he had done at the church earlier in the day. Here the stall walls were a foot off the tiled floor, and anyone walking into the restroom would immediately see the gun in plain view.

And no doubt go screaming like a banshee into the corridor.

He looked from the floor to the back side of

443

the door. There was a standard metal hook there, and he turned the gun upside down and slipped its trigger guard over the hook.

That works good.

He then undid his pants to inspect the damage.

He saw red.

That's a lot of blood.

Not good . . .

He kicked off his black athletic shoes, then slipped off the slacks and hung them by a belt loop on the hook. Then he peeled off his fouled underwear and wrapped it in paper towels.

He was now naked from the waist down, and he suddenly felt very cold, chilled to the core.

And then there was a rumble in his abdomen.

A half hour later, feeling clammy and completely spent, Will managed to dress himself and exit the stall.

Washing his hands, he looked in the mirror and truly didn't recognize himself. He was saddened by the ashen-faced, sickly old man staring back at him. He thought he looked worse than ever.

I know I damn sure feel worse than ever.

And I keep passing blood.

He dried his hands, then started for the door. Feeling dizzy, he took his steps carefully. At the door, he pulled it inward, then stopped.

Damn! The gun!

He retrieved the pistol from the toilet stall's coat hook, stuck it behind his belt buckle, then made his way out of the cinema and across the complex to the car park.

The white Ford minivan was where he'd left it, but the full-size SUVs that had been on either side were gone, as were half the vehicles in the lot.

He got behind the wheel and started the engine. Looking at the dashboard, he saw the small stack of the four remaining FedEx envelopes. He picked them up and flipped through them.

The first had a Last Known Address that was in far South Philly, almost to Philadelphia International Airport. The second was on Richmond, the other side of Kensington. The third was on Ontario, near Eighteenth Street. And the fourth was the Last Known Address that had been a dead end — the house that had burned to the ground.

The Richmond one is too close to here for tonight.

445

He flipped back and looked at the Ontario address.

That's Allegheny West, on the way home.

What the hell . . .

He put the minivan in gear, flicked on the headlights, and drove out into the night.

He took Girard Avenue west to Broad Street — giving a wide berth to Jefferson and Hancock, where he'd shot LeRoi Cheatham earlier in the day — then drove north on Broad all the way to Ontario. There, he made a left.

Just before crossing over Germantown Avenue, Will considered pulling to a stop to reapply the FedEx signs to the doors of the vehicle. But he decided that the signage really didn't matter at night.

The guy is going to see the new white minivan and my uniform. That's enough.

And I really don't want them on the doors if the cops are still out looking for a white FedEx minivan.

Who knows what that retard Michael told them?

Then, after this, I'll take Germantown home and finish the rest tomorrow.

Then he did pull over, but only to hit the overhead light and reread the waybill on the FedEx envelope. It had:

In his research at CrimeFreePhilly.com, Will Curtis had learned that originally it had been Miffin's girlfriend who'd turned in the thirty-year-old to the police. Miffin had been babysitting her eleven-year-old daughter at her house when she had left work early to surprise him.

And surprise him she had.

She walked into the living room carrying a store-bought angel food cake in a plastic to-go bag and a long slicing knife.

She found the two of them on the sofa.

He was teaching the girl how to masturbate.

The daughter, after quickly pulling on her pants, had loudly defended Miffin, declaring it all a simple misunderstanding. Using the vernacular of the street, she explained that Miffin had been teaching her self-stimulation only because he'd told her that it was very wrong for him to continue orally stimulating her with his tongue.

Her mother had responded to that information by also drawing from the street: She lunged for Miffin and tried cutting out his tongue with the angel food knife.

She failed, but did manage to slash a nasty gash on his left cheek in the shape of, oddly, a J.

After his arrest, Jossiah Miffin had been found guilty of indecent assault and corruption of a minor. (The mother claimed it had been self-defense that had led to the cheek cut.) Miffin was sentenced to probation, which included his getting and keeping a job, obtaining intense sex-offender treatments, and maintaining absolutely no unsupervised contact with minors.

Having made no effort whatsoever to meet even one of the requirements of his probation, Miffin's Wanted sheet hit the Megan's Law list.

And it hit Will Curtis's Law of Talion pervert list.

On Ontario Street, just shy of Nineteenth Street and the SEPTA train tracks, Will Curtis slowed and started looking for 1822. It was damn difficult on the dark street. Here, too, there were huge gaps where row houses had once stood. And he had to start with a known address and try to count from there to 1822, guessing how many ghost addresses there were between existing houses.

And this easily could turn out like that other

address — nonexistent.

He was amazed that his decent middle-class house was only a couple miles from this run-down ruin of a neighborhood. The houses were literally falling apart. And all the cars here were older models, some very much older, including the carcasses of two that clearly had been wrecked and abandoned long before.

As the minivan rolled down the street, its headlights picked up an occasional address — and, twice, a group of young boys walking down the broken sidewalk, trying to stay in the shadows.

They look like they're up to no good.

He finally saw 1818 in the headlight beam, counted the gap next to that house as 1820, and decided the next ratty row house had to be 1822.

He stopped the minivan at what he presumed was 1824, parked, grabbed the envelope, peeled off his denim jacket, and got out.

As he looked at the darkened house — he could not see one light on inside — he now worried that this address may be deserted.

One step away from falling down and becoming a gap, too.

But when he knocked on the old wooden door's glass pane, which was covered on the inside by a dusty curtain, a dog barked loudly from deep inside the house.

He faintly heard footsteps inside, then the lone bulb of the porch light came on.

Bony fingers pulled aside the dusty curtain, and an elderly black woman with a deeply wrinkled face and thinning gray hair peered out at him. She looked half asleep, and judging by her expression, she was not expecting to find a white man in a FedEx uniform on her porch.

"Can I help you?" she squeaked out.

"Sorry to bother you so late, ma'am. It's my last delivery." He held up the envelope. "Got a special delivery from the U.S. Treasury for a Jossiah Miffin at this address."

"A what?"

"It's an envelope from the Treasury Department in Washington. Been delivering these all day. I'm guessing they're some kind of refund check."

"Check?" she repeated, taking a long moment to consider that. "Just leave it. At the door be good."

"Sorry, ma'am. Can't do that. Need for this" — he glanced at the bill of lading and pretended to read it — "Jossiah Miffin to personally sign for it. He live here?"

She nodded. "He my grandson. I sent him to the drugstore in my car. You can wait if you want."

Will Curtis felt his stomach start to knot up again.

He looked at the woman, nodded, and said, "I'm going to wait in the van."

"Suit yourself," she said, and the dusty curtain fell closed.

In the fifteen minutes that Will Curtis had sat in the minivan, hoping not to experience another unfortunate personal accident, he'd again seen the group of three boys who'd been walking down the sidewalk earlier.

They simply have nothing better to do.

Or choose not to find something better to do.

No wonder they get in such trouble. You look long enough for trouble, you're damn sure going to find it.

There was still a knot in his stomach. And he still felt terribly weak and drained. The dizziness had not completely gone away.

He pulled the Glock out from under his shirt and laid it on his lap, then realized he hadn't been keeping track of how many rounds he'd fired.

More important, how many I have left.

All I know for sure is that there's one round chambered.

He pushed the magazine release on the side

of the weapon and the magazine dropped out of the grip. Its capacity was ten rounds.

He held the magazine up to the overhead light. Numbered holes up its back side allowed for a visual count of the bullets, but in the poor lighting he had trouble seeing exactly how many were there.

With some effort, he started thumbing the rounds out the top of the magazine and into his lap. He counted a total of five left.

Six, including the one in the throat.

He reloaded the magazine with some effort, slipped it into the pistol, and, using the heel of his left hand, slammed it home.

Okay, now where the hell are you, Jossiah?

A minute or so later, his eyes were slightly blinded by lights reflected in his rearview mirrors.

He blinked, then looked. He saw a yellowish pair of big, round headlight beams bouncing up and down the street toward him. Then he heard the sound of the engine valves knocking noisily as the driver accelerated.

That's one old damn car.

The shocks are shot. And it sounds like the engine is just about to go, too.

The car rattled to a stop at the weed-choked curb in front of the row house at 1822 Ontario Street. The air became heavy with the smell of raw gasoline and half-burned exhaust.

Will Curtis pulled on his grease-smeared FedEx cap and swung open the minivan's door. He stepped out, swaying a bit, then walked back and stood in the beam of the car's left headlight so that the FedEx logos on his hat, shirt, and the envelope were clearly visible to the driver.

He held the envelope in front of his crotch, concealing his hand holding the pistol.

As Will Curtis carefully continued stepping toward the car — which he now could see was a mid-1970s AMC Gremlin, in his opinion one of the ugliest and most worthless vehicles that had ever been produced — there came the sound of tortured metal as the driver pushed open the rusted-out door.

"You stay there, girl," the driver, a black man with shoulder-length hair, said to someone in the passenger seat.

Curtis could barely make out what he thought was a thin young teenage girl sitting there. She wore a white sleeveless jacket.

So he's still got a taste for the young ones. . . .

The black male turned to Will Curtis and aggressively said: "What the hell you want?"

"Your grandmother said I should wait for you to deliver this envelope," Curtis said.

"You're Jossiah Miffin, right?"

As Curtis stepped closer, he saw the black man's attention turn to the envelope. Then, despite the now-long black hair, Will saw the face from the mug shot, including the J-shaped scar.

"What up with the envelope? What's in it?"

Unexpectedly, a delirious Will Curtis heard in his head Stan Colt's voice. Colt, playing an over-the-top tough-cop character, was saying one of the lines in the shoot-'em-up movie that Curtis had just sat through twice.

Curtis tossed the envelope at Miffin's feet.

Miffin instinctively tried to catch it.

Will Curtis then leveled the Glock at Miffin's head and, in his best deep gravelly Stan Colt voice, recited the line "A heavy diet of lead, with a side order of penance."

Curtis squeezed the trigger twice.

The first round pierced the hook of the J-shaped scar, causing Miffin's head to jerk backward. The second round then went into the roof of his open mouth and exited through the top of his skull.

Miffin collapsed to the asphalt street.

The teenage girl in the car began screaming hysterically.

And suddenly, feeling very dizzy, Will

Curtis saw nothing but black. He collapsed beside Miffin, dropping the Glock as he went down.

Will Curtis didn't know how long he'd been passed out, only that he'd definitely been out cold. He had a lump on his forehead from where it had hit the pavement.

He figured that he couldn't have been out too long, because the teenage girl was still screaming in the passenger seat.

And Jossiah Miffin, of course, was still where he'd fallen dead.

As Will Curtis tried to stand, he quickly discovered that he had almost no energy whatever.

He made it up to his hands and knees and began crawling back to the Ford minivan.

It took an eternity to pull himself up into the driver's seat, then get the door closed.

With a lot of effort, he started the engine, put the shifter in drive, and rolled forward.

He looked in the mirror and saw three young black teens rush out to the Gremlin. He watched as one reached under the car and pulled something out.

What was . . . oh, the envelope!

Those savages will steal anything they think is worth something.

Won't they be surprised when they find the

Wanted sheet.

Then again, maybe they'll turn him in for the reward.

The kid shoved it inside his sweatshirt, then took off running.

Will Curtis turned at the corner and headed for Germantown Avenue.

[THREE]
Hops Haus Tower, Unit 2180
1100 N. Lee Street, Philadelphia
Sunday, November 1, 9:58 P.M.

In the middle of the plush king-size bed facing a panoramic view of the lights along the Delaware River and beyond, Matt Payne and Amanda Law were lying on their left sides, spoon fashion, resting in the glow of the carnally exhausted. Matt had his arms wrapped around Amanda and across her slowly rising and falling bosoms. His right leg was draped over her right hip, his toes tucked back in just above her ankles. When he inhaled, he marveled at her soft warm scent — at once sweet and, from the perspiration, lightly salty — that felt rich in pheromones.

This is as good as it gets, he thought, and

he gently kissed the back of her neck.

She grunted softly, appreciatively.

Then, even though his cell phone was in the pocket of his khaki pants that had been unceremoniously dropped on the floor at the far side of the bed and were now under a curled-up Luna, he heard the phone's distinctive *ping!* that announced he had an incoming text message.

Okay, we've been lying here like this for at least ten minutes, neither of us saying a word. Or moving an inch.

Just intimately intertwined.

And it's been nice. Incredibly nice.

So would I really ruin everything by checking that message?

I really really really don't want to fuck up the moment, because — wow! — what a helluva romp that was.

Where does she get the energy? And the deep passion?

Incredible.

Then he heard another *ping!*

In his arms, Amanda moved a little.

"You're not," she softly said. But it was more of a question.

He didn't reply.

"Are you?" she then said, her tone somewhat incredulous.

He thought: *You probably would if it was*

yours going off.

He said: "Of course not, baby."

And then there was another: *Ping!*

Then two others in a row: *Ping! Ping!*

What the hell?

"What's going on, Matt?"

"I don't know, baby. I told you I'm not going to check those."

But I should. What the hell?

Ping!

She moved again, then suddenly squirmed out from under him.

"Well," she said, "if you're not, I sure as hell am."

She reached down the side of the bed and grabbed the waistband of the khakis, tugging hard when she felt the weight of Luna on them.

"Sorry, girl," Amanda said as she dug in the pocket and pulled out the phone.

Luna slinked across the room and went into her crate in the master bath. It sounded as if she threw herself down onto the hard plastic liner. Then Luna gave a heavy sigh.

Amanda looked at the phone's screen.

She said, "Three from Tony —"

"What the hell?" he said, sitting up and adjusting the pillow to lean back on.

"— one from Kerry, and the last one's from Denny."

"Denny?" he said.

She held the phone out to him.

"That can't be good," Matt said. "He doesn't like texting and only does it out of necessity. Wonder why he didn't just call."

He glanced at them, then saw that the time stamps of the various messages were not all from the last few minutes, as the multiple *ping-ping*s would have suggested. Instead, the first one, from Harris, went back almost an hour. That suggested the messages had been stacked up somewhere, unable to get through. He then looked at his signal-strength icon, and it was flickering from the weakest signal to the icon that read: NO SIGNAL.

Payne shook his head, then read the first message from Tony Harris:

— **ANTHONY HARRIS**-

YO, MATTY. TURN ON KEYCOM CABLE CHANNEL 555 & BACK IT UP TO THE TOP OF THE HOUR. TROUBLE BREWING . . .

When Hops Haus Tower had been built, the entire property had been wired, so to speak, with super-high-speed KeyCom plastic fiber-optic digital transmission cables. The lines allowed for the advanced technology of KeyCom's various communications packages — telephone, Internet, television — to be exclusively provided by KeyCom to the residents and the retailers.

There was a simple reason for this select relationship: KeyProperties was heavily invested financially in the complex. And while some complained that such a noncompetitive environment effectively violated at least a dozen antitrust laws in the Commonwealth of Pennsylvania alone, the man who controlled both companies argued differently.

Frances Franklin Fuller the Fifth said that everyone did indeed have other options: "They are free to choose to live anywhere else and purchase the inferior communications packages offered there."

Matt looked at Amanda and said, "Tony says I need to see something on channel 555 real quick."

She nodded. "But be aware: If you run out the door on me two nights in a row . . ."

Matt smiled, then picked up the remote control, turned on the sixty-inch flat-screen television mounted on the wall, and hit the 5 button on the keypad three times.

Because the high-speed system was all digital, the control box for the television had a function that allowed any recorded program to be replayed or fast-forwarded for up to two hours. The fast-forward mode did not, of course, work for anything that was airing live. ("Now, that'd be revolutionary," Payne had said when an installation tech was showing him all the system's bells and whistles, "because if it could do that, it'd be tantamount to looking into the future.") But a live newscast, once recorded on KeyCom's massive servers, could be replayed.

"Hey," Matt said, "this is the cable channel for the live streaming news from Mickey O'Hara's CrimeFreePhilly website."

The news live stream looked exactly like any conventional television network newscast. It had a slick "News Center," a studio set that consisted of a brightly lit anchor desk, behind which sat a pair of young, perky, and polished talking heads. On the wall behind them, CRIMEFREEPHILLY.COM NEWSCAST was spelled out in gleaming chrome letters that were splashed with various colors from filters on unseen klieg carbon arc lamps that hung from the studio ceiling. Below the chrome letters, the wall held a bank of four giant flat-screen studio monitors, each showing some working news story.

Matt hit the button on the remote control that restarted the newscast at its beginning.

461

"Good evening," said the good-looking male talking head with dark hair and a bright smile. "Welcome to the nine-o'clock edition of tonight's newscast at CrimeFreePhilly-dot-com. I'm Dusty Meyers."

"And I'm Jessi Sabatini," said the attractive redhead with a dazzling display of teeth who was sitting beside him. "Tonight's top news: This weekend's Halloween Homicides continue to mount in Philadelphia."

Matt saw that the image behind her on the upper-right flat-screen studio monitor was of Francis Fuller standing at a lectern.

Matt hit the FAST FORWARD button, causing the audio to go temporarily silent and the two talking heads to begin bobbing as if on coil springs. They made very fast gestures.

Then the camera zoomed in on Jessi Sabatini. As she jabbered, a box popped up beside her bobbing head. In the box appeared a progression of photographs, mostly mug shots, of all the pop-and-drops with their names shown beneath them. Then there was a picture of Francis Fuller with his name underneath, and Payne hit the NORMAL PLAY button on the remote.

Jessi Sabatini was saying: "Corporate titan Frances Fuller, whose Lex Talionis has been very busy this weekend, gave a press conference earlier at which he presented ten-thousand-dollar rewards to some heroic citizens of Philadelphia. Our own Michael J. O'Hara was there and has the story."

The image of Fuller filled the entire television screen.

"And so the circus continues," Matt said to Amanda. "Hell, it was inevitable Five-Eff, my favorite Puritan, would make an appearance."

There was a text box to the right of Fuller's head reading: FRANCIS FULLER, C.E.O. LEX TALIONIS, DISTRIBUTES $10,000 REWARDS.

Along the bottom of the screen was a line of text that moved from right to left reading: *BREAKING NEWS* . . . MAYOR CARLUCCI ANNOUNCES POLICE DEPARTMENT EMERGENCY TASK FORCE AS HALLOWEEN HOMICIDES CONTINUE TO RISE . . . BODY COUNT IN OLD CITY NOW UP TO FIVE. . . .

The voice of O'Hara, who was off-screen, came from the television speakers: "This is Michael J. O'Hara reporting from Lex Talionis in Old City, where Frank Fuller has just made some Philly residents much richer for having helped make the city much safer."

The camera pulled back and showed more of the room.

Francis Franklin Fuller the Fifth was in

what appeared to be a conference room of his Richard Saunders Holdings office building. The short, portly forty-four-year-old, wearing his customary Benjamin Franklin outfit, stood behind a solid black lectern, both hands gripping its top. The front of the black lectern had a bronze plaque bearing the Lex Talionis logotype with the stylized-eyeball "o."

The camera then pulled farther back and showed a line of people standing to the side. Between them they held three ceremonial bank checks fashioned from heavy white plastic sheeting three feet high and six feet long. Each had in the upper left-hand corner a large red representation of the Lex Talionis logotype. And each had been filled out in handwritten lettering with a fat-tipped black permanent marker.

Payne immediately recognized one of the women who held the reward checks. She was the first on the left, closest to the lectern.

"And look who he's with," Matt said. "That's the mother of one of the dead pop-and-drops."

It was confirmed by the name written in her check's payee field: *Shauna Mays*.

Matt added: "We think that my mystery shooter popped her son, and then she and a gypsy cabbie dropped the body at Five-Eff's."

Matt thought: *Women really can be the more ruthless of our species.*

Despite her face and hand being deeply bruised, and still looking malnourished and dirty in the torn clothing she'd been wearing when Payne interviewed her earlier in the day, Shauna Mays stood there beaming.

She held — barely, as it was bigger than she was — a ceremonial check made out in the amount of ten thousand dollars. To her right — behind another ten-thousand-dollar ceremonial check that was written out to: *Paco Ramirez, Yvette Iglesia, et alii, for Sasha Bazelon* — stood a small pack of teenagers. Holding the check at each end were a tough-looking Latin male wearing baggy jeans and an oversize jacket, and a pretty, petite Latina with fiery eyes.

Matt said, "Those in the middle must be the crowd Javier told me about. The ones who caught the punk responsible for Principal Bazelon's death. And that pretty teen girl looks like she is probably Javier's baby sister."

Matt did not recognize the woman holding the third oversize reward check, but like Shauna Mays, she appeared rough-looking and underfed. Judging by the name on the check, it was most likely Michael Floyd's mother.

Then Matt noticed the two extra legs standing beside her, and when the check moved, Michael's head appeared around its right end.

Matt turned to Amanda and said, "That's the kid I was going to tell you about. Very strange."

Hanging on the wall behind them was a white banner emblazoned with:

YOUR HOME FOR HELPING CLEAN UP
YOUR HOMETOWN:
WWW.LEXTALIONIS.COM
AND
WWW.CRIMEFREEPHILLY.COM

The camera went back to Fuller. And the voice of O'Hara said: "Let's now go directly to Fuller's press conference. . . ."

As if trying to bring attention to them, Francis Fuller took an inordinate amount of time to straighten the tiny round Ben Franklin glasses at the tip of his big nose. Then he cleared his throat. He smiled and leaned forward to speak into the black stalk microphone that curved up from the lectern.

"Thank you for coming," Fuller began.

"I do have an important announcement today. My assistant, however, tells me we're to start with your questions." He pointed forward, toward the unseen reporters. "Yes, madam?"

A female reporter's voice asked, "There've been a total of six dead dropped here —"

"Five dead evildoers," he corrected, "and one looking like he soon may join them."

"Okay, five dead, one nearly so. What is your reaction to Mayor Carlucci's statement earlier today that clearly was triggered by these dead men left here at Lex Talionis?"

"Well, of course I agree with Mayor Carlucci, whom I consider not only a fine leader of our city but also a close personal friend."

"Bullshit," Matt said.

Fuller went on: "We agree that evildoers must be held accountable for their actions. I fully support Jerry's efforts and those of our hardworking police department. Which is why today it's been my great honor as a citizen of Philadelphia to present the reward checks for ten thousand dollars" — he gestured toward those holding the ceremonial checks — "to these fine folks who have helped rid our society of those who chose not to be law-abiding. Today alone we have two additional evildoers who will never again roam our free society to harm the innocent. And we have Xavier Smith — now at Hahnemann University Hospital in critical condition and under police guard — a career criminal with more than twoscore arrests who has been brought to justice. Regardless of any differences the mayor and I may or may not have, I would suggest that real progress in cleaning up our city is being made here at Lex Talionis."

Amanda said, "You know, rationally, I can't say that I disagree with Fuller."

"Not you, too?" Matt said incredulously.

She shrugged and said, "It's really no different from what my father said about humans not being very far removed from other animals. He compared the criminals, particularly the most heinous, to hyenas, saying they were nothing more than opportunistic savages. And that it took a predator, like a lion, to weed them out, essentially cleaning up its environment. If someone had done that a long time ago with Delgado and Jiménez, a lot of people would never have been hurt."

Matt looked at her for a moment.

Well, I can understand her wanting vengeance for being abducted.

He then said: "I'm afraid to ask what you think about the mating ritual of the female

468

praying mantis."

She looked at him out of the corner of her eye, grinned playfully, and replied, "Nothing to lose your head over, sweetie."

On-screen, Fuller was taking his time pointing toward the crowd, then said, "You, sir. Your question?"

A male voice said, "How do you respond to those who say that your reward to 'remove evildoers from free society' actually encourages killing, as opposed to simple capture and arrest?"

Fuller tried to square up his short, paunchy body, and then said with strong conviction, "I believe the results, as noted, speak for themselves. Next question."

"And the Law of Talion is above our legal system?" the same reporter asked.

"No. Of course not. I would simply characterize it as a more effective system, both for dealing with the worst of our criminal element and for discouraging others who consider crime acceptable. People have choices. Some make very bad ones, time and again."

He picked up from the lectern the Wanted sheet for Kendrik LeShawn Mays. He held it out toward the crowd and cameras. The mug shot was clearly visible on the television.

"Take, as an example, this latest evildoer. Among his many other crimes, Kendrik Mays preyed on children, forever corrupting their innocence for his sexual pleasure. He was a fugitive, on the run for years after serving time for involuntary deviant sexual intercourse and rape of an unconscious or unaware person. It is my understanding that his victim was a fourteen-year-old girl whom he drugged and then committed unspeakable acts upon. Mays's mother told me that he continued such corrupt and contemptible behavior right up until his moment of *Lex Talionis*."

Fuller paused dramatically, then went on: "I put to you that the traditional legal system failed not only to either change or stop Mays, but that it also failed to protect us citizens from him. And there are countless other evildoers just like him, ones fearless of the legal system."

Amanda said, "And I don't disagree with that, either."

Matt caught himself nodding, then he stopped himself just before he said aloud: *That's what's known in my business as job security, baby.*

Fuller pointed to another reporter: "Yes?"

"What are your thoughts about Operation Clean Sweep?"

Matt said, "Now, this should be interesting."

Fuller nodded solemnly, took a long moment to gather his thoughts, then said: "My first thought on the police department's task force is this: If anyone can make it successful, it's the Wyatt Earp of the Main Line."

He paused and almost grinned.

Matt blurted, "Five-Eff, you sonofabitch!"

Fuller went on: "And I mean that sincerely. Sergeant Payne is not only a fine law-enforcement officer, but a fine friend of mine, too."

"Bullshit," Matt said again.

"Now," Fuller said, "with all due respect to my good friend Mayor Carlucci, I say this to his statement concerning this new task force: Why waste effort trying to stop someone who is doing good by removing the evildoers from our city? Such people should not be condemned and hunted but, rather, encouraged in whatever way. Indeed, *rewarded.* And that's why Lex Talionis is here today. And it's why it will be here tomorrow and the days after."

Francis Franklin Fuller the Fifth then smiled and raised his right index finger, wagging it at shoulder height.

"And *that* brings me to today's big announcement," he said. "I am genuinely honored to say that, henceforth, Lex Talionis will double each new reward to" — he poked the air with his index finger for each word — *"twenty thousand dollars!"*

The microphone picked up the loud and indignant voice of a young male just out of camera view: "Say *what?* And we only get ten grand, muthafucka?"

Matt Payne chuckled. "That was that backward kid."

Then he thought: *Wait. He's doubling the reward?*

He thumbed the remote control to back up to where Fuller raised his finger, then watched him poke the air and say, *"Twenty thousand dollars!"*

"Sonofabitch! There'll be mayhem in the streets!"

Amanda said, "You're right. Now what happens?"

Matt looked at her. "I don't know exactly, but it's going to have to come from someone with stars on his white shirt. Or higher. And soon."

Matt looked at his phone and quickly read through the other texts.

The second one from Harris, time-stamped almost thirty minutes earlier than the other, read:

> — ANTHONY HARRIS-
>
> GOOD NEWS: THE PRINTS CAME BACK FROM IAFIS ON REGGIE JONES.
>
> ONE WAS A NO-MATCH. BUT THE OTHER WAS A HIT FOR (I SHIT YOU NOT) A DRUG DEALER NAMED MARCUS CICERO, AKA MARC JAMES, WHITE MALE, AGE 28. LONG LIST OF PRIORS.

Matt shook his head.

Some druggie murderer trying to pass himself off as a Roman emperor? What's up with that?

Then he read Harris's third text, the most recent, which was time-stamped fifteen minutes after the second one:

> — ANTHONY HARRIS-
>
> FYI — THERE'S NOW AN UNDERCOVER SITTING ON JAMES'S LKA IN PORT RICHMOND. HE'S WORKING A COUPLE CI'S TOO.

Well, maybe one or both confidential informants will want to cash in the wannabe Roman

473

for a twenty-grand reward. . . .

Matt then went to Rapier's message:

```
- CPL KERRY RAPIER-

THOUGHT  YOU'D  LIKE  TO  KNOW
THAT  I  HEARD  FROM  FORENSICS  ON
THE  PRINTS  FROM  KENDRIK  MAYS'S
HOUSE.  GOT  A  HIT:  IT'S  YOUR  OLD
BUDDY  SNU  2010-56-9280
```

Damn. But no surprise there. The mystery shooter strikes again.

Finally, he got to Coughlin's.

Payne was amazed that Coughlin had actually thumbed out a cleanly written text message, and he wondered how long the two sentences had taken him. They read:

```
- UNCLE DENNY-

BE  PREPARED  FOR  CONFERENCE  IN
ECC  TOMORROW  0800.

YOUR  PAL  5-F  JUST  CAUSED  CAR-
LUCCI  TO  REALLY  BLOW  HIS  CORK
AGAIN.
```

"Oh, shit," Matt said as he quickly thumbed

and sent the reply: "Yes, sir. I'll be there."

"What, Matt?" Amanda asked.

"I was right. Something from very high up. Uncle Denny says that Carlucci has blown his cork and that he will hold another conference first thing in the morning. Which means I'll have to be there at oh-dark-thirty. Anytime he plays the Boy Scout motto card, it's code for me to really be on my toes."

"Be Prepared?" she said, reading the screen.

"Uh-huh."

Amanda then reached over and picked up the television remote from beside his knee. She hit its red OFF button.

She then snuggled up to him and tugged his cell phone out of his hands. She turned it off, too, and slipped the phone back into his pants pocket.

Then she put her head on his shoulder and softly said, "That's tomorrow, sweetie. Now it's Be Prepared for tonight."

[FOUR]
Two Liberty Place,
Thirty-seventh Floor
50 South Sixteenth Street,
Philadelphia
Sunday, November 1, 10:12 P.M.

"Seriously?" Jan Harper said, her tone sharp and incredulous. She tried keeping her voice low to avoid being overheard in the five-star restaurant high atop one of Philly's tallest buildings. "Rapp, I don't know if you can cover your ass this time. Those guys are dead. And the demolition company is raising hell that we — HUD — said it was clear to take down those condemned buildings. And I don't know who gave them the go-ahead."

Badde heard Jan, but he was paying more attention to how she looked in the posh Vista Fiume restaurant. And thinking how, when they'd walked in, she'd looked like she owned the place. The young bankers and lawyers and other professionals had turned.

The beautiful people, Badde thought.

And I'm with one of the prettiest women in the room.

Not bad for the son of a barber from South Philly.

This really is a classy joint.

Maybe after I get through all this, and the fund makes a little more money, I'll get a condo here. Move on up. I heard Risken bought a six-million-dollar one just before he ran for governor. Not bad company for me to be associated with. . . .

Taking up half of the entire thirty-seventh floor, "River View" had a high-class international feel, more like a large open-air nightclub than a restaurant. All its gleaming wood-inlaid tables featured undulating lounge seats that faced the windows and their commanding views of the city and the rivers bracketing it. The ambience thrummed with a high energy.

While Vista Fiume set a new nightlife standard for Philadelphia, it still wasn't on par with the chicest and toniest restaurants and nightclubs that were offered in New York, the City That Never Sleeps. And the Philly nightlife certainly wasn't anywhere near that of, say, Buenos Aires, where the Argentines began partying well past ten-thirty and did not slow down until the sun came up.

But judging by the international clientele, Badde thought, scanning the room, *it's coming.*

Those foreign models are gorgeous — and Jan fits right in.

When he had driven the Range Rover up to the cobblestone circle drive of the Hops Haus Tower, Jan had been waiting just inside the main glass doors. The bright lights of the lobby made her look like a model. Her curvy body looked stunning in a black velvet dress, her silky light-brown face complemented with an elegant short strand of pearls.

Although Badde — who had stopped by his City Hall office and changed into a plain dark two-piece suit and open-collared shirt he'd worn two days earlier — would never have admitted to it, he felt far out of her league.

And that had only become more apparent to him when they'd arrived at Two Liberty Place, a first-class high-rise that was the city's third-tallest building. It featured executive offices and condominiums costing upward of seven million dollars, among the most expensive in town.

Then Jan had really proven she owned the place when she told the maître d': "The reservation is under Harper, and it's for table eighty-two, please."

After they were seated, and Rapp Badde could tell the table had the best view in the place, he said, "You've been here before!"

She smiled. "No, I just made a few calls while getting ready. Then made the reservation. A friend said table eighty-two is supposed to have the best sunset view. And she said I should have crab cakes and lobster, and my date should get either the tenderloin or veal. Or, if you're feeling adventurous, the mini cheesesteaks. Get some before Yuri arrives."

Badde then thought: *And what the hell does the Russian want to talk about all of a sudden? I've been racking my brain over that since Jan said we were coming here.*

He really is an impatient one — an impatient one with a temper.

Forty-eight-year-old Yuri Tikhonov was an international investor who had earned his first billion dollars between the ages of thirty-five and forty — after, it was rumored, having more or less left the employ of the Sluzhba Vneshney Razvedki, Russia's external spying and intelligence gathering agency, formerly the KGB.

Tikhonov now had investments in companies around the world, though primarily in Russia, Europe, and the United States. He held forty-nine percent of Diamond Develop-

479

ment in Philadelphia, while the other fifty-one percent — the majority of shares — was owned by minority investors or minority-owned companies, including one Urban Ventures LLC.

Tikhonov was quietly friendly with various members of the Russian mafia, a group viewed as far more merciless than the Italian mob. It was said that the only reason the Russians hadn't come in and simply wiped out La Cosa Nostra was that they felt the crimes of the Sicilians — petty by comparison — weren't really competition. The Wops kept the cops plenty busy chasing cheap hookers and sports bookies, and were thus a convenient diversion from the Russians' own high-dollar illicit activities, everything from corporate fraud to money laundering.

Badde had learned that it didn't take a mathematical whiz to put two and two together and figure out that a lot of the investment money going into the Diamond Development projects was dirty cash getting cleansed.

But no one — particularly a politician hoping to run for mayor of Philadelphia in the next election — was ever going to question the minority lead investors (brought together by Tikhonov) about where their funds had been borrowed from (venture capital firms serving as shells for the Russian mob).

If that happened, the money — and the "multipurpose professional entertainment venue" and other major projects — would find a city not so inquisitive and unfriendly to capital investment.

Jan Harper took a bite of her crab cake appetizer, then carefully picked up her martini glass and sipped the bright green appletini.

"Seriously," Badde said, nodding after taking a swallow of his vodka-and-tonic cocktail. "Who's anyone going to believe more? The office of a city councilman or a bunch of Dago dirt movers? I've got that possible liability —"

"*Plausible deniability,* Rapp," she interrupted, her tone now slightly disgusted. "I told you that it's called plausible deniability. What you deny is believable. And to that point, I'm not sure that's the case here. Three people are dead, and it looks like HUD sent a crew out to do it."

She looked at him as she went to sip her martini.

He looks pissed. And he is.

But it's not because I corrected him.

It's because I interrupted.

Badde then shrugged. "I don't know. If we didn't do it, then we didn't do it."

"It's perception," Jan said. "People believe what they see, not necessarily what the facts are."

"Then maybe we can blame it on miscommunications. Throw some poor campaign volunteer under the bus." He paused in thought. "Actually, that might be a really good idea. An extra diversion."

Jan Harper didn't say anything, but she was coming to realize that the more she knew H. Rapp Badde, Jr., the more she found that he wasn't at all shy about making people sacrificial lambs for his purposes.

Sure, it's not unusual in politics, where the rule is always to protect the politician.

But he almost does it for blood sport.

And who's to say he wouldn't do it to me?

Jan glanced around the room, then looked at Badde, who she saw was also scanning the crowd. Suddenly, his eyes went wide.

"Don't look now," he said, looking behind her toward the entrance. "Wait till I tell you."

"What?"

"Yuri just walked in."

She turned. When she saw him, she smiled and waved once, then turned back toward Badde.

Yuri Tikhonov had a slender, compact, five-foot-five frame. His dark hair was cut stylishly long, the back touching his collar. He had a narrow face with piercing blue-gray eyes. He wore a custom-made dark two-piece suit and ice-blue shirt with French cuffs.

Tikhonov was making a direct line for the table, stopping only to shake hands with a few of the well-dressed men and kiss the cheeks of many more ladies.

Badde, still looking in his direction, was starting to stand. He said somewhat disgustedly, "The bastard acts like he owns the place."

Jan said simply, "He does, Rapp. I thought you knew."

When she saw him standing, she suddenly said in a loud whisper: "Badde!"

He looked at her with an annoyed expression that was meant to say *What now?*

She nodded toward his crotch and waved her hand over hers. "Your napkin!"

He looked down, said, "Shit," then removed the black linen napkin from where he'd tucked it into his belt.

He tossed the napkin onto the lounge seat just in time to hold out his right hand. He turned on his best politician's charm. "Yuri! How very good to see you again."

The Russian ignored Badde's hand and, instead, first leaned over and lightly kissed

Jan on both cheeks.

"It is a pleasure to see you, Janelle," he said, taking a step back and spreading his arms. "You look fabulous! A movie star!"

Then he turned to Badde and offered his hand.

"We do need to talk," he said by way of greeting.

Badde motioned for him to have a seat, and he took it.

"This won't take long," the Russian said, all businesslike. A waiter arrived and delivered to him a glass of ice water. "How soon does the project move forward, now that the holdouts have left the property?"

Rapp looked to Jan.

She said, "Theoretically, crews could start tomorrow. Realistically? Probably a month."

They watched as Tikhonov sipped his ice water and considered that.

"Not good enough," he then said. "Sooner. Too much time has been wasted."

Ever the politician, Badde smiled and lied, "Of course, Yuri. Sooner."

He looked at Jan and said, "Sooner, right?"

"Rapp, I'm not sure —"

"Sooner," Badde repeated, almost as if it were an order, then looked at Tikhonov.

Tikhonov locked eyes with him.

"No promises," the Russian said. "I want it done."

Badde then said, "Just so you know, there may be a small delay. We first have to manage a misunderstanding that we killed one of the holdouts by sending the wrecking crew and —"

Tikhonov interrupted him: "It will be no problem. That will be found to be nothing more than an unfortunate accident —"

Rapp interrupted: "That's what I thought," he said, giving Jan a glance.

"— and they will find that the others died of natural causes unknown," Tikhonov concluded.

"How can you be so sure?" Badde asked, clearly surprised.

Tikhonov considered his reply a long moment, then simply said: "Succinylcholine."

"What?"

"A muscle relaxant," Tikhonov said conversationally, "sometimes called suxamethonium. Injected, it causes the heart muscle to relax till it stops. Has a very short half-life. Undetectable after perhaps an hour."

Badde again glanced at Jan, then at Tikhonov. "You did it?"

Tikhonov, stone-faced, took a sip of his ice water, then said, "Of course not. Friends."

Badde thought, *Ice water is fitting. Just like*

the blood in his veins.

Badde said, "So then you called the demo-lition crew?"

Tikhonov shook his head. "Dimitri."

His assistant passed himself off as the new HUD expediter!

Yuri Tikhonov sighed. "Time is money, and it is time for the development to move forward." He paused and locked eyes with Badde. "Just make sure it continues to do so."

Tikhonov suddenly stood and said, "You'll please excuse me." Then he leaned over and kissed Janelle Harper once on the cheek, and left.

As Jan and Rapp looked at each other word-lessly, his business cell phone vibrated in his pocket. In the dim light under the table, its glowing screen read: ROGER WYNNE.

Badde slipped it back into his pocket, then looked at Jan, who was downing her mar-tini.

"I need to visit the men's room."

He stood and made his way toward the bar, then to the windows on the other side. He called Wynne back as he looked out at the grand view the thirty-seventh floor of-fered.

"Found him, Rapp," Wynne said when he answered. "Well, where Kenny's been, anyway. A nice old woman by the name of Irma Graham just called here looking for Kenny. Said she missed him tonight at Fernwood Manor's bingo, and that she hadn't seen him since he put a bunch of boxes in the storage room of their Community Activity Center."

That was *bingo I heard in the background!*

"Get someone over there to whatever you said —"

"Fernwood Manor at Cobbs Creek," Wynne furnished. "And I'm already on my way."

"Destroy every goddamn shred of paper. I don't care if we ever have those votes again."

Badde ended the call. Looking out the window over the city, he thought, *Well, at least that'll get rid of the absentee-voter stuff. Now Kenny can't squeal — who's going to believe him without proof?*

I may again have just dodged going to jail. . . .

On the way back to the table, Badde paused at the magnificent bar.

There was a muted large flat-screen television tuned to the Eagles–Broncos National Football League game. Badde, acting as if he'd stopped to catch the score — Philadelphia was just barely beating Denver — took in the crowd, particularly all the attractive women.

Well, I'll damn sure be coming back here.

The TV broadcast went to a commercial break.

One of the TV news talking heads came on with a tease for the eleven P.M. newscast. The box that popped up next to the news anchor's head showed Francis Fuller awarding at least three ceremonial ten-thousand-dollar reward checks. The text below the pop-up box said HALLOWEEN HOMICIDES: COLD-BLOODED MURDER TURNS INTO COLD CASH.

And Kenny — and that drug dealer Cicero — are going to be next.

X

[ONE]
The Roundhouse, Third Floor
Eighth and Race Streets,
Philadelphia
Monday, November 2, 9:12 A.M.

The Executive Command Center's main bank of monitors — all nine sixty-inch flat-screen televisions — was filled with the beet-red, angry face of the Honorable Jerome H. "Jerry" Carlucci, Mayor of the City of Philadelphia, Pennsylvania.

He stared right into the camera with a searing fire in his intense brown eyes as he said with great force: "And never in all my years in this city — both during my years in the Philadelphia Police Department and my time in elected office as your mayor — *never* have I witnessed such careless disregard for our laws. And I am here to tell you that this is lawless chaos of the worst sort" — his fist could be heard pounding the lectern — *"and I will not let it stand!* There will be law and order in the great city of Philadelphia if I have to bring in the state police and our National Guard troops.

"And I am also telling you again that if you have information about any crime, you are to call our police department or the tips hotline — and no one else — and the police department will respond appropriately. This will not in any way cause anyone to be ineligible for any possible reward. It will, however, restore decorum to our fine city and dignity to its citizens.

"Now, to show how absolutely serious I am in this regard, just this morning four people who went to Lex Talionis in Old City —"

The image on the screen then cut to a shot of what had become the familiar scene at Third and Arch. Except this time there was a sea of dark blue — uniformed police lining the sidewalks shoulder to shoulder as far as the eye could see. And there were police cruisers parked bumper to bumper all along the curbs. There was a Medical Examiner's Office van parked on the sidewalk, its rear doors open and a gurney with a full body bag being pushed inside.

And in front of the van were four people, their hands cuffed behind their backs, being led by blue shirts to the open rear doors of two Chevy Impala police cars parked at the curb. The first was a tiny, ancient, gray-haired black woman in a sacklike dress, then a skinny young teenage black girl in a white sleeveless jacket, and two teenage black males in jeans and hoodie sweatshirts.

A Tow Squad wrecker rolled past on Arch Street, a rusted-out mid-1970s AMC Gremlin hanging backward behind it.

"— were each arrested on multiple counts of suspicion of murder, tampering with evidence at the scene of a crime, and various other criminal charges in connection with the murder last night of one Jossiah Miffin. Arrested were his grandmother and three teenagers, two boys who identified themselves as Miffin's neighbors, and a girl who said she was his niece."

The image went back to Carlucci's face.

He went on pointedly: "If these people had followed the proper procedure and called 911 for the police to handle the case of Miffin's murder — and *not* brought the deceased to Lex Talionis — certain charges would never have been brought against them." He paused, exhaled audibly, and in a calmer manner added, "So, in conclusion, let there be no mistake that, as I swore to do when I took my oath of office, I will see that the laws of this fine and just city are enforced to the letter. And, together, you and I will see Philadelphia return to normalcy. Thank you for your time. And may God bless you and the great city of Philadelphia."

Corporal Kerry Rapier was in his wheeled nylon-mesh-fabric chair at the control panel, manipulating the images on the three banks of monitors. He rewound the recording back to where Carlucci was forcefully saying: "And never in all my years in this city . . ."

"I think three times is enough, Kerry," Sergeant Matthew Payne said. "It was difficult enough to watch live the first time. I was convinced that his anger was being directed at the head of Task Force Operation Clean Sweep, who has accomplished exactly

491

zero in his appointed duty."

Payne was sitting at Conference Table One. Detective Anthony Harris sat beside him. Each had a commanding view of the three banks of TV monitors, all brightly lit with various images, ones that now included the new pop-and-drops. Before them on the table, each had a notebook computer wired into the communications network. Matt's screensaver image showed a hundred tiny .45 ACP rounds continually ricocheting across the screen, looking like a copper-jacketed hollow-point meteor shower.

Next to Matt's computer was a coffee-stained mug with the representation of a patch. On the patch was the downtown Philadelphia skyline with the statue of William Penn atop City Hall. Overlooking that was a Grim Reaper in a black cape and holding a golden scythe. And in gold letters the words PHILADELPHIA POLICE HOMICIDE DIVISION — OUR DAY BEGINS WHEN YOURS ENDS circled the patch.

Kerry Rapier said: "But, Matt, I just love that part where the spittle starts flying and he pounds the lectern with his iron fist while declaring, '. . . and I will not let it stand!' Brilliant, just brilliant theater."

Payne raised an eyebrow. "I'm pretty damn sure he wasn't acting. I've seen him blow his

492

cork a time or three before." He looked to the second bank of monitors. "Getting back to the task force task at hand, so to speak, let's see if we can turn over some damn stone under the stone."

Kerry Rapier checked the notes he'd written on his pad, then looked at the banks of monitors and said, "We have new information in the case files of Kendrik Mays, LeRoi Cheatham, Reggie Jones, and now Jossiah Miffin." He paused, then added, "Oh, and those three dead we saw at the demolition site in Northern Liberties."

"Not those now," Payne said. "They were a block away from where Cheatham got popped, but they're not even remotely connected to any of the pop-and-drops, including Cheatham's."

"I agree," Harris said. "Unless the medical examiner finds some obvious cause of death — maybe poisoning? — my gut tells me that those are fast on their way to becoming cold cases. All we know is what caused the blunt trauma on the one — a damn wrecking ball — but that wasn't necessarily the cause of death."

"Gotcha," Rapier said. He manipulated his control panel.

Kendrik Mays's case file went to the main bank of monitors, his ugly mug staring down at them.

Rapier took the Colt .45 cursor and clicked on the link that took them to the crime-scene video. But the pointing device didn't fire or have any muzzle smoke.

"What happened to that?" Payne asked.

"I disabled it before the mayor came in this morning," Kerry said. "Decided it was a bit over the top. Anyway, as I told you in that text last night, Matt, forensics matched the prints at the Mays house to our mystery shooter, SNU 2010-56-9280."

The video showed the Mays basement with inverted-V evidence markers everywhere. Rapier moved the cursor over the marker bearing the numeral "05" in the corner of the basement. It was next to a pistol on a dirt-encrusted, sweat-stained T-shirt. A box with a series of digitized buttons at its bottom then popped up. It held a sharp image of the revolver that they'd seen being photo-graphed on the live feed the day before.

"Matt, you were right about the snub-nosed. It was a Chief's Special, not a Body-guard."

Manipulating the console joystick, Rapier rotated the image of the pistol, showing all the angles at which it had been photo-graphed. He then moved the cursor to the series of digitized buttons. He clicked the button with a question mark on it, and up popped a translucent text box over the image of the pistol. It read:

Weapon: <u>Smith & Wesson Model 637-1</u> .38 Special revolver.

Serial Number: (Unknown; removed by grinding or filing)

Sold: (Unknown)

Seller: (Unknown)

Buyer: (Unknown)

Notes: <u>Airweight Chief's Special</u>. 5-shot stainless-steel cylinder and 2-inch barrel, aluminum alloy J-frame. Black rubber Uncle Mike's grips. Only two (2) rounds of Federal .38 caliber +p loaded in cylinder; other three (3) were spent shell casings of same round. Barrel riflings show evidence of firing. Fingerprints belonging to <u>Kendrik LeShawn MAYS 2008-18-063914-POP-N-DROP</u>.

"Then the 'boom' that killed Mays was the .38?" Payne said. "Not our mystery man's .45 cal.?"

"No, no. It was almost certainly the forty-five," Rapier said.

"What do you want to bet that when we run the ballistics on those plus-p rounds, the .38 will be linked to some other murder?" Harris said.

Payne nodded as they watched Rapier move the cursor to the basement floor, to the marker with a black "03" at the foot of the dirty mattress lying on wooden pallets. Next to it was a single spent brass casing.

Rapier put the cursor over the marker, and a box popped up with a digital photo close-up of the brass round. He clicked on the box's question mark button:

Spent casing, .45 GAP.
Notes: Possible bullet that killed Kendrik LeShawn MAYS 2008-18-063914-POP-N-DROP. SNU 201-56-9280.

Then he went to the opposite end of the bed, to the basement wall that had the blood splatter.

He clicked on the evidence maker, and up popped a box showing a close-up photograph of a Crime Scene Unit tech's hands in tan-colored synthetic polymer gloves holding a heavy-duty needle-nose pliers device that had just extracted a mushroomed copper-covered lead bullet from a wooden stud.

The question mark button brought up:

Copper-Jacketed Hollow-Point, .45 caliber. Notes: Possible/Probable bullet that killed <u>Kendrik LeShawn MAYS 2008-18-063914-POP-N-DROP.</u> <u>SNU 201-56-9280.</u>

"Okay," Payne said, "so we know it's our mystery shooter."

"Next," Rapier then said, working the control panel. Mays's case file was replaced with LeRoi Cheatham's on the main bank of monitors.

They read the Notes section and chuckled at Detective Harry Mudd's thoroughness. He'd written: "Michael FLOYD, age 12, nephew of deceased, when asked about possible involvement of a driver of a FedEx white minivan, responded with, 'What be a FedEx, motherfucker?' "

"I forget who it was," Harris said, "but someone once questioned Mudd about leaving something out of a report once, and he's never not put everything he knew into one. I heard that once, when a guy got shot in the pisser of a bar, he included all those 'for a good time, call Suzy' phone numbers he copied off the walls."

"Only some pompous ass like Howard Walker would question a pro like him," Payne said, then he immediately realized Rapier probably had heard him speak ill about his boss. When he glanced his way, Rapier was nodding. "That, and I like Mudd's sense of humor."

Rapier then went to the Crime Scene Unit's imagery of the Cheatham scene in Northern Liberties, and then went through the same motions with the spent .45-caliber casings there.

Payne felt his cell phone vibrate once. Staring at its screen, and seeing that he had no tower signal and that the time stamp of the new text was twenty minutes old, he blurted: "Goddamn cell service! Or I should say: goddamn lack of service!"

He glanced at Rapier. "Kerry, how come text messages are more reliable than voice? Call me skeptical, but it seems like it's the phone company's evil plan to screw the consumer. You either pay the outrageous price for an unlimited usage plan, or you pay through the nose for each individual text."

Rapier swiveled in his chair and replied: "Texts use less data than voice, making them easier to get through the pipes. They actually use the tiniest part of the bandwidth that the cell tower uses to constantly link to your phone. The rest of the bandwidth is for the heavier data users, the actual talking and Internet surfing." He paused and smiled. "But I'm betting you're right about it being an evil plan."

Matt grunted as he read the text from Amanda. All morning he'd figured that he was going to catch hell from her after she woke up and found on the pillow beside her only a note — and not him.

He'd written: *You look like such an angel while you sleep. I couldn't find the halo — I looked! — but there's definitely a heavenly glow. Sorry I had to leave so early. See you soon. — M*

He'd then gone back to his Rittenhouse Square apartment atop the Cancer Society Building that he rented from his father. He'd shaved and showered, and changed into nicer clothes.

He now wore a navy blazer, gray woolen cuffed trousers, a crisply starched light-blue shirt with a red striped tie, and highly polished black lace-up shoes.

But apparently I missed that bullet, he thought, rereading it:

```
AMANDA LAW

GOT YOUR NOTE. THANKS.

I WAY OVERSLEPT & WOKE UP NOT
FEELING WELL.

GOING DOWN TO DRUGSTORE.

THEN IT'S BACK TO BED . . .

XOXO -A
```

Hmmm . . . back to bed?
But no fun there if she's ill.
Guess that glow was a fever.
Hope it's not me she's sick of.
Could be from sheer exhaustion.
Then he thumbed the reply:

```
I'M REALLY SORRY, BABY.

CAN I BRING YOU ANYTHING?

ASPIRIN? CHICKEN SOUP?

HOW ABOUT ETERNAL HAPPINESS?

SEE YOU SOON . . .
```

He hit SEND. Then he put the phone back
in his pants pocket.

[TWO]

A minute later, the main door to the ECC suddenly began to swing open. Payne, Harris, and Rapier could hear the soft humming sound of an electric motor on the other side. Then in the doorway appeared a black male in his late teens. He was in a wheelchair, but it was a highly maneuverable power chair. He controlled its speed and direction with a joystick on the right armrest.

He fluidly rolled inside the ECC.

"Well, hell," Matt Payne said, "look who's still on the right side of the law. How are you, Andy?"

"Great, Marshal," Andy Radcliffe said with a smile.

Radcliffe, with gentle black eyes and a round, kind face, had a full head of dark hair trimmed to his scalp. His jeans and slightly oversize cotton dress shirt were neatly pressed. His navy blazer was somewhat worn.

Payne admired the intern, not only because he was a sophomore at La Salle doing a double major in computer science and criminal justice, and planning to get on with the department. He was also genuinely impressed with Andy's attitude after the teen had been robbed three years before in North Philly — then paralyzed when the robbers viciously stabbed him in the back.

Radcliffe looked at Rapier.

"Anything I can do to help?" he asked. He pointed at Payne's mug. "More java, Marshal?"

And there's that positive attitude, Payne thought. *Willing to fetch coffee, anything.*

"We're reviewing some cases," Payne said. "Never hurts to have a fresh set of eyes and ears. Make yourself comfortable. At the miserable rate we're going, we'll be here some time."

Radcliffe nodded. "Yessir."

"Okay, Kerry, let's move on to Reggie Jones —"

"Can I first read this one on Cheatham?" Radcliffe asked. "Wait. I'll pull it all up on the laptop. You guys go ahead."

Payne looked at him and thought, *And he's got confidence. Just walks in as if he's been doing it for years.*

The motor of Andy's power chair hummed as he went over to the end of the conference table, close to Rapier, and pulled out a laptop from a sleeve behind his chair. He

plugged the box into the department's communications system and started pounding
its keyboard.

Payne and Harris exchanged glances, then
looked back to the main monitor. The fat
baby face of Reginald Jones was looking
down on them.

Radcliffe looked up from his laptop and
saw Rapier's custom-made .45 pointer on-
screen.

He snorted. "That's some sweet cursor,
Kerry."

"Watch this," Rapier said. He typed a
command on his keyboard, then put the
cursor over REGINALD "REGGIE" JONES
Case No.: 2010-81-039 613-Pop-n-Drop
and clicked.

The overhead speakers then filled with
the report of a gunshot, and a puff of smoke
blew from the muzzle of the pistol pointer.

"Now, that," Radcliffe said, shaking his
head, "might be a bit too much."

"Finally!" Payne said. "A clear voice of reason is heard on the task force."

Harris snorted.

Radcliffe looked at him as if wondering
if he was being mocked, then judging by
Payne's expression realized that wasn't the
case. He returned his attention to his laptop,
fingers tapping the keyboard as he stared

thoughtfully at the screen.

Rapier did something at the control panel, and when he went to the Notes section of Reggie Jones's case file and clicked on FINGERPRINTS, the gunfire and smoke effects were gone.

He turned it off again, Payne thought. *But he doesn't look like he's pissed or anything.*

"Here's this new guy James, Matt," Rapier said as two boxes popped up with digitized images of fingerprints. One was headlined "Suspect Name Unknown #2010-56-9327." The second had the new live link: MARC JAMES Case No.: 2002-41-093631.

Harris said, "The prints on the still-unknown doer are being run again. Forensics got a hit with James's only because they reran his, too. They said they didn't find a match the first time because his prints on record from a previous arrest didn't have sufficient ridge detail for comparison. But the second go-round, they lit up just enough."

Payne looked at Rapier. "Punch up James, Kerry."

Reggie Jones's fat baby face was now replaced with that of a shiny-skinned black male with a round face and male-pattern baldness.

Toilet seat hair, Payne remembered hearing

someone describe it. Its shape was similar to those seats found on public commodes.

And the upper part of his garment looks like a hospital gown — or Roman-like robe.

"Who does this Cicero guy think he is?" Payne said. "Looks like he's in a toga, too."

"All kinds of crackpots in this city try to stand out from the crowd," Andy Radcliffe said.

"There's that voice of reason again," Payne said.

This time Radcliffe didn't at all feel like he was bring mocked.

Payne read off the screen: "'Marc James aka Marcus Cicero, age twenty-eight.' Looks like a nice guy, if you can just overlook all those unfortunate priors for running meth and roofies. And, for good measure, he racked up a conviction on involuntary deviant sexual intercourse. Guess he wanted to test his product."

Harris snorted. "Yeah. Really nice guy."

"Who's sitting on him now?"

"Charley Bell, in that old PECO van."

Payne nodded. The Philadelphia Electric Company van was always a good choice, its paint shot but the faded PECO logotype on it easily recognizable.

"Okay," Payne then said, "it's no doubt way too soon to have much on this new one that's got Hizzonor spitting mad. But punch up number twelve on the main bank, please."

Rapier worked the keyboard and the case sheet for Jossiah Miffin appeared. It showed both his mug shot, in which he had close-cropped hair, and his Medical Examiner's Office photo, where he had long black hair. Both showed the nasty J-shaped scar on his left cheek.

Name: Jossiah A. MIFFIN

Description: Black Male, age 30, 5'7", 180 lbs.

L.K.A.: 1822 W. Ontario St, Phila.

Prior Arrests: 8 total: possession of marijuana (6); possession of Methamphet-amine (1); convicted of Indecent assault & corruption of a minor (1) and sentenced to probation of intense sex offender treat-ments & no unsupervised contact with minors.

Call Received: 02 Nov, 0730 hours.

Cause of Death: Gunshots (2) to head (99 percent probability).

Case No.: 2010-81-039617-POP-N-DROP

> **Notes:** Fugitive. Warrants issued for multiple probation violations. Has prominent J-shape scar on left cheek. Takeeta Smith, 14-year-old female witness who claims to be niece of deceased, stated in interview that she saw him killed 01 Nov 2130 hrs by SNU in street at L.K.A. & described SNU as a skinny white male approximately 40 years of age wearing delivery uniform. Assailant left Wanted sheet at scene in FedEx envelope that was discarded. Body transported to Lex Talionis, Old City.

"Check out the Notes, Matt," Harris was saying, looking at the main monitor.

Payne looked up at the main monitor and read it.

"A FedEx delivery there at nine-thirty on a Sunday night?"

Then he turned to Rapier: "Punch up that interview with the girl, the animal's so-called niece."

The main bank of screens then showed Homicide Detective Jeff Kauffman — a tall, dark-haired thirty-four-year-old who had a quick laugh when he wasn't interviewing murder suspects — in Homicide Interview Room II with Takeeta Smith. She was sipping from a plastic bottle of grape-flavored soda. The empty wrapper of a Tastykake lay on the metal table.

They were almost exactly halfway through the interview when Takeeta's scratchy voice coming through the speakers in the ECC ceiling said:

"It be a FedEx envelope. And dude had a FedEx uniform."

"You're positive?"

She looked at Kauffman like he was from another planet, then said:

"Yeah, fool. I be positive. I mean, he be standing in the headlight, clear as damn day. Can't miss no FedEx sign. It be on every box my cousin's black tar shit come in from Texas."

Harris chuckled, then said, "Look at her *Oh shit, what'd I just say?* expression. Now who's the fool, Takeeta?"

"What a brain trust," Payne said. "They just don't know better. Reminds me of that arrogant Hank Whatshisname, the U.S. congressman from somewhere near Atlanta, who was grilling an admiral on Capitol Hill about the Navy's plans to station some eight thousand sailors and their families on Guam. He lectured the admiral that the island was only twenty-four miles long, seven 'at its least widest' — that's what he said, 'least widest, shore to shore' — and that he was afraid that with all those extra people, the island would tip over and capsize."

Harris laughed. "You're kidding."

Payne shook his head. "I shit you not, my friend. That's the kind of brilliant example of the 'geniuses' in our government that kids like her get to look up to as role models."

He looked over at Radcliffe. "Andy, who've been your role models in life?"

"Well, my momma, of course," he said immediately, clearly without thought. "She taught me hard work, discipline, never to give up. And there's Will Parkman, that really good cop who was a Marine and helps me go to school so I can eventually get a job here." He paused and thought, then added, "And you, Marshal."

Payne looked at Radcliffe, thinking that he now was being mocked. But when Matt saw Andy's face, he knew Andy was sincere.

Payne said, "I'd be damned careful about that last guy. He'll only lead you to trouble." He sighed. "And damn sure not to catch any bad guys."

"What's up with the bad-guy pop-and-drops having histories of sex crimes," Radcliffe said, "*and* STDs?"

"Where'd you get that?" Payne said, impressed.

He pointed at his laptop screen. "From the master file case notes."

"You've gone all the way back to the beginning?"

"Sure. Isn't that what you're supposed to do when trying to turn over a rock under a rock?"

Payne nodded. "Yes, indeed it is. And, to answer your question, there's not any single answer — with the exception of what Kerry recently suggested. None apparently knows what the hell a condom is."

Radcliffe said, "I've been feeding key data into my skunk-works search engine."

Radcliffe had managed to get his hands on an early version of a super-powerful software program developed at MIT, and Payne had seen him use it before.

"And?" Payne said.

"All the pop-and-drops who'd been shot had either been charged with or served time for a sex crime, all but the lawyer and his client."

"Right."

"Jay-Cee," Harris put in, "had charges against him of involuntary deviant sexual intercourse and rape of an unconscious or unaware person in one case that Gartner got tossed."

"Tossed on a technicality," Radcliffe said.

"The chain of evidence of the rape kit was broken. It was deemed inadmissible in the trial. But the results still are on file. They state that the blood test from the girl he raped showed that she had really early stages of the bacterial disease gonorrhea."

"And?" Payne said.

Radcliffe shrugged. "Nguyen's master case file from those charges says that he was undergoing treatment for gonorrhea."

"So Nguyen gave the girl the clap," Payne said.

"Would appear that way."

"Nothing new. Kerry has a story about one where the rape victim got whatever disease in her throat," Payne said. He then appeared to be in deep thought. He said: "Which puts Nguyen in line with the other pop-and-drops, leaving only Gartner with no sex-crime link. He may just have been in the wrong place at the wrong time when Jay-Cee got popped." He paused, then added, "Lucky us."

"You didn't like Gartner?"

"Nobody liked that slimy sonofabitch."

Andy Radcliffe raised his eyebrows, nodded once, then looked back to the laptop screen. "Maybe I can find a link with Gartner and some sex crime. . . ."

"Kerry, let's take another look at the interview I had with Shauna Mays."

Rapier worked his control panel, and the image of Matt with the malnourished and badly bruised woman in Homicide's Interview Room II came on the monitor. In the right-hand bottom corner was a small date stamp: 01 NOV, 13:20:01.

"Run it up to about 13:30," Payne said.

Rapier fast-forwarded to that point on the clock, hit play, and shortly thereafter the sound of Payne exhaling came through the speakers in the ceiling. Then his voice, slightly frustrated, said:

"Okay, let's start from the beginning. Who had the gun?"

"A delivery guy. He come in with Kendrik's paper. That paper I had that the cop took?"

"The Wanted sheet?"

"Yeah, that's it. He come in and — No, wait. First he say he got a check for Kendrik. And when I let him in, he give me the paper. The sheet. Said there was no check."

"This began at what time?"

She cocked her head. "Time? This morning, all I know. Ain't no clocks in a crack house!"

In the ECC, there was a chorus of chuckles from Harris, Radcliffe, and Rapier.

As they watched Payne in the video nodding while writing in his notepad, Kerry said, "Gee, Marshal, I thought everyone knew crack houses didn't have clocks."

Payne gave him the finger as his voice came through the speakers:

"What did this guy look like? And was he alone, anyone else in the house?"

"Just him. Old white guy, maybe my age. Tall. Kinda skinny."

"Okay, you can stop it, Kerry," Payne said. He looked at Harris. "So, a delivery guy. A FedEx delivery guy? And Mudd said the blue shirt had seen a FedEx minivan rolling through right before Cheatham took a bullet."

"But that kid, his nephew, told Mudd that he didn't see one. Which of course, as Mudd pointed out, could've been a straight-out lie."

They were quiet a long moment, each in deep thought.

Then Harris said: "You have any idea how many FedEx trucks there are in Philadelphia?"

"But it was on a Sunday, not a normal day for deliveries."

"I'll say it again, Matt. You have any idea how many FedEx trucks there are in Philadelphia? And just because they may not be delivering, they're still moving around the city for logistical and other reasons, like maintenance. And, then again, for all we know, this one was stolen."

Matt nodded. "Agreed. But it's a rock to look under. Maybe we'll find another under it."

Looking at the image of Marc James, Payne said, "Whoever he is, our mystery shooter's bright. He's doing the reverse of a sweepstakes sting."

"A sweepstakes sting?" Radcliffe repeated.

Payne explained: "You mail out, say, a thousand letters to the LKA of people wanted on outstanding warrants. The letter says the recipient is guaranteed a prize worth up to a couple hundred bucks, and the first fifty people who show up have a chance to win a car. The official-looking but bogus letter-head has the address of some empty store in a strip center you get a civic-minded owner to let you borrow. The day of the 'event,' you furnish it with a couple desks and some chairs, then put signs in the window that say 'Keystone State Sweepstakes Headquarters.' And you borrow a nice new luxury sports car or SUV to park in front with a sign saying 'Win This!' Then, when the wanted ones show up, an undercover posing as a secretary matches the letter to the warrant list to make sure it's still outstanding, then sends the idiot back to another room for his photograph and prize — a nice shiny pair of handcuffs."

Radcliffe grinned. "Sounds like it works."

"Not as good as it used to, but yeah, there's still plenty of stupid critters out there. One really bright one even brought his court papers as his proof of ID."

"So," Radcliffe said, "instead of the guy sending out letters to the LKAs, he went to them individually, saying he was delivering FedEx envelopes containing checks?"

"That appears to be it," Payne said.

Everyone was silent a moment.

Then Radcliffe went back to his keyboard and stared at the screen, then quickly typed something and smacked the enter key.

"There," he said, pointing at the screen. "I don't know if it means anything, but in Nguyen's file?"

"Yeah?" Payne said.

"The district attorney's case notes say that William Curtis is employed by FedEx here. Says he lives on Mount Pleasant."

Payne casually sipped from his Homicide coffee mug, then said, "Who the hell is William Curtis?"

Twenty minutes later, Harris returned the receiver to the cradle of the multiline phone on the conference desk. He looked at Payne.

"This Will Curtis called in sick today. His supervisor" — he looked at his notes — "a guy named Jeff Allan, said he's in a bad way. Curtis has been out sick most of the month. And he said that, judging by the look of him, it's the real deal. He guessed it's something terminal. He asked, but Curtis wouldn't own up to it."

Payne and Harris looked at each other.

"And there's no answer at his house on Mount Pleasant," Payne said.

Harris's cell phone started ringing.

He checked the caller ID, then answered the phone with: "Whatcha got, Charley?"

Payne looked at Harris and saw his expression brighten.

"How many?" Harris said. Then: "Okay, got it. Let me know if anything changes. We're on our way."

He looked at Matt as he broke off the call.

"Bell says two black males just entered the James place on Richmond carrying a black duffel bag."

Payne quickly stood up. "Kerry, you and Andy run things here and call me the minute you find anything else on this Curtis guy."

As Payne pulled on his blazer and dug in his pocket for the Crown Vic keys, he said to Harris, "Let's roll."

[THREE]
3118 Richmond Street, Philadelphia
Monday, November 2, 10:45 A.M.

Allante Williams saw an open parking spot one block south of 3118. He liked it for two good reasons: It was close enough to reach if the deal went sour and he had to run, and his black Dodge Charger would be well hidden by the old PECO truck right in front of it.

He shut off the car, looked at Kenny Jones sitting in the passenger seat, then reached back and pulled the black duffel from the backseat. He unzipped it and took out a monster of a stainless-steel pistol. Even Kenny appeared impressed at the sight of the Ruger Redhawk, a double-action revolver chambered for .44 Magnum.

"You ever shoot a wheel gun?" Allante asked. "Any gun?"

"Damn right, Big Al!"

Allante wasn't sure if he believed him.

"This Redhawk is a cannon," Allante said,

517

handing it to him. "It's mine, dude, and I want it back, so don't get any goddamn ideas."

"Yeah, sure, man," Kenny said, wrapping his hand around its big black grip and aiming it out the windshield.

"Keep it down, dammit!"

"Okay," Kenny said, putting it on his lap and swinging out the cylinder to check if all the bullets were live rounds.

"There ain't no damn bullets in this gun!" Kenny blurted. "What the hell's it good for if it ain't got no bullets?"

"Calm down, dude. You saw how it looked when you first saw it. That's all you need to do with Cicero. Door opens, you move inside with the bag of money first, then hold the tip of this badass barrel in his face."

And with no bullets you won't be able to shoot me later.

"Besides, I'll be backing you up with this going in," Allante said, pulling back his jacket to reveal the Ruger 9-millimeter semi-automatic in a holster on his belt.

Kenny clearly looked as if he didn't like the idea, but then shrugged. He reached in his pocket and pulled out five or six foot-long white zip ties.

"Not gonna shoot the bastard, anyway,"

Kenny said, pointing to the zip ties. "Gonna do to him what he did to Reggie."

With Allante Williams just to the right of the door at 3118 Richmond Street, Kenny Jones banged on the door.

What are the fucking odds that some hothead inside is going to look out the peephole, see this dumbass holding the sack of cash, then drill the door — and him — with lead?

Damn good, that's what the odds are.

This better be worth forty Gs. . . .

The door opened a crack, and Kenny said, "Cicero, I got it like I said, man."

He held up the bag with his left hand. The hand cannon was in his right, hidden by the bag.

The door closed, and there was the clanking sound of its two chains being removed, then the door swung open.

And Kenny, surprising the hell out of Allante, did exactly as he'd been told.

Allente went in behind him.

"What're you doing, Kenny?" Cicero said, staring at the business end of the barrel.

Then Kenny swung the heavy stainless-steel Ruger, fiercely pistol-whipping Cicero's mostly bald head.

Cicero quickly backed up, shielding his head from the blows with his arms.

"Kenny! Wait!" Allante yelled. "Stop!"

Cicero then turned and tried to run down the basement steps — but Kenny got one last hard swing in.

And Cicero went tumbling down the steps.

In the basement were two small dirty rooms, one with a twin-size bed and a wooden table. There were bags of pills stacked two feet high.

Kenny dragged the limp but breathing body to the bed, then pulled the zip ties from his pocket and cinched them tightly around Cicero's neck. Cicero's body began to convulse. But within a minute, it went slack.

Damn, that was fast, Allante thought.

Kenny turned and said, "I'm gonna look for some acid. Be right back."

And he ran back up the stairs.

After Allante was sure Kenny was out of earshot, he called Rapp Badde.

"Hey, man, I know you were worried. Everything's under control. The Cicero guy is gone and —"

"Look," Badde interrupted, "you don't have to do Kenny, too. We got back everything that he stole. All's good. Just turn him in for the reward, too."

"Okay, man. You're the boss," he said, but

realized that he was talking to a broken connection.

Badde had already hung up.

Then Allante, starting to paw the bags of
pills, wondering what they might be, heard
banging on the front door upstairs.

What the — ?

He threw all the bags of pills he could fit in
the duffel, then headed for the stairs.

Will Curtis, curiosity getting the best of him
on his way to Port Richmond, drove to where
LeRoi Cheatham had had his Lex Talionis
moment. Because of the various one-way
streets, he had to make a huge circle around
the block.

Then, there on Hancock, was a shred of
yellow POLICE LINE tape flapping in the
breeze.

And that's all.

Then he thought he saw a bloodstain on
the alleyway. But it was in shadow and he
couldn't be sure.

A block later, he did a double take at the
cleared city block.

Down there's where all those cops were.

*But I thought there were some houses on
that corner.*

Now it's all smelly raw dirt.

He drove on, and ten minutes later, just

521

before eleven o'clock, he turned the white Ford minivan onto Richmond Street, then rolled up the street, looking for 3118.

During the drive, Will Curtis had decided he wasn't going to handle this delivery like the others. He didn't think he could go through the whole charade, then maybe have to wait if the bastard wasn't here.

He felt so ill, in fact, that he almost had not come at all. Even after a night's sleep he had not felt significantly better. He'd regained a little energy from forcing himself to eat a banana and half a turkey sandwich on the drive over. But he was still weak, far more so than usual.

The only good thing, he decided, was that he hadn't had another unfortunate accident. The lump on his forehead hurt enough.

But I really want this evildoer to pay.

The sonofabitch not only sold those damn date-rape pills, but he'd been convicted of using them, too.

So, the minute the door opens, I'm just going to go in. I know what the bastard looks like.

Then it's Wham Bam Thank You Ma'am, and I'm done.

[FOUR]
3118 Richmond Street, Philadelphia
Monday, November 2, 10:59 A.M.

Flying up the Delaware Expressway in the gray unmarked Crown Victoria, Matt Payne killed the siren over Ann Street — where this part of I-95 went from being elevated to ground level — then caught the next exit. The off-ramp actually went over Allegheny, and he had to go up a block to Westmoreland, then double back around a park.

As he did so, he listened to Tony Harris talking on his cell phone with Charley Bell, the hefty thirty-year-old detective who was sitting undercover in the old Philadelphia Electric Company van.

"Okay, got it," Harris said into the phone. He broke the connection and looked at Payne. "He said nobody's come or gone since the last two went in. And that it'd be a good idea to go around the back and check that first. Said it's the house with the black Cadillac Escalade in the drive."

Payne nodded.

Harris then said, "Give me your phone."

Payne did, and he saw Harris key in a number, then call it.

"It's Harris," Tony said. "Just making sure you have Matt Payne's number. Now you both have each other's number ready to speed-dial in your LAST CALL list."

He ended the call without another word, then handed the phone back to Payne.

Because the Crown Vics had been on loan from Homeland Security and no one knew for sure how long the loan program would last — *What the Fed Giveth, the Fed Can Taketh Away at Any Damn Time* — the police department had had no intention of spending the money to buy more of its police radios and installing them in the cars when they'd have to uninstall them at the end of the loan. It had been decided that the portable handheld police radio units could be used. And, failing that, a cell phone.

As Matt made the right turn onto westbound Allegheny, he reached down and tugged the plug for the light bar out of the cigarette lighter receptacle. Harris then flipped the two sun visors up, concealing the light bar and the POLICE sticker.

Payne turned left onto Richmond, then left again at the next street, which provided access to the rear of the properties. It was next to the interstate highway, and there was plenty of traffic noise along the back side of the buildings.

Some of the row house backyards still had grass, but it wasn't well kept. Others were cluttered with anything from storage buildings to busted aboveground swimming pools to junk cars.

And one had a shiny black luxury SUV.

"There's the ride," Payne said as he pulled out his Colt Officer's Model .45 from inside his waistband. With the muzzle pointed at the floorboard, he thumbed back the hammer to cock it, then thumbed up the lever at the back of the slide to lock it. Then, as he continued to scan the area, he held it on his right thigh. "But I don't see anything happening at the house — or any of the others, for that matter."

"Me neither. Go up a couple more drives past it, and I'll get out and cover this back here while you and Charley take the front."

Just before making the right turn to get back to Richmond, Matt saw in his rearview mirror that Tony was rolling two rusty drums from the yard next door and putting them behind the Escalade.

That probably won't stop someone trying to

get away, but it ought to slow them.

Then Matt saw ahead of him, at the corner of Richmond, the nose of Charley Bell's PECO van. It was parked against the right curb.

The row houses here were mostly identical, all three-story and faced with red brick, the front door right at the sidewalk. And many of them had plastic garbage bags stacked at the curb.

As Matt rolled toward Richmond, he saw a late-model plain white Ford minivan going up Richmond. Its brake lights were lit. In the split second when it passed, Payne saw a white male at the wheel, and he thought that the driver wore some kind of uniform shirt.

He stopped the Crown Vic just shy of Richmond, nosing it up on the sidewalk. He shut off the car. Then he put in his left ear a wireless speaker-microphone device for his phone, speed-dialed Charley Bell, and slipped the live phone into his pocket.

Matt heard Bell's voice in the earbud: "Hey, Matt, that white minivan that just went by has pulled up to our house."

"No shit?" Payne said, opening his door. "Can you make out the driver?"

"Just that he's a white male, older. He's getting out now. Moving slowly."

Payne closed the door of the Crown Vic.

He quickly went to the corner, near the front door of an abandoned storefront. He held his Colt along his right leg as he peered around the brick edge of the wall and up the street. He thumbed down the pistol's lock lever. Now when he went to squeeze the trigger, the hammer could freely fall to fire the round in the chamber.

Matt could clearly see the man.

That is a FedEx uniform, and he's carrying an envelope.

But he is moving really slow. Almost like he's not going to make it to the door.

No doubt whatsoever that's Will Curtis. . . .

Bell said: "What do you want to do, Matt?"

"Let's hold and see what happens. Be ready to move. Tony's covering the back door."

They watched as the man banged on the faded maroon metal door, then waited for an answer.

Then he banged again, and after a moment the door opened.

"Charley, I can't see who opened the door."

"Shit, Matt. Me neither."

They watched as Will Curtis held up the envelope in his left hand. Curtis said something, but he was too far away for them to hear it.

Then suddenly they watched as he surged at the open door — and disappeared inside.

"Oh, shit! Let's go!" Payne said. He started up the sidewalk in a crouch.

After a few strides, Payne glanced over his left shoulder and saw the hefty Bell lumbering after him. Like Matt, Charley had his police badge clearly visible, its leather holder hanging from a chain around his neck. Charley had his service Glock out of the belt holster on his right hip.

"I think I saw him pull something from his waist, Matt. Maybe a pistol."

Before they reached the front door, which was still open, Matt could hear angry voices inside.

"I told you I ain't him, old man!" a male voice said. "Put down the fucking gun!"

Curtis, in a weak voice, said, "Then where's this James?"

"Put down the gun, old man!" the other male repeated.

Matt got to the edge of the doorway and carefully looked inside.

There were only the two males visible, Will Curtis in the FedEx uniform and a black-skinned man with scraggly long hair and a full beard. They were in the large front room of the row house. Curtis was to the left and had a Glock aimed at the chest of the black male, who held up his hands shoulder high, the FedEx envelope in his right one.

Payne saw that a wood-floored hallway led to the back of the house and to the flight of stairs leading to the second floor. Under that flight, just barely visible, was the entrance for the flight that went downstairs to the basement.

He felt a hand on his shoulder and turned to see that Charley Bell was now right behind him. Payne reached into his pocket and broke the connection for their call, then speed-dialed Harris. Charley listened in as Matt told Tony what he'd seen inside, ending with, "Going to take it now."

Payne then yelled around the corner of the doorway: "Police! Put down your weapons!"

When he peered around the corner, he was amazed that Will Curtis had actually complied with the order on the first shout. He was looking with tired eyes toward the front door.

Sergeant Matt Payne, with his Colt .45 raised in both hands close to his chest, smoothly rushed through the doorway, Detective Charley Bell lumbering on his heels.

Payne was shouting, "Police! Nobody move! Hands on your head!"

The black male still had his hands raised

and now moved them to his head.

Will Curtis, as quickly as he could, complied, too.

They could hear Detective Tony Harris kicking in the back door.

Matt motioned for Charley to go let Tony in, and he hustled down the hall.

Just as Payne said to the black male, "Where's the other guy?" the old man pointed under the stairs and yelled, "Coming out of the basement!"

Payne looked toward the basement entrance in time to see the head of a black male — whose hand was bringing up a black semiautomatic pistol.

The shooter swung the pistol at Payne. But before Matt could squeeze off a shot, Will Curtis stepped between them — and then came three shots from the black male.

Two of the bullets hit Curtis in the left shoulder, the third in his left chest.

As Matt dove for cover at the foot of the steps leading upstairs, he thought, *Did he step in the way on purpose?*

He did! He took those damn bullets for me!

Matt saw Charley Bell peering around a corner at the back end of the hall. The shooter did, too, and fired three shots at him. Two struck the wall at the corner, sending Sheetrock flying. The third found

Bell's forearm.

"Fuck! I'm hit!" he shouted.

Curtis fell forward and grabbed the Glock he'd been told to drop, then remarkably squeezed off five shots in the direction of the shooter.

Then Will Curtis finally collapsed, blood from his wounds beginning to pool around him.

The long-haired black male was now cowering behind Payne, lying flat on the floor against the wall.

Payne carefully looked past the edge of the stairs toward the basement entrance, trying to get a clear line of fire on the shooter.

He saw the entrance but not the shooter.

Sonofabitch!

Keeping low, he stepped into the hallway and moved toward the basement entrance. The worn wooden flooring squeaked under his weight.

"You okay, Charley?" Payne called out.

"Get that sonofabitch, Matt!"

Payne looked back at the black male. He was still cowering against the wall, but now he stared wide-eyed at the old man lying in the pool of blood.

As Payne moved closer to the basement entrance, Tony Harris appeared from around the bullet-pocked corner. He motioned toward the basement, then motioned that he'd cover Matt. Matt nodded.

When Payne got to the top of the stairs, he saw a heavy blood trail leading down the wooden treads.

Will Curtis hit the bastard.

"Police!" Matt yelled down the steps. "Drop your weapons!"

Payne and Harris slowly descended the stairs.

When they reached the bottom, there were two rooms. They cleared the first, then followed the blood trail to the door of the second. A light was on inside it, and when Payne looked around the edge of the door frame, he saw two black males — both dead.

One was on the floor at the end of the heavy blood trail. The shooter had at least one enormous hole through his neck. The semiautomatic 9-millimeter Baretta was still in his right hand. The other dead male was lying on an old twin bed. He had been strangled. Two foot-long plastic zip ties strung end-to-end cut deeply into his bruised neck.

A black duffel bag with stacks of banded cash and clear plastic bags full of pills was on the floor.

Matt and Tony then heard fast footfalls on the wooden flooring above their heads.

Then they heard Charley Bell yell, "Stop! Police!"

Payne exchanged a fast glance with Harris, then bolted up the steps.

At the top, Payne turned toward the open front door as he heard the minivan starting and then its tires spinning as it squealed away.

He looked toward the back of the house and saw Bell standing with what looked like a dirty dish towel wrapped around his left forearm. It was blood-soaked.

"The sonofabitch grabbed the old man's keys," Bell said. "And got his Glock, too!"

Matt looked at the towel.

"I'm okay," Bell said. "Go! Go! Go!"

Matt pointed down the basement stairs.

"Clear the house with Tony," he said.

Then, stepping around the dead body of the old man who'd sacrificed his life for Matt's, Payne was out the door.

[FIVE]

The first thing Matt Payne saw when he came running out of the row house was a huge, nasty-looking garbage truck. It was stopped right beside the PECO van, and

Payne realized that if he didn't run faster to reach the Crown Vic, the truck was going to move up and block him.

As he ran, he yelled "Stop! Police!" to the driver, holding his left-hand palm out, anxiously signaling him to stay put. But after he got in the car and finally had it moving off the sidewalk, he saw the last plastic garbage bag from the corner being tossed into the back of the garbage truck as the truck moved forward.

Matt hammered the heel of his right hand on the horn as he floored the accelerator. Yanking the steering wheel to the right, he had to hop the curb to narrowly miss both the front of the garbage truck and the rear of a parked car.

Payne pursued the Ford minivan as it raced up Richmond Street.

He thought about calling in for backup, but dismissed that immediately.

No police radio. And I'm not about to try juggling my cell right now.

He flipped down the sun visors, then reached down and plugged in the emergency lights and threw the switch for the siren.

Two cars were stopped up ahead, waiting for the traffic light at Allegheny Avenue. He watched as the minivan's brake lights came on for a second, then went off. The van then swung into the oncoming traffic lane to get around the two cars. Then it blew through the red light, cutting a hard right and going down Allegheny Avenue.

Matt came up on the two cars but could not pass because a pickup truck had just turned down Richmond, blocking his way. He could see the red-and-blue strobes reflecting off the back glass of the vehicle ahead of him. He hammered the horn out of habit, but its sound was mostly lost in the loud *whoop-whoop* of the siren.

The traffic light cycled to green, the first car started to roll, then both finally moved quickly out of the way.

Matt made the corner just in time to see the tail of the minivan going up an on-ramp, headed southbound on the Delaware Expressway.

He pulled on the gear-selector stalk on the steering column, dumping the transmission into second gear, then floored the accelerator.

Just before the ramp at the next block, with the high-revving engine roaring, Matt tapped the brakes once before turning, then put the Police Interceptor into a squealing right turn. He corrected the skid, then floored the accelerator again and bumped the transmission into high gear.

This section of Interstate 95 was four lanes in each direction, and Matt saw that the minivan was weaving through the heavy traffic.

Sonofabitch is using all the lanes!

The other vehicles were quickly becoming aware of the reckless minivan. Just past the point where the expressway became elevated, some began moving out of the wild driver's way. Matt figured that the driver of a full-size Dodge SUV must have seen the Ford minivan flying up on its tail. It tried to move quickly into the lane to its left — and immediately sideswiped the Honda Accord that was traveling in that lane.

Oh, shit!

The impact from the heavier truck forced the lighter compact car into the far inside lane, which fortunately was unoccupied.

That Honda was damn lucky it didn't slam into the concrete divider.

Or completely lose control.

The Ford minivan, apparently anticipating the Dodge SUV swerving back into its lane, then darted through a gap in the right lane. It flew past a half-dozen vehicles before again having to brake heavily, this time almost at the Vine Street Expressway.

After checking the nearby lanes for traffic, Matt calmly steered to follow it.

I wonder how many violations I've made so far of our department's pursuit policies.

Plenty, I'm sure.

And I'm also sure someone will be more than happy to point them out as we review the video of it in the ECC.

His cell phone began ringing, and he dug it out of his pocket and glanced at the caller ID. Payne was amazed the earbud was still in his ear. When he answered the call, he wondered if all Harris would hear would be his siren wails and horn honks.

"Tony, how's Charley? All okay?"

"He's fine. We've got the scene under control. Where the hell are you?"

"Southbound Delaware Expressway, about to Vine. Hot on the tail of the white minivan. You want to call in for units to try to head off this guy? He's running hard, and about to make a big mess out here."

Payne, closing the distance between them, watched the Ford minivan make jerky movements as the driver tried getting around four vehicles that were driving abreast and effectively forming a wall across the expressway. They did try to get out of the way, but every time a driver anticipated the minivan's next move, another driver wound up blocking him again.

The minivan was in the far right lane, and

when it came up to the two-lane split leading to the exit for the Vine Street Expressway, it shot the gap and accelerated.

"Tony, he just took the Vine exit. Hell, we're almost to the Roundhouse, about a quarter-mile out. Maybe he's going there to give himself up."

He heard Harris snort, then start relaying that updated information.

Payne made the exit for the Vine Street Expressway, and as the two lanes of the elevated concrete thoroughfare widened to four, Matt looked in the distance and saw the minivan heading toward the Center City skyline.

Also ahead, at the point where the expressway crossed over Fourth Street, there was a series of flashing caution lights and signage that read: CAUTION! ROAD REPAIR AHEAD! YO, GIVE US A BRAKE!

The minivan was now just passing the first of the flashing lights.

The lights and signs became thicker as the expressway approached the Fifth Street overpass, and Payne remembered that that was where two eighteen-wheelers had collided a few weeks earlier. The mass of them together had taken out five sections of the three-foot-tall concrete divider that separated the eastbound and westbound lanes.

As a temporary patch, a double line of fifty-five-gallon drums, orange with reflective tape, had been put in place with more caution signage. And a temporary speed-limit sign had been posted.

Matt saw ahead of the Ford minivan that traffic in all the westbound lanes was slowing to a stop just past the construction crew.

"Looks like the Vine Expressway is shut down, Tony."

The minivan was beginning to make jerky moves from lane to lane, looking for a route around the slow traffic.

Matt moved into the far outside lane behind the minivan and eased up on the accelerator as he closed the distance between them.

No exit here. Nowhere to run.

Looks like the end of the road.

But then he saw that not only was the minivan not slowing to the posted twenty-five miles an hour, it was accelerating.

And then it suddenly shot from the right lane and across the other three — then went right through the orange barrels, scattering them and causing the construction workers to dive for cover.

"Jesus H. Christ!"

"What, Matt?"

"He just crossed into the oncoming lanes."

"How the hell did he do that?"

"He blew through a hole in the construction zone."

More important, how the hell did he miss those oncoming cars?

At least they're driving slow because of the roadwork.

The minivan then drove to the far left of the expressway and turned left onto a lane that was carrying oncoming traffic coming off the Benjamin Franklin Bridge. The vehicles swerved to miss hitting the minivan head-on.

"Jesus! And now he's headed the wrong way toward the Ben Franklin Bridge!"

Payne, with his hands on the steering wheel at three and nine o'clock, looked over his left shoulder, then cut across the westbound lanes of the expressway, stopping in the hole that the minivan had plowed through the rows of orange drums. Then he checked for a gap in the eastbound traffic. There wasn't one immediately, but as he waited, one driver, then two and three and more, began to heed the siren and red-and-blue strobes, either slowing to a crawl or coming to a complete stop.

Jesus! Here we go!

Payne put his right foot to the floor, and the Crown Vic burned rubber as it shot forward.

The minivan had momentarily disappeared around the curves of the turns leading up to the bridge. But its tail came back into view as soon as Payne reached the first overhead gantry.

The five vehicles that had just crashed also came into view.

Payne steered around them and headed for the bridge.

The eighty-year-old steel suspension bridge spanned the Delaware River, connecting Center City to Camden, New Jersey. It had a total of seven lanes for automotive traffic. Separating the east- and westbound lanes was an articulated concrete wall called a "zipper" barrier. Depending on traffic demand, the three-foot-tall zipper could be moved to create more or fewer lanes in either direction.

Payne saw that the zipper had been positioned so that there were four lanes westbound.

Which gives me more room.

The minivan was going right down the center white-dotted lines, the oncoming cars parting to either side. That created a path for Payne, and he gunned the Crown Vic, closing more quickly than before.

Need to do this PIT fast.

He pulled up almost to the minivan, setting up with his reinforced front bumper to the left rear of the minivan, just forward of its rear bumper. Then he quickly turned the steering wheel to the right, causing his front bumper to smack the minivan's rear — and the minivan to suddenly break loose and skid sideways.

Matt slammed both of his feet on the brake pedal, which triggered the chattering kickback of the antilock-brake system.

He watched the minivan slide sideways toward the concrete zipper barrier, then go into a counterclockwise spin. On its second almost complete revolution, the right front bumper impacted the zipper barrier, then the whole right side of the vehicle slammed into it, forcing the van to almost flip over into the eastbound lanes. The impact moved the zipper barrier into them, causing two cars to collide on that side.

Payne let off the brakes and, dodging an oncoming Volvo, its woman driver looking terrified, drove beyond the minivan. He nosed the Crown Vic against the barrier at an angle so that it would serve as a buffer. As he got out, he saw that the minivan driver had already fled the vehicle and now was running with the pistol in his right hand. He also saw that blood flowed from a gash on his forehead.

It was a feeble escape attempt. He almost immediately tripped in a crack just before an expansion joint in the suspension bridge, and bounced as he landed on top of the joint. When he hit, he loosened his grip on the pistol — and it slid toward the gap in the expansion joint.

That Glock's going to fall into the Delaware!

But then it kept sliding and stopped in the middle of the westbound lanes.

Payne then suddenly heard the horrible roar of screaming tires behind him, and he immediately ran to the pocket that the minivan had made by moving the zipper barrier. When he turned, it was just in time to see a woman in a brand-new Toyota Land Cruiser slam into the side of the Crown Vic, the SUV's windshield instantly filling with multiple inflated air bags.

Jesus!

Guess the car can go back to the feds now. . . .

Payne looked back at the black male. He was still trying to get up.

Payne ran toward him, his pistol aimed at his back.

He shouted, "Police! Don't move!"

But then the black male did move, bolting toward the zipper barrier.

Now Payne no longer had a clear field of fire; there were countless vehicles zipping by in the three eastbound lanes just beyond the man.

"Stop!" Payne yelled again as the man went over the low barrier.

The man paused there on the other side, waiting for a gap in traffic — and causing a six-wheeled big box delivery truck in the inside lane to lock up its brakes trying to avoid hitting him.

That suddenly slowed traffic, and there was a gap, and the black male decided to make his dash across. But as he bolted into the next lane, the large profile of the delivery truck obstructed his view — and he ran right into the path of a fast-moving, low-profile sports car.

Payne watched as the car hit him in the lower legs. The impact caused him to tumble like a rag doll over the top of the sports car. He flipped through the air twice before hitting the bridge decking and then being run over by three other vehicles, including a bus.

Traffic came to a stop.

Matt Payne shook his head. He decocked his Colt, then slipped it back under his blazer and beneath the waistband of his woolen slacks. He could hear the sirens of the squad cars that Harris had called in screaming toward him and what sounded like the heavy horns of the fire department's rapid-intervention and major crash-rescue vehicles.

Then he saw one of the Aviation Unit's Bell 206 L-4 helicopters approaching from the north.

Glancing at the overhead traffic cameras, he thought, *Kerry probably called in every last one of the cavalry, too.*

Standing there in his navy blazer, his gray woolen cuffed trousers, a once crisply starched light-blue shirt with a red-striped tie, and his highly polished black shoes all scuffed, he forced a smile and waved at the cameras.

And Rapier and Ratcliff and whoever the hell else is in the ECC.

The eastbound traffic slowly parted, and two Philadelphia Police Department Chevy Impalas rolled up to the dead black male. The blue shirts began routing traffic around the scene. Another Impala arrived and went to the cars that had stopped after hitting the man. And there were paramedics talking with the woman sitting behind the wheel of the SUV that had hit the Crown Vic.

Payne turned and walked back to the minivan.

The window on the sliding center door had popped out on impact. Payne looked in through the hole. The first thing he saw was a plastic sign with the FedEx HOME DELIVERY logo. And then he noticed on the floorboard several scattered rounds of .45-caliber GAP hollow-points.

There's the rest of Will Curtis's story.

So the pop-and-drops are over. . . .

[SIX]
Hops Haus Brewery
1101 N. Lee Street, Philadelphia
Monday, November 2, 12:44 P.M.

H. Rapp Badde, Jr., was sitting at the massive rectangular stainless-steel-topped bar. He chewed on his lunch of a steak sandwich while watching with fascination the police chase playing out live on the two giant flat-screen televisions behind the bar.

What the hell drives, so to speak, people to act that way? he thought. *That's just insane to run from the cops, then go the wrong way on the freeway.*

Who plays with fire like that?

He reached for his pint glass of lager, which was almost empty. He drained it, then tried to get the barmaid's attention. It took a minute, because everyone was glued to the image of the white minivan racing the wrong way into westbound traffic on the Ben Franklin Bridge. Even some of the chefs had come out of the kitchen to watch. After Badde waved his hand for help for a bit longer, one of the busboys saw him and flagged the barmaid, and she got the signal to bring him a fresh pint.

Who the hell am I kidding?

All I've been doing is playing with fire lately — and coming damn close to being incinerated.

But what's the saying?

"Close only counts with horseshoes and hand grenades"?

Badde was more or less hiding under a plain cloth cap and blending in with the crowd. He wore an Eagles sweatshirt, faded blue jeans, and athletic shoes, trying to keep a low profile until the thing with Allante Williams, Kenny Jones, and that drug dealer was finally finished.

And I get back my ten grand from Allante.

I wonder how much I can really trust him. I did just feed him a job that made him forty grand richer.

Badde had come to the brewery after visiting the demolition site and checking on the progress there. It had been damned lucky that the cops had not released the scene until late the night before. Lucky because by then it had been too late and dark to move the heavy demolition equipment. They'd been able to get the crews there at the crack of dawn for an early start.

By the time Badde had arrived, the crews were mostly done. And he'd taken a picture with his cell phone camera of that almost perfectly flat property, then sent it to Janelle Harper with explicit instructions for her to e-mail it immediately to the Russian.

I don't know for sure if what he said about those holdouts being killed with a muscle relaxer is true or not.

But I do know that it's smart to proceed with caution.

I don't want to get on his bad side, and there's no question that that was a threat last night.

Which is why I had Janelle send those photos to him. And why he'll get more photos the minute the damn construction crews arrive.

There was a huge gasp from the crowd as the televisions showed the gray police sedan racing up behind the minivan — then ramming it.

The minivan slid sideways, then spun twice before smacking the divider wall.

Jesus! It hit so hard it moved the wall!

He'd already heard from Roger Wynne that the last of the recovered absentee ballots had been shredded into a fine confetti, so that was not going to come back to haunt him.

Unless Wynne gets wise and thinks he can use that against me.

I'm going to have to keep an eye on him.

As he picked up his new pint of lager and downed a third of it in one swallow, his Go To Hell cell phone rang. He put down the glass and looked at the caller ID.

What? It's gobbledlygook. Nothing but "010101010."

"Yes?" he said, answering it.

"I got your photograph. The site is looking better."

The Russian? How the hell did he get this number?

"Yuri?" Badde said.

"I think we now better understand each other."

Badde began, "I'm glad . . ." But then he realized that the line was dead.

He anxiously sipped at his beer as he tried to figure out just what the hell had happened.

There was another gasp from the crowd, and he looked again to the televisions.

The camera showed a remarkably clear shot of a man running from the minivan, being chased by a man in a coat and tie from the gray sedan.

That first one looks like it could be Kenny!

Being chased by a plainclothes cop?

And then the camera caught a clear shot of the man in the coat and tie.

Someone said, "Look! It's the Wyatt Earp of the Main Line!"

Then Badde saw the man who was being chased trip, get up, and go over the concrete divider. What happened next was obstructed by the big box of a delivery truck. But the crowd's gasp made it obvious what had happened.

Damn! Talk about being thrown under a bus.

He took another sip of beer and thought a long moment.

Bottom line: I'm going to have to watch my back a helluva lot more closely.

"Waitress!" he called out to the barmaid, and when she stepped over, he said, "I'll take a double Jameson's rocks. No, make it a triple."

[SEVEN]
Ben Franklin Bridge, Philadelphia
Monday, November 2, 1:05 P.M.

Matt stood next to the zipper wall, watching the Tow Squad wrecker — its flatbed tilted down and touching the deck of the bridge — winch up the demolished gray Crown Victoria Police Interceptor.

Every lane of traffic was backed up in both directions on the bridge, and there was a cacophony of horns honking.

As Matt scanned the maddening scene, he thought about all the craziness that had led up to this very moment — all the crimes that had been committed against the innocent, which had led to all the shootings and brutal beatings of the career criminals.

And there are all the others still out there.

More crimes, more killings — it's not going to stop.

I just slowed it. But I'm never going to be able to stop it.

He suddenly felt very small and alone.

Is there any sanity left in this world?

As he ran his fingers through his hair and

shook his head, his cell phone began ringing in his pocket.

He pulled it out and glanced at the caller ID — then smiled as he closed his eyes and visualized the last time he'd seen Amanda Law.

The angel goddess peacefully asleep — there is sanity.

"Hey, baby," he said, answering it. "Feeling any better?"

"Yeah, thanks. I am. Are you too busy to talk?" She didn't wait for an answer. "Say, I'm on the balcony looking at the Ben Franklin Bridge. It's shut down in both directions. Any idea what that's about?"

"A little. I'll tell you in a bit. What's on your mind?"

"I really don't want to tell you this on the phone. How long do you think — ?"

Oh, shit! What the hell else can go wrong today?

"What? Everything okay?"

"Yeah, it is."

Now he could hear the excitement in her voice.

"What is it, Amanda?"

There was a long pause, then she said: "Okay, okay. Matt, I'm . . . I'm pregnant! *We're* pregnant!"

What? A baby?

Then he realized: *No wonder the goddess was glowing.*

She was saying: "I knew I was a little late with my cycle, Matt, but when I went and got out the calendar, I saw that I was *very* late. And then I thought the nausea might be, well, from being late, so in the drug-store I got one of those self-tests. It came up positive, and I thought, 'How could that be?' We're *always* careful, you know? But then I remembered that first night we were just so . . . well, you remember, in a hurry and not careful. And then I counted the days and went back and got another brand to test with. And then it showed positive. Soooo . . ."

Matt was quiet a long time as he absorbed the news.

He looked past the cables of the suspension bridge in the direction of the Hops Haus Tower, then up to where Amanda would be standing on the balcony and looking toward him.

"Matt . . . ?" she said very softly. "What are you thinking?"

Matt Payne then smiled broadly and said, "I'm thinking that's wonderful, Amanda. Absolutely wonderful, my angel goddess."

ABOUT THE AUTHORS

W.E.B. Griffin is the author of six best-selling series: The Corps, Brotherhood of War, Badge of Honor, Men at War, Honor Bound, and Presidential Agent. He has been invested into the orders of St. George of the U.S. Armor Association and St. Andrew of the U.S. Army Aviation Association, and is a life member of the U.S. Special Operations Association; Gaston-Lee Post 5660, Veterans of Foreign Wars; China Post #1 in Exile of the American Legion; the Police Chiefs Association of Southeast Pennsylvania, South New Jersey, and Delaware; and the Flat Earth Society (Pensacola, Florida, and Buenos Aires, Argentina, chapters). He is an honorary life member of the U.S. Army Otter & Caribou Association, the U.S. Army Special Forces Association, the U.S. Marine Corps Raider Association, and the USMC Combat Correspondents Association.

William E. Butterworth IV has been an editor and writer for more than twenty-five years, and has worked closely with his father for several years on the editing of the Griffin books. He is the coauthor of the bestselling OSS Men at War novels *The Saboteurs* and *The Double Agents* and *Death and Honor* in the Honor Bound series. He lives in Texas.